PRAISE FOR

His Majesty's Dragon

AND THE TEMERAIRE SERIES

"These are beautifully written novels—not only fresh, original, and fast paced, but full of wonderful characters with real heart. [The Temeraire series] is a terrific meld of two genres that I particularly love—fantasy and historical epic."

—PETER JACKSON

"A terrifically entertaining fantasy novel . . . Is it hard to imagine a cross between Susanna Clarke, of Norrell and Strange fame, and the late Patrick O'Brian? Not if you've read this wonderful, arresting novel."

—STEPHEN KING

"A splendid series . . . Not only is it a new way to utilize dragons, it's a very clever one and fits neatly into the historical niche this author has used."

—ANNE MCCAFFREY

BY NAOMI NOVIK

THE SCHOLOMANCE

A Deadly Education
The Last Graduate

Uprooted
Spinning Silver

TEMERAIRE

His Majesty's Dragon
Throne of Jade
Black Powder War
Empire of Ivory
Victory of Eagles
Tongues of Serpents
Crucible of Gold
Blood of Tyrants
League of Dragons

BLACK POWDER WAR

BLACK POWDER WAR

Book Three of Temeraire

NAOMI NOVIK

NEW YORK

2021 Del Rey Trade Paperback Edition

Copyright © 2006 by Temeraire LLC
Excerpt from *Empire of Ivory* by Naomi Novik
copyright © 2007 by Temeraire LLC

Published in the United States by Del Rey,
an imprint of Random House,
a division of Penguin Random House LLC, New York.

DEL REY is a registered trademark and the CIRCLE colophon
is a trademark of Penguin Random House LLC.

Originally published in the United States
by Del Rey, an imprint of Random House,
a division of Penguin Random House LLC, in 2006.

ISBN 978-0-593-35956-3
Ebook ISBN 978-0-345-49343-9

Printed in the United States of America on acid-free paper

randomhousebooks.com

4 6 8 9 7 5 3

Book design by Alexis Capitini

for my mother
in small return for many
bajki cudowne

BLACK
POWDER
WAR

PROLOGUE

Even looking into the gardens at night, Laurence could not imagine himself home; too many bright lanterns looking out from the trees, red and gold under the upturned roof-corners; the sound of laughter behind him like a foreign country. The musician had only one string to his instrument, and he called from it a wavering, fragile song, a thread woven through the conversation which itself had become nothing more than music: Laurence had acquired very little of the language, and the words soon lost their meaning for him when so many voices joined in. He could only smile at whoever addressed him and hide his incomprehension behind the cup of tea of palest green, and at the first chance he stole quietly away around the corner of the terrace. Out of sight, he put his cup down on the window-sill half-drunk; it tasted to him like perfumed water, and he thought longingly of strong black tea full of milk, or better yet, coffee; he had not tasted coffee in two months.

The moon-viewing pavilion was set on a small promontory of rock jutting from the mountain-side, high enough to give an odd betwixt-and-between view of the vast imperial gardens laid out beneath: neither as near the ground as an ordinary balcony nor so high above as Temeraire's back, where trees changed into matchsticks and the great pavilions into children's toys. He stepped out from under the eaves and went to the railing: there was a pleasant coolness to the air after the rain, and Laurence did not mind the damp, the mist on his face welcome and more familiar than all the rest of his surroundings, from years at sea. The wind had obligingly cleared away the last of the lingering storm-bank; now steam curled languidly upon the old, soft, rounded stones of the pathways, slick and grey and bright under a moon nearly three-quarters full, and the breeze was full of the smell of over-ripe apricots, which had fallen from the trees to smash upon the cobbles.

Another light was flickering among the stooped ancient trees, a thin white gleam passing behind the branches, now obscured, now seen, moving steadily towards the shore of the nearby ornamental lake, and with it the sound of muffled footfalls. Laurence could not see very much at first, but shortly a queer little procession came out into the open: a scant handful of servants bowed down under the weight of a plain wooden bier and the shrouded body lying atop; and behind them trotted a couple of young boys, carrying shovels and throwing anxious looks over their shoulders.

Laurence stared, wondering; and then the tree-tops all gave a great shudder and yielded to Lien, pushing through into the wide clearing behind the servants, her broad-ruffed head bowed down low and her wings pinned tight to her sides. The slim trees bowed out of her way or broke, leaving long strands of willow-leaves draped across her shoulders. These were her only adornment: all her elaborate rubies and gold had been stripped away, and she looked pale and queerly vulnerable with no jewels to relieve the white translucence of her color-leached skin; in the darkness, her scarlet eyes looked black and hollow.

The servants set down their burden to dig a hole at the base of one old majestic willow-tree, blowing out great sighs here and again as they flung the soft dirt up, and leaving black streaks upon their pale broad faces as they labored and sweated. Lien

paced slowly around the circumference of the clearing, bending
to tear up some small saplings that had taken root at the edges,
throwing the straight young trees into a heap. There were no
other mourners present, save one man in dark blue robes trailing
after Lien; there was a suggestion of familiarity about him, his
walk, but Laurence could not see his face. The man took up a
post at the side of the grave, watching silently as the servants
dug; there were no flowers, nor the sort of long funerary procession Laurence had before witnessed in the streets of Peking: family tearing at their clothes, shaven-headed monks carrying
censers and spreading clouds of incense. This curious night-time
affair might almost have been the scene of a pauper's burial, save
for the gold-roofed imperial pavilions half-hidden amongst the
trees, and Lien standing over the proceedings like a milk-white
ghost, vast and terrible.

The servants did not unwrap the body before setting it in the
ground; but then it had been more than a week since Yongxing's
death. This seemed a strange arrangement for the burial of an
imperial prince, even one who had conspired at murder and
meant to usurp his brother's throne; Laurence wondered if his
burial had earlier been forbidden, or perhaps was even now
clandestine. The small shrouded body slipped out of view, a soft
thump following; Lien keened once, almost inaudibly, the sound
creeping unpleasantly along the back of Laurence's neck and
vanishing in the rustling of the trees. He felt abruptly an in-
truder, though likely they could not see him amid the general
blaze of the lanterns behind him; and to go away again now
would cause the greater disturbance.

The servants had already begun to fill in the grave, scraping
the heaped earth back into the hole in broad sweeps, work that
went quickly; soon the ground was patted level once again under
their shovels, nothing to mark the grave-site but the raw de-
nuded patch of ground and the low-hanging willow-tree, its
long trailing branches sheltering the grave. The two boys went
back into the trees to gather armfuls of forest-cover, old rotted
leaves and needles, which they spread all over the surface until
the grave could not be told from the undisturbed ground, van-

ishing entirely from view. This labor accomplished, they stood
uncertainly back: without an officiant to give the affair some
decent ceremony, there was nothing to guide them. Lien gave
them no sign; she had huddled low to the ground, drawn in
upon herself. At last the men shouldered their spades and drifted
away into the trees, leaving the white dragon as wide a berth as
they could manage.

The man in blue robes stepped to the graveside and made the
sign of the cross over his chest; as he turned away, his face came
full into the moonlight, and abruptly Laurence knew him: De
Guignes, the French ambassador, and almost the most unlikely
mourner imaginable. Yongxing's violent antipathy towards the
influence of the West had known no favorites, nor made distinc-
tions amongst French, British, and Portuguese, and De Guignes
would never have been admitted to the prince's confidence in
life, nor his company tolerated by Lien. But there were the long
aristocratic features, wholly French; his presence was at once
unmistakable and unaccountable. De Guignes lingered yet a moment in the clearing and spoke to Lien: inaudible at the distance,
but a question by his manner. She gave him no answer, made no
sound at all, crouched low with her gaze fixed only upon the
hidden grave, as if she would imprint the place upon her memory. After a moment he bowed himself away gracefully and left
her.

She stayed unmoving by the grave, striped by scudding clouds
and the lengthening shadows of the trees. Laurence could not
regret the prince's death, yet pity stirred; he did not suppose
anyone else would have her as companion now. He stood watching her for a long time, leaning against the rail, until the moon
traveled at last too low and she was hidden from view. A fresh
burst of laughter and applause came around the terrace corner:
the music had wound to a close.

PART I

CHAPTER 1

The hot wind blowing into Macao was sluggish and unre-
freshing, only stirring up the rotting salt smell of the harbor, the fish-corpses and great knots of black-red seaweed,
the effluvia of human and dragon wastes. Even so the sailors
were sitting crowded along the rails of the *Allegiance* for a
breath of the moving air, leaning against one another to get a
little room. A little scuffling broke out amongst them from time
to time, a dull exchange of shoving back and forth, but these
quarrels died almost at once in the punishing heat.

Temeraire lay disconsolately upon the dragondeck, gazing towards the white haze of the open ocean, the aviators on duty
lying half-asleep in his great shadow. Laurence himself had sacrificed dignity so far as to take off his coat, as he was sitting in
the crook of Temeraire's foreleg and so concealed from view.

"I am sure I could pull the ship out of the harbor," Temeraire
said, not for the first time in the past week; and sighed when this
amiable plan was again refused: in a calm he might indeed have
been able to tow even the great dragon transport, but against
a direct headwind he could only exhaust himself to no purpose.

"Even in a calm you could scarcely pull her any great distance," Laurence added consolingly. "A few miles may be of some use out in the open ocean, but at present we may as well stay in harbor, and be a little more comfortable; we would make very little speed even if we could get her out."

"It seems a great pity to me that we must always be waiting on the wind, when everything else is ready and we are also," Temeraire said. "I would so like to be home *soon:* there is so very much to be done." His tail thumped hollowly upon the boards, for emphasis.

"I beg you will not raise your hopes too high," Laurence said, himself a little hopelessly: urging Temeraire to restraint had so far not produced any effect, and he did not expect a different event now. "You must be prepared to endure some delays; at home as much as here."

"Oh! I promise I will be patient," Temeraire said, and immediately dispelled any small notion Laurence might have had of relying upon this promise by adding, unconscious of any contradiction, "but I am quite sure the Admiralty will see the justice of our case very quickly. Certainly it is only fair that dragons should be paid, if our crews are."

Having been at sea from the age of twelve onwards, before the accident of chance which had made him the captain of a dragon rather than a ship, Laurence enjoyed an extensive familiarity with the gentlemen of the Admiralty Board who oversaw the Navy and the Aerial Corps both, and a keen sense of justice was hardly their salient feature. The offices seemed rather to strip their occupants of all ordinary human decency and real qualities: creeping, nip-farthing political creatures, very nearly to a man. The vastly superior conditions for dragons here in China had forced open Laurence's unwilling eyes to the evils of their treatment in the West, but as for the Admiralty's sharing that view, at least so far as it would cost the country tuppence, he was not sanguine.

In any case, he could not help privately entertaining the hope that once at home, back at their post on the Channel and engaged in the honest business of defending their country, Temeraire might, if not give over his goals, then at least moderate them. Laurence could make no real quarrel with the aims, which were natural and just; but England was at war, after all, and he was conscious, as Temeraire was not, of the impudence in demanding concessions from their own Government under such circumstances: very like mutiny. Yet he had promised his support and would not withdraw it. Temeraire might have stayed here in China, enjoying all the luxuries and freedoms which were his birthright as a Celestial. He was coming back to England largely for Laurence's sake, and in hopes of improving the lot of his comrades-in-arms; despite all Laurence's misgivings, he could hardly raise a direct objection, though it at times felt almost dishonest not to speak.

"It is very clever of you to suggest we should begin with pay," Temeraire continued, heaping more coals of fire onto Laurence's conscience; he had proposed it mainly for its being less radical a suggestion than many of the others which Temeraire had advanced, such as the wholesale demolition of quarters of London to make room for thoroughfares wide enough to accommodate dragons, and the sending of draconic representatives to address Parliament, which aside from the difficulty of their getting into the building would certainly have resulted in the immediate flight of all the human members. "Once we have pay, I am sure everything else will be easier. Then we can always offer people money, which they like so much, for all the rest; like those cooks which you have hired for me. That is a very pleasant smell," he added, not a non sequitur: the rich smoky smell of well-charred meat was growing so strong as to rise over the stench of the harbor.

Laurence frowned and looked down: the galley was situated directly below the dragondeck, and wispy ribbons of smoke, flat and wide, were seeping up from between the boards of the deck. "Dyer," he said, beckoning to one of his runners, "go and see what they are about, down there."

Temeraire had acquired a taste for the Chinese style of dragon cookery which the British quartermaster, expected only to provide freshly butchered cattle, was quite unable to satisfy, so Laurence had found two Chinese cooks willing to leave their country for the promise of substantial wages. The new cooks spoke no English, but they lacked nothing in self-assertion; already professional jealousy had nearly brought the ship's cook and his assistants to pitched battle with them over the galley stoves, and produced a certain atmosphere of competition.

Dyer trotted down the stairs to the quarterdeck and opened the door to the galley: a great rolling cloud of smoke came billowing out, and at once there was a shout and halloa of "Fire!" from the look-outs up in the rigging. The watch-officer rang the bell frantically, the clapper scraping and clanging; Laurence was already shouting, "To stations!" and sending his men to their fire crews.

All lethargy vanished at once, the sailors running for buckets, pails; a couple of daring fellows darted into the galley and came out dragging limp bodies: the cook's mates, the two Chinese, and one of the ship's boys, but no sign of the ship's cook himself. Already the dripping buckets were coming in a steady flow, the bosun roaring and thumping his stick against the foremast to give the men the rhythm, and one after another the buckets were emptied through the galley doors. But still the smoke came billowing out, thicker now, through every crack and seam of the deck, and the bitts of the dragondeck were scorching hot to the touch: the rope coiled over two of the iron posts was beginning to smoke.

Young Digby, quick-thinking, had organized the other ensigns: the boys were hurrying together to unwind the cable, swallowing hisses of pain when their fingers brushed against the hot iron. The rest of the aviators were ranged along the rail, hauling up water in buckets flung over the side and dousing the dragondeck: steam rose in white clouds and left a grey crust of salt upon the already warping planks, the deck creaking and moaning like a crowd of old men. The tar between the seams was liquefying, running in long black streaks along the deck with a sweet, acrid smell as it scorched and smoked. Temeraire was standing on all four legs now, mincing from one place to another for relief from the heat, though Laurence had seen him lie with pleasure on stones baked by the full strength of the mid-day sun.

Captain Riley was in and among the sweating, laboring men, shouting encouragement as the buckets swung back and forth, but there was an edge of despair in his voice. The fire was too hot, the wood seasoned by the long stay in harbor under the baking heat; and the vast holds were filled with goods for the journey home: delicate china wrapped in dry straw and packed in wooden crates, bales of silks, new-laid sailcloth for repairs. The fire had only to make its way four decks down, and the stores would go up in quick hot flames running all the way back to the powder magazine, and carry her all away.

The morning watch, who had been sleeping below, were now fighting to come up from the lower decks, open-mouthed and gasping with the smoke chasing them out, breaking the lines of water-carriers in their panic: though the *Allegiance* was a behemoth, her forecastle and quarterdeck could not hold her entire crew, not with the dragondeck nearly in flames. Laurence seized one of the stays and pulled himself up on the railing of the deck, looking for his crew in and amongst the milling crowd: most had already been out upon the dragondeck, but a handful remained unaccounted for: Therrows, his leg still in splints after the battle in Peking; Keynes, the surgeon, likely at his books in the privacy of his cabin; and he could see no sign of Emily Roland, his other runner: she was scarcely turned eleven, and could not easily have pushed her way out past the heaving, struggling men.

A thin, shrill kettle-whistle erupted from the galley chimneys, the metal cowls beginning to droop towards the deck, slowly, like flowers gone to seed. Temeraire hissed back in instinctive displeasure, drawing his head back up to all the full length of his neck, his ruff flattening against his neck. His great haunches had already tensed to spring, one foreleg resting on the railing. "Laurence, is it quite safe for you there?" he called anxiously.

"Yes, we will be perfectly well, go aloft at once," Laurence said, even as he waved the rest of his men down to the forecastle, concerned for Temeraire's safety with the planking beginning to give way. "We may better be able to come at the fire once it has come up through the deck," he added, principally for the encouragement of those hearing him; in truth, once the dragondeck fell in, he could hardly imagine they would be able to put out the blaze.

"Very well, then I will go and help," Temeraire said, and took to the air.

A handful of men less concerned with preserving the ship than their own lives had already lowered the jolly-boat into the water off the stern, hoping to make their escape unheeded by the officers engaged in the desperate struggle against the fire; they dived off in panic as Temeraire unexpectedly darted around the ship and descended upon them. He paid no attention to the men, but seized the boat in his talons, ducked it underwater like a ladle, and heaved it up into the air, dripping water and oars. Carefully keeping it balanced, he flew back and poured it out over the dragondeck: the sudden deluge went hissing and spitting over the planks, and tumbled in a brief waterfall over the stairs and down.

"Fetch axes!" Laurence called urgently. It was desperately hot, sweating work, hacking at the planks with steam rising and their axe blades skidding on the wet and tar-soaked wood, smoke pouring out through every cut they made. All struggled to keep their footing each time Temeraire deluged them once again; but the constant flow of water was the only thing that let them keep at their task, the smoke otherwise too thick. As they labored, a few of the men staggered and fell unmoving upon the deck: no time even to heave them down to the quarterdeck, the minutes too precious to sacrifice. Laurence worked side by side with his armorer, Pratt, long thin trails of black-stained sweat marking their shirts as they swung the axes in uneven turns, until abruptly the planking cracked with gunshot sounds, a great section of the dragondeck all giving way at once and collapsing into the eager hungry roar of the flames below.

For a moment Laurence wavered on the verge; then his first lieutenant, Granby, was pulling him away. They staggered back together, Laurence half-blind and nearly falling into Granby's arms; his breath would not quite come, rapid and shallow, and his eyes were burning. Granby dragged him partway down the steps, and then another torrent of water carried them in a rush the rest of the way, to fetch up against one of the forty-two-pounder carronades on the forecastle. Laurence managed to pull himself up the railing in time to vomit over the side, the bitter taste in his mouth still less strong than the acrid stink of his hair and clothes.

The rest of the men were abandoning the dragondeck, and now the enormous torrents of water could go straight down at the flames. Temeraire had found a steady rhythm, and the clouds of smoke were already less: black sooty water was running out of the galley doors onto the quarterdeck. Laurence felt queerly shaken and ill, heaving deep breaths that did not seem to fill his lungs. Riley was rasping out hoarse orders through the speaking-trumpet, barely loud enough to be heard over the hiss of smoke; the bosun's voice was gone entirely: he was pushing the men into rows with his bare hands, pointing them at the hatchways; soon there was a line organized, handing up the men who had been overcome or trampled below: Laurence was glad to see Therrows being lifted out. Temeraire poured another torrent upon the last smoldering embers; then Riley's coxswain Basson poked his head out of the main hatch, panting, and shouted, "No more smoke coming through, sir, and the planks above the berth-deck ain't worse than warm: I think she's out."

A heartfelt ragged cheer went up. Laurence was beginning to feel he could get his wind back again, though he still spat black with every coughing breath; with Granby's hand he was able to climb to his feet. A haze of smoke like the aftermath of cannon-fire lay thickly upon the deck, and when he climbed up the stairs he found a gaping charcoal fire-pit in place of the dragondeck, the edges of the remaining planking crisped like burnt paper. The body of the poor ship's cook lay like a twisted cinder amongst the wreckage, skull charred black and his wooden legs burnt to ash, leaving only the sad stumps to the knee.

Having let down the jolly-boat, Temeraire hovered above uncertainly a little longer and then let himself drop into the water beside the ship: there was nowhere left for him to land upon her. Swimming over and grasping at the rail with his claws, he craned up his great head to peer anxiously over the side. "You are well, Laurence? Are all my crew all right?"

"Yes; I have made everyone," Granby said, nodding to Laurence. Emily, her cap of sandy hair speckled grey with soot, came to them dragging a jug of water from the scuttlebutt: stale and tainted with the smell of the harbor, and more delicious than wine.

Riley climbed up to join them. "What a ruin," he said, looking over the wreckage. "Well, at least we have saved her, and thank Heaven for that; but how long it will take before we can sail now, I do not like to think." He gladly accepted the jug from Laurence and drank deep before handing it on to Granby. "And I am damned sorry; I suppose all your things must be spoilt," he added, wiping his mouth: senior aviators had their quarters towards the bow, one level below the galley.

"Good God," Laurence said, blankly, "and I have not the least notion what has happened to my coat."

"FOUR; FOUR DAYS," the tailor said in his limited English, holding up fingers to be sure he had not been misunderstood; Laurence sighed and said, "Yes, very well." It was small consolation to think that there was no shortage of time: two months or more would be required to repair the ship, and until then he and all his men would be cooling their heels on shore. "Can you repair the other?"

They looked together down at the coat which Laurence had brought him as a pattern: more black than bottle-green now, with a peculiar white residue upon the buttons and smelling strongly of smoke and salt water both. The tailor did not say *no* outright, but his expression spoke volumes. "You take this," he said instead, and going into the back of his workshop brought out another garment: not a coat, precisely, but one of the quilted jackets such as the Chinese soldiers wore, like a tunic opening down the front, with a short upturned collar.

"Oh, well—" Laurence eyed it uneasily; it was made of silk, in a considerably brighter shade of green, and handsomely embroidered along the seams with scarlet and gold: the most he could say was that it was not as ornate as the formal robes to which he had been subjected on prior occasions.

But he and Granby were to dine with the commissioners of the East India Company that evening; he could not present himself half-dressed, or keep himself swathed in the heavy cloak which he had put on to come to the shop. He was glad enough to have the Chinese garment when, returning to his new quarters on shore, Dyer and Roland told him there was no proper coat to be had in town for any money whatsoever: not very surprising, as respectable gentlemen did not choose to look like aviators, and the dark green of their broadcloth was not a popular color in the Western enclave.

"Perhaps you will set a new fashion," Granby said, somewhere between mirth and consolation; a lanky fellow, he was himself wearing a coat seized from one of the hapless midwingmen, who, having been quartered on the lower decks, had not suffered the ruin of their own clothes. With an inch of wrist showing past his coat sleeves and his pale cheeks as usual flushed with sunburn, he looked at the moment rather younger than his twenty years and six, but at least no one would look askance. Laurence, being a good deal more broad-shouldered, could not rob any of the younger officers in the same manner, and though Riley had handsomely offered, Laurence did not mean to present himself in a blue coat, as if he were ashamed of being an aviator and wished to pass himself off as still a naval captain.

He and his crew were now quartered in a spacious house set directly upon the waterfront, the property of a local Dutch merchant more than happy to let it to them and remove his household to apartments farther into the town, where he would not have a dragon on his doorstep. Temeraire had been forced by the destruction of his dragondeck to sleep on the beach, much to the dismay of the Western inhabitants; to his own disgust as well, the shore being inhabited by small and irritating crabs which persisted in treating him like the rocks in which they made their homes and attempting to conceal themselves upon him while he slept.

Laurence and Granby paused to bid him farewell on their way to the dinner. Temeraire, at least, approved Laurence's new costume; he thought the shade a pretty one, and admired the gold buttons and thread particularly. "And it looks handsome with the sword," he added, having nosed Laurence around in a circle the better to inspect him: the sword in question was his very own gift, and therefore in his estimation the most important part of the ensemble. It was also the one piece for which Laurence felt he need not blush: his shirt, thankfully hidden beneath the coat, not all the scrubbing in the world could save from disgrace; his breeches did not bear close examination; and as for his stockings, he had resorted to his tall Hessian boots.

They left Temeraire settling down to his own dinner under the protective eyes of a couple of midwingmen and a troop of soldiers under the arms of the East India Company, part of their private forces; Sir George Staunton had loaned them to help guard Temeraire not from danger but over-enthusiastic well-wishers. Unlike the Westerners who had fled their homes near the shore, the Chinese were not alarmed by dragons, living from childhood in their midst, and the tiny handful of Celestials so rarely left the imperial precincts that to see one, and better yet to touch, was counted an honor and an assurance of good fortune.

Staunton had also arranged this dinner by way of offering the officers some entertainment and relief from their anxieties over the disaster, unaware that he would be putting the aviators to such desperate shifts in the article of clothing. Laurence had not liked to refuse the generous invitation for so trivial a reason, and had hoped to the last that he might find something more respectable to wear; now he came ruefully prepared to share his travails over the dinner table, and bear the amusement of the company.

His entrance was met with a polite if astonished silence, at first; but he had scarcely paid his respects to Sir George and accepted a glass of wine before murmurs began. One of the older commissioners, a gentleman who liked to be deaf when he chose, said quite clearly, "Aviators and their starts; who knows what they will take into their heads next," which made Granby's eyes glitter with suppressed anger; and a trick of the room made some less consciously indiscreet remarks audible also.

"What do you suppose he means by it?" inquired Mr. Chatham, a gentleman newly arrived from India, while eyeing Laurence with interest from the next window over; he was speaking in low voices with Mr. Grothing-Pyle, a portly man whose own interest was centered upon the clock, and in judging how soon they should go in to dinner.

"Hm? Oh; he has a right to style himself an Oriental prince now if he likes," Grothing-Pyle said, shrugging, after an incurious glance over his shoulder. "And just as well for us, too. Do you smell venison? I have not tasted venison in a year."

Laurence turned his own face to the open window, appalled and offended in equal measure. Such an interpretation had never even occurred to him; his adoption by the Emperor had been purely and strictly *pro forma,* a matter of saving face for the Chinese, who had insisted that a Celestial might not be companion to any but a direct connection of the imperial family; while on the British side it had been eagerly accepted as a painless means of resolving the dispute over the capture of Temeraire's egg. Painless, at least, to everyone but Laurence, already in possession of one proud and imperious father, whose wrathful reaction to the adoption he anticipated with no small dismay. True, that consideration had not stopped him: he would have willingly accepted anything short of treason to avoid being parted from Temeraire. But he had certainly never sought or desired so signal and queer an honor, and to have men think him a ludicrous kind of social climber, who should value Oriental titles above his own birth, was deeply mortifying.

The embarrassment closed his mouth. He would have gladly shared the story behind his unusual clothing as an anecdote; as an excuse, never. He spoke shortly in reply to the few remarks offered him; anger made him pale and, if he had only known it, gave his face a cold, forbidding look, almost dangerous, which made conversation near him die down. He was ordinarily good-humored in his expression, and though he was not darkly

tanned, the many years laboring in the sun had given his looks a
warm bronzed cast; the lines upon his face were mostly smiling:
all the more contrast now. These men owed, if not their lives, at
least their fortunes to the success of the diplomatic mission to
Peking, whose failure would have meant open warfare and an
end to the China trade, and whose success had cost Laurence a
blood-letting and the life of one of his men; he had not expected
any sort of effusive thanks and would have spurned them if offered, but to meet with derision and incivility was something
entirely different.

"Shall we go in?" Sir George said, sooner than usual, and at
the table he made every effort to break the uneasy atmosphere
which had settled over the company: the butler was sent back to
the cellar half-a-dozen times, the wines growing more extravagant with each visit, and the food was excellent despite the limited resources accessible to Staunton's cook: among the dishes
was a very handsome fried carp, laid upon a ragout of the small
crabs, now victims in their turn, and for centerpiece a pair of fat
haunches of venison roasted, accompanied by a dish full of
glowing jewel-red currant jelly.

The conversation flowed again; Laurence could not be insensible to Staunton's real and sincere desire to see him and all the
company comfortable, and he was not of an implacable temper
to begin with; still less when encouraged with the best part of a
glorious burgundy just come into its prime. No one had made
any further remarks about coats or imperial relations, and after
several courses Laurence had thawed enough to apply himself
with a will to a charming trifle assembled out of Naples biscuits
and sponge-cake, with a rich brandied custard flavored with orange, when a commotion outside the dining room began to in-
trude, and finally a single piercing shriek, like a woman's cry,
interrupted the increasingly loud and slurred conversation.

Silence fell, glasses stopped in mid-air, some chairs were
pushed back; Staunton rose, a little wavering, and begged their
pardon. Before he could go to investigate, the door was thrust
abruptly open, Staunton's anxious servant stumbling back into
the room still protesting volubly in Chinese. He was gently but

with complete firmness being pressed aside by another Oriental man, dressed in a padded jacket and a round, domed hat rising above a thick roll of dark wool; the stranger's clothing was dusty and stained yellow in places, and not much like the usual native dress, and on his gauntleted hand perched an angry-looking eagle, brown and golden feathers ruffled up and a yellow eye glaring; it clacked its beak and shifted its perch uneasily, great talons puncturing the heavy block of padding.

When they had stared at him and he at them in turn, the stranger further astonished the room by saying, in pure drawing-room accents, "I beg your pardon, gentlemen, for interrupting your dinner; my errand cannot wait. Is Captain William Laurence here?"

Laurence was at first too bemused with wine and surprise to react; then he rose and stepped away from the table, to accept a sealed oilskin packet under the eagle's unfriendly stare. "I thank you, sir," he said. At a second glance, the lean and angular face was not entirely Chinese: the eyes, though dark and faintly slanting, were rather more Western in shape, and the color of his skin, much like polished teak wood, owed less to nature than to the sun.

The stranger inclined his head politely. "I am glad to have been of service." He did not smile, but there was a glint in his eye suggestive of amusement at the reaction of the room, which he was surely accustomed to provoking; he threw the company all a final glance, gave Staunton a small bow, and left as abruptly as he had come, going directly past a couple more of the servants who had come hurrying to the room in response to the noise.

"Pray go and give Mr. Tharkay some refreshment," Staunton said to the servants in an undertone, and sent them after him; meanwhile Laurence turned to his packet. The wax had been softened by the summer heat, the impression mostly lost, and the seal would not easily come away or break, pulling like soft candy and trailing sticky threads over his fingers. A single sheet within only, written from Dover in Admiral Lenton's own hand, and in the abrupt style of formal orders: a single look was enough to take it in.

... and you are hereby required without
the loss of a Moment to proceed to
Istanbul, there to receive by the Offices of
Avraam Maden, in the service of H.M.
Selim III, three Eggs now through
agreement the Property of His Majesty's
Corps, to be secured against the Elements
with all due care for their brooding and
thence delivered straightaway to the charge
of those Officers appointed to them, who
shall await you at the covert at Dunbar . . .

The usual grim epilogues followed, *herein neither you nor any of you shall fail, or answer the contrary at your peril;* Laurence handed the letter to Granby, then nodded to him to pass the letter to Riley and to Staunton, who had joined them in the privacy of the library.

"Laurence," Granby said, after handing it on, "we cannot sit here waiting for repairs with a months-long sea-journey after that; we must get going at once."

"Well, how else do you mean to go?" Riley said, looking up from the letter, which he was reading over Staunton's shoulder. "There's not another ship in port that could hold Temeraire's weight for even a few hours; you can't fly straight across the ocean without a place to rest."

"It's not as though we were going to Nova Scotia, and could only go by sea," Granby said. "We must take the overland route instead."

"Oh, come now," Riley said impatiently.

"Well, and why not?" Granby demanded. "Even aside from the repairs, it's going by sea that is out of the way, we lose ages having to circle around India. Instead we can make a straight shot across Tartary—"

"Yes, and you can jump in the water and try to swim all the way to England, too," Riley said. "Sooner is better than late, but late is better than never; the *Allegiance* will get you home quicker than that."

Laurence listened to their conversation with half an ear, reading the letter again with fresh attention. It was difficult to separate the true degree of urgency from the general tenor of a set of orders; but though dragon eggs might take a long time indeed to hatch, they were unpredictable and could not be left sitting indefinitely. "And we must consider, Tom," he said to Riley, "that it might easily be as much as five months' sailing to Basra if we are unlucky in the way of weather, and from there we should have a flight overland to Istanbul in any case."

"And as likely to find three dragonets as three eggs at the end of it, no use at all," Granby said; when Laurence asked him, he gave as his firm opinion that the eggs could not be far from hatching; or at least not so far as to set their minds at ease. "There aren't many breeds who go for longer than a couple of years in the shell," he explained, "and the Admiralty won't have bought eggs less than halfway through their brooding: any younger than that, and you cannot be sure they will come off. We cannot lose the time; why they are sending us to get them instead of a crew from Gibraltar I don't in the least understand."

Laurence, less familiar with the various duty stations of the Corps, had not yet considered this possibility, and now it struck him also as odd that the task had been delegated to them, being so much farther distant. "How long ought it take them to get to Istanbul from there?" he asked, disquieted; even if much of the coast along the way were under French control, patrols could not be everywhere, and a single dragon flying should have been able to find places to rest.

"Two weeks, perhaps a little less flying hard all the way," Granby said. "While I don't suppose we can make it in less than a couple of months, ourselves, even going overland."

Staunton, who had been listening anxiously to their deliberations, now interjected, "Then must not these orders by their very presence imply a certain lack of urgency? I dare say it has taken three months for the letter to come this far. A few months more, then, can hardly make a difference; otherwise the Corps would have sent someone nearer."

"If anyone nearer could be sent," Laurence said, grimly. England was hard-up enough for dragons that even one or two could not easily be spared in any sort of a crisis, certainly not for a month going and coming back, and certainly not a heavy-weight in Temeraire's class. Bonaparte might once again be threatening invasion across the Channel, or launching attacks against the Mediterranean Fleet, leaving only Temeraire, and the handful of dragons stationed in Bombay and Madras, at any sort of liberty.

"No," Laurence concluded, having contemplated these un-pleasant possibilities, "I do not think we can make any such as-sumption, and in any case there are not two ways to read *without the loss of a moment,* not when Temeraire is certainly able to go. I know what I would think of a captain with such orders who lingered in port when tide and wind were with him."

Seeing him thus beginning to lean towards a decision, Staunton at once began, "Captain, I beg you will not seriously consider taking so great a risk," while Riley, more blunt with nine years' acquaintance behind him, said, "For God's sake, Laurence, you cannot mean to do any such crazy thing."

He added, "And I do not call it *lingering in port,* to wait for the *Allegiance* to be ready; if you like, taking the overland route should rather be like setting off headlong into a gale, when a week's patience will bring clear skies."

"You make it sound as though we might as well slit our own throats as go," Granby exclaimed. "I don't deny it would be awkward and dangerous with a caravan, lugging goods all across Creation, but with Temeraire, no one will give us any trouble, and we only need a place to drop for the night."

"And enough food for a dragon the size of a first-rate," Riley fired back.

Staunton, nodding, seized on this avenue at once. "I think you cannot understand the extreme desolation of the regions you would cross, nor their vastness." He hunted through his books and papers to find Laurence several maps of the region: an inhospitable place even on parchment, with only a few lonely small towns breaking up the stretches of nameless wasteland, great expanses of desert entrenched behind mountains; on one dusty and crumbling chart a spidery old-fashioned hand had written *heere ys no water 3 wekes* in the empty yellow bowl of the desert. "Forgive me for speaking so strongly, but it is a reckless course, and I am convinced not one which the Admiralty can have meant you to follow."

"And I am convinced Lenton should never have conceived of our whistling six months down the wind," Granby said. "People do come and go overland; what about that fellow Marco Polo, and that nearly two centuries ago?"

"Yes, and what about the Fitch and Newbery expedition, after him," Riley said. "Three dragons all lost in the mountains, in a five-day blizzard, through just such reckless behavior—"

"This man Tharkay, who brought the letter," Laurence said to Staunton, interrupting an exchange which bade fair to end in hot words, Riley's tone growing rather sharp and Granby's pale skin flushing up with tell-tale color. "He came overland, did he not?"

"I hope you do not mean to take him for your model," Staunton said. "One man can go where a group cannot, and manage on very little, particularly a rough adventurer such as he. More to the point, he risks only himself when he goes: you must consider that in your charge is an inexpressibly valuable dragon, whose loss must be of greater importance than even this mission."

"OH, PRAY LET us be gone at once," said the inexpressibly valuable dragon, when Laurence had carried the question, still unresolved, back to him. "It sounds very exciting to me." Temeraire was wide-awake now in the relative cool of the evening, and his tail was twitching back and forth with enthusiasm, producing moderate walls of sand to either side upon the beach, not much above the height of a man. "What kind of dragons will the eggs be? Will they breathe fire?"

"Lord, if they would only give us a Kazilik," Granby said. "But I expect it will be ordinary middle-weights: these kinds of bargains are made to bring a little fresh blood into the lines."

"How much more quickly would we be at home?" Temeraire asked, cocking his head sideways so he could focus one eye upon the maps, which Laurence had laid out over the sand. "Why, only see how far out of our way the sailing takes us, Laurence, and it is not as though I must have wind always, as the ship does: we will be home again before the end of summer," an estimate as optimistic as it was unlikely, Temeraire not being able to judge the scale of the map so very well; but at least they would likely be in England again by late September, and that was an incentive almost powerful enough to overrule all caution.

"And yet I cannot get past it," Laurence said. "We were assigned to the *Allegiance,* and Lenton must have assumed we would come home by her. To go haring-off along the old silk roads has an impetuous flavor; and you need not try and tell me," he added repressively to Temeraire, "that there is nothing to worry about."

"But it *cannot* be so very dangerous," Temeraire said, undaunted. "It is not as though I were going to let you go off all alone, and get hurt."

"That you should face down an army to protect us I have no doubt," Laurence said, "but a gale in the mountains even you cannot defeat." Riley's reminder of the ill-fated expedition lost in the Karakorum Pass had resonated unpleasantly. Laurence could envision all too clearly the consequences should they run into a deadly storm: Temeraire borne down by the frozen wind, wet snow and ice forming crusts upon the edges of his wings, beyond where any man of the crew could reach to break them loose; the whirling snow blinding them to the hazards of the cliff walls around them and turning them in circles; the dropping chill rendering him by insensible degrees heavier and more sluggish—and worse prey to the ice, with no shelter to be found. In such circumstances, Laurence would be forced to choose between ordering him to land, condemning him to a quicker death in hopes of sparing the lives of his men, or letting them all continue on the slow grinding road to destruction together: a horror beside which Laurence could contemplate death in battle with perfect equanimity.

"So then the sooner we go, the better, for having an easy crossing of it," Granby argued. "August will be better than October for avoiding blizzards."

"And for being roasted alive in the desert instead," Riley said.

Granby rounded on him. "I don't mean to say," he said, with a smoldering look in his eye that belied his words, "that there is anything old-womanish in all these objections—"

"For there is not, indeed," Laurence broke in sharply. "You are quite right, Tom; the danger is not a question of blizzards in particular, but that we have not the first understanding of the difficulties particular to the journey. And that we must remedy, first, before we engage either to go or to wait."

"IF YOU OFFER the fellow money to guide you, of course he will say the road is safe," Riley said. "And then just as likely leave you halfway to nowhere, with no recourse."

Staunton also tried again to dissuade Laurence, when he came seeking Tharkay's direction the next morning. "He occasionally brings us letters, and sometimes will do errands for the Company in India," Staunton said. "His father was a gentleman, I believe a senior officer, and took some pains with his education; but still the man cannot be called reliable, for all the polish of his manners. His mother was a native woman, Thibetan or Nepalese, or something like; and he has spent the better part of his life in the wild places of the earth."

"For my part, I should rather have a guide half-British than one who can scarcely make himself understood," Granby said afterwards, as he and Laurence together picked their way along the backstreets of Macao; the late rains were still puddled in the gutters, a thin slick of green overlaid on the stagnating waste. "And if Tharkay were not so much a gypsy he wouldn't be of any use to us; it is no good complaining about that."

At length they found Tharkay's temporary quarters: a wretched little two-story house in the Chinese quarter with a drooping roof, held up mostly by its neighbors to either side, all of them leaning against one another like drunken old men, with a landlord who scowled before leading them within, muttering.

Tharkay was sitting in the central court of the house, feeding the eagle gobbets of raw flesh from a dish; the fingers of his left hand were marked with white scars where the savage beak had cut him on previous feedings, and a few small scratches bled freely now, unheeded. "Yes, I came overland," he said, to Laurence's inquiry, "but I would not recommend you the same road, Captain; it is not a comfortable journey, when compared against sea travel." He did not interrupt his task, but held up another strip of meat for the eagle, which snatched it out of his fingers, glaring at them furiously with the dangling bloody ends hanging from its beak as it swallowed.

It was difficult to know how to address him: neither a superior servant, nor a gentleman, nor a native, all his refinements of speech curiously placed against the scruff and tumble of his clothing and his disreputable surroundings; though perhaps he could have gotten no better accommodations, curious as his appearance was, and with the hostile eagle as his companion. He made no concessions, either, to his odd, in-between station; a certain degree of presumption almost in his manner, less formal than Laurence would himself have used to so new an acquaintance, almost in active defiance against being held at a servant's distance.

But Tharkay answered their many questions readily enough, and having fed his eagle and set it aside, hooded, to sleep, he even opened up the kit which had carried him there so that they might inspect the vital equipment: a special sort of desert tent, fur-lined and with leather-reinforced holes spaced evenly along the edges, which he explained could be lashed quickly together with similar tents to form a single larger sheet to shield a camel, or in larger numbers a dragon, against sandstorm or hail or snow. There was also a snug leather-wrapped canteen, well-waxed to keep the water in, and a small tin cup tied on with string, marks engraved into it halfway and near the rim; a neat small compass, in a wooden case, and a thick journal full of little hand-sketched maps, and directions taken down in a small, neat hand.

All of it showed signs of use and good upkeep; plainly he knew what he was about, and he did not show himself over-eager, as Riley had feared, for their custom. "I had not thought of returning to Istanbul," Tharkay said instead, when Laurence at last came around to inquiring if he would be their guide. "I have no real business there."

"But have you any elsewhere?" Granby said. "We will have the devil of a time getting there without you, and you should be doing your country a service."

"And you will be handsomely paid for your trouble," Laurence added.

"Ah, well, in that case," Tharkay said, a wry twist to his smile.

"WELL, I ONLY wish you may all not have your throats slit by Uygurs," Riley said in deep pessimism, giving up, after he had tried once more at dinner to persuade them to remain. "You will dine with me on board tomorrow, Laurence?" he asked, stepping into his barge. "Very good. I will send over the raw leather, and the ship's forge," he called, his voice drifting back over the sound of the oars dipping into the water.

"I will not let anyone slit your throats at all," Temeraire said, a little indignantly. "Although I would like to see an Uygur; is that a kind of dragon?"

"A kind of bird, I think," Granby said; Laurence was doubtful, but he did not like to contradict when he was not sure himself.

"Tribesmen," Tharkay said, the next morning.

"Oh." Temeraire was a little disappointed; he had seen people before. "That is not very exciting, but perhaps they are very fierce?" he asked hopefully.

"Have you enough money to buy thirty camels?" Tharkay asked Laurence, after he had finally escaped a lengthy interrogation as to the many other prospective delights of their journey, such as violent sandstorms and frozen mountain passes.

"We are going by air," Laurence said, confused. "Temeraire will carry us," he added, wondering if Tharkay had perhaps misunderstood.

"As far as Dunhuang," Tharkay said equably. "Then we will need to buy camels. A single camel can carry enough water for a day, for a dragon of his size; and then of course he can eat the camel."

"Are such measures truly necessary?" Laurence said, in dismay at losing so much time: he had counted on crossing the desert quickly, on the wing. "Temeraire can cover better than a hundred miles in a day at need; surely we can find water over such an expanse."

"Not in the Taklamakan," Tharkay said. "The caravan routes are dying, and the cities die with them; the oases have mostly failed. We ought to be able to find enough for us and the camels, but even that will be brackish. Unless you are prepared to risk his dying of thirst, we carry our own water."

This naturally putting a period to any further debate, Laurence was forced to apply to Sir George for some assistance in the matter, having had no expectation, on his departure from England, that his ready funds should need to stretch to accommodate thirty camels and supplies for an overland journey. "Nonsense, it is a trifle," Staunton said, refusing his offered note of hand. "I dare say I will have cleared fifty thousand pounds in consequence of your mission, when all is said and done. I only wish I did not think I was speeding you on the way to your destruction. Laurence, forgive me for making so unpleasant a suggestion; I would not like to plant false suspicions in your head, but the possibility has been preying on me since you decided upon going. Could the letter by any chance have been forged?"

Laurence looked at him in surprise, and Staunton went on, "Recall that the orders, if honest, must have been written before news of your success here in China reached England—if indeed that news has reached them yet. Only consider the effect upon the negotiations so lately completed if you and Temeraire had unceremoniously gone away in the midst of them: you would have had to sneak out of the country like thieves to begin with, and an insult of such magnitude would surely have meant war. I am hard-pressed to imagine any reason the Ministry should have sent such orders."

Laurence sent for the letter and for Granby; together they studied it fresh in the strong sunlight from the east-facing windows. "I am damned if I am any judge of such things, but it seems Lenton's hand to me," Granby said doubtfully, handing it back.

To Laurence also; the letters were slant and wavering, but this kind of affliction, he did not say to Staunton, was not uncommon; aviators were taken into service at the age of seven, and the most promising among them often became runners by ten, with studies neglected sadly in favor of practical training: his own young cadets were inclined to grumble at his insistence that they should learn to write a graceful hand and practice their trigonometry.

"Who would bother with it, any road?" Granby said. "That French ambassador hanging about Peking, De Guignes—he left even before we did, and by now I expect he is halfway to France. Besides, he knows well enough that the negotiations are over."

"There might be French agents less well-informed behind it," Staunton said, "or worse, with knowledge of your recent success, trying to lure you into a trap. Brigands in the desert would hardly be above taking a bribe to attack you, and there is something too convenient in the arrival of this message, just when the *Allegiance* has been damaged, and you are sure to be chafing at your enforced delay."

"Well, I make no secret I had as lief go myself, for all this nay-saying and gloom," Granby said as they walked back to their residence: the crew had already begun the mad scramble of preparation, and haphazard bundles were beginning to be piled upon the beach. "So it may be dangerous; we are not nursemaids to a colicky baby, after all. Dragons are made to fly, and another nine months of this sitting about on deck and on shore will be the ruin of his fighting-edge."

"And of half the boys, if they have not been spoilt already," Laurence said grimly, observing the antics of the younger officers, who were not entirely reconciled to being so abruptly put back to work, and were engaging in more boisterous behavior than he liked to see from men on duty.

"Allen," Granby called sharply, "mind your damned harness-straps, unless you want to be started with them." The hapless young ensign had not properly buckled on his flying-harness, and the long carabiner straps were dragging on the ground behind him, bidding fair to trip him and any other crewman who crossed his path.

The ground-crew master Fellowes and his harness-men were still laboring over the flying rig, not yet repaired after the fire: a good many straps stiff and hard with salt, or rotted or burnt through, which needed replacing; too, several buckles had twisted and curled from the heat, and the armorer Pratt panted over his makeshift forge on shore as he pounded them straight and flat once more.

"A moment, and I will see," Temeraire said, when they had put it on him to try, and leapt aloft in a stinging cloud of sand. He flew a small circuit and landed, directing the crew, "Pray tighten the left shoulder-strap a little, and lengthen the crupper," but after some dozen small adjustments he pronounced himself satisfied with the whole.

They laid it aside while he had his dinner: an enormous horned cow spit-roasted and dressed with heaps of green and scarlet peppers with blackened skins, and also a great mound of mushrooms, for which he had acquired a taste in Capetown; meanwhile Laurence sent his men to dinner and rowed over to the *Allegiance* to have a final meal with Riley, convivial though quiet; they did not drink very much, and afterwards Laurence gave him a last few letters for his mother and for Jane Roland, the official post having already been exchanged.

"Godspeed," Riley said, seeing him down the side; the sun was low and nearly hidden behind the buildings of the town as Laurence was rowed back to shore. Temeraire had nibbled the last of the bones clean, and the men were coming out of the house. "All lies well," Temeraire said, when they had rigged him out once more, and then the crew climbed aboard, latching their individual harnesses onto Temeraire's with their locking carabiners.

Tharkay, his hat buttoned on with a strap under the chin, climbed easily up and tucked himself away near Laurence, close to the base of Temeraire's neck; the eagle, hooded, was in a small cage strapped against his chest. Abruptly from the *Allegiance* came the sudden thunder of cannon-fire: a formal salute, and Temeraire roared out gladly in answer while the flag-signal broke out from the mainmast: *fair wind.* With a quick bunching of muscle and sinew, a deep hollow rushing intake of breath beneath the skin, all the chambers of air swelling out wide, Temeraire was aloft, and the port and the city went rolling away beneath him.

CHAPTER 2

They went quickly, very quickly; Temeraire delighting in the chance to stretch his wings for once with no slower companions to hold him back. Though Laurence was at first a little cautious, Temeraire showed no sign of over-exertion, no heat in the muscles of his shoulders, and after the first few days Laurence let him choose the pace as he wished. Baffled and curious officials came hurrying out to meet them whenever they came down for some food near a town of sufficient size, and Laurence was forced on more than one occasion to put on the heavy golden dragon-robes, the Emperor's gift, to make their questions and demands for paperwork subside into a great deal of formal bowing and scraping: though at least he did not need to feel improperly dressed, as in his makeshift green coat. Where possible they began to avoid settlements, instead buying Temeraire's meals directly from the herdsmen out in the fields, and sleeping nightly in isolated temples, wayside pavilions, and once an abandoned military outpost with the roof long fallen in but the walls still half-standing: they stretched a canopy made of their lashed-together tents over the remnants, and built their fire with the old shattered beams for tinder.

"North, along the Wudang range, to Luoyang," Tharkay said. He had proven a quiet and uncommunicative companion, directing their course most often with a silent pointing finger, tapping on the compass mounted upon Temeraire's harness, and leaving it to Laurence to pass the directions on to Temeraire. But that night he sketched at Laurence's request a path in the dirt as they sat outside by the fire, while Temeraire peered down interestedly. "And then we turn west, towards the old capital, towards Xian." The foreign names meant nothing to Laurence, every city spelled seven different ways on his seven different maps, which Tharkay had eyed sidelong and disdained to consult. But Laurence could follow their progress by the sun and the stars, rising daily in their changed places as Temeraire's flight ate up the miles.

Towns and villages one after another, the children running along the ground underneath Temeraire's racing shadow, waving and calling in high indistinct voices until they fell behind; rivers snaking below them and the old sullen mountains rising on their left, stained green with moss and girt with reluctant clouds unable to break free from the peaks. Dragons passing by avoided them, respectfully descending to lower ranks of the air to give way to Temeraire, except once one of the greyhound-sleek Jade Dragons, the imperial couriers who flew at heights too cold and thin for other breeds, dived down with a cheerful greeting, flitting around Temeraire's head like a hummingbird, and as quickly darted up and away again.

As they continued north, the nights ceased to be so stiflingly hot and became instead pleasantly warm and domestic; hunting plentiful and easy even when they did not come across one of the vast nomadic herds, and good forage for the rest of them. With less than a day's flight left to Xian, they broke their traveling early and encamped by a small lake: three handsome deer were set to roasting for their dinner and Temeraire's, the men meanwhile nibbling on biscuit and some fresh fruit brought them by a local farmer. Granby sat Roland and Dyer down to practice their penmanship by the firelight while Laurence attempted to make out their attempts at trigonometry. These, having been carried out mid-air and with the slates subject to all the force of the wind, posed quite a serious challenge, but he was glad to see at least their calculations no longer produced hypotenuses shorter than the other sides of their triangles.

Temeraire, relieved of his harness, plunged at once into the lake: mountain streams rolled down to feed it from all sides, and its floor was lined with smooth tumbled stones; it was a little shallow now on the cusp of August, but he managed to throw water over his back, and he frolicked and squirmed over the pebbles with great enthusiasm. "That is very refreshing; but surely it must be time to eat now?" he said as he climbed out, and looked meaningfully at the roasting deer; but the cooks waved their enormous spit-hooks at him threateningly, not yet satisfied with their work.

He sighed a little and shook out his wings, spattering them all with a brief shower that made the fire hiss, and settled himself down upon the shore next to Laurence. "I am very glad we did not wait and go by sea; how lovely it is to fly straight, as quickly as one likes, for miles and miles," he said, yawning.

Laurence looked down; certainly there was no such flying in England: a week such as the last would have seen them from one end of the isles to the other and back. "Did you have a pleasant bathe?" he asked, changing the subject.

"Oh, yes; those rocks were very nice," Temeraire said, wistfully, "although it was not *quite* as agreeable as being with Mei."

Lung Qin Mei, a charming Imperial dragon, had been Temeraire's intimate companion in Peking; Laurence had feared since their departure that Temeraire might privately be pining for her. But this sudden mention seemed a non sequitur; nor did Temeraire seem very love-lorn in his tone. Then Granby said, "Oh, dear," and stood up to call across the camp, "Mr. Ferris! Mr. Ferris, tell those boys to pour out that water, and go and fetch some from the stream instead, if you please."

"Temeraire!" Laurence said, scarlet with comprehension.

"Yes?" Temeraire looked at him, puzzled. "Well, do you not find it more pleasant to be with Jane, than to—"

Laurence stood up hastily, saying, "Mr. Granby, pray call the men to dinner now," and pretended not to hear the unsteady stifled mirth in Granby's voice as he said, "Yes, sir," and dashed away.

XIAN WAS AN ancient city, the former capital of the nation and full of the memory of glory, the thin scattering of carts and travelers lonely on the wide and weed-choked roads leading in to the city; they flew over high moated walls of grey brick, pagoda towers standing dark and empty, only a few guards in their uniforms and a couple of lazy scarlet dragons yawning. From above, the streets quartered the city into chessboard squares, marked with temples of a dozen descriptions, incongruous minarets cheek by jowl with the sharp-pointed pagoda roofs. Narrow poplars and old, old pines with fragile wisps of green needles lined the avenues, and they were received in a marble square before the main pagoda by the magistrate of the city, officials assembled and bowing in their robes: news of their approach was outrunning them, likely on the wings of the Jade Dragon courier. They were feasted on the banks of the Wei River in an old pavilion overlooking rustling wheat fields, on hot milky soup and skewers of mutton, three sheep roasted together on a spit for Temeraire, and the magistrate ceremonially broke sprigs of willow in farewell as they left: wishes for a safe return.

Two days later they slept near Tianshui in caves hollowed from red rock, full of silent unsmiling Buddhas, hands and faces reaching out from the walls, garments draped in eternal folds of stone, and rain falling outside beyond the grotto openings. Monumental figures peered after them through the continuing mist as they flew onward, tracking the river or its tributaries now into the heart of the mountain range, narrow winding passes not much wider than Temeraire's wingspan. He delighted in flying through these at great speed, stretching himself to the limit, his wing-tips nearly brushing at the awkward saplings that jutted out sideways from the slopes, until one morning a freak-ish start of wind came suddenly whistling through the narrow pass, catching Temeraire's wings on the upswing, and nearly flung him against the rock face.

He squawked ungracefully, and managed with a desperate snaking twist to turn round in mid-air and catch himself on his legs against the nearly vertical slope. The loose shale and rock at once gave way, the little scrubby growth of green saplings and grass inadequate to stabilize the ground beneath his weight; "Get your wings in!" Granby yelled, through his speaking-trumpet: Temeraire by instinct was trying to beat away into the air again, and only hastening the collapse. Pulling his wings tight, he managed a clawing and flailing scramble down the loose slope, and landed awkwardly athwart the stream bed, his sides heaving.

"Order the men to make camp," Laurence said quickly to Granby, unhooking his carabiner rings, and scrambled down in a series of half-controlled drops, barely grasping the harness with his fingers before letting himself down another twenty feet, hurrying to Temeraire's head. He was drooping, the tendrils and ruff all quivering with his too-quick panting, and his legs were trembling, but he held himself up while the poor bellmen and the ground crew let themselves off staggering, all of them half-choking and caked with the grey dirt thrown up in the frantic descent.

Though they had scarcely gone an hour, everyone was glad to stop and rest, the men throwing themselves down upon the dusty yellow grass-banks even as Temeraire himself did. "You are sure it does not pain you anywhere?" Laurence asked anx-iously while Keynes clambered muttering over Temeraire's shoulders, inspecting the wing-joints.

"No, I am well," Temeraire said, looking more embarrassed than injured, though he was glad to bathe his feet in the stream, and hold them out to be scrubbed clean, some of the dirt and pebbles having crept under the hard ridge of skin around the talons. Afterwards he closed his eyes and put his head down for a nap, and showed no inclination to go anywhere at all; "I ate well yesterday; I am not very hungry," he answered when Laurence suggested they might go hunting, saying he preferred to sleep. But a few hours later Tharkay reappeared—if it could be called reappearing, when his initial absence had gone quite unnoticed—and offered him a dozen fat rabbits which he had taken with the eagle. Ordinarily they would hardly have made a few bites for him, but the Chinese cooks stretched them out by stewing them with salt pork fat, turnips, and some fresh greens, and Temeraire made a sufficiently enthusiastic meal out of them, bones and all, to give the lie to his supposed lack of hunger.

He was a little shy even the next morning, rearing up on his haunches and tasting the air with his tongue as high up as he could stretch his head, trying to get a sense of the wind. Then there was a little something wrong with the harness, somehow not easy for him to describe, which required several lengthy adjustments; then he was thirsty, and the water had become overnight too muddy to drink, so they had to pile up stones for a makeshift dam to form a deeper pool. Laurence began to wonder if perhaps he had done badly not to insist they go aloft again directly after the accident; but abruptly Temeraire said, "Very well, let us go," and launched himself the moment everyone was aboard.

The tension across his shoulders, quite palpable from where Laurence sat, faded after a little while in the air, but still Temeraire went with more caution now, flying slowly while they remained in the mountains. Three days passed before they met and crossed over the Yellow River, so choked with silt it seemed less a waterway than a channel of moving earth, ochre and brown, with thick clods of grass growing out onto the surface of the water from the verdant banks. They had to purchase a bundle of raw silk from a passing river barge to strain the water through before it could be drunk, and their tea had a harsh and clayey taste even so.

"I never thought I would be so glad to see a desert, but I could kiss the sand," Granby said, a few days later: the river was long behind them and the mountains had abruptly yielded that afternoon to foothills and scrubby plateau. The brown desert was visible from their camp on the outskirts of Wuwei. "I suppose you could drop all of Europe into this country and never find it again."

"These maps are thoroughly wrong," Laurence agreed, as he noted down in his log once more the date, and his guess as to miles traversed, which according to the charts would have put them nearly in Moscow. "Mr. Tharkay," he said, as the guide joined them at the fire, "I hope you will accompany me tomorrow to buy the camels?"

"We are not yet at the Taklamakan," Tharkay said. "This is the Gobi; we do not need the camels yet. We will only be skirting its edges; there will be water enough. I suppose it would be as well to buy some meat for the next few days, however," he added, unconscious of the dismay he was giving them.

"One desert ought to be enough for any journey," Granby said. "At this rate we will be in Istanbul for Christmas; if then."

Tharkay raised an eyebrow. "We have covered better than a thousand miles in two weeks of traveling; surely you cannot be dissatisfied with the pace." He ducked into the supply-tent, to look over their stores.

"Fast enough, to be sure, but little good that does everyone waiting for us at home," Granby said, bitterly; he flushed a little at Laurence's surprised look and said, "I am sorry to be such a bear; it is only, my mother lives in Newcastle-upon-Tyne, and my brothers."

The town was nearly midway between the covert at Edinburgh and the smaller at Middlesbrough, and provided the best part of Britain's supply of coal: a natural target, if Bonaparte had chosen to set up a bombardment of the coast, and one which would be difficult to defend with the Aerial Corps spread thin. Laurence nodded silently.

"Do you have many brothers?" Temeraire inquired, unrestrained by the etiquette which had kept Laurence from similarly indulging his own curiosity: Granby had never spoken of his family before. "What dragons do they serve with?"

"They are not aviators," Granby said, adding a little defiantly, "My father was a coal-merchant; my two older brothers now are in my uncle's business."

"Well, I am sure that is interesting work too," Temeraire said with earnest sympathy, not understanding, as Laurence at once had: with a widowed mother, and an uncle who surely had sons of his own to provide for, Granby had likely been sent to the Corps because his family could not afford to keep him. A boy of seven years might be sponsored for a small sum and thus assured of a profession, if not a wholly respectable one, while his family saved his room and board. Unlike the Navy, no influence or family connections would be required to get him such a berth: the Corps was more likely to be short of applicants.

"I am sure they will have gun-boats stationed there," Laurence said, tactfully changing the subject. "And there has been some talk of trying Congreve's rockets for defense against aerial bombardment."

"I suppose that might do to chase off the French: if we set the city on fire ourselves, no reason they would go to the trouble of attacking," Granby said, with an attempt at his usual good humor; but soon he excused himself, and took his small bedroll into a corner of their pavilion to sleep.

ANOTHER FIVE DAYS of flying saw them to the Jiayu Gate, a desolate fortress in a desolate land, built of hard yellow brick that might have been fired from the very sands that surrounded it, outer walls thrice Temeraire's height and nearly two foot thick: the last outpost standing between the heart of China and the western regions, her more recent conquests. The guards were sullen and resentful at their posts, but even so more like real soldiers to Laurence's eye than the happier conscripts he had seen idling through most of the outposts in the rest of the country; though they had but a scattering of badly neglected muskets, their leather-wrapped sword hilts had the hard shine of long use. They eyed Temeraire's ruff very closely as if suspecting him of an imposture, until he put it up and snorted at one of them for going so far as to tug on the spines; then they grew a little more circumspect but still insisted on searching all the party's packs, and they made something of a fuss over the one piece Laurence had decided to bring along instead of leaving on board the *Allegiance:* a red porcelain vase of extraordinary beauty which he had acquired in Peking.

They brought out an enormous text, part of the legal code which governed exports from the country, studied articles, argued amongst themselves and with Tharkay, and demanded a bill of sale which Laurence had never obtained in the first place; in annoyance he exclaimed, "For Heaven's sake, it is a gift for my father, not an article of trade," and this being translated seemed at last to mollify them. Laurence narrowly watched them wrap it back up: he did not mean to lose the thing now, after it had come through vandalism and fire and three thousand miles intact; he thought it his best chance for conciliating Lord Allendale, a notable collector, to the adoption, which would certainly inflame a proud temper already none too pleased with Laurence's having become an aviator.

The inspection dragged on until mid-morning, but they none of them had any desire to remain another night in the unhappy place: once the scene of joyous arrivals, caravans reaching their safe destination and others setting forth on their return journeys, it was now only the last stopping-place of exiles forced to leave the country; a miasma of bitterness lingered.

"We can reach Yumen before the worst heat of the day," Tharkay said, and Temeraire drank deeply from the fortress cistern. They left by the only exit, a single enormous tunnel passing from the inner courtyard and through the whole length of the front battlements, dim sputtering lanterns at infrequent intervals flickering over walls almost covered with ink and in places etched by dragon claws, the last sad messages before departure, prayers for mercy and to one day come home again. Not all were old; fresh broad cuts at the tunnel's edge crossed over other, faded letters, and Temeraire stopped and read them quietly to Laurence:

> Ten thousand *li* between me and your grave,
> Ten thousand *li* more I have yet to travel.

I shake out my wings and step into the
merciless sun.

Past the shade of the deep tunnel, the sun was indeed merciless and the ground dry and cracked, drifted over with sand and
small pebbles. As they loaded up again outside, the two Chinese
cooks, who had grown quiet and unhappy overnight despite not
the least signs of homesickness over the whole course of their
journey thus far, walked a little way off and each picked up a
pebble and flung it at the wall, in what seemed to Laurence an
odd hostility: Jing Chao's pebble bounced off, but the other,
thrown by Gong Su, skittered and rolled down the sloping wall
to the ground. At this he made a short gasp and came at once to
Laurence with a torrent of apology, of which even Laurence
with his very scant supply of Chinese could make out the meaning: he did not mean to come any farther.

"He says that the pebble did not come back, and that means
he will never return to China," Temeraire translated; meanwhile
Jing Chao was already handing up his chest of spices and cooking tools to be bundled in with the rest of the gear, evidently as
reassured as Gong Su was distressed.

"Come now, this is unreasonable superstition," Laurence
said to Gong Su. "You assured me particularly you did not mind
leaving China; and I have given you six months' wages in advance. You cannot expect me to pay you still more for your
journey now, when you have been at work less than a month's
time, and are already reneging upon our contract."

Gong Su made still further apologies: he had left all the
money at home with his mother, whom he made out to be thoroughly destitute and friendless otherwise, though Laurence had
met the stout and rather formidable lady in question along with
her eleven other sons when they had all come to see Gong Su off
from Macao. "Well," Laurence said finally, "I will give you a
little more to start you on the way, but still you had much better
come with us. It will take you a wretchedly long time to get
home going by land, apart from the expense, and I am sure you
would soon feel very foolish at having indulged your fancy in

such a manner." Truthfully, of the two Laurence would much rather have spared Jing Chao, who was proving generally quarrelsome and given to berating the ground crew in Chinese if they did not treat his supplies with what he considered appropriate care. Laurence knew some of the men were beginning to inquire quietly of Temeraire about the meaning of some words to understand what was being said to them; Laurence suspected himself that many of Jing Chao's remarks were impolite, and if so the situation would certainly become difficult.

Gong Su wavered, uncertainly; Laurence added, "Perhaps it only means you will like England so very well you will choose to settle there, but in any case I am sure nothing good can come of taking fright at such an omen, and trying to avoid whatever your fate may be." This made an impression, and after a little more consideration Gong Su did climb aboard; Laurence shook his head at the silliness of it all, and turned to say to Temeraire, "It is a great deal of nonsense."

"Oh; yes," said Temeraire with a guilty start, pretending he had not been eyeing a convenient boulder, roughly half the size of a man, which if flung against the wall would likely have brought the guards boiling out in alarm, convinced they were under bombardment by siege weaponry. "We will come back someday, Laurence, will we not?" he asked, a little wistfully: he was leaving behind not only the handful of other Celestial dragons who were all his kin in the world, and the luxury of the imperial court, but the ordinary and unconscious liberties which the Chinese system showed to all dragons as a matter of course, in treating them very little different from men at all.

Laurence had no such powerful reasons for wanting to return: to him China had been the scene only of deep anxiety and danger, a morass of foreign politics, and if he were honest even a degree of jealousy; he did not himself feel any desire ever to come back. "When the war is over, whenever you would like," he said quietly, however, and put a hand on Temeraire's leg, comforting, while the crew finished getting him rigged-out for the flight.

CHAPTER 3

They left the green oasis of Dunhuang at dawn, the camel-bells in a querulous jangle as the beasts reluctantly trudged away over the dune-crests, their shaggy flat feet muddling the sharp lines of the ridges which cut the sunlight into parts: the dunes like ocean waves captured in pen and ink, on one side perfectly white and on the other pure shadow, printed on the pale caramel color of the sand. The caravan trails unknotted themselves one at a time and broke away to north and south, joinings marked by heaps of bones with staring camel-skulls piled atop. Tharkay turned the lead camel's head southward, the long train following: the camels knew their work even if their still-awkward riders did not. Temeraire padded after like a disproportionate herd-dog, at a distance far enough to comfort them, near enough to keep any of them from trying to bolt the way they had come.

Laurence had expected the terrible sun, but so far north the desert did not hold its heat: by mid-day a man was soaked through with sweat; an hour after nightfall he was chilled to the bone, and a white frost crept over the water-casks during the night. The eagle kept itself fed on brown-spotted lizards and small mice, seen otherwise only as shadows darting uneasily beneath rocks; Temeraire daily reduced the camel-train by one; the rest of them ate thin, tough strips of dried meat, chewed for hours, and coarse tea mixed into a vile but nourishing slurry with oat flour and roasted wheat berries. The casks were reserved for Temeraire; their own supply came from the water-bags each man carried for himself, filled every other day or so from small decaying wells, mostly tainted with salt, or shallow pools overgrown with tamarisk-trees, their roots rotting in the mud: the water yellow and bitter and thick, scarcely drinkable even when boiled.

Each morning Laurence and Temeraire took Tharkay aloft and scouted some little distance ahead of the camel-train for the best path, though always a shimmering haze distorted the horizon, limiting their view; the Tianshan range to the south seemed to float above the blurred mirage, as though the blue jutting mountains were divided from the earth, upon another plane entirely.

"How lonely it is," Temeraire said, though he liked the flying: the heat of the sun seemed to make him especially buoyant, perhaps acting in some peculiar way upon the air-sacs which enabled dragons to fly, and he needed little effort to keep aloft.

He and Laurence would often pause during the day together: Laurence would read to him, or Temeraire recite him attempts at poetry, a habit acquired in Peking, it being there considered a more appropriate occupation for Celestials than warfare; when the sun dipped lower they would take to the air to catch up the rest of the convoy, following the plaintive sound of the camel-bells through the dusk.

"Sir," Granby said, jogging to meet Laurence as they descended, "one of those fellows is missing, the cook."

They went aloft again at once, searching, but there was no sign of the poor devil; the wind was a busy house-keeper, sweeping up the camel-tracks almost as quickly as they had been made, and to be lost for ten minutes was as good as for eternity. Temeraire flew low, listening for the jingle of camel-bells, fruitlessly;

night was coming on quickly, and the lengthening shadows of the dunes blurred together into a uniform darkness. "I cannot see anything more, Laurence," Temeraire said sadly: the stars were coming out, and there was only a thin sliver of moon.

"We will look again tomorrow," Laurence said to comfort him, but with little real hope; they set down again by the tents, and Laurence shook his head silently as he climbed down into the waiting circle of the camp; he gladly took a cup of the thick tea and warmed his chilled hands and feet at the low wavering campfire.

"The camel is a worse loss," Tharkay said, turning away with a shrug, brutal but truthful: Jing Chao had endeared himself to no one. Even Gong Su, his country-man and longest acquaintance, heaved only one sigh, and then led Temeraire around to the waiting roast camel, today cooked in a fire-pit with tea-leaves, an attempt at changing the flavor.

THE FEW OASIS towns they passed through were narrow places in spirit, less unfriendly than perplexed by strangers: the market-places lazy and slow, men in black skull-caps smoking and drinking spiced tea in the shade and watching them curiously; Tharkay exchanged a few words now and again, in Chinese and in other tongues. The streets were not in good repair, mostly drifted over with sand and cut by deep channels pitted with the ancient marks of nail-studded waggon wheels. They bought bags of almonds and dried fruit, sweet pressed apricots and grapes, filled their water-bags at the clean deep wells, and continued on their way.

The camels began moaning early in the night, the first sign of warning; when the watch came to fetch Laurence, the constellations were already being swallowed up by the low oncoming cloud.

"Let Temeraire drink and eat; this may last some time," Tharkay said: a couple of the ground crewmen pried off the cover from two of the flat-sided wooden butts and brushed the damp, cooling sawdust away from the swollen leather bags inside, then Temeraire lowered his head so they might pour out the mixture of water and ice into his mouth: having had nearly a week's practice, he did not spill a drop, but closed his jaws tight before raising his head up again to swallow. The unburdened camel rolled its eyes and fought at being separated from its fellows, to no avail; Pratt and his mate, both of them big men, dragged it around behind the tents; Gong Su drew a knife across its neck, deftly catching the spurting blood in a bowl; and Temeraire unenthusiastically fell-to: he was getting tired of camel.

There were still some fifteen left to get under cover, and Granby marshaled the midwingmen and the ensigns while the ground crewmen anchored the tents more securely; already the layer of loose fine sand was whipping across the surface of the dunes and stinging their hands and faces, though they put up their collars and wrapped their neckcloths over their mouths and noses. The thick fur-lined tents, which they had been so glad to have during the cold nights, now grew stifling hot as they struggled and pushed and crowded in the camels, and even the thinner leather pavilion which they got up to shield Temeraire and themselves was smotheringly close.

And then the sandstorm was upon them: a hissing furious assault, nothing like the sound of rain, falling without surcease against the leather tent wall. It could not be ignored; the noise rose and fell in unpredictable bursts, from shrieks to whispers and back again, so they could only take brief unrestful snatches of sleep; and faces grew bruised with fatigue around them. They did not risk many lanterns inside the tent; when the sun set, Laurence sat by Temeraire's head in a darkness almost complete, listening to the wind howl.

"Some call the karaburan the work of evil spirits," Tharkay said out of the dark; he was cutting some leather for fresh jesses for the eagle, presently subdued in its cage, head hunched invisibly into its shoulders. "You can hear their voices, if you listen," and indeed one could make out low and plaintive cries on the wind, like murmurs in a foreign tongue.

"I cannot understand them," Temeraire said, listening with

interest rather than dread; evil spirits did not alarm him. "What language is that?"

"No tongue of men or dragons," Tharkay said seriously: the ensigns were listening, the older men only pretending not to, and Roland and Dyer had crept close, eyes stretched wide. "Those who listen too long grow confused and lose their way: they are never found again, except as bones scoured clean to warn other travelers away."

"Hm," Temeraire said skeptically. "I would like to see the demon that could eat *me*," which would certainly have required a prodigious kind of devil.

Tharkay's mouth twitched. "That is why they have not dared to bother us; dragons of your size are not often seen in the desert." The men huddled rather closer to Temeraire, and no one spoke of going outside.

"Have you heard of dragons having their own languages?" Temeraire asked Tharkay a little later, softly; most of the men were drifting, half-asleep. "I have always thought we learned them from men only."

"The Durzagh tongue is a language of dragons," Tharkay said. "There are sounds in it men cannot make: your voices more easily mimic ours than the reverse."

"Oh! will you teach me?" Temeraire asked, eagerly; Celestials, unlike most dragons, kept the ability to easily acquire new tongues past their hatching and infancy.

"It is of little use," Tharkay said. "It is only spoken in the mountains: in the Pamirs, and the Karakoram."

"I do not mind that," Temeraire said. "It will be so very useful when we are back in England. Laurence, the Government cannot say we are just animals if we have invented our own language," he added, looking to him for confirmation.

"No one with any sense would say it regardless," Laurence began, to be interrupted by Tharkay's short snorting laugh.

"On the contrary," he said. "They are more likely to think you an animal for speaking a tongue other than English; or at least a creature unworthy of notice: you would do better to cultivate an elevated tone," and his voice changed quite on the final words, taking on the drawling style favored by the too-fashionable set for a moment.

"That is a very strange way of speaking," Temeraire said dubiously, after he had tried it, repeating over the phrase a few times. "It seems very peculiar to me that it should make any difference how one says the words, and it must be a great deal of trouble to learn how to say them all over again. Can one hire a translator to say things properly?"

"Yes; they are called lawyers," Tharkay said, and laughed softly to himself.

"I would certainly not recommend you to imitate this particular style," Laurence said dryly, while Tharkay recovered from his amusement. "At best you might only impress some fellow on Bond Street, if he did not run away to begin with."

"Very true; you had much better take Captain Laurence as your model," Tharkay said, inclining his head. "Just how a gentleman ought to speak; I am sure any official would agree."

His expression was not visible in the shadows, but Laurence felt as though he were being obscurely mocked, perhaps without malice, but irritating to him nonetheless. "I see you have made a study of the subject, Mr. Tharkay," he said a little coldly. Tharkay shrugged.

"Necessity was a thorough teacher, if a hard one," he said. "I found men eager enough to deny me my rights, without providing them so convenient an excuse to dismiss me. You may find it slow going," he added to Temeraire, "if you mean to assert your own: men with powers and privileges rarely like to share them."

This was no more than Laurence had said, on many an occasion, but a vein of cynicism ran true and deep beneath Tharkay's words which perhaps made them the more convincing: "I am sure I do not see why they should not wish to be just," Temeraire said, but uncertainly, troubled, and so Laurence found he did not after all like to see Temeraire take his own advice to heart.

"Justice is expensive," Tharkay said. "That is why there is so little of it, and that reserved for those few with enough money and influence to afford it."

"In some corners of the world, perhaps," Laurence said, unable to tolerate this, "but thank God, we have a rule of law in Britain, and those checks upon the power of men which prevent any from becoming tyrannical."

"Or which spread the tyranny over more hands, piecemeal," Tharkay said. "I do not know that the Chinese system is any worse; there is a limit to the evil one despot alone can do, and if he is truly vicious he can be overthrown; a hundred corrupt members of Parliament may together do as much injustice or more, and be the less easy to uproot."

"And where on the scale would you rank Bonaparte?" Laurence demanded, growing too indignant to be polite: it was one thing to complain of corruption, or propose judicious reforms; quite another to lump the British system in with absolute despotism.

"As a man, a monarch, or a system of government?" Tharkay asked. "If there is more injustice in France than elsewhere, on the whole, I have not heard of it. It is quixotic of them to have chosen to be unjust to the noble and the rich, in favor of the common; but it does not seem to me naturally worse; or, for that matter, likely to last long. As for the rest, I will defer to *your* judgment, sir; who would you take on the battlefield: good King George or the second lieutenant of artillery from Corsica?"

"I would take Lord Nelson," Laurence said. "I do not believe anyone has ever suggested he likes glory less than Bonaparte, but he has put his genius in service to his country and his King, and graciously accepted what rewards they chose to give him, instead of setting himself up as a tyrant."

"So shining an example must vanquish any argument, and indeed I should be ashamed to be the cause of any disillusionment." Tharkay's faint half-smile was visible now: it was growing lighter outside. "We have a little break in the storm, I think; I will go and look in on the camels." He wrapped a veil of cotton several times around his face, pulling his hat firmly down over all, and drew on his gloves and cloak before ducking out through the flaps.

"Laurence, but the Government must listen in our case, because there are so many dragons," Temeraire said, interrogatively, when Tharkay had gone out, returning to the point of real concern to him.

"They *shall* listen," Laurence said, still smoldering and indignant, without thinking; and regretted it the next instant: Temeraire, only too willing to be relieved of doubt, brightened at once and said, "I was sure it must be so," and whatever good the conversation might have done, in lowering his expectations, was lost.

THE STORM LINGERED another day, fierce enough to wear holes, after a while, in the leather of their pavilion; they patched it as best they could from inside, but dust crept in through all the cracks, into their garments and their food, gritty and unpleasant when they chewed the cold dried meat. Temeraire sighed and shivered his hide now and again, little cascades of sand running off his shoulders and wings onto the floor: they had already a layer of desert inside the tent with them.

Laurence did not know just when the storm ended: as the blessed silence began to fall, they all drifted into their first real sleep in days, and he woke to the sound of the eagle outside giving a red cry of satisfaction. Stumbling out of the tent, he found it tearing raw flesh from the corpse of a camel lying across the remains of the campfire pit, neck broken and white rib cage already half-stripped clean by the sands.

"One of the tents did not hold," Tharkay said, behind him. Laurence did not at once take his meaning: he turned and saw eight of the camels, tethered loosely near a heap of piled forage, swaying a little on legs grown stiff from their long confinement; the tent which had sheltered them was still up, leaning somewhat askew with a sand-drift piled up against one side. Of the second tent there was no sign except two of the iron stakes still planted deeply in the ground, and a few scraps of brown leather pinned down, fluttering with the breeze.

"Where are the rest of the camels?" Laurence said, in growing horror. He took Temeraire aloft at once, while the men spread out, calling, in every direction, in vain: the scouring wind had left no tracks, no signs, not so much as a scrap of bloody hide.

By mid-day they had given it up, and began in desolate spirits to pack up the camp; seven camels lost, and their water-casks with them, which had been left on to keep them weighted down and quiet. "Will we be able to buy more in Cherchen?" Laurence asked Tharkay, wearily, wiping a hand across his brow; he did not recall seeing many animals in the streets of the town, which they had left nearly three days before.

"Only with difficulty," Tharkay said. "Camels are very dear here, and men prize them highly; some may object to selling healthy beasts to be eaten. We ought not turn back, in my opinion." At Laurence's doubtful look, he added, "I set the number at thirty deliberately high, in case of accidents: this is worse than I had planned for, but we can yet manage until we reach the Keriya River. We will have to ration the camels, and refill Temeraire's water-casks as best we can at the oases, forgoing as much as we can ourselves; it will not be pleasant, but I promise you it can be done."

The temptation was very great: Laurence bitterly grudged the loss of more time. Three days back to Cherchen, and likely a long delay there acquiring new pack-animals, all the while having to manage food and water for Temeraire in a town unaccustomed to supporting any dragons at all, much less one of his size; a clear loss of more than a week, certainly. Tharkay seemed confident, and yet—and yet—

Laurence drew Granby behind the tents, to consult in privacy: considering it best to keep their mission secret, so far as possible, and not to spread any useless anxiety over the state of affairs in Europe, Laurence had not yet shared their purpose with the rest of the crew, and left them to believe they were returning overland only to avoid the long delay in port.

"A week is enough time to get the eggs to a covert *somewhere*," Granby said, urgently. "Gibraltar—the outpost on Malta—it might be the difference between success and failure. I swear to you there is not a man among us who would not go hungry and thirsty twice as long for the chance, and Tharkay is not saying there is a real risk we shall run dry."

Abruptly Laurence said, "And you are easy in your mind, trusting his judgment on the matter?"

"More than any of ours, surely," Granby said. "What do you mean?"

Laurence did not know quite how to put his unease into words; indeed he hardly knew what he feared. "I suppose I only do not like putting our lives so completely into his hands," he said. "Another few days of travel will put us out of reach of Cherchen, with our present supplies, and if he is mistaken—"

"Well, his advice has been good so far," Granby said, a little more doubtfully, "though I won't deny he has a damned queer way of going on, sometimes."

"He left the tent once, during the storm, for a long while," Laurence said quietly. "That was after the first day, halfway through—he said he went to look in on the camels."

They stood silently together. "I don't suppose we could tell by looking how long that camel has been dead?" Granby suggested. They went to try an inspection, but too late: Gong Su already had what was left of the dead beast jointed and spitted over a fire, browning to a turn, and offering no answers whatsoever.

When consulted, Temeraire said, "It seems a very great pity to turn around to me also. I do not mind eating every other day," and added under his breath, "especially if it must be camel."

"Very well; we continue on," Laurence said, despite his misgivings, and when Temeraire had eaten, they trudged onward through a landscape rendered even more drear by the storm, scrub and vegetation torn away, even the scattering of colorful pebbles blown away, leaving no relief to the eye. They would have gladly welcomed even one of the grisly trail-markers, but there was nothing to guide their steps but the compass and Tharkay's instincts.

The rest of the long dry day passed by, as terrible and monotonous in its turn as the storm, miles of desert grinding slowly away under their feet; there was no sign of life, nor even one of the old crumbling wells. Most of the crew were riding on Temeraire now, trailing the sad little string of camels remaining; as the day wore on, even Temeraire's head drooped: he, too, had only had half his usual ration of water.

"Sir," Digby said through cracked lips, pointing, "I see something dark over there, though it's not very big."

Laurence saw nothing; it was late in the day, with the sun beginning to make queer long shadows out of the small twisted rocks and stumps of the desert landscape, but Digby had the sharp eyes of youth and was the most reliable of his lookouts, not given to exaggeration. So they went on towards it: soon they could all see the round dark patch, but it was too small to be the mouth of a well. Tharkay stopped the camels beside it, looking down, and Laurence slid down from Temeraire's neck to walk over: it was the lid of one of the lost water-casks, lying incongruously all alone atop the sand, thirty miles of empty desert away from the morning's camp.

"EAT YOUR RATION," Laurence said sternly, when he saw Roland and Dyer putting down their strips of meat half-eaten: they were all hungry, but the long chewing was painful in a dry mouth, and every sip of water now had to be stolen from Temeraire's casks; another long day had gone, and still they had found no well. Temeraire had eaten his camel raw, so as not to lose any of the moisture in cooking: only seven left, now.

Two days later they stumbled across a dry, cracked irrigation channel, and on Tharkay's advice turned northward to follow its path, hoping to find some water still at its source. The wizened and twisted remains of dead fruit-trees still overhung the sides, their small gnarled branches dry as paper to the touch, and as light, reaching for the vanished water. The city took shape out of the desert haze as they rode onwards: shattered timbers jutting out of the sand, sharpened by years of wind into pointed stakes; broken pieces of mud-and-wattle bricks; the last remnants of buildings swallowed by the desert. The bed of the river that had once given life to the city was filled with fine dust; there was nothing living in sight but some brown desert grass clinging to the tops of dunes, which the camels hungrily devoured.

Another day's journey would put them beyond the hope of turning back. "I am afraid this is a bad part of the desert, but we will find water soon," Tharkay said, bringing an armful of old broken timbers to the campfire. "It is just as well we have found the city; we must be on an old caravan route now."

Their fire leapt and crackled brightly, the dry seasoned wood going up hot and quick; the warmth and light was comforting in the midst of the ashes and broken relics of the city, but Laurence walked away brooding. His maps were useless: there were no marked roads, nothing to be seen in any direction for miles; and his patience was badly frayed at seeing Temeraire go hungry and thirsty. "Pray do not worry, Laurence, I am very well," Temeraire had assured him; but he had not been able to keep his eyes from lingering on the remaining camels, and it hurt Laurence to see how quickly he tired, each day, with his tail now often dragging upon the sand: he did not wish to fly, but plodded along in the wake of the camels, and lay down often to rest.

If they turned back in the morning, Temeraire could eat and drink his fill; they might even load two of the water-casks upon him, slaughter an additional camel for him to carry, and try to make Cherchen by air. Laurence thought two days' flight would see them there, if Temeraire went lightly burdened and had food and water enough. He would take the youngest of the crew: Roland and Dyer and the ensigns, who would slow the others down on the ground and need less water and food for Temeraire to carry; though he would not like leaving the rest of the men, by his calculation the water carried by the last four camels would be just sufficient to see them back to Cherchen by land, if they could manage twenty miles in a day.

Money would then present difficulties: he did not have so much silver he could afford to purchase another great string of camels even if the beasts could be found, but perhaps someone might be found who would take the risk of accepting a note on the strength of his word, offered at an exorbitant rate; or they might exchange some labor: there did not seem to be dragons living in the desert towns, and Temeraire's strength could accomplish many tasks quickly. In the worst case, he might pry the gold and gems off the hilt of his sword, to be later replaced, and sell the porcelain vase if he could find a taker. God only knew how much delay it would all mean: weeks if not a month, and many fresh risks taken; Laurence took his turn at watch and went to sleep still undecided, unhappy, and woke with Granby shaking him in the early morning, before dawn: "Temeraire hears something: horses, he thinks."

The light crept along the crests of the low dunes just outside the town: a knot of men on shaggy, short-legged ponies, keeping a good distance; even as Laurence and Granby watched, another five or six rode up onto the top of the dune to join them, carrying short curved sabers, and some others with bows. "Strike the tents, and get the camels hobbled," Laurence said grimly. "Digby, take Roland and Dyer and the other ensigns and stay by them: you must not let them run off. Have the men form up around the supplies; backs to that wall, over there, the broken one," he added to Granby.

Temeraire was sitting up on his haunches. "Are we going to have a battle?" he asked, with less alarm than eager anticipation. "Those horses look tasty."

"I mean to be ready, and let them see it, but we are not going to strike first," Laurence said. "They have not threatened us yet; and in any case, we had much better buy their help than fight them. We will send to them under a flag of truce. Where is Tharkay?"

Tharkay was gone: the eagle also, and one of the camels, and no one remembered seeing him go. Laurence was conscious at first of only shock, more profound than he ought to have felt, having been suspicious. The sensation yielded to a cold savage anger, and dread: they had been drawn just far enough that the camel stolen meant they could not turn back to Cherchen, and the bright beacon of the fire, last night, perhaps had drawn down this hostile attention.

With an effort he said, "Very well; Mr. Granby, if any of the men know a little Chinese, let them come with me under the flag; we will see if we can manage to make ourselves understood."

"You cannot go yourself," Granby said, instantly protective; but events obviated any need for debate on the matter: abruptly the horsemen wheeled around as one and rode away, vanishing into the dunes, the ponies whinnying with relief.

"Oh," Temeraire said, disappointed, and drooped back down onto all fours; the rest of them stood uncertainly awhile, still alert, but the horsemen did not reappear.

"Laurence," Granby said quietly, "they know this ground, I expect, and we do not; if they mean to have at us and they have any sense, they will go away and wait for tonight. Once we have encamped, they can be on us before we know they are there, and maybe even do Temeraire some mischief. We oughtn't let them just slip away."

"And more to the point," Laurence said, "those horses were not carrying any great deal of water."

The soft dented hoofprints led them a wary trail west- and southward, climbing over a series of hills; a little hot wind came into their faces as they walked, and the camels made low, eager moaning noises and quickened their pace unasked: over the next rise the narrow green tops of poplar-trees came unexpectedly into view, waving, beckoning them on over the rise.

The oasis, hidden in a sheltered cleft, looked only another small brackish pool, mostly mud, but desperately welcome for all that. The horsemen were there gathering on the far edge, their ponies milling around nervously and rolling their eyes as Temeraire approached, and among them was Tharkay, with the missing camel. He rode up to them as if unconscious of any wrong, and said to Laurence, "They told me of having seen you; I am glad you thought to follow."

"Are you?" Laurence said.

That stopped him a moment; he looked at Laurence, and the corner of his mouth twisted upwards a little; then he said, "Follow me," and led them, their hands still full of pistols and swords, around the edges of the meandering pond: clinging to the side of one grassy dune was a great domed structure built of long narrow mud bricks, the same pale straw color as the yellowed grass, with a single arched opening looking in, and a small window in the opposite wall which presently let in a shaft of sunlight to play upon the dark and shining pool of water that filled the interior. "You can widen the sardoba opening for him to drink, only be careful you do not bring down the roof," Tharkay said.

Laurence kept a guard facing the horsemen across the oasis, with Temeraire at their backs, and set the armorer Pratt to work with a couple of the taller midwingmen to help. With his heavy mallet and some pry-bars they shortly had tapped away more bricks from the sides of the ragged opening: it was only just large enough before Temeraire had gratefully plunged in his snout to drink, great swallows going down his throat; he lifted his muzzle out dripping wet and licked even the drops away with his long, narrow forking tongue. "Oh, how very nice and cool it is," he said, with much relief.

"They are packed with snow during the winter," Tharkay said. "Most have fallen into disuse and are now left empty, but I hoped we might find one here. These men are from Yutien; we are on the Khotan road, and in four more days we will reach the city: Temeraire can eat as he likes, there is no more need to ration."

"Thank you; I prefer to yet exercise a little caution," Laurence said. "Pray ask those men if they will sell us some of their animals: I am sure Temeraire would enjoy a change from camel."

One of the ponies had gone lame, and the owner professed himself willing to accept in exchange five Chinese taels of silver. "It is an absurd amount," Tharkay commented, "when he cannot easily get the animal home again," but Laurence counted the money well-spent as Temeraire tore into the meal with a savage delight. The seller looked equally pleased with his end of the bargain, if less violently demonstrative, and climbed up behind one of the other riders; they and some four or five others at once left the oasis, riding away southward in a cloud of rising dust. The rest of the horsemen stayed on, boiling water for tea over small grass fires and sending sideways, covert looks across the pond at Temeraire, who now lay drowsy and limp in the shade of the poplars, snorting occasionally in his sleep and otherwise inert. They might only have been nervous for the sake of their mounts, but Laurence began to fear he had by his free-spending given the horsemen cause to think them rich and tempting prey, and he kept the men on close watch, letting them go to the sardoba only by twos.

To his relief, in the waning light the horsemen broke camp and left; their passage away could be followed by the dust which they kicked up, lingering like a mist against the deepening twilight. At last Laurence went himself to the sardoba and knelt by the edge to cup the cold water directly to his mouth: fresh and more pure than any he had tasted in the desert, only a faint earthen taste from lying sheltered inside the clay brick. He put his wet hands to his face and the back of his neck, coming away stained yellow and brown with the dust which had collected upon his skin, and drank another few handfuls, glad of every drop, before he rose again to oversee their making camp.

The water-casks were brimming again and heavy, which displeased only the camels, and even they were not unhappy; they did not spit and kick while being unloaded, as was their usual practice, but submitted quietly to the handling and to their tethers, and eagerly bent their heads to the tender green shrubs around the water-hole. The men's spirits all were high, the younger boys even playing a little in the cool evening at a makeshift bit of sport with a dead branch as bat and a rolled-up pair of stockings for a ball. Laurence felt certain that some of the flasks being passed from hand to hand held something considerably stronger than water, though he had ordered all liquor poured out and replaced with water before they entered the desert; and they made a merry dinner, the dried meat far more palatable for having been stewed with grain and some wild onions growing near the water's edge, which Gong Su had pointed out to them as fit for human consumption.

Tharkay took his portion and planted his small tent a little way off, speaking in low voice only to the eagle, resting hooded and silent on his hand after its own meal of a couple of plump and unwary rats. The isolation was not wholly self-imposed: Laurence had not spoken of his suspicions to the men, but his anger that morning at Tharkay's disappearance had transmitted itself without words, and in any case no-one thought much of his having gone off in such a manner. At worst he might have meant to strand them deliberately: certainly none of them would have been able to find the oasis alone, without the trail accidentally provided by the horsemen; or, only a little less bad, he might instead have chosen to abandon them to an uncertain fate, and to secure his own safety by taking a camel and water enough to last him a long time alone. He might have returned to them, having discovered the oasis, but that he had left them only to scout ahead, Laurence could not credit— without a word? with no companion?—if not entirely disprovable, still unsatisfying.

What was to be done about him an equal puzzle: they could not manage without a guide, though Laurence could not see continuing with one untrustworthy; yet how another was to be found, he could not well conceive. At least any decision by necessity would be deferred to Yutien: he would not abandon the man alone in the desert, even if Tharkay had meant to do as much to them; at least not with so little proof. So Tharkay was left to sit alone untroubled for the moment, but as the men began to seek their beds, Laurence quietly arranged with Granby a doubled guard on the camels, and let the men think it was only for fear of the horsemen returning.

THE MOSQUITOES SANG loudly, all round them, after the sun had gone down; even hands pressed over the ears could not drown out their thin whining voices. The first sudden howling was at first almost a relief, a clear reasonable human noise; then the camels were bellowing and plunging as the horses came stampeding through the middle of the camp, their riders yelling loud enough to drown out any orders Laurence might shout, and scattering the embers of the campfire with long raking branches dragged along the ground.

Temeraire sat up from behind the tents and roared: the camels began struggling all the more wildly against their hobbles, and many of the ponies whinnying in terror bolted away; Laurence heard pistols going off in all directions, the white muzzle-flashes painfully bright in the dark. "Damn you; don't waste your shot," he bellowed, and seized young Allen, pale and frightened, as he stumbled backwards out of a tent with a pistol shaking in his hand. "Put that down, if you cannot—" Laurence said, and caught the pistol as it fell; the boy was sliding limp to the ground, blood spurting from a neat pistol-hole in his shoulder.

"Keynes!" Laurence shouted, and thrust the fainting boy into the dragon-surgeon's arms; he drew his own sword and dashed towards the camels, the guards all staggering uselessly to their feet, with the thick confused look of men woken from drunken slumber, a couple of hip-flasks rattling empty on the ground beside them. Digby was clinging to the animals' tethers, nearly dangling by them to keep the camels from rearing: the only one being of any use, even though his gangly young frame was hardly enough weight to keep their heads down, and he was nearly bouncing at the ends of the reins with his fair hair, grown long and unkempt, flopping wildly.

One of the raiders, thrown from his fear-maddened horse, gained his feet; if he could get at the tethers and cut them, the unleashed camels would do half the work, for they would surely bolt directly out of the camp in their present state of confusion and terror; on horseback the raiders could then herd them together and away, and vanish amongst the hills and valleys of the surrounding dunes.

Salyer, one of the midshipmen on watch, was fumbling his pistol one-handed, trying to cock the hammer and rub at his gummy eyes with the other, while the man bore down on him with saber raised; suddenly Tharkay was there, snatching the pistol from Salyer's slack grip. He fired into the raider's chest, dropping him to the ground, and drew in his other hand a long knife; another of the raiders swung at his head, from horseback, and Tharkay ducking underneath coolly slit open the animal's belly. It fell screaming and thrashing, the man pinned underneath and howling almost as loudly, and Laurence's naked sword swept down once, twice, and silenced them both.

"Laurence, Laurence, here!" Temeraire called, and lunged in the dark towards one of the supply-tents, the red scattered remnants of the fire giving off a little light, enough to see shadows moving around the edges, and the silhouettes of rearing, snorting horses. Temeraire struck with his talons, fabric ripping as the tent collapsed around the body of a man, and all the other horsemen were suddenly going, drumming hooves going quiet and muffled as they fled from the hard-packed campground onto loose sand, leaving only the mosquitoes behind to raise up their song again.

They had accounted for five men and two horses all told; their losses one of the midwingmen, Macdonaugh, who had taken a saber-thrust to the belly and now lay gasping quietly upon a makeshift cot; and young Allen: his tent-mate Harley, who had fired off the shot in panic as the horses went thundering by, wept quietly in a corner, until Keynes in his brusque way told the boy, "Cease to behave like a watering-pot, if you please; you had better practice your aim: a shot like that would not kill anyone," and set him to cutting up bandages for his fellow ensign.

"Macdonaugh is a strong fellow," Keynes said to Laurence quietly, "but I will not give you false hope," and a few hours before morning, he gave a choked rattling sigh and died. Temeraire dug him a grave in the dry earth some little distance from the watering-pool, in the shade of the poplars; very deep, so that sandstorms would not expose the body. The bodies of the other men they buried more shallowly, in a mass grave. The raiders had carried off very little in exchange for their blood: a few cooking pots, a bag of grain, some blankets; and one of the tents had been ruined by Temeraire's attack.

"I doubt they will make another attempt, but we had better move on as quickly as we can," Tharkay said. "If they choose to carry a false report of us back to Khotan, we might find an unpleasant welcome there."

LAURENCE DID NOT know what to make of Tharkay: if he were the most brazen traitor alive, or the most inconsistent; or his own suspicions wholly unjust. That had been no coward standing up beside him during the fight, with the panicked animals on every side and the attackers intent only on gain: easy enough for Tharkay to duck away quietly, or even to let the bandits have their way and snatch a camel for himself in the confusion. Still, a man might be brave enough with swords drawn and that say nothing for his character otherwise, though Laurence felt awkward and ungrateful for entertaining the thought.

He would not take further chances, however, at least none unnecessary: if four days' time brought them safely to Yutien, as Tharkay had promised, well and good; but Laurence would not put them in a position to starve if the promise did not hold true. Fortunately, having gorged himself on the two dead horses, Temeraire was able now without pain to leave the remaining camels unmolested for a couple of days: and at evening on the third he took Laurence aloft, and in the distance they saw the narrow ribbon of the Keriya River shining silver-white in the sunset, interrupting the desert and garlanded with a swath of thick and verdant green.

Temeraire ate his camel that night with pleasure, and they all drank their fill; the next morning they soon came to farmland, bordered on all sides by tall swaying stands of cannabis plants growing higher than a man's head, planted in perfectly squared rows to anchor the dunes; and vast groves of mulberry-trees, leaves rustling against one another in the whisper of breeze, on the approach to the great desert city.

The marketplace was divided into separate quarters, one full of gaily painted waggons that were both transport and shop, drawn by mules or the small shaggy ponies, many of them adorned also with waving colored plumes; in the other, tents of breezy cotton were set up on frameworks of poplar-branches to provide a kind of storefront, and smallish dragons in bright spangly jewelry curled around them in company with the traders, raising their heads curiously to watch Temeraire go by; he eyed them with equal interest, and some covetous gleam. "It is only tin and glass," Laurence said hurriedly, hoping to forestall any desire Temeraire might have to deck himself out in similar wise. "It is not worth anything."

"Oh; it is very pretty, though," Temeraire said regretfully, lingering on a dramatic ensemble rather like a tiara of purple and crimson and brass, with long swooping chains of glass beads draped down the neck.

Like the horsemen they had met, the faces were more Turkish than Oriental, nut-brown in the desert sun, but for the heavily veiled Mahommedan women of whom only their hands and feet could be seen; other women did not cover their faces, but wore only the same four-cornered caps as the men, embroidered lavishly in dyed silks, and watched them with open curious dark eyes: interest returned in at least full measure by the men. Laurence turned to give Dunne and Hackley, the rather exuberant young riflemen, a hard look: they started guiltily and dropped their hands, which they had raised to kiss to a pair of young women across the road.

Trade goods were laid out in every corner of the bazaar: sturdy sacks of cotton canvas standing upon the ground full of grains and rare spices and dried fruit; bolts of silks in queer many-colored patterns of no meaning, neither flowers nor any other image; gleaming treasure-vault walls of stacked chests, with strips of brass hammered on like gilding; bright copper jugs hanging and white conical jars half-buried in the ground, for keeping water cool; and notably many wooden stands displaying an impressive array of knives, their hilts cunningly worked, some inlaid and jeweled, and the blades long and curving and wicked.

They went at first warily through the streets of the bazaar, keeping their eyes on the shadows, but their fears of another ambush proved unfounded: the natives only smiled and beckoned from the stalls, even the dragons themselves calling out invitations to come and buy, some in clear fluting song which Temeraire paused now and again to try and answer with snatches of the dragon language that Tharkay had begun to teach him. Here and there a merchant of Chinese ancestry came out of his stall and bowed low to the ground as Temeraire went by, in respect, and stared in puzzlement at the rest of them.

Tharkay led them unerringly through the dragon quarter and skirting a small mosque beautifully painted, the square before it full of men and even a handful of dragons prostrating themselves on soft woven prayer-rugs; on the outskirts of the market they came to a comfortable pavilion large enough to accommodate even Temeraire, tall slim wooden columns holding up a roof of canvas, with poplar-trees shading the square all around. A little of Laurence's dwindling supply of silver bought them sheep for Temeraire's dinner, and a rich pilaf of mutton and onion and moist sweet sultanas for their own, with flat rounds of roasted bread and juicy water-melons to eat in thick slices down to the pale green rind.

"Tomorrow we can sell the rest of the camels," Tharkay said, after the scant leavings had been carried away and the men had disposed themselves around the pavilion, to drowse upon comfortable rugs and cushions; he was feeding the eagle on scraps of sheep's liver, discarded by Gong Su from the preparations for Temeraire's meal. "From here to Kashgar the oases are not so far apart, and we need only carry enough water for a day."

No news could have been more welcome; comfortable again in body and spirit, and greatly relieved by their safe crossing, Laurence was inclined to make allowances. To find another guide would take time, and the poplar-trees murmuring together around the clearing said that time was short: their leaves had begun to turn gold, early heralds of autumn. "Walk with me a moment," he said to Tharkay, when the guide had settled the eagle back into its cage and draped it for the night; together they went a little distance back into the lanes of the marketplace, the tradesmen beginning to pack their things away, rolling up the lips of the sacks to cover their dry goods.

The street was busy and crowded, but English was enough privacy; Laurence stopped in the nearest shade and turned to Tharkay, whose face was all polite untroubled inquiry. "I hope you have some notion already what I wish to say to you," Laurence began.

"I am sorry it is not so, Captain, and I must put you to the trouble of explication," Tharkay said. "But perhaps that is best: misunderstandings shall be thus avoided; and I am sure I know of no reason why you should scruple to be frank with me."

Laurence paused; this sounded to him again more sly half-mockery, for Tharkay was no fool, and he had not spent four days nearly shunned by all their company without noticing. "Then I will oblige you," Laurence said, more sharply. "You have brought us so far successfully, and I am not ungrateful for your efforts; but I am very heartily displeased with your conduct in having abandoned us unannounced in the midst of the desert.

"I do not want excuses," he added, seeing Tharkay's brow lift. "I count them useless, when I cannot know whether to believe them. But I will have your promise that you will not again leave our camp without permission: I want no more of these unannounced departures."

"Well, I am sorry not to have given satisfaction," Tharkay said thoughtfully, after a moment. "And I would never wish to keep you to what now seems to you a bad bargain, out of some sense of obligation. I am perfectly willing we should part ways here if you like. You will be able to find a local guide, in a week or two, perhaps three; but I am sure that cannot mean very much: you will certainly still arrive home in Britain quicker than the *Allegiance* should have brought you there."

This answer neatly evaded the required promise, and brought Laurence up directly: they could not easily give up three weeks or one—if that were not an optimistic estimate to begin with, as they knew neither the local language, which seemed closer to Turkish than Chinese, nor the customs. Laurence was not even sure they were still in territory claimed by China, or in some smaller principality.

He swallowed anger, renewed suspicion, and a hasty reply, though all three stuck unpleasantly in his throat. "No," he said, grimly. "We have no time to waste; as I think you know very well," he added: Tharkay's tone had been bland, unreadable, but a little too much so; and there was something knowing in his look, as though he understood their special urgency. Laurence still had the letter from Admiral Lenton secure in his baggage, but now he recalled the smudged softness of the red wax seal, when the letter had first been given him: easy enough, bringing the letter across all these miles, to have pried it open and then sealed it up again.

But Tharkay's expression did not change at the hint of accusation; he only bowed and said mildly, "As you wish," and turning went back to the pavilion.

CHAPTER 4

The red dry mountains looked as though they had been folded directly up out of the desert plain, cliffs painted with broad stripes of white and ochre, without any softening foothills at their base. They remained stubbornly distant: for a whole day Temeraire flew at a steady pace and seemed to come no closer, the mountains drawing themselves ever upwards and out of reach, until suddenly canyon walls were rising to either side. In the space of ten minutes' flight the sky and desert vanished away behind them, and abruptly Laurence understood the red mountains were themselves the foothills for the towering white-clad peaks beyond.

They camped in wide meadowlands high in the mountains, fortressed by the peaks and sparsely furred with sea-green grass, small yellow flowers standing up like flags from the dusty ground. Horned black cattle with bright red tassels dangling over their foreheads eyed them warily as Tharkay negotiated their price with the herdsmen in their round, conical-roofed huts. At night a few white flakes came silently drifting down, glittering against the night; they melted snow in a great leather pot for Temeraire to drink.

Occasionally, they heard a faint, far-off call of dragons that made Temeraire prick up his ruff; and once in the distance saw a feral pair go spiraling up chasing each other's tails, crying out in shrill joyful voices before they vanished around the other side of a mountain. Tharkay made them put veils over their eyes, to shield against the brilliant glare; even Temeraire had to submit to this treatment, and very odd he looked with the thin white silk wrapped around his head like a blindfold. Even with such precautions, their faces grew pink and sunburnt for the first few days.

"We will need to take food with us, past Irkeshtam," Tharkay said, and when they had made camp outside the old run-down fortress, he went away and returned nearly an hour later with three locals herding along a small band of fat, short-legged pigs.

"You mean to take them up alive?" Granby cried, staring. "They will squeal themselves hoarse and then die of terror."

But the pigs seemed curiously somnolent and indifferent to Temeraire's presence, much to his puzzlement: he even leaned over and nudged at one with his nose, and it only yawned and sat down thump on its hindquarters in the snow. One of the others kept attempting to walk into the brick wall of the fortress, and had to be hauled repeatedly back by its minders. "I put opium in their feed," Tharkay said, in answer to Laurence's confusion. "We will let the drug wear off when we make camp, and he will eat after we have rested; then the rest we dose again."

Laurence was wary of this notion, and not inclined to trust Tharkay's offhand assurance; he watched closely after Temeraire ate the first pig. It went to its death perfectly sober and kicking all the way, and Temeraire showed no inclination afterwards to begin flying in mad circles; although he did fall into rather a deeper sleep than usual, and snored loud enough to rattle.

⁂

THE PASS ITSELF climbed so high they left the clouds below them, and all the rest of the earth; only the nearby mountain peaks kept them company. Temeraire panted for breath, now and again, and had to let himself down to rest wherever the ground permitted, leaving his body outlined in the snow as he lifted away. There was a queer sense of watchfulness, all the day long; Temeraire kept looking around as he flew, and pausing to hover in mid-air, with a low uneasy rumbling.

Having cleared the pass, they set down for the evening in a small valley sheltered from the wind between two great peaks with the ground clear of snow, and anchored their tents at the bottom of the cliff face; the pigs they penned up with a fence of kindling and rope, and let them range freely. Temeraire paced his side of the valley a few times, and then settled himself down with his tail still twitching; Laurence came to sit beside him with his tea. "It is not that I hear anything," Temeraire said, uncertainly, "but I feel as though I *ought* to be hearing something."

"We have a good position here: we cannot be come upon by surprise, at least," Laurence said. "Do not let it keep you from sleeping: we have posted a watch."

"We are very high in the mountains," Tharkay said unexpectedly, startling Laurence: he had not heard the guide come towards them. "You may only be feeling the change, and the difficulty of breathing: the air has less body."

"Is that why it is so hard to breathe?" Temeraire said, and abruptly sat up on his haunches; the pigs began to squeal and run as nearly a dozen dragons, motley in colors and size, came winging down towards them. Most of them landed skillfully clinging to the cliff face, peering down towards the tents, faces sleek and clever and hungry looking; the largest three dropped down between Temeraire and the makeshift pen, and sat up on their haunches, challengingly.

They were none of them large: the lead fellow something smaller than a Yellow Reaper, pale grey with brown markings and a single crimson patch across half his face and down his neck, with a great many spiny horns around his head; he bared his teeth and hissed, the horns bristling. His two companions were of slightly larger size, one a collection of bright blues and the other dark grey; and all three heavily scarred with the relics of a great many battles, the marks of tooth and claw.

Temeraire outweighed nearly all three of them together: he sat up very straight and his ruff opened wide, stretching like a frill around his head, and gave a small growling roar in answer: a warning. The ferals, so isolated from all the world, likely would not know to fear Celestials as anything other than large dragons, for their size and strength; but the strange ability of the divine wind was by far their most dangerous weapon, and without visible means could shatter stone and wood and bone. Temeraire did not now raise the divine wind against them, but there was an edge of it in his roaring, enough to rattle Laurence's bones; before it, the ferals quailed, the red-patch leader's horns flattening against his neck, and like a flock of alarmed birds they all flung themselves up and out of the valley.

"Oh; but I did not do anything, yet," Temeraire said, puzzled and a little disappointed. Above them the mountains were still grumbling with the echoes of his roar, piling them one on another into a continuous roll of thunder, a sound almost magnified beyond the original. The white face of the peak stirred at the noise, sighed, and let go its hold upon the stone, the entire slab of snow and ice sliding gently free; for a moment yet it kept its shape, moving with slow and stately grace, then cracks like spiderwebs spread across its surface, and the whole collapsed into a great billowing cloud and came galloping down the slope towards the camp.

Laurence felt like the captain of a ship on her beam-ends, seeing the wave that would make her broach-to: in perfect consciousness of disaster and powerless to avert it; there was no time to do anything at all but watch. So quickly did the avalanche come that a couple of the luckless ferals, though they had all tried at once to flee, were swept up in its path. Tharkay was shouting, "Get away! Get away from the cliff!" to the men standing around the tents, pitched directly in the path; but even as he cried out, the vast eruption spilled off the slope, swept over the camp, and then the boiling mass came seething and roaring across the green valley floor.

First there came a shock of cold air, almost physical in its force; Laurence was flung back against Temeraire's great bulk, reaching out to catch Tharkay's arm as the guide stumbled back, and then the cloud itself struck and tore away the world: like being thrust abruptly face-forward into deep snow and held down, a cool muffling eerie blue all around him, a hollow rushing sound in his ears. Laurence opened his mouth for air that was not there, flakes and slivers of ice like knives scraping his face, his lungs heaving against the pressure on his chest, on his limbs, his arms spread-eagled and pressed back so that his shoulders ached.

And then as quickly as it had come, the terrible weight was gone. He was buried standing-up in snow, solidly to the knees and thinning to a solid icy crust over his face and shoulders; with a great desperate heave he broke his arms free, and scraped at his mouth and nostrils with clumsy, benumbed hands, lungs burning until he could drag in the first raw, painful breaths; next to him Temeraire was looking more white than black, like a pane of glass after a frost, and sputtering as he shook himself off.

Tharkay, who had managed to turn his back to the cloud, was in a little better case, already dragging his feet out of the snow. "Quickly, quickly, there is not a moment to lose," he said, hoarsely, and began to flounder across the valley towards the tents: or where the tents had been, now a sloping heap of snow, piled ten feet deep or more.

Laurence dragged himself free and went after him, pausing to pull up Martin when he saw the midshipman's straw-yellow hair breaking the snow: he had been only a short way off, but, having been knocked flat, he was more deeply buried beneath the snow. Together they struggled through the great drifts: thankfully nearly all soft wet snow, not ice or rock, but dreadfully heavy nonetheless.

Temeraire followed anxiously after and heaved great mounds

of snow this way and that at their direction, but he was forced to be careful with his talons. They soon uncovered one of the ferals, struggling like mad to get herself free: a little blue-and-white creature not much bigger than a Greyling; Temeraire seized her by the scruff of her neck and dragged her loose, shaking her free, and in the pocket underneath her body they found one of the tents half-crushed, a handful of the men gasping and bruised.

The feral tried to fly away as soon as Temeraire set her down, but he caught her again and hissed at her, some broken words of the dragon-tongue mingling with ordinary anger. She startled and fluted something back, and then, after he hissed again, turned abashed and began to help them dig; her smaller claws were better for the more delicate work of getting out the men. The other feral, slightly larger, in motley of orange and yellow and pink, they found pinned at the very bottom of the slope in much worse case: one wing hanging torn and wildly askew, he made low terrible keening noises and only crouched, shivering and huddled against the ground, when they had freed him.

"Well, it took you damned long enough," Keynes said, when they had dug him out: he had been sitting placidly in the sick-tent, waiting, while the terrified Allen hid his face in his cot. "Come along; you can be of some use for once," he said, and at once loaded the boy down with bandages and knives and dragged him over to the poor injured creature, who warily hissed them away until Temeraire turned his head and snapped at him; then, cowed, he hunched down and let Keynes do as he liked, only whimpering a little as the surgeon moved the broken spines back into their places.

Granby they found unconscious and blue-lipped, buried nearly upside-down, and Laurence and Martin together carried him carefully to cleared ground, covering him with the folds of the one tent they had managed to extract, lying beside the rifle-men, who had been standing together very near the slope: Dunne, Hackley, and Lieutenant Riggs, all of them pale and still. Emily Roland managed to dig her own head out, nearly swimming up through the snow, after Temeraire had swept away most of the top layers, and called until they came and got her and Dyer free, the two clutching at each other's hands.

"Mr. Ferris, I make all accounted for?" Laurence asked, near half-an-hour later; his hand came away bloody from his eyelids, rubbed raw with snow.

"Yes, sir," Ferris said, low: Lieutenant Baylesworth had just been dug out, dead of a broken neck, the last man missing.

Laurence nodded, stiffly. "We must get the wounded under cover, and manage some shelter," he said, and looked around for Tharkay: the guide was standing a little distance away, head bent, holding the small, still body of the eagle in his hands.

UNDER TEMERAIRE'S NARROW gaze, the ferals led them to a cold, encrusted cave in the mountain wall; as they went in deeper, the passage grew warmer, until it opened up without warning into a great hollowed-out cavern, with a pool of steaming sulfurous water in the middle, and a crudely carved channel for fresh snow-melt running into it. Several more ferals were disposed around the cavern, napping; the leader with the red patch was curled up on an elevated perch, atop a leveled-off rise, chewing meditatively upon the leg bone of a sheep.

They all startled and made small hissing noises as Temeraire ducked into the chamber, with the injured feral clinging onto his back and the rest of them following behind; but the little blue-and-white dragon sang out some reassurances, and after a moment a few more of the dragons came forward to help the injured one climb down.

Tharkay stepped forward and spoke to them in their language, approximating several sounds of it with whistles and cupping his hands around his mouth, gesturing towards the cave passage. "But those are *my* pigs," Temeraire said, indignantly.

"They are all certainly dead by now from the avalanche, and will only rot," Tharkay said, looking up surprised, "and there are too many for you to eat alone."

"I do not see what that has to do with anything," Temeraire said; his ruff was still bristling wide, and he looked over the other dragons, particularly the red-patch one, with a martial eye. They in turn uneasily shuffled and stirred, wings half-rising from their backs and folding in again, and watched Temeraire sidelong.

"My dear," Laurence said quietly, laying a hand on Temeraire's leg, "only look at their condition; I dare say they are all very hungry, and would never else have tried to encroach upon you. It would be unkind in the extreme, were you to chase them away from their home that we might shelter here, and if we mean to ask their hospitality, it is only right we should share with them."

"Oh," Temeraire said, considering, and the ruff began slightly to curl back down against his neck: the ferals truly did look hungry, all whipcord muscle and taut leathery hide, narrow faces and bright eyes watching, and many of them showed signs of old illness or injury. "Well, I would not like to be unkind, even if they did try to quarrel, first," he at last agreed, and addressed them himself; their first expressions of surprise gave way to a wary half-suppressed excitement, and then the red-patch one gave a quick short call and led a handful of the others out in a flurry.

They came presently back, carrying the bodies of the pigs, and watched with fixed and staring interest as Gong Su began to butcher them. Tharkay having managed to convey a request for wood, a couple of the smaller flew out and returned dragging some small dead pine-trees, grey and weathered, which they inquiringly offered; shortly Gong Su had a crackling fire going, smoke drawing up a crevice into the high recesses of the cave, and the pigs were roasting deliciously. Granby stirred and said vaguely, "Would there be spareribs?" much to Laurence's relief; he was soon roused and drinking tea, hands shaking so he needed help to hold the cup, though they seated him as near the fire as they could.

The crew were all of them inclined to cough and sneeze, the boys particularly, and Keynes said, "We ought put them all in the water: to keep the chest warm must be the foremost concern."

Laurence agreed without thinking and was shortly appalled by the sight of Emily bathing with the rest of the young officers, innocent of both clothing and modesty. "You must not bathe with the others," Laurence said to her urgently, having bundled her out and into a blanket.

"Mustn't I?" she said, gazing up at him damp and bewildered.

"Oh, Christ," Laurence said, under his breath. "No," he told her firmly, "it is not suitable; you are beginning to be a young lady."

"Oh," she said dismissively, "Mother has told me all about that, but I have not started bleeding yet, and anyway I would not like to go to bed with any of them," and a thoroughly routed Laurence feebly fell back on giving her some make-work, and fled to Temeraire's side.

The pigs were coming to a turn, and meanwhile Gong Su had been stewing the intestines and offal and hocks, judiciously adding from the various ingredients which the ferals had begun offering him, the fruit of their own collections, not all entirely legitimate: some greens and native roots, but also a bushel of turnips in a torn sack, and another bag of grain, which evidently they had snatched and found inedible.

Temeraire was engaged in a conversation of rapidly increasing fluency with the red-patch leader. "His name is Arkady," Temeraire said to Laurence, who bowed to the dragon. "He says he is very sorry they should have troubled us," he added.

Arkady inclined his head graciously and made a pretty speech of welcome, not looking particularly repentant; Laurence doubted not that they would set on the next travelers with as good a will. "Temeraire, do express to him the dangers of this sort of behavior," he said. "They will all end by being shot, likely enough, if they continue to waylay men: the populace will grow exasperated and lay out a bounty on their heads."

"He says it is only a toll," Temeraire said doubtfully, after some further discussion, "and that no one minds paying it, though of course they ought to have waived it for me." Arkady here added something more in a slightly injured tone, which puzzled Temeraire into scratching at his forehead. "Although the last one like me did not object, and gave them a pair of very nice cows, if they should lead her and her servants through the passes."

"Like you?" Laurence said, blankly; there were only eight dragons in the world like Temeraire, all of them five thousand miles away in Peking; and even in so broad a quality as color he was very nearly unique, being a solid glossy black save for the pearlescent markings at the very edges of his wings, while most dragons were patterned in many colors like the ferals themselves.

Temeraire made further inquiry. "He says she was just like me, except white all over, and her eyes were red," he said, his ruff coming straight back up, and his nostrils flaring redly; Arkady edged away, looking alarmed.

"How many men were with her?" Laurence demanded. "Who were they; did he see which way she left, after the mountains?" Questions, anxieties at once came tumbling over one another: the description left no doubt as to the identity of the dragon. It could only be Lien, the Celestial whose color had been leached away by some strange mischance of birth, and surely in her heart their bitter enemy: in her startling choice to leave China he could read nothing but the worst intentions.

"There were some other dragons traveling with them, to carry the men," Temeraire said, and Arkady called over the little blue-and-white dragon, whose name was Gherni: being in some measure familiar with the Turkish dialect of these parts, as well as the draconic speech, she had served as interpreter with the pack-dragons and could tell them a little more.

The news was as bad as could be imagined: Lien was traveling with a Frenchman, by the description surely Ambassador De Guignes, and from what Gherni said, she had already mastered the language, from her ability to converse with De Guignes. She was certainly on her way to France, and there could be only one motive for her to have made such a journey.

"She won't let them put her to any real use," Granby offered as consolation, in their hasty discussion. "They cannot just throw her into the front lines, without a crew or captain, and she'll never let them put a harness on her after all the fuss they made about our putting one on Temeraire."

"At the very least they can breed her," Laurence said, grimly, "but I do not think for a moment that Bonaparte will not find some way to turn her to good account. You saw what Temeraire did, on our way to Madeira: a frigate of forty-eight guns, sunk in a single pass, and I do not know the same trick would not do for a first-rate." The Navy's wooden walls were yet Britain's surest defense, and the still-more-vulnerable merchantmen carried the trade which was her lifeblood; the threat Lien represented alone might well alter the balance of power across the Channel.

"I am not afraid of Lien," Temeraire said, still in a bristling mood. "And I am not in the least sorry Yongxing is dead, either: he had no business trying to kill you, and she had none letting him try, if she did not like it served back again."

Laurence shook his head; such considerations would surely hold no water with Lien. Her strange ghostly coloration had rendered her outcast among the Chinese, and all her world had been bound up in Yongxing, even more than most dragons with their companions; she would certainly not forgive. He had not imagined, proud and disdainful of the West as she was, that she would ever go into such an exile: if revenge and hatred had moved her so far, they would suffice for more.

CHAPTER 5

"Any delay now is disaster," Laurence said, and Tharkay sketched out the last stretch of their journey upon the smooth floor of the cavern, using pale rocks for chalk; a course which would avoid the great cities, past golden Samarkand and ancient Baghdad, between Isfahan and Tehran, and take them on a meandering road through wilderness and skirting the edges of the great deserts.

"We will have to spend more time hunting," Tharkay warned, but that was small cost by comparison: Laurence wanted to risk neither challenge nor hospitality from the Persian satraps, which would consume far more time in either case. There was something a little unpleasant and skulking about creeping through the countryside of a foreign nation, without permission, and it would be at the very least embarrassing if they were caught, but he was willing to trust their caution and Temeraire's speed to guard against the last.

Laurence had meant to stay another day, to let the men worst injured by the avalanche make some recovery on the ground, but there could be no question of that now with Lien on her way to France, where she might wreak merry havoc at the Channel, or upon the Mediterranean Fleet. The Navy and the merchant marine would be wholly unsuspecting and vulnerable; her appearance would not be a warning, for her white coloration would not be found in any of the dragon-books which ships carried, to warn their captains of fire-breathers and the like. She was many years older than Temeraire, and though she had never been trained in battle, she lacked nothing in agility and grace and likely was more practiced in the use of the divine wind; it made him shudder to think of so deadly a weapon placed in Bonaparte's hands, and aimed nearly at the heart of Britain.

"We will leave in the morning," he said, and stood up from the floor to find a disgruntled audience of dragons; the ferals had gathered around in curiosity while Tharkay made his diagrams, and, having demanded some explanation from Temeraire, they were now indignant to find their own mountain range little more than a scattering of hatch-marks dividing the vast expanse of China from Persia and the Ottoman Empire.

"I am just telling them that we have been all the way from England to China," Temeraire informed Laurence, smugly, "and round Africa, too; they have none of them ever been very much outside the mountains."

Temeraire made some further remarks to them, in a tone of no little condescension. He had indeed some experience to brag of, having been fêted lavishly at the imperial court of China after a journey halfway around the world, not to mention several notable actions to his credit; besides these adventures, his jeweled breastplate and talon-sheaths had already drawn envy from the unadorned ferals, and Laurence even discovered himself the subject of a gallery of appraising slit-pupiled stares after Temeraire had finished telling them he knew not what.

He was not unhappy for Temeraire to have an example before him of dragons in their natural state, without any influence of men: the ferals' existence offered a happy contrast with the elevated circumstances of the Chinese dragons, by which comparison the lot of British dragons need not look so very ill, and he was glad Temeraire so plainly felt his own position superior to theirs; but Laurence was dubious of the wisdom of thus provoking them into a more active envy and perhaps to belligerence.

The more Temeraire spoke, the more the ferals murmured and looked sideways at their own leader Arkady, with a jaundiced air; jealously aware that he was losing some of his luster in their eyes, he was ruffling up the collar of spikes around his neck and bristling.

"Temeraire," Laurence said, to interrupt, even though he did not know what else to say, but when Temeraire looked towards him in inquiry Arkady leapt at once into the breach: puffing out his chest, he made an announcement in grandiose tones which sent a quick murmur of excitement around the other ferals.

"Oh," Temeraire said, tail twitching doubtfully, and regarding the red-patch dragon.

"What is it?" Laurence said, alarmed.

"He says he will come with us to Istanbul, and meet the Sultan," Temeraire explained.

This amiable project, while less violent than the challenge Laurence had feared, was nearly as inconvenient, and argument was of no use: Arkady would not be dissuaded, and many of the other dragons now began to insist that they too would come along. Tharkay gave up the effort after a short while and turned away, shrugging. "We may as well resign ourselves; there is little we can do to prevent their following, unless you mean to attack them."

Nearly all the ferals set out with them the next morning, saving a few too indolent or too incurious to be bothered, and the little broken-winged one they had rescued from the avalanche, who stood looking after them at the mouth of the cave and making small unhappy cries as they left. They made difficult company, noisy and excitable, and quick to fall to squabbling in mid-air, two or three of them tumbling head-over-tail in a wild flurry of hissing and claws until Arkady or one of his two larger lieutenants dived at them and knocked them apart with loud remonstrances to sulk in private.

"We will never pass through the countryside unnoticed with

this circus following behind us," Laurence said in exasperation after the third such incident, the echoes of the shrieks still ringing off the peaks.

"Likely they will get tired of it in a few days and turn back," Granby said. "I have never heard of ferals wanting to go anywhere near people, except to steal food; and I dare say we'll see them turn shy as soon as we leave their territory."

The ferals indeed grew nervous towards the afternoon, as the mountains began abruptly to diminish into foothills, and the smooth rolling curve of the horizon came clear, green and dusty and endlessly wide under the great bowl of the sky: a wholly different landscape. They whispered and rustled their wings together uneasily at the edge of the camp, and were very little use at all in hunting. As evening fell, the lights of a nearby village began to gleam faintly orange in the distance, half-a-dozen farmhouses some miles away. By morning several of the ferals had agreed amongst themselves that this must be Istanbul, it was not nearly so nice as they had expected, and they were quite ready to go home.

"But that is not Istanbul at all," Temeraire said indignantly, and subsided only at Laurence's hurried gesture.

They were thus rid of the better part of their company, much to their relief. Only the youngest and most adventurous remained, chief among them little Gherni, who had hatched in the lowlands and thus had a little more experience of this foreign landscape, and was quite pleased with this newfound distinction among her peers. She was loud in professing herself not at all afraid, and making mock of those turning back; in the face of her taunting, a couple of the others determined on continuing also, and sadly these were the most chest-puffing quarrelsome of the lot.

And Arkady was unwilling to turn back while any others of his flock remained: Temeraire had told too many stories, and those too vivid, of treasures and feasts and dramatic battles; now the feral leader evidently feared one of his erstwhile subjects might return at some future date covered in glory real or contrived, and challenge his standing; a standing founded less in raw strength—both his lieutenants outstripping him in this arena—than on a certain alchemy of charisma and quickness of thought, rendering his position the less easily defensible.

But he was hardly enthusiastic, for all the strutting bravado with which he concealed his anxiety, and Laurence hoped that he would shortly have persuaded the others to go. His lieutenants, called Molnar and Wringe—as best as Laurence could make out—would certainly have been happier to stay behind even without him, and Wringe, the dark grey, even ventured to suggest as much to her chief, which only succeeded in making Arkady fly into a passion and beat her vigorously about the head, accompanied by a verbal harangue which required no translation.

But that night he huddled close with them for comfort, the mountains having dwindled to distant blue majesty, and the rest of the ferals cuddled about them also, paying only half-hearted attention to Temeraire's attempts at conversation. "They are not very venturesome," Temeraire said, disappointed, coming to settle down beside Laurence. "They only ask me all the time about food, and how soon they shall be feasted by the Sultan, and what he will give them, and when they can go home: though they have all the liberty in the world, and could go anywhere they like at all."

"When you are very hungry, my dear, it is hard for your ambitions to rise above your belly," Laurence said. "There is not much to be said for the sort of liberty which they enjoy: the freedom to starve or to be slaughtered is hardly one to which most would aspire, and," he added, seizing the moment, "both men and dragons may with good sense choose to sacrifice some personal liberty for the sake of the general good, which shall advance their own condition with those of their fellows."

Temeraire sighed, and did not argue, but prodded at his dinner dissatisfied, at least until Molnar noticed and made a cautious gesture at taking a bit of the half-abandoned meat for himself: which made Temeraire growl him away, and devour all the rest in three tremendous gulps.

They had fine weather the next day, the sky clear and vast,

which worked to excellent discouraging effect upon their traveling companions; Laurence was sure that evening would see the
last of them turn tail for home. But they made only a poor show
of hunting again, and Laurence was forced to send Tharkay
with some of the men to try and find a farm nearby, and buy
some cattle to make up the difference.

The ferals grew round-eyed at the great, horned brown beasts
as they were dragged into the camp lowing in pitiful fear, and
even more so when they were given four to divide up amongst
themselves, gorging near to ecstasy. The littler ones lay on their
backs afterwards, with their wings splayed awkwardly out of
the way and their limbs curled over their distended bellies, be-
atific expressions on their faces, and even Arkady, who had done
his best to eat nearly an entire cow alone, sprawled limp-legged
on his side. Laurence sinkingly gathered they had never tasted
beef before, and certainly not like this farm-raised cattle, fat and
sweet-flavored; they would have made very good eating even for
the finest table in England, and must have been ambrosial to the
ferals, accustomed to subsistence on thin goats and mountain
sheep, and the occasional stolen pig.

Temeraire put the seal to the matter by saying blithely, "No,
I am sure the Sultan will give us something much nicer," after
which Istanbul took on the roseate glow of Paradise: there was
no more hope of shaking them.

"Well, we had better go on by night, as much as we can,"
Laurence said, in reluctant surrender. "At least I expect any ordinary peasant who sees us will imagine we are part of their
native aerial corps, as much a cavalcade as we are."

The ferals were at least some use once having gotten over
their fright; one of the littler fellows, Hertaz, greenish yellow
stripes over dusty brown, proved their best hunter in the summer-
yellowed grasslands: he could flatten himself in the tall grass and
hide downwind while the other dragons stampeded animals out
of forests and hills with their roaring; the hapless beasts would
run very nearly straight into his path, and he often brought
down as many as half-a-dozen in a single lunge.

The ferals were wary, too, for the scent of men, as Temeraire was not; it was Arkady's warning that saved them from notice by a Persian cavalry company, all the dragons only barely managing to get behind some hills as the troop came riding over the crest of the road and into sight. Laurence lay concealed a long time, listening to the banners snapping and bridle-bits jingling as the company went gradually by, until the sound had wholly faded into the distance, and twilight advanced far enough they could risk taking to the air once again.

The feral leader was smug and prancing afterwards, and while Temeraire was still eating that afternoon, Arkady seized the opportunity to take back pride of place, regaling his troop with a long and involved performance, half-storytelling, half-dance, which Laurence at first took to be a re-creation of his achievements as a hunter, or some similarly savage activity; the other dragons were all chiming in now and again with their own contributions.

But then Temeraire put down his second deer to listen in with great interest, and shortly began to put in his own remarks. "What is he speaking of?" Laurence asked him, puzzled that Temeraire should have anything to add to the narrative.

"It is very exciting," Temeraire said, turning to him eagerly, "it is all about a band of dragons, who find a great heap of treasure hidden in a cave, that belonged to an old dragon who died, and they are quarreling over how to divide it, and there are a great many duels between the two strongest dragons, because they are equally strong, and really they want to mate and not fight, but neither of them knows that the other also wants to mate, and so they each think they have to win the treasure, and then they can give it to the other, and then the other one will agree to mate to get the treasure. And one of the other dragons is very small but clever, and he is playing tricks on the others and getting lots of the treasure away for himself bit by bit; and also there is a mated pair who have argued over their own share, because the female was too busy brooding the egg to help him fight the others and get a bigger share, and then he did not want to share equally with her, and then she got angry and took away the egg and hid with it, and now he is sorry but he cannot find her, and there is another male who wants to mate with her, and he has found her and is offering her some of his own share of the treasure—"

Laurence was by now lost in the sea of events, even so summarized; he did not understand how Temeraire was following it at all, or what there was to be interested in about it; but certainly Temeraire and the ferals took passionate enjoyment in the entire tangle. At one stage Gherni and Hertaz even came to blows, evidently over a disagreement on what ought to happen next, batting at each other's heads until Molnar, annoyed at the interruption of the tale, snapped at them and hissed them into submission.

Arkady flung himself down at last panting and very pleased, and the other dragons all whistled in approval and thumped their tails; Temeraire clicked his talons against a broad rock, in the Chinese mode of approval.

"I must remember it so I can write it down, when we are home, and I can have another writing-box like the one I had in China," Temeraire said, with a deeply satisfied sigh. "I tried to recite some parts of the *Principia Mathematica* to Lily and Maximus once, but they did not find it very interesting; I am sure they would like this better. Perhaps we can have it published, Laurence, do you suppose?"

"You will have to teach more dragons to read, first," Laurence said.

A handful of the crew were making some shifts at picking up the Durzagh language; pantomime ordinarily worked quite well, as the ferals were quite clever enough to make out the meaning, but they were also quite happy to pretend they did not understand anything they did not like, such as being told to move from a comfortable place so tents might be pitched, or being roused up from naps for an evening stretch of flying. As Temeraire and Tharkay were not always handy to translate, learning to speak to them became rather a form of self-defense for the younger officers responsible for setting up the camp. It was rather comical to see them whistling and humming bits of it at the dragons.

"Digby, that will be enough; don't let me catch you encouraging them to make up to you," Granby said, sternly.

"Yes, sir; I mean, no, sir, yes," Digby said, gone crimson and tongue-tied, and scurried away to busy himself with a contrived task on the other side of the camp.

Laurence looked up from his consultation with Tharkay at hearing this, surprised, as the boy was ordinarily the steadiest of the ensigns, for all he was scarcely turned thirteen; he had never needed to be taken-down before, so far as Laurence recalled.

"Oh, no real harm; he has only been saving the choice bits aside for that big fellow Molnar, and some of those other boys too, for their own favorites," Granby said, joining them. "It's only natural they should like to pretend themselves captains, but it is no good making pets of the creatures: you don't make a feral tame by feeding him."

"Although they do seem to be learning some manners; I had thought ferals would be wholly uncontrollable," Laurence said.

"So would they be, if Temeraire weren't at hand," Granby said. "It is only him making them mind."

"I wonder; they seem to govern themselves well enough when given sufficient interest in so doing," Tharkay observed, a little dry, "which seems an eminently rational philosophy; to me it is rather more remarkable that any dragon should mind under other circumstances."

THE GOLDEN HORN glittered from a long way off, the city sprawling lavishly over its banks and every hill crowned with the minarets and smooth shining marble domes of the mosques, blue and grey and pink amidst the terra-cotta roofs of the houses and the narrow green blades of the cypress-trees. The sickle-shaped river emptied itself into the mighty Bosphorus, which in its turn snaked away in either direction, black and dazzled with sunlight in Laurence's glass; but he had little attention for anything but the farther shore, the first glimpse of Europe.

His crew were all of them tired and hungry; as they had drawn closer to the great city, there was a good deal more trouble to avoid settlements, and they had not stopped for more than a cold meal and an uncomfortably broken mid-day sleep in ten days, the dragons hunting on the wing and eating what little meat they caught raw. When they came up over the next rank of hills and saw the great herd of grey cattle grazing upon the wide banks of the Asian side of the strait, Arkady gave an eager bloodthirsty roar and dived at them instantly.

"No, no, you cannot eat those!" Temeraire said, too late: the other ferals were already plunging with cries of delight after the panicked, bellowing herd, and at the southern end of the plain, from behind the ramparts of a squat stone-and-mortar wall, the heads of several dragons, brightly adorned with the plumes of the Turkish service, hove up into view.

"Oh, for all Heaven's sake," Laurence said. The Turkish dragons leapt aloft and came on in a furious rush towards the ferals, who were too busy to notice their danger, snatching at first one cow and then another and comparing them in an ecstasy over their sudden riches, too overwhelmed even to settle down and begin eating. That alone saved them: as the Turkish dragons stooped towards them, the ferals jumped and scattered away, leaving almost a dozen cattle crumpled or dead upon the ground, just in time to avoid the reaching claws and teeth.

Arkady and the others at once darted straight back to Temeraire for shelter, flurrying around behind him, and making shrill taunting cries at the Turkish dragons, now sweeping up from their dive and coming on furious and roaring in pursuit.

"Run up the colors, and fire off a gun to leeward," Laurence called to his signal-ensign Turner, and the British flag, still brightly colored after their long journey but for the pale creases along the folds, unfurled with a crisp snapping noise.

The Turkish guard-dragons slowed as they drew near, baring teeth and talons, belligerent but uncertain: they were none of them more than middling in size, not much bigger than the ferals themselves, and as they drew nearer, Temeraire's great wingspan threw a long shadow across them: they were five in number, plainly unused to any great exertions, with odd, dimpled ridges of fat collected in front of their haunches. "Gone to seed,"

Granby said, disapproving; and indeed they were puffing a little after their first enraged rush, sides heaving visibly: Laurence supposed that they could have very little work, ordinarily, placed here at the capital and on such trivial duty as guarding cattle.

"Fire!" Riggs called: the volley was a little ragged, he and the other riflemen not wholly recovered yet from their temporary entombment in the ice and all inclined to sneeze at inopportune moments. Still the signal had the salutary effect of slowing the oncoming dragons, and to Laurence's great relief, the captain in the lead lifted his speaking-trumpet to his mouth to bellow at them, at some length.

"He says to land," Tharkay translated, with improbable brevity; at Laurence's frowning look he added, "and he calls us a great many impolite names; do you wish them all translated?"

"I do not see why I should have to land first and go underneath them," Temeraire said, and he descended only with an uneasy grumble, cocking his head at an awkward angle to keep an eye always on the dragons above him. Laurence also disliked the vulnerable position, but the offense had been given on their side: a few of the cows had staggered back up onto their feet and now stood trembling and dazed, but most of them were unmoving and certainly dead, a great waste that Laurence was not sure he could even make good, without application to the British ambassador locally, and he could hardly blame the Turkish captain for insisting they make some show of better faith.

Temeraire had to speak sharply to the ferals before they would land beside him, and at last even to give a low warning roar, enough to frighten all the remaining cattle into running even farther away. Arkady and the others came down with a surly, reluctant air, and they stayed only uneasily on the ground, wings scarce-furled and fidgeting.

"I ought never have allowed them to come with us so near, without giving the Turks warning first," Laurence said, grimly, watching them. "They cannot be trusted to behave among men or cattle."

"I do not see it is Arkady's fault at all, or the others'," Temeraire said loyally. "If I did not understand about property, *I* would not have known there was anything wrong in taking those cows, either." He paused and added, more low, "And in any case those dragons had no business lying out of sight like that and leaving the cows for anyone to take, if they did not like it."

Even once the ferals had at last descended, the Turkish dragons did not themselves land but set to flying in a slow but showy circle pattern overhead, very much to drive home their position of lofty superiority. Watching this display, Temeraire snorted and mantled a little, his ruff beginning to flare wide. "They are very rude," he said angrily, "I do not like them at all; and I am sure that we could beat them; they look like birds, with all that flapping."

"There would be another hundred to deal with shortly once you had run these off, and those like to be a different proposition: the Turkish corps are no joke, even if this handful have fallen out of fighting-trim," Laurence said. "Pray be patient and they will get tired of it presently." But in truth his own temper was scarcely less short; upon the hot, dusty field they were exposed to the full force of the sun, the baked ground unforgiving, and they had not carried much water with them.

The ferals were not long abashed, and began shortly to eye the slaughtered cows and to make muttered remarks amongst themselves; their tone was perfectly comprehensible, even where their words were not, and Temeraire himself said discontentedly, "And those cows will only go bad, if they are not eaten soon," much to Laurence's alarm.

"You might try and make the Turks think it does not bother you," he proposed, a happy inspiration. Temeraire brightened and spoke to the ferals in a loud whisper; shortly they had all sprawled out comfortably upon the grass, yawning elaborately; a couple of the little ones even began to whistle rudely through their nostrils, and the play occupied them all. The Turkish dragons soon tired of exercising to so little point, and at last circled down and landed opposite them, the lead dragon discharging his captain; a fresh occasion for dismay, for Laurence did not look forward to making either explanation or apology; with reason, as the event proved.

The Turkish captain, a gentleman named Ertegun, was hotly suspicious and his behavior alone insulting: he returned Laurence's bow with barely a twitch of his head, left his hand upon the hilt of his sword, and spoke coldly in Turkish.

After some brief discussion with Tharkay, Ertegun repeated himself in a middling sort of French, heavily accented: "Well? Explain yourself, and this vicious assault." Laurence's own command of even that language was sadly halting, but at least he could make some pretense of communication. He stumbled over an explanation, which had not the least softening effect upon Ertegun's offended mien nor his suspicions, which found vent in something very much like an interrogation on Laurence's mission, his rank, the course of his journey, and even his funds, until Laurence began to grow impatient himself in his turn.

"Enough; do you imagine that we are thirty dangerous lunatics, who have all together decided to launch an attack against the walls of Istanbul, with a company of seven dragons?" Laurence said. "Nothing is served by keeping us waiting here in the heat; have one of your men take word to the British ambassador in residence, and I trust he will be able to satisfy you."

"Not without great difficulty, since he is dead," Ertegun said.

"Dead?" Laurence said blankly, and in mounting incredulity heard Ertegun insist that the ambassador, Mr. Arbuthnot, had been killed only the week past in some sort of hunting accident, the details vague; and furthermore that there was no other representative of the Crown in the city at present.

"Then, sir, I suppose I must present my bona fides directly, in the absence of such a representative," Laurence said, very much taken aback, and wondering privately what he should do for lodging for Temeraire. "I am here on a mission arranged between our nations, one which can allow of no delay."

"If your mission were of so great importance, your Government might have chosen a better messenger," Ertegun said, offensively. "The Sultan has many affairs to occupy him, and is not to be disturbed by every beggar who wishes to come knocking at the Gate of Felicity; nor are his vezirs to be lightly troubled, and I do not believe that you are from the British at all."

There was a conscious satisfaction visible in Ertegun's face at having produced these objections, a deliberate hostility, and Laurence said coldly, "These discourtesies, sir, are as dishonorable to your Sultan's government as insulting to myself; you cannot seriously imagine we should invent such a story."

"And yet I must imagine that you and this rag-tag of dangerous animals coming out from Persia are British representatives, I see," Ertegun said.

Laurence had no opportunity to respond to this incivility as it deserved. Temeraire was perfectly fluent in French, having spent several months of his life in the shell aboard a French frigate, and he now intruded his massive head into the conversation. "We are not animals, and my friends only did not understand that the cows were yours," he said angrily. "They would not hurt anyone, and they have come a long way to see the Sultan, too."

Temeraire's ruff had stretched wide and bristling, and his wings half-rising from his back threw a long shadow, his shoulders coming forward with the taut cords of his tendons standing out against the flesh as he thrust his head with its foot-long serrated teeth towards the Turkish captain. Ertegun's dragon gave a small shrill cry and jerked forward, but the other Turkish dragons all by instinct backed away from the fierce display and gave him no support; and Ertegun himself took a step back, involuntary, towards the shelter of his anxious dragon's reaching forelegs.

"Let us have an end to this dispute," Laurence said, quick to seize the advantage, with Ertegun thus momentarily silenced. "Mr. Tharkay and my first lieutenant will go into the city with your man, while the rest of us remain: I am quite confident the ambassador's staff will be able to arrange our visit entirely to the satisfaction of the Sultan and his vezirs, even if you are quite correct there is no official delegate at present; and I trust will also assist me in making good the losses to the royal herd; which as Temeraire has said were the result of accident and not malice."

Plainly Ertegun was not pleased with this proposal, but he did not know how to refuse with Temeraire still hovering; he opened and closed his mouth a few times, then began weakly, "It is quite impossible," which made Temeraire growl in refreshed temper. The Turkish dragons all edged a little further away yet; and suddenly his ears were full of howling, caterwauling dragon voices: Arkady and the ferals were all leaping into the air, tails lashing, talons clawing the air, wings flapping, all of them yowling as loud as they could go. The Turkish dragons too began to bellow, fanning their wings, about to go aloft. The noise was horrific, drowning out any hope of orders, and then to add to the cacophony Temeraire sat up and roared out over their heads: a long threatening roll like thunder.

The Turkish dragons tumbled back upon their haunches with cries and hisses, fouling one another's wings, snapping at the air and each other with instinctive alarm. In the confusion, the ferals seized their moment: they darted at the dead cows, snatched them out from under the noses of the Turks, and turned tail as one to flee. Already mid-air, the others flurrying away ahead of him, Arkady turned back with one cow clutched in each foreleg and bobbed his head in thanks at Temeraire; then they were gone: flying at a great pace, on a line straight back for the safe harbor of the mountains.

THE SHOCKED SILENCE lasted scarcely half-a-minute, and then Ertegun, still upon the ground, burst out into an indignant stammering flood of Turkish which Laurence, deeply mortified, thought it was better he did not understand: he could cheerfully have shot the whole lot of bandits himself. They had made him a liar in front of his own men and the Turkish captain, already eager to latch upon any excuse to deny them.

Ertegun's earlier obduracy had now been superseded by a

more honest indignation, violent and very real; he was grown hot with anger, great fat droplets of sweat beading and rolling in long trails down from his forehead to be lost in his beard, furious threats falling over one another in mingled Turkish and French.

"We will teach you how we deal with invaders here; we will slaughter you as the thieves have slaughtered the Sultan's cattle, and leave your bodies to rot," he finished, making wild flourishes to the Turkish dragons.

"I will not let you hurt Laurence or my crew at all," Temeraire said hotly, and his chest swelled out with gathering breath; the Turkish dragons all looked deeply anxious. Laurence had before noted that other dragons seemed to know to fear Temeraire's roar, even if they had not yet felt the true divine wind, some instinct warning them of the danger. But their riders did not share that understanding, and Laurence did not think the dragons would refuse orders to attack; even should Temeraire prove able to singly defeat a force of half-a-dozen dragons, they could win only a Pyrrhic victory thereby.

"Enough, Temeraire; stand down," Laurence said; to Ertegun he said, stiffly, "Sir, the wild dragons I have already made plain to you were not under my command, and I have promised to make good your losses. I do not suppose you seriously propose to offer an act of war against Britain without the approval of your government; we will certainly offer no such hostility ourselves."

Tharkay unexpectedly translated this into Turkish, though Laurence had muddled through it in French, and spoke loudly enough that the other Turkish aviators might overhear; they looked uneasily at one another, and Ertegun threw him an ugly look, full of savage frustration. He spat, "Remain, and you will learn otherwise to your peril," and flung himself back towards his dragon, shouting orders; the whole flight together backed away some little distance and settled themselves in the shade of a small grove of fruit-trees bordering upon the road leading to the city, which they disposed themselves across; and the smallest of them leapt aloft and flew away towards the city at an energetic pace; shortly he grew too small to see, and vanished against the haze.

"And carrying no good news of us, to be sure," Granby said, watching his progress through Laurence's glass.

"Not without cause," Laurence said grimly.

Temeraire scratched at the ground, with a guilty air. "They were not very friendly," he said, defensively.

There was very little shelter to be had, without retreating a great distance away out of sight of the guard-dragons, which Laurence did not mean to do; but they found a place between two low hillocks and pitched a little canvas on poles stuck into the dirt, to give the sick men a piece of shade. "It is a pity they took *all* the cows," Temeraire said, wistfully, looking after the vanished ferals.

"A little patience would have seen them fed and you also, as guests instead of as thieves," Laurence said, his own sorely tried. Temeraire did not protest the reproof, but only hung his head, and Laurence stood up and walked some distance away under the excuse of looking again towards the city through his glass: no change, except now some herdsmen were driving cattle towards the encamped Turkish dragons, so they might eat; and the men were taking refreshment also. He put down the glass and turned from the scene. His own mouth was dry and crack-lipped; he had given his water ration to Dunne, who could hardly stop coughing. It was already grown too late to forage; but in the morning, he would have to send some of the men to hunt and find water, at great risk to themselves in strange country, where they could answer no challenge; and he had no clear idea what they might do next, if the Turks remained obdurate.

"Ought we not go round the city and try it again, from the European side?" Granby suggested, as Laurence came back to their makeshift camp.

"There are look-outs posted upon the hills to the north, against invasion from Russia," Tharkay said briefly. "Unless you mean to travel an hour out of the way, you will rouse all the city."

"Sir, someone is coming," Digby said, pointing, and the de-

bate was moot: a courier-dragon was coming quickly from the
city, with an escort of two heavy-weight beasts; and though the
lowering sun was full on them, blotting out their colors, Laurence saw clearly silhouetted against the sky the two great horns
thrust up from their foreheads, the narrower spikes like thorns
bristling along the twisting serpentine lengths of their bodies: he
had seen a Kazilik once before thus, framed against the billowing tower of smoke and flame rising from the *Orient,* at the Nile,
as the dragon set her magazine alight and burnt the great
thousand-man ship to the waterline.

"Get all the sick aboard, and unload all the powder and the
bombs," he said, grimly; a scorching Temeraire could survive, if
he could not evade, but even a small unlucky lick of flame might
set off the store of gunpowder and incendiaries packed into his
belly-rigging, with as deadly result for him as for that ill-fated
French flagship.

They worked double-quick, leaving the round bombs heaped
in small pyramids upon the ground, while Keynes strapped the
sickest men down to boards to be secured into the belly-rigging;
canvas and cloth were flung down billowing, and the spare
leather also. "I can make a polite noise, Laurence; do you go
aboard, until we know what they mean," Granby suggested; to
Laurence's impatient refusal. The rest of the men Laurence sent
aboard, however, so that only he and Granby remained on foot,
well in reach of Temeraire.

The Kazilik pair landed together a short distance away, their
scarlet hides vivid with markings of black-edged green, like
leopard-spots, and licking at the air with their long black
tongues; so close that Laurence could hear emanating from their
bodies a low, faint rumbling something like the purr of a cat and
the hiss of a kettle combined, and see even against the still-light
sky the thin lines of steam which wisped upwards and away
from the narrow spikes along the ridges of their back.

Captain Ertegun came towards them again, eyes narrowed
and dark with satisfaction; from the courier dismounted two
black slaves, who with great care assisted another man to de-
scend smoothly from the dragon's shoulders; grasping their

hands he stepped down onto a small folding set of steps, which they laid upon the ground. He wore a gorgeously appointed kaftan embroidered in silks of many colors, and a white many-plumed turban concealing his hair; Ertegun bowed low before him, and presented him to Laurence as Hasan Mustafa Pasha; the last a title rather than surname, Laurence vaguely recalled, and a senior rank among the vezirs.

This at least was better than an immediate assault, and when the introductions had been coldly concluded by Ertegun, Laurence began awkwardly, "Sir, I hope you will permit me to express my apologies—"

"No, no! Enough, come, let us hear no more of this," Mustafa said, his French a great deal more fluent and voluble than Laurence's, and easily overrunning his stumbling tongue; and reaching out the vezir grasped Laurence's hand in his own, with enthusiasm. While Ertegun, outraged, stared and colored to his cheekbones, Mustafa waved away all further apology and explanation, and said, "It is only unfortunate that you should have been taken in by those wretched creatures; but then it is as the imams have said, that the dragon born in the wild does not know the Prophet, and is as a servant of the Devil."

Temeraire bridled at this, snorting, but Laurence was in no mood to quarrel, full of relief. "You are more than generous, sir; and you may well believe me grateful for it," he said. "It is paltry in me to be asking your hospitality, having so abused it already—"

"Ah, no!" Mustafa said, dismissing this as of no moment. "Of course you are very welcome, Captain; you have come a long way. You will follow us to the city: the Sultan, peace be upon him, has already commanded from his generosity that you shall be housed in the palace. We have made quarters ready for you, and a cool garden for your dragon; you will rest and refresh yourselves after your journey, and we will think no more of this unhappy misunderstanding."

"I confess your suggestion is by far more appealing than the demands of my duty," Laurence said. "We would indeed be thankful for some little refreshment, whatever you can provide, but we cannot linger in port, as it were, and must soonest be on our way again: we have come to collect the dragon eggs, as has been arranged, and we must straightaway get them to England."

Mustafa's smile wavered, for a moment, and his hands still clasping Laurence's between them tightened. "Why, Captain, surely you have not come so far for nothing?" he cried. "You must know we cannot give you the eggs."

PART II

CHAPTER 6

The small ivory fountain, many-jetted, flung off a fine cooling mist that gathered upon the orange-tree leaves and fruit hanging low over the pool, ripe and fragrant and trembling. In the vast palatial gardens below the terrace railing, Temeraire lay sun-dappled and drowsy after his substantial meal, and the little runners, having cleaned him off, were sleeping tucked against his side. The chamber itself was fairytale-lovely, tiles of lapis-blue and white laid upon the walls from floor to gilt-painted ceiling, shutters inlaid with mother-of-pearl, velvet-cushioned window seats, thick carpets in a thousand shades of red heaped over the floors, and in the center of the room a tall painted vase half the height of a man stood upon a low table, full of a profusion of flowers and vines. Laurence could gladly have hurled it across the room.

"It is the outside of enough," Granby said, blazing away as he paced. "Fobbing us off with a pack of excuses, and then to heap on such vile insinuations, and as good as call this poor wretch Yarmouth a thief—"

Mustafa had been full of apology, of regret: the agreements

had never been signed, he explained, fresh concerns having
arisen to delay the matter; and as a consequence the payment
had not yet been delivered when the ambassador had met with
his accident. When Laurence had received these excuses with all
the suspicion the circumstances commanded, and demanded at
once to be taken to the ambassador's residence and to speak
with his staff, Mustafa had with an air of faint discomfort confided that upon the ambassador's death, his servants had departed post-haste for Vienna, and *one*, his secretary James
Yarmouth, had vanished entirely.

"I will not say I know any evil of him, but gold is the great
tempter," Mustafa had said, spreading his hands wide, his implications plain. "I am sorry, Captain, but you must understand we
cannot bear the responsibility."

"I do not believe a word of it; not a word," Granby went on,
furiously, "the notion they would send to us, in China, to come
here with an agreement only half-made—"

"No, it is absurd," Laurence agreed. "Lenton would have
spoken quite differently in his orders, had the arrangement been
uncertain in the least; they can only want to renege upon it, with
as little embarrassment to themselves as possible."

Mustafa had smiled and smiled relentlessly in the face of all
Laurence's objections, and repeated his apologies, and offered
hospitality once again; with all the crewmen weary and thick
with dust, and no alternative to hand, Laurence had accepted,
supposing besides that they would only find it easier to work out
the truth of the affair, and exert some influence to see matters set
right, once ensconced in the city.

He and his crew had been settled into two elaborate kiosques
upon the inner grounds, the buildings nestled amidst rich lawns
vast enough for Temeraire to sleep in. The palace crowned the
narrow spur of land where the Bosphorus and the Golden Horn
together met the sea, and endless prospects showed in every direction during their descent: horizons full of ocean, and a great
crowd of shipping on the water. Laurence only too late recognized that they had stepped into a gilded cage: the matchless
views were so because the palace hill was encircled all around

with high windowless walls that barred all communication with the outside world, and their quarters looked upon the sea through windows barred with iron.

From the air, the kiosques had seemed joined with the sprawling palace complex, but the connection proved only a roofed cloister, open to the air: all the doors and windows which might have led into the palace proper were locked and forbidding, black and shuttered against even the entry of their gaze. More of the black slaves stood guard at the foot of the terrace stairs, and in the gardens the Kazilik dragons lay in sinuously knotted heaps, their glittering yellow eyes slitted open and resting watchfully on Temeraire.

For all his genial welcome, Mustafa had vanished away as soon as he had seen them neatly locked up, with vague promises to return very soon. But the call to prayer had come thrice since then; they had explored the limits of their handsome prison twice over, and still there was no sign of his returning. The guards made no objections if any of them came down to speak with Temeraire, in the gardens just beneath the kiosques, but they shook their heads genially when Laurence pointed over their shoulders to the paved walkway that led towards the rest of the grounds.

Held at this remove, from the terraces and windows they could watch the life of the palace as much as they wished, a curious kind of frustration: other men walking about the grounds, busy and preoccupied; officials in high turbans, servants carrying trays, young pages darting back and forth with baskets and letters; once even a gentleman who looked like a medical man, long-bearded and in plain black clothing, who disappeared into a small kiosque of his own some distance away. Many looked over curiously at Laurence and his crew, the boys slowing in their progress to stare at the dragons sitting in the garden, but they made no answer if called-to, only hurrying on prudently.

"Look; do you suppose that is a woman, over there?" Dunne and Hackley and Portis were jostling one another for the glass, hanging nearly halfway over the terrace railing with twenty feet down to solid stone pavement, trying recklessly to peer across the garden: an official was speaking with a woman—or a man, or an orang-utang, so far as could be told from externals. She was wearing a veil not of heavy silk but dark, which was wrapped around her head and shoulders and left only her eyes uncovered; and despite the heat of the day her gown was covered with a long coat, reaching to her jewel-slippered feet, and a deep-slashed pocket in the front concealed even her hands from view.

"Mr. Portis," Laurence said sharply; the older midshipman was actually putting fingers to his lips to whistle, "as you have nothing better to do, you will go below and see to digging Temeraire a fresh necessary; and when he has done with it you may fill it in again; at once, if you please." Dunne and Hackley hastily lowered the glass as Portis slunk off abashed, attempting without much success an air of innocence; Tharkay silently relieved them of it, while Laurence added, "And you two gentlemen—"

He paused in mingled outrage and dismay to see Tharkay himself peering through the glass at the veiled woman; "Sir," Laurence said, against his teeth, "I will thank *you* not to ogle the palace women either."

"She is not a woman of the harem," Tharkay said. "The harem quarters are to the south, beyond those high walls, and the women are not permitted outside; I assure you, Captain, we would not be seeing nearly so much of her, were she an odalisque." He straightened away from the glass: the woman had turned to look at them, a pale narrow strip of skin all that the robes did not cover, only just large enough to leave her dark eyes exposed.

Thankfully she made no outcry, and in a moment she and the official had walked out of sight again. Tharkay shut up the glass and gave it to Laurence, and walked away, insouciant; Laurence closed his fist around the barrel. "You will go and ask Mr. Bell to find you some way to assist him with the newest leather he has to hand," he said to Dunne and Hackley, restraining himself from giving them a sharper punishment duty; he would not make them scapegoat for Tharkay.

They made their grateful escape, and Laurence paced the terrace length again, stopping at the far end to look out over the city and the Golden Horn; dusk was descending: Mustafa would surely not come today.

"And there is the day wasted," Granby said, joining him as the last call to prayer came: the raw straining voices of the muezzin mingled from distant minarets and near, one so close it might have been only on the other side of the high brick wall that divided their courtyard from the harem.

The call woke Laurence again at dawn: he had left the shutters all open for the breeze, and so that he might lift his head during the night and see Temeraire safe and asleep in the faint eldritch glow of the scattered lanterns hung on the palace walls. And once again they heard it five times over with still no communication: not a visit nor a word nor any sign that their existence was even acknowledged, beyond the meals which were brought them by a quick and silent handful of servants, there and gone before any questions could be asked them.

At Laurence's request, Tharkay tried to bespeak the guards in Turkish, but they only shrugged inarticulate and opened their mouths to show where their tongues had been cut out, a piece of barbarity. When asked to take a letter, they shook their heads firmly, whether from unwillingness to leave their posts for such a purpose, or perhaps under instructions to keep them incommunicado.

"Do you suppose we could bribe them?" Granby said, when night began to come on, and still no word had come. "If only we could get out, a few of us: someone in this damned city must know what has happened to the ambassador's staff; not all of them can have gone away."

"We might; if we had anything to bribe them with," Laurence said. "We are wretchedly short, John; I dare say they would sniff at what I can afford. I doubt it would see us out of the palace, when it would mean their positions if not their heads."

"Then we might have Temeraire knock down a wall to let us

out; at least that might draw some notice," Granby said, not entirely joking, and flung himself down onto the nearest couch.

"Mr. Tharkay, do you translate for me again," Laurence said, and went to address the guards once more; though at first they had tolerated their guest-prisoners with good humor, they were now grown visibly annoyed, this being the sixth time Laurence had accosted them over the course of the day. "Pray tell them we require some more oil for the lamps, and candles," Laurence said to Tharkay, "also perhaps some soap, and other toilet articles," improvising some small requests.

These presently, as he had hoped, brought one of the young pages they had seen from afar, to fetch and carry for them; the boy was sufficiently impressed at the offer of a silver coin to agree to convey a message to Mustafa. Having first sent him off to bring the candles and sundry, to forestall any suspicion on the part of the guards, Laurence sat down with pen and paper to compose as severe a formal letter as he could manage, which he hoped would convey to that smiling gentleman that he did not mean to sit quietly in this bower.

"I am not sure what you mean by the beginning of the third paragraph," Temeraire said doubtfully, when Laurence read over the letter, written in French, to him.

"'Whatever your design may be, in leaving unanswered all the questions which—'" Laurence began.

"Oh," Temeraire said, "I think you want *conception* instead of *dessin*. Also, Laurence, I do not think you want to say you are his obedient *domestique*."

"Thank you, my dear," Laurence said, correcting the words, and guessing at the spelling of *heuroo*, before he folded up the missive and handed it over to the boy, who had now returned with a basket of candles and of small cakes of soap, heavily perfumed.

"I only hope he will not throw it in the fire," Granby said, after the boy had trotted away, coin clutched in one fist, not very discreetly. "Or I suppose Mustafa might hurl it in himself."

"We will not hear anything tonight, regardless," Laurence said. "We had better sleep while we can. If we get no answer, we will have to think of making a dash for Malta tomorrow. They do not have much of a shore battery here, and I dare say they will answer us very differently if we come back with a first-rate and a couple of frigates behind us."

"LAURENCE," TEMERAIRE CALLED from outside, rousing him from a thick, too-real dream of sailing; Laurence sat up and rubbed his wet face: a change in the wind had carried the fountain-spray onto him during the night.

"Yes," he answered, and went to wash in the fountain, still half-asleep; he went down into the gardens, nodding civilly to the yawning guards, and Temeraire nudged at him with interest.

"That is a nice smell," he said, diverted, and Laurence realized he had washed with the perfumed soap.

"I will have to scrub it off later," he said, dismayed. "Are you hungry?"

"I would not mind something to eat," Temeraire said, "but I must tell you something: I have been talking to Bezaid and Sherazde, and they say their egg will hatch very soon."

"Who?" Laurence said, puzzled, then stared at the pair of Kazilik dragons, who blinked their glossy eyes at him in return, with mild interest. "Temeraire," he said, slowly, "do you mean that we are to have *their* egg?"

"Yes, and two others, but those have not started to harden," Temeraire said. "I think," he added. "They only know a little French, and a little of the dragon-language, but they have been telling me words in Turkish."

Laurence paid this no attention, too staggered by the news; very nearly since any organized sort of dragon-breeding had begun, Britain had been trying to acquire a line of fire-breathers. A few of the Flamme-de-Gloire had been brought over after Agincourt, but the last had died out scarcely a century later, and since then there had been only failure after failure: France and Spain had naturally denied them, too-close neighbors to wish to yield so great an advantage, and for a long while the Turks had been no more eager to deal with infidels than the British with heathen.

"And we were in negotiations with the Inca, not twelve years ago," Granby said, his face flushed bright with passionate excitement, "but it all came to nothing, in the end; we offered them a kingdom's ransom, and they seemed pleased, then overnight they returned us all the silk and tea and guns we had brought them, and ran us out of the place."

"How much did we offer to them, do you recall?" Laurence asked, and Granby named a sum which made him sit abruptly down. Sherazde, with an air of smugness, informed them in her broken French that *her* egg had commanded a higher price still, almost impossible to believe.

"Good God; how half such a sum was raised, I am at a loss to imagine," Laurence said. "They might build half-a-dozen first-rates for the same price, and a pair of dragon transports besides."

Temeraire was sitting up and very still, his tail wound tight around his body and his ruff bristling. "We are *buying* the eggs?" he said.

"Why—" Laurence was surprised; he had not before realized Temeraire did not understand the eggs were to be acquired for money. "We are, yes, but you see yourself that your acquaintances do not object to giving over their egg," he said, glancing anxiously at the Kazilik pair, who indeed seemed unconcerned at being parted from their offspring.

But Temeraire dismissed this with an impatient flick of his tail. "Of course they do not mind that, they know we will take care of the egg," he said. "But as you have told me yourself, if you buy a thing, then you own it, and may do as you like with it. If I buy a cow I may eat it, and if you buy an estate then we may live upon it, and if you buy me a jewel I may wear it. If eggs are property, then the dragons that hatch out of them are also, and it is no wonder that people treat us as though we are slaves."

There was very little way to answer this; raised in an abolitionist household, Laurence understood without question that men ought not be bought and sold, and when put on terms of principle he could hardly disagree; however, there was plainly a vast difference in the condition of dragons and the unfortunate wretches who lived in bondage.

"It's not as though we can make the dragonets do as we want, once they hatch," Granby offered, a useful inspiration. "You could say that we are only buying the chance to persuade them to go into harness with us."

But Temeraire said, with a militant gleam, "And if instead when hatched they wished to fly away, and come back here?"

"Oh, well," Granby said, lamely, and looked awkward; naturally in such a case, the feral dragonet would be taken to the breeding-grounds instead.

"At least consider that in this case, we are taking them away to England, where you will have the opportunity of improving their condition," Laurence tried as consolation, but Temeraire was not so easily mollified, and curled brooding in the garden to consider the problem.

"Well, he has taken the bit in his teeth and no mistake," Granby said to Laurence, with a worried querying note in his voice, as they went back inside.

"Yes," Laurence said dismally. He did have some expectation of winning real improvement in the comforts of the dragons, once back home; he was sure Admiral Lenton and the other senior admirals of the Corps would be quite willing to adopt all such measures which their authority should allow. Laurence had with him plans for a pavilion in the Chinese style, with the heating-stones beneath and the pipe-fed running fountains, which had been so much to Temeraire's liking; Gong Su might easily train others in the art of dragon cookery, and the *Allegiance* was carrying home besides the reading frames and sand writing tables, which surely could be adapted to Western usage. Privately Laurence doubted whether most dragons would have any interest; Temeraire was unique not only in his gift for language but his passion for books. But whatsoever interest there was could be satisfied easily and without great cost, and could hardly provoke any objections.

But beyond these measures, which might be undertaken

within the discretion and the funds of the Corps, Government was hardly likely to go with a good-will, and the degree of coercion required to force anything more, Laurence could not bear to endorse. A mutiny of dragons would terrify all the country, and surely injure the cause as much as promote it; and fix the Ministry in the prejudice that dragons were not to be depended upon. The effects of such a conflict upon the prosecution of the war were hardly to be overstated, and as distraction alone might prove fatal: there were not enough dragons in England for those available to be worrying more about their pay and their rights in law than about their duty.

He could not help but wonder if another captain, a proper aviator and better-trained, might have kept Temeraire from growing so preoccupied and discontented, and channeled his energies better. He would have liked to ask Granby if such difficulties were at all common, if there were any advice to be had on the matter, but he could not be asking a subordinate for help in managing Temeraire; and in any case, he was not sure advice would be of use any longer. To call it slavery, when a dragon egg was purchased at a cost of half-a-million pounds, and the only change whether it should be hatched in England rather than in the Sublime Porte, was unreasonable as a practical matter, and all the philosophy in the world could not change that.

"If the egg has begun to harden, how long do you expect we have?" he asked Granby instead, putting his hand up to the wind that came in at the archway facing the sea, and calculating in his mind how long it should be to bring a ship from Malta; they could reach the island in three days' flying, he felt sure, if Temeraire was well-rested and well-fed beforehand.

"Well, certainly it is down to weeks, but whether it is three or ten I cannot tell you without I see the thing, and even then I could be wrong: you will have to ask Keynes for that," Granby said. "But it's not enough to lay our hands upon the egg at the last moment, you know. This dragonet shan't be like Temeraire and pop out knowing three tongues at once, I never heard of anything like; we must get hold of the egg and start it on English straight off."

"Oh, Hell," Laurence said, dismayed, and let fall his hand; he had not even considered the matter of language. He had captured Temeraire's egg scarcely a week before hatching, and had not known enough to be surprised to find him speaking English, more astonished that a new-hatched creature could speak at all. Yet another gap in his training; and another fresh source of urgency.

"IT WOULD GIVE the Sultan a strange appearance among the ranks of rulers," Laurence said, only just contriving to present an appearance of equanimity, "to tolerate the disappearance of half-a-million pounds meant for his treasury and the death of an ambassador within his territory, with no inquiry; mere courtesy to an ally would dictate greater concern, sir, at the circumstances which you have described to me."

"But, Captain, I assure you, all inquiries are being made," Mustafa said, in great earnest, and tried to press a platter of honey-soaked pastry upon him.

Mustafa had at last appeared shortly after the hour of noon, pleading as excuse for his absence an unexpected affair of state which had drawn away his attention; by way of apology he had come accompanied by their dinner, and an extravagant entertainment besides. Two dozen servants or more bustled around with great noise, setting rugs and cushions for them upon the terrace, all around the marble pool, and ferrying great platters from the kitchens, laden with fragrant pilaff and heaps of mashed aubergines, cabbage leaves and green peppers stuffed with meat and rice, skewers and thin-sliced roasted meats redolent of rich smoke.

Temeraire, his head craned over the railing to observe the event, sniffed these with especial appreciation, and, despite having been well-fed on two tender lambs only an hour earlier, surreptitiously cleared in a few bites a serving-dish set down for a moment within his reach, and left the servants staring at the empty platter, its gold scraped and dented by his teeth.

In case this should have proved inadequate distraction, Mustafa had brought with him musicians, who at once set up a great noise, and a crowd of dancing-girls in loose and translucent pantaloons. Their gyrations were so plainly indecent, and so little concealed by the veils which they swung round themselves, that Laurence could only blush for them, though their performance was much applauded by many of his younger officers. The riflemen were the most outrageous: Portis had learnt his lesson, at least, but Dunne and Hackley, younger and more exuberant, were comporting themselves shamelessly, trying to catch at the trailing veils and whistling approval; Dunne even went so far as to get up onto one knee and reach out a hand before Lieutenant Riggs caught his ear smartly and pulled him down.

Laurence was in no danger of being so led astray; the women were beautiful, white-limbed and dark-eyed Circassians, but his wrath at these plain efforts to keep them from business was rather more in force than any other base emotion, and superseded any temptation he might otherwise have felt. But when he tried at first to speak to Mustafa, one went so far as to approach him more directly, her arms spread wide to display her lovely breasts to good effect, these being covered inadequately and moving in counter-point to her hips. Gracefully she seated herself upon his couch and stretched her slender arms out towards him in blatant invitation; an effective bar to any conversation, and it was no part of his character to thrust a woman forcibly away.

Fortunately, his virtue had an effective guardian: Temeraire put his head down to inspect her with jealous suspicion, eyes narrowing further at her many dazzling chains of gold, and snorted; the girl, unprepared for such a reception, sprang hurriedly up from the divan and back to the safety of her fellows.

At last Laurence was able to press Mustafa for some relief; only to have the pasha put him off with vague assurances that the investigations would bear fruit "soon, very soon, of course; although the labors of government are many, Captain, I am certain you understand."

"Sir," Laurence said bluntly, "I understand well enough you

may drag things out to suit you; but when you have delayed too long and rendered all discussion moot, what hold you presently have on our patience will be gone, and you may find such treatment will merit an answer you will not enjoy receiving."

This pointed remark was as near as he felt he could come to a threat, or ought to; no minister of the Sultan's could fail to understand how very vulnerable the city was to blockade or even attack by sea, with the Navy in easy striking distance at Malta. Indeed, for once Mustafa was left without a ready answer, and his mouth was pressed tight.

"I am no diplomat, sir," Laurence added, "and I cannot wrap my meaning up in fine language. When you know as well as do I that time is of the essence, and yet I am left to cool my heels to no purpose, I do not know what to call it but deliberate; and I cannot easily believe that my ambassador dead and his secretary missing, all his staff should have unceremoniously departed, though knowing to expect us and with so vast a sum unaccounted for."

But to this, Mustafa sat up and spread his hands. "How may I convince you, Captain? Will you be satisfied to visit his residence, and inspect for yourself?"

Laurence paused, taken aback; his intention had been to press Mustafa for just such a liberty, and he had not expected to have it offered him unsolicited. "I would indeed be glad of the opportunity," he answered, "and to speak with whatever servants of his household remain in the neighborhood."

"I do not like it in the least," Granby said, when a pair of mute guards arrived shortly after their dinner, to escort Laurence on the foray. "You ought to remain here; let me go instead with Martin and Digby, and we will bring back anyone I can find."

"They are not likely to permit you to bring men freely into the palace; nor can they be so lost to reason as to murder us in the street, with Temeraire and two dozen men here to carry away the news," Laurence said. "We will do very well."

"I do not like your going away, either," Temeraire said discontentedly. "I do not see why I cannot come." He had grown used to walking about freely in Peking, and so long as they had been in the wilderness, of course, his movements also had not been restricted.

"I am afraid the conditions here are not as they were in China," Laurence said. "The streets of Istanbul will not admit of your passage, and if they did we would begin a panic among the populace. Now; where is Mr. Tharkay?"

There was a moment of general silence and confusion, heads turning all around: Tharkay was nowhere to be seen. A hurried questioning made sure that no one had seen him since the previous evening, and then Digby pointed out his small bedroll neatly tucked away and still bound up among their baggage, unused. Laurence regarded it with a tight-lipped expression. "Very well; we cannot delay in hopes he will come back. Mr. Granby, if he returns, you will put him under guard until I have opportunity to speak with him."

"Yes, sir," Granby said, darkly.

Certain phrases which might form a part of that conversation sprang forcefully to Laurence's mind, as he stood in bafflement outside the elegant ambassador's residence: the windows tight-shuttered, the door barred, dust and rat-droppings beginning to collect upon the front stoop. The guards only looked at him uncomprehendingly when he tried to make gestures suggesting the servants, and though he went so far as to apply at the neighboring houses, he found no one who understood a word of English or French, nor even his wretched gasping scraps of Latin.

"Sir," Digby said, low, when Laurence came back unsuccessful once more, from the third house, "I think that window on the side there is unlocked, and I dare say I could scramble in, if Mr. Martin would give me a leg up."

"Very good; only mind you do not break your neck," Laurence said; he and Martin together heaved Digby up close enough to reach the balcony. Squirreling up over an iron railing was no great difficulty for a boy raised to clamber all over a dragon's back in mid-flight, and though the window stuck halfway, the young ensign was still slim enough he could wriggle through.

The guards made an uneasy wordless protest when Digby opened the front door from within, but Laurence ignored them and went inside, Martin at his back. They stepped over straw and tracked dirt in the hallway, marks of bare dusty feet on the floor, signs of a hasty packing and departure. Inside the rooms were dark and echoing even when the shutters were thrown open, sheets draped across furnishings all left in place, the ghostly quality of a house abandoned and waiting, and the low muttering *tick-tick* of the great clock beside the staircase queerly loud in the hush.

Laurence went upstairs and through the chambers; but though there were some papers scattered and left here and there, these were little more than scraps left from packing: torn rags and fragments of kindling paper. One leaf he found beneath the writing-desk in a large bedchamber, in a lady's hand, an excerpt of a cheerful and ordinary letter home, full of news of her small children and curious stories of the foreign city, broken off mid-page and never finished; he put it down again, sorry to have intruded.

A smaller chamber down the hall, Laurence thought must have been Yarmouth's; it seemed as though the occupant had stepped out only for an hour: two coats hanging with a clean shirt, a suit of evening wear, a pair of buckled shoes; a bottle of ink and a pen lying trimmed upon the desk, with books left on the shelves and a small cameo left inside the desk: a young woman's face. But the papers had been taken away: or at least, there were none left which had any useful intelligence.

He went down again none the wiser; and Digby and Martin had met with no better luck belowstairs. At the least there was no sign of foul play, or of looting, though everywhere an untidy mess and all the furniture left behind; they had gone in a great hurry, certainly, but not it seemed by force. Her husband so suddenly dead and his secretary vanished, under such irregular circumstances and with so vast a sum of gold involved: caution alone might have reasonably driven the ambassador's wife to take her children and the remains of her household and retreat, rather than remain alone and friendless in a city so foreign and far away from allies.

But a letter to Vienna might take weeks to go and bring back a reply; they would not have time to learn the truth, not before the egg was irretrievably lost to them, and there was certainly nothing here to disprove Mustafa's story. Disheartened, Laurence left the house, the guards beckoning them impatiently on, and Digby barred the door again from within and scrambled down from the balcony to rejoin them.

"Thank you, gentlemen, I think we have learned all we can," Laurence said; there was no sense in letting Martin and Digby share in his own sense of dismay, and as best he could he concealed his anxiety as they followed in the guards' train back towards the river. Yet he was deep in a brown study, and gave little attention to their surroundings but to watch they did not lose the guards in the enormous crowd. The ambassador's residence had stood in the Beyoglu quarter across the Golden Horn, full of foreigners and tradesmen; there was a great press of people in the streets, strangely narrow after the broad avenues of Peking, and a din of voices calling: merchants outside their storefronts beckoning the instant they caught the eye of any passerby, trying to draw them inside.

But the crowd fell abruptly off, and the noise with it, as they came nearer to the shore: houses and shops all shuttered together, though now and again Laurence saw a face look out momentarily from behind a curtain, peering up at the sky, then vanish again as quickly. Above them broad shadows flickered by, blotting out for a moment the sun: dragons wheeling overhead, so near their bellmen could be counted by the head. The guards looked up apprehensively, and hurried them onward, though Laurence would have liked to stop for a better look, to see what they were about, lingering over so populous an area, and so crushing all the commerce of the day. Only a handful of men were to be seen in the streets beneath the shadows of the dragons, and those hurrying by anxious and quick; one dog stood barking with more courage than sense, its piercing voice carrying across the expanse of the harbor; the dragons paid it no more notice than a man might a buzzing fly, calling to one another aloft.

Their chief ferryman was waiting uneasily, passing the end of his anchor-cable through his hands, on the verge perhaps of abandoning them; he beckoned hurriedly while they came down the hill. Laurence turned himself around in the boat to see, as they drew away across the river: at first he thought the dragons, perhaps half-a-dozen of them, were only sporting in the air. But then he saw there were thick cables stretching down over the harbor, and the dragons were hauling upon these, drawing up whole waggons which carried, unmistakable, the barrels of long guns.

When they had reached the far shore of the river, Laurence leapt out ahead of the guards and went to the dockside to look more closely: already he could tell these were no trivial works. A host of low-bellied barges stood in the harbor, swarmed with some hundreds of men arranging the next waggon-loads, and a crowd of horses and mules somehow being kept obedient despite the dragons so nearby; perhaps because the dragons were above and out of their direct sight. Not only guns, but cannon-balls, barrels of powder, heaps of brick; such a mass of matériel Laurence would have allowed weeks to shift it up the steep hill, all of it traveling upwards quick as winking. And higher upon the hillside itself, the dragons were lowering the massive cannon-barrels into their waiting wooden cradles, as easily as a pair of men might move a plank of wood.

Laurence was by no means the only curious observer; a great press of natives of the city were gathered along the docks, staring at the scene, and whispering amongst themselves doubtfully; a company of Janissaries, in their plumed helmets, stood frowning not a dozen yards away, with their hands restless and toying with their carbines. One enterprising young man was going about offering the use of a glass to the onlookers, for a small fee; it was not very powerful, and the lenses mazed, but good enough for a closer look.

"Ninety-six-pounders, unless I quite mistake it, maybe so many as twenty of them, and I think there were as many more already ensconced on the Asian coast. This harbor will be a death-trap for any ship that comes in range," Laurence said grimly to Granby, as he washed the dust of the streets from his face and hands in the basin set on the wall, and ducked his head in the water for good measure, wringing his hair out with some savagery: soon he would resort to hacking off the ends with his sword, he thought, if he did not come to a barber; it had always refused to grow long enough for a proper queue, only enough to be an irritation and drip endlessly when wet. "And they were not at all sorry to let me see it; those guards were urging us along all the day, but they were pleased enough for me to stop and stare as long as I liked."

"Mustafa might as well have thumbed his nose at us," Granby agreed. "And Laurence, I am afraid that is not the only—well, you will see for yourself," and together they went around to the garden-side: the Kazilik dragons had gone, but in their stead another dozen dragons had been set around Temeraire, so that the garden was grown crowded, and a couple of them were obliged even to perch atop the backs of others.

"Oh, no; they are all quite friendly, and have only come to talk," Temeraire said earnestly; he was already making himself understood somehow in a mélange of French scattered with Turkish and the dragon-language, and with some labor and repetition he presented Laurence to the Turkish dragons, who all nodded their heads to him politely.

"They will still give us no end of difficulty if we need to leave with any haste," Laurence said, eyeing them sidelong; Temeraire was fast, very fast, for a dragon of his size; but the couriers at least could certainly outdistance him, and Laurence rather thought a couple of the middle-weight beasts might be able to match his speed long enough to slow him for a dragon more up to his fighting-weight.

But they were at least not unpleasant guard-dogs, and proved informative. "Yes; some of them have been telling me about the harbor works, they are here in the city helping," Temeraire said, when the operations Laurence had seen were described to him; and the visiting dragons willingly confirmed a good deal of what Laurence had surmised: they were fortifying the harbor, with a great many cannon. "It sounds very interesting; I would like to go and see, if we might."

"I would dearly like a closer look myself," Granby said. "I have no idea how they are managing it with horses involved. It is the very devil of a time having cattle around dragons; we count ourselves lucky not to stampede them, much less to get any useful work out of them. It is not enough to keep them out of sight; a horse can smell a dragon more than a mile off."

"I doubt Mustafa will be inclined to let us inspect their works very closely," Laurence said. "To let us have a glimpse across the harbor to impress upon us the futility of attack is one thing; to show all his hand would be something else. Has there been any word from him, any further explanation?"

"Not a peep, and neither hide nor hair of Tharkay, either, since you left," Granby said.

Laurence nodded, and sat down heavily upon the stairs. "We cannot keep going through all these ministers and official channels," he said finally. "Time is too short. We must demand an audience with the Sultan; his intercession must be the surest way to gain their quick cooperation."

"But if he has let them put us off, this far—"

"I cannot credit an intention on his part to wreck all relations," Laurence said, "not with Bonaparte nearer his doorstep than ever, since Austerlitz; and if he would be as pleased to keep the eggs, that is not as much to say he would choose them over an open and final breach. But so long as his ministers serve as intercessionaries, he has not committed himself and his state: he can always blame it upon them; if indeed it is not some sort of private political tangle behind these delays to begin with."

CHAPTER 7

Laurence occupied his evening with writing a fresh letter, this one still more impassioned and addressed directly to the Grand Vezir. He was only able to dispatch it by the cost of two pieces of silver instead of one: the boy servant had grown conscious of the strength of his position, and kept his hand outstretched firmly when Laurence put the first piece into his palm, staring silent but expectantly until Laurence at last set another down; an impudence Laurence was powerless to answer otherwise.

The letter brought no answer that night; but in the morning, at first he thought he had at last won some reply, for a tall and impressive man came walking briskly and with energy into their courtyard shortly past first light, trailed by several of the black eunuch guards. He created something of a noise, and then came out to the gardens where Laurence was sitting with Temeraire and laboring over yet another letter.

The newcomer was plainly a military officer of some rank; an aviator, by his long sweeping coat of leather gorgeously embroidered around the borders, and by the short-trimmed hair that set the Turkish aviators apart from their turbaned fellows; and a gifted one, by the sparkling jeweled *chelengk* upon his chest, a singular mark of honor among the Turks, rarely bestowed, which Laurence recognized from its having been granted Lord Nelson after the victory of the Nile.

The officer mentioned Bezaid's name, which made Laurence suspect him the Kazilik male's captain, but his French was not good, and at first Laurence thought he was speaking over-loud to try and make himself understood. He went on at length, his words tumbling together, and turned to address the watching dragons noisily also.

"But I have not said anything that is not the truth," Temeraire said, indignantly, and Laurence, still puzzling out the words he had managed to pick out of the flood, realized the officer was deeply, furiously agitated, and his spitting words rather a sign of high temper than inarticulate speech.

The officer actually shook his fist in Temeraire's teeth and said to Laurence violently, in French, "He tells more lies, and—" Here he dragged his hand across his throat, a gesture requiring no translation. Having finished this incoherent speech, he turned and stormed out of the garden; and in his wake a handful of the dragons sheepishly leapt into the air and flew away: plainly they were not under any orders to guard Temeraire at all.

"Temeraire," Laurence said, in the following silence, "what have you been saying to them?"

"I have only been telling them about property," Temeraire said, "and how they ought to be paid, and not need to go to war unless they wish it, but might do more work such as they are doing upon the harbor, or some other sort of labor, which might be more interesting, and then they could earn money for jewels and food, and go about the city as they liked—"

"Oh, good God," Laurence said, with a groan; he could imagine very well how these communications would have been viewed by a Turkish officer whose dragon expressed a desire not to go into battle and to take up some other profession which Temeraire might have suggested from his experience in China, such as poetry or nursemaiding. "Pray send the rest of them away, at once; or I dare say every officer of the Turkish corps in reach will come and rail at us in turn."

"I do not care if they do," Temeraire said obstinately. "If he had stayed, I should have had a great deal to say to him. If he cared for his dragon, he would want him treated well, and to have liberty."

"You cannot be proselytizing now," Laurence said. "Temeraire, we are guests here, and very nearly supplicants; they can deny us the eggs and make all our work to come here quite useless, and surely you see that they are putting obstacles enough in our path, without we give them any further cause to be difficult. We must rather conciliate the good-will of our hosts than offend them."

"Why ought we conciliate the men at the dragons' expense?" Temeraire said. "The eggs are theirs, after all, and indeed, I do not see why we are not negotiating with *them*, rather."

"They do not tend their own eggs, or manage their hatching; you know they have left the eggs to their captains, and given over their handling," Laurence said. "Else I should be delighted to address them; they could scarcely be less reasonable than our hosts," he added with some frustration. "But as matters stand, we are at the mercy of the Turks, and not their dragons."

Temeraire was silent, though his tail twitching rapidly betrayed his agitation. "But they have never had the opportunity to understand their own condition, nor that there might be a better; they are as ignorant as I myself was, before I saw China, and if they do not learn that much, how would anything ever change?"

"You will accomplish no change solely by making them discontented and offending their captains," Laurence said. "But in any case, our duty to home and to the war effort must come first. A Kazilik alone, on our side of the Channel, may mean the difference between invasion and security, and tip the balance of war; we can hardly weigh any concerns against such a potential advantage."

"But—" He stopped, and scratched at his forehead with the side of his claw. "But how will matters at all be different, once we are at home? If men will be upset at giving dragons liberty, would this not interfere with the war in England, too, and not only by keeping us from the eggs here? Or, if some British dragons did not want to fight anymore, that would hurt the war also."

He peered down with open curiosity at Laurence, waiting an answer; an answer which Laurence could not give, for indeed he felt precisely so, and he could not lie and say otherwise, not in the face of a direct question. He could think of nothing to say which would satisfy Temeraire, and as his silence stretched, Temeraire's ruff slowly drooped down, flattening against his neck, and his tendrils hung limply.

"You do not want me to say these things when we are at home, either," Temeraire said quietly. "Have you only been humoring me? You think it is all foolishness, and we ought not make any demands."

"No, Temeraire," Laurence said, very low. "Not foolishness at all, you have all the right in the world to liberty; but selfish— yes; I must call it so."

Temeraire flinched, and drew his head back a little, bewildered; Laurence looked down at his own tight-wrung hands; there could be no softening of it now, and he must pay for his long delay of the inevitable, at an usurious rate of interest.

"We are at war," he said, "and our case is a desperate one. Against us is ranged a general who has never been defeated, at the head of a country with twice over and more the native resources of our own small British Isles. You know Bonaparte has once massed an invasion force; he can do it again, if only he should subdue the Continent to his satisfaction, and perhaps with more success in a second attempt. In such circumstances, to begin a campaign for private benefit, which should have material risks of injuring the war effort, in my opinion can bear no other name; duty requires we put the concerns of the nation above our own."

"But," Temeraire protested, in a voice as small as could be produced from his deep chest, "but it is not for my own benefit, but for that of all the dragons, that I wish to press for change."

"If the war be lost, what will anything else matter, or whatever progress you have made at the expense of such a loss?" Laurence said. "Bonaparte will tyrannize over all Europe, and no one will have any liberty at all, men or dragons."

Temeraire made no answer; his head drooped over his forelegs, curling in on himself.

"I beg you, my dear, only to have patience," Laurence said after a long and painful moment of silence, aching to see him so downcast; and wishing he might in honesty recall his own words. "I do promise you, we will make a beginning; once we are home in England, we will find friends who will listen to us, and I hope I may have some small influence to call upon also. There are many real advances," he added, a little desperately, "practical improvements, which can be made without any unhappy effect upon the progress of the war; and with these examples to open the way, I am confident you will soon find a happier reception for your more lavish ideas, a better success at the cost only of time."

"But the war must come first," Temeraire said, low.

"Yes," Laurence said, "—forgive me; I would not for the world give you pain."

Temeraire shook his head a little, and leaned over to nuzzle him briefly. "I know, Laurence," he said, and rose up to go and speak to the other dragons, who were still gathered behind them in the garden, watching; and when he had seen them all flit away again, he padded away with head bowed low to curl himself brooding in the shade of the cypress-trees. Laurence went inside and sat watching him through the window-lattice, wondering wretchedly if Temeraire would have been happier, after all, to stay the rest of his days in China.

"You could tell him—" Granby said, but he stopped and shook his head. "No, it won't do," he agreed. "I am damned sorry, Laurence, but I can't see how you can sweeten it. You would not credit the stupid display in Parliament anytime we ask for funds only to keep up a covert or two, or get some better provisions for them; even if we only start building them pavilions, we will have a second war at home on our hands, and that is the least of his notions."

Laurence looked at him. "Will it hurt your chances?" he asked, quietly; these could not be very good in any case, with more than a year so far from home, out from under the eye of the senior officers who decided which lieutenants should be allowed a chance to put a hatchling into harness, not with ten eager men or more to every egg.

"I hope I am not so selfish a dog as to cavil for a reason such as that," Granby said with spirit. "I never knew a fellow to get an egg who was forever worrying about it; pray don't consider it. Damned few fellows who come into the Corps fresh, like me, ever get their step; there are too many dragons who go by inheritance, and the admirals like to have fellows from Corps families. But if I ever have a boy, now I am far enough along I can give him a leg up, or one of my nephews; that is good enough for me, and serving with a prime goer like Temeraire."

But he could not quite keep a wistful note from his voice; of course he would want his own dragon, and Laurence was certain that service as first lieutenant aboard a heavy-weight like Temeraire would ordinarily have meant a very good opportunity. Consideration for Granby was not an argument which could be made to Temeraire himself, of course, being a wholly unfair sort of pressure. On Laurence, however, it weighed heavily; he had been himself the beneficiary of a great deal of influence in his naval service, much of it even earned by merit, and he considered it a point of honor to do properly by his own officers.

He went outside. Temeraire had retreated further within the gardens; when Laurence at last came on him, Temeraire was still sitting curled quietly, his distress betrayed only by the furrows which he had gouged deep in the ground before him. His head was lowered upon his forelegs, and his eyes distant and narrow-slitted; the ruff nearly flat against his neck, sorrowful.

Laurence had no very clear notion of what to say, only wishing desperately to see him less unhappy, and almost willing to lie again if it would not hurt him the more. He stepped closer, and Temeraire lifted his head and looked at him; they neither of them spoke, but he went to Temeraire's side and put his hand on him, and Temeraire made a place in the crook of his foreleg for Laurence to sit.

A dozen nightingales were singing, pent in some nearby aviary; no other sound disturbed them a long while, and then Emily came running through the garden and calling, "Sir, sir," until panting she reached them and said, "Sir, pray come, they want to take Dunne and Hackley and hang them."

Laurence stared, leapt down from Temeraire's arm, and dashed back up the stairs to the court, Temeraire sitting up and putting his head anxiously over the terrace railing: nearly all the crew were out in the arched cloister, figuring in a wild noisy struggle with their own door guards and several other palace eunuchs: men of far greater position, judging by their golden-hilted scimitars and rich garb, and of more powerful mien, bull-necked and plainly not mutes, with furious imprecations flying from their lips as they wrestled slighter aviators to the ground.

Dunne and Hackley were in the thick of it; the two young riflemen were panting and fighting against the grip of the heavy-set men who clutched at them. "What the devil do you all mean by this?" Laurence bellowed, and let his voice carry over their heads; Temeraire added emphasis with his own rumbling growl, and the struggle subsided: the aviators fell back, and the guards stared up at Temeraire with expressions to suggest they would have gone pale if they could. They did not loose their captives, but at least did not attempt at once to drag them away.

"Now then," Laurence said grimly, "what goes toward here; Mr. Dunne?" He and Hackley hung their heads and said nothing, an answer in itself; plainly they had engaged in some sort of skylarking, and disturbed the guards.

"Go and fetch Hasan Mustafa Pasha," Laurence said to one of their own guards, a fellow he recognized, and repeated the name a few times over, the man glancing reluctantly at the others; abruptly one of the stranger eunuchs, a tall and imposing man in a high turban, snow-white against his dark skin and adorned by a sizable ruby set in gold, spoke commandingly to the guard; at this the mute at last nodded and set off down the stairs, hurrying away towards the rest of the palace grounds.

Laurence turned around. "You will answer me, Mr. Dunne, at once."

"Sir, we didn't mean any harm," Dunne said, "we only thought, we thought—" He looked at Hackley, but the other rifleman was dumb and staring, pale under his freckled skin, no help. "We only went up over the roof, sir, and then we thought we might have a look round at the rest of the place, and—and then those fellows started chasing us, and we got over the wall again and ran back here, and tried to get back inside."

"I see," Laurence said, coldly, "and you thought you would do this without application to myself or Mr. Granby, as to the wisdom of this course of action."

Dunne swallowed and let his head fall again. There was an uneasy, uncomfortable silence, a long wait; but not so very long, before Mustafa came around the corner at a rapid clip, the guard leading him, and his face red and mottled with haste and anger. "Sir," Laurence said, forestalling him, "My men without permission left their posts; I regret that they should have caused a disturbance—"

"You must hand them over," Mustafa said. "They shall at once be put to death: they attempted to enter the seraglio."

Laurence said nothing a moment, while Dunne and Hackley hunched themselves still lower and darted their eyes at his face anxiously. "Did they trespass upon the privacy of the women?"

"Sir, we never—" Dunne began.

"Be silent," Laurence said savagely.

Mustafa spoke to the guards; the chief eunuch beckoned forward one of his men, who answered in a voluble flow. "They looked in upon them, and made to them beckoning gestures through the window," Mustafa said, turning back. "More than sufficient insult: it is forbidden that any man but the Sultan should look upon the women of the harem and have intercourse with them; only the eunuchs, otherwise, may speak with them."

Temeraire, listening to this, snorted forcefully enough to

blow the fountain-spray into their faces. "That is very silly," he said hotly. "I am not having any of my crew put to death, and anyway I do not see why anyone should be put to death for talking to someone else at all; it is not as though that could hurt anyone."

Mustafa did not try to answer him, but instead turned a narrow measured look on Laurence. "I trust you do not mean to thus defy the Sultan's law, Captain, and give offense; you have, I think, had something to say on the subject of courtesy between our nations before."

"On *that* subject, sir—" Laurence said, angry at this bald-faced attempt at pressure; and then swallowed the words which leapt to his tongue: such as a pointed remark that Mustafa had been quick enough to come at once on this occasion, though previous entreaties had found him so occupied he could not spare a moment.

Instead he controlled himself, and said after a moment, "Sir, I think perhaps your guard may have from zeal thought more transpired than did in fact occur; I dare say my officers did not see the women at all, but only were calling in hopes of catching sight of them. That is a great folly; and you may be sure," he added, with heavy emphasis, "that they will suffer punishment for it; but to hand them over to death for it, I will not do, not on the word of a witness who has every cause to accuse them of doing rather *more* than *less* than they did, from a natural desire of protecting his charges from insult."

Mustafa, frowning, appeared ready to dispute further; Laurence added, "If they had outraged the virtue of any of the women, I would without hesitation deal with them according to your notion of justice; but so uncertain a circumstance, with a single witness to speak against them, must argue for a degree of mercy."

He did not move his hand to the hilt of his sword, nor signal to his men; but as best he could without turning his head, he considered their positions, and the disposal of their baggage, most of which had been stowed away inside the kiosques; if the Turks wished to seize Dunne and Hackley by force, he should have to order the men aboard directly, and leave all behind: if half-a-dozen dragons got into the air before Temeraire was aloft, it would be all up with them.

"Mercy is a great virtue," Mustafa said finally, "and indeed it would be sorrowful to mar relations between our countries by unhappy and false accusations. I am sure," he added, looking at Laurence significantly, "that you would grant an equal presentiment of innocence in any reverse case."

Laurence pressed his lips together. "You may rely upon it," he said, through his teeth, well aware he had committed himself to at least tolerate the inadequacies of the Turkish explanations so long as he had no proof of the reverse. But there was very little choice; he would not see two young officers under his care put to death for kissing their hands to a handful of girls through a window, dearly as he would have liked to wring their necks.

Mustafa's mouth turned up at the corner, and he inclined his head. "I believe we understand one another, Captain; we will leave their correction to you, then, and I trust you will ensure no similar incident occurs: gentleness shown once is mercy, shown twice is folly."

He collected the guards and led them away into the grounds, not without some low and angry protest on their part; there were some sighs of relief as they at last reluctantly went out of sight, and a couple of the other riflemen went so far as to clap Dunne and Hackley on the back: behavior which had at once to be stopped. "That will be enough," Laurence said dangerously. "Mr. Granby, you will note for the log that Mr. Dunne and Mr. Hackley are turned out of the flight crew, and you will put their names in the ground-crew roll."

Laurence had no very good idea whether an aviator might so be turned before the mast, as it were; but his expression did not allow of argument, and he did not receive any, only Granby's quiet, "Yes, sir." A harsh sentence, and it would look ugly upon their records even after they had been restored to their positions, as Laurence meant to do once they had learned a lesson. But he had little other choice, if they were to be punished; he could call no court-martial here, so far from home, and they were too old to be started with a cane. "Mr. Pratt, take these men in irons; Mr. Fellowes, I trust our supply of leather will allow you to prepare a lash."

"Aye, sir," Fellowes said, clearing his throat uncomfortably.

"But Laurence, Laurence," Temeraire said into complete silence, the only one who would have dared intercede. "Mustafa and those guards have gone, you need not flog Dunne and Hackley now—"

"They deserted their posts and willfully risked all the success of our enterprise, all for the satisfaction of the most base and carnal impulses," Laurence said flatly. "No; do not speak further in their defense, Temeraire: any court-martial would hang them for it, and high spirits make no excuse; they knew better."

He saw with some grim approval the young men flinching, and nodded shortly. "Who was on guard when they left?" he asked, surveying the rest of the crew.

Eyes dropped all around; then young Salyer stepped forward and said, "I was, sir," in a trembling voice, which cracked mid-word.

"Did you see them go?" Laurence asked quietly.

"Yes, sir," Salyer whispered.

"Sir," Dunne said hurriedly, "sir, we told him to keep quiet, that it was only for a lark—"

"That will be quite enough, Mr. Dunne," Granby said.

Salyer himself did not make excuses; and he was indeed a boy, only lately made midwingman, though tall and gangly with his adolescent growth. "Mr. Salyer, as you cannot be trusted to keep watch, you are reduced to ensign," Laurence said. "Go and cut a switch from one of those trees, and go to my quarters." Salyer stumbled away hiding his face, which beneath his hand was blotchy red.

To Dunne and Hackley, Laurence turned and said, "Fifty lashes each; and you may call yourselves damned lucky. Mr. Granby, we will assemble in the garden for punishment at the stroke of eleven; see to it the bell is rung."

He went to his kiosque, and when Salyer came gave him ten

strokes; it was a paltry count, but the boy had foolishly cut the switch from springy green wood, far more painful and more like to cut the skin, and the boy would be humiliated if he was driven to weeping. "That will do; see you do not forget this," Laurence said, and sent him away, before the trembling gasps had broken into tears.

Then he drew out his best clothes; he still had no better coat than the Chinese garment, but he set Emily to polish his boots fresh, and Dyer to press his neckcloth, while he went out and shaved himself over the small hand-basin. He put on his dress-sword and his best hat, then went out again and found the rest of the crew assembling in their Sunday clothing, and makeshift frames of bare signal-flag shafts thrust deep into the ground. Temeraire hovered anxiously, shifting his weight from side to side, and plowing up the earth.

"I am sorry to ask it of you, Mr. Pratt, but it must be done," Laurence said to the armorer quietly, and Pratt with his big head hung low between his shoulders nodded once. "I will keep the count myself, do you not count aloud."

"Yes, sir," Pratt said.

The sun crept a little higher. All the crew were already assembled and waiting and had been ten minutes and more; but Laurence neither spoke nor moved until Granby cleared his throat and said, "Mr. Digby, ring the bell for eleven, if you please," with great formality; and the eleven strokes tolled away, if softly.

Stripped to the waist and in their oldest breeches, Dunne and Hackley were led up to the poles; they at least did not disgrace themselves, but silently put their shaking hands up to be tied. Pratt was standing unhappily, ten paces back, running the long strap of the whip through his hands, folding it upon itself every few inches. It looked like an old scrap of harness, hopefully softened by use and much of the thickness worn away; better at any rate than new leather.

"Very well," Laurence said; a terrible silence fell, broken only by the crack of the descending lash, the gasps and cries growing slowly fainter, the count going on and on with their bodies slackening in the frames, hanging heavy from their wrists and dripping thin trickles of blood. Temeraire keened unhappily and put his head under his wing.

"I make that fifty, Mr. Pratt," Laurence said; nearer to forty if even so far, but he doubted any of his men had been counting very closely, and he was sick to his heart of the business. He had rarely ordered floggings of more than a dozen strokes, even as a naval captain, and the practice was entirely less common among aviators. For all the gravity of the offense, Dunne and Hackley were still very young; and he blamed himself in no small part that they should have come to run so wild.

Still it had to be done; they had known better, much better, and been reined in scarcely days before; so flagrant a breach, left unchecked, would have wholly ruined them. Granby had not been so far off, in Macao, to worry about the effect of their long travels on the young officers; the long idleness of their sea-journey followed by their more recent excess of adventure was no substitute for the steady pressure of ordinary day-to-day discipline, in a covert; it was not enough for a soldier to be brave. Laurence was not sorry to see a strong impression from the punishment on the faces of the other officers, particularly the young men, that at least this small good might come of the unhappy incident.

Dunne and Hackley were cut down, and carried not unkindly back up to the larger kiosque, and laid in a screened-off corner upon a pair of cots which Keynes had prepared; they lay on their faces still gasping softly in half-consciousness, while he with a tight mouth sopped away the blood from their backs, and gave them each a quarter-glass of laudanum to drink.

"How do they do?" Laurence asked the dragon-surgeon, later in the evening; they had fallen quiet after the drug, and lain still.

"Well enough," Keynes said shortly. "I am grown used to having them as patients; they had only just risen from their sick-beds—"

"Mr. Keynes," Laurence said quietly.

Keynes looking up at his face fell silent, and turned his attention back to the wounded men. "They are inclined to be a little feverish, but that is nothing wonderful. They are young and strong, the bleeding has stopped nicely; they ought to be on their feet by morning, for a little while in any case."

"Very good," Laurence said, and turned away to find Tharkay standing before him, in the low circle of the candle-light, looking at Dunne and Hackley where they lay; their striped backs were bare, and the weals bright red and purpling along the edges.

Laurence stared, drew in a sharp breath, then with controlled fury said, "Well, sir, and do you return? I wonder you should show your face here again."

Tharkay said, "I hope my absence has not been too great an inconvenience," with calm impudence.

"Only of too short duration," Laurence said. "Take your money and your things and get out of my sight, and I wish you may go to the devil."

"Well," Tharkay said, after a moment, "if you have no further need of my services, I suppose I may as well be on my way; I will give Mr. Maden your apologies, then, and indeed I ought not to have committed you."

"Who is Mr. Maden?" Laurence said, frowning; the name was distantly familiar, and then he slowly reached into his coat and drew out the letter which had come to them in Macao all those long months ago, which Tharkay had brought to him: flaps still marked with seals, and one of those marked with a solid *M*. "You are speaking of the gentleman who engaged you to bring us our orders?" he asked sharply.

"I am," Tharkay said. "He is a banker here in the city, and Mr. Arbuthnot desired him to find a reliable messenger for the letter; alas, only I was to be had." There was a little mocking quality to his voice. "He invites you to dine; will you come?"

CHAPTER 8

"Now," Tharkay said, soft, soft, they were at the palace wall, and the night-guards had just gone past; he flung a grappling-line, and they scrambled up and over: no great trick for a sailor, the stone wall ragged-faced and generous with footholds. In the outer gardens, pleasure-pavilions stood overlooking the sea, and a single great towering column loomed up against the half-moon while they ran across the lawns; then they were safely across the open ground and into the thickets left wild upon the hillside, ivy blanketing scraps of old, old ruins, arches built of brick and columns tumbled onto their sides.

They had another wall to scramble over, but this one, traveling as it did all around the circumference of the vast grounds, was too long to be well-patrolled; then they made their way down to the shores of the Golden Horn, where Tharkay calling softly roused a ferryman to carry them across the span in his little damp boat. The tributary glimmered to match its name even in the darkness, reflections stretching long from window-light and boat lanterns on both of its banks, people taking the air on balconies and terraces, and the sound of music carrying easily over the water.

Laurence would have liked to stop and look over the harbor for some closer detail of the works he had seen the previous day, but Tharkay led him on without a pause away from the dock-yards and into the streets, not in the same direction as the embassy, but towards the ancient spire of Galata Tower, standing sentinel upon the hill. A low wall encircled the district around the watchtower, soft and crumbling and very old, unattended; inside the streets were much quieter; only a handful of coffee-houses owned by Greeks or Italians still lit, small handfuls of men at tables talking in low voices over cups of the sweet-smelling apple tea, and here and there a devoted hookah-smoker gazing out upon the street while the fragrant steam emitted in slow, thin trails from between his lips.

Avraam Maden's house was handsome, wider by twice than its nearest neighbors and framed by broad-spreading trees, established on an avenue with a clear prospect on the old tower. A maid welcomed them, and within were all the signs of prosperity and long residence: carpets old but rich and still bright; portraits upon the walls in gilt frames, of dark-eyed men and women: rather more Spanish than Turkish in character, Laurence would have said.

Maden poured them wine as the maid laid out a platter of thin bread with a dish of paste made from aubergines, very piquant, and another of sweet raisins and dates chopped together with nuts, flavored with red wine. "My family came from Seville," he said, when Laurence mentioned the portraits, "when the King and the Inquisition expelled us; the Sultan was kinder to us."

Laurence hoped he might not have a very dismal meal ahead of him, having some vague impression of restrictions upon the Jewish diet, but the late dinner was more than respectable: a very good leg of lamb, roasted to a turn in the Turkish manner and carved off the spit into thin slices, with new potatoes dressed in their skins and a fragrant glaze of olive oil and strong herbs; and besides a whole fish roasted with peppers and tomatoes, pungent and strongly flavored with the common yellow spice, and a tenderly stewed fowl which no one could have objected to.

Maden, who in his trade often served as a factor for British visitors, spoke excellent English, and his family also; they sat to table five, Maden's two sons being already established in their own homes; besides his wife only his daughter Sara remained at home, a young woman well out of the schoolroom: not yet thirty but old to be unmarried with so good a dowry as Maden seemed able to provide, and her looks and manner were pleasing if in a foreign mode, dark hair and brows striking against fair skin, very like her elegant mother. Seated opposite the guests, she from either modesty or shyness kept her eyes lowered, though she spoke easily enough when addressed, in a self-possessed manner.

Laurence did not broach his urgent inquiries himself, feeling it a species of rudeness, but rather fell back on a description of their journey westward, prompted by his hosts' inquiries; these were polite to begin with, but soon began to be truly curious. Laurence had been raised to consider it a gentleman's duty to make good dinner conversation, and their passage had furnished him with material enough for anecdotes to make it very little burden in the present case. With the ladies present, he made somewhat light of the worst dangers of the sandstorm and the avalanche, and did not speak of their encounter with the horsemen-raiders, but there was interest enough without it.

"And then the wretches lighted on the cattle and were off again without a by-your-leave," he said, finishing ruefully with the account of the ferals' mortifying performance at the city gates, "with that villain Arkady wagging his head at us as he went, and all of us left at a standstill, our mouths hanging open. They went back well-pleased with themselves, I am sure, and as for us, it is of all things wonderful we were not thrown into prison."

"A cold welcome for you after a difficult road," Maden said, amused.

"Yes, a very difficult road," Sara Maden said in her quiet

voice, without looking up. "I am glad you all came through in safety."

There was a brief pause in the conversation; then Maden reached out and handed to Laurence the bread-platter, saying, "Well, I hope you are comfortable enough now; at least in the palace you must not be subjected to all this noise we have."

He was referring to the construction in the harbor, evidently a source of much aggrievance. "Who can get anything done with those great beasts overhead?" Mrs. Maden said, shaking her head. "Such a noise they make, and if they were to drop one of those cannon? Terrible creatures; I wish they were not let into civilized places. Not to speak of your dragon, of course, Captain; I am sure he is beautifully behaved," she said hastily, catching herself, and speaking apologetically to Laurence, with some confusion.

"I suppose we sound to you complainers over nothing, Captain," Maden said, coming to her rescue, "when you daily must tend to them at close quarters."

"No, sir," Laurence said, "indeed I found it wonderful to see a flight of dragons in the middle of the city here; we are not permitted to come so near to settled places, in England, and must follow particular courses to navigate overhead in the cities, that we do not distress the populace or the cattle, and even then there is always something of a noise made about our movements. Temeraire has often found it a burdensome stricture. Then is it a new sort of arrangement?"

"Of course," Mrs. Maden said. "I never heard of such a thing before, and I hope I never do again when it is over with. Not a word of warning, either; they appeared one morning as soon as the call to prayer was over; and we were left quaking in our houses all the day."

"One grows accustomed," Maden said, with a philosophical shrug. "It has been a little slow the last two weeks, but the stores are opening again, dragons or no."

"Yes, and none too soon," Mrs. Maden said. "How we are to arrange everything, in less than a month—Nadire," she called to the maid, "give me the wine, please," with only the barest pause, scarcely noticeable.

The little maid came in and handed over the decanter, which stood in easy reach on the sideboard, and whisked herself out again; while the bottle went around, Maden said quietly, while he poured for Laurence, "My daughter is to be married soon." He spoke in a queerly gentle tone, almost apologetic.

An uncomfortable, waiting silence fell, which Laurence did not understand; Mrs. Maden looked down at her plate, biting her lip. Tharkay broke it, lifting his glass, and said to Sara, "I drink to your health and happiness." She raised her dark eyes at last and looked across the table at him. Only for a moment, and then he broke from her gaze, raising the glass between them; but that was long enough.

"My congratulations," Laurence said, to help fill the silence, lifting his glass to her in turn.

"Thank you," she said. There was a little high color in her face, but she inclined her head politely, and her voice did not waver. The silence yet lingered; Sara herself broke it, straightening with a little jerk of her shoulders, and addressed Laurence across the table, a little firmly, "Captain, may I ask you, what has happened to the boys?"

Laurence would have liked to oblige her courage, but was puzzled how to understand the question, until she added, "Were they not from your crew, the boys who looked in on the harem?"

"Oh; I am afraid I must own it," Laurence said, mortified that the story should have somehow traveled so far, and hoping he was not compounding the situation by speaking of such a thing; he would not have thought the harem any fit subject for a young Turkish lady, any more than questions about a *demi-mondaine* or an opera singer from an English debutante. "They have been well-disciplined for their behavior, I assure you, and there will be no repetition of the event."

"But they were not put to death, then?" she said. "I am glad to hear it; I will be able to reassure the women of the harem; it was all they were talking of, and they indeed hoped the boys would not suffer too greatly."

"Do they go out into society so often, then?" Laurence had always imagined the harem very much in the nature of a prison, and no communication with the outer world permitted.

"Oh, I am *kira,* business agent, for one of the *kadin,*" Sara said. "Although they do leave the harem on excursions, it is only with a great deal of trouble; no one is allowed to see them, so they must be shut up in coaches, and take many guards, and they must have the Sultan's permission. But being a woman, I can come in to them and go out again freely myself."

"Then I hope I may beg you also to pass on to them my apologies for the intrusion, and those of the young men," Laurence said.

"They would indeed have been better satisfied with a more successful one, of longer duration," she said, with a ghost of amusement, and smiled at Laurence's tinge of embarrassment. "Oh, I do not mean any indiscretion; only they suffer from a great deal of boredom, being permitted little but indolence, and the Sultan is more interested in his reforms than in his favorites."

The meal being done, she rose with her mother and they left the table; she did not look round, but went out of the room tall and straight-shouldered, and Tharkay went to look silently out of the windows, into the garden behind the house.

Maden sighed, soundlessly, and poured more of the strong red wine into Laurence's glass. Sweets were carried in, a platter of marchpane. "I understand you have questions for me, Captain," he said.

He had served Mr. Arbuthnot not only by arranging for Tharkay to carry the message, but also as banker, and, it transpired, had been the foremost agent of the transaction. "You can conceive of the precautions which we arranged," he said. "The gold was not conveyed all at once, but on several heavily escorted vessels, at various intervals, all in chests marked as iron ingots; and brought directly to my vaults until the whole was assembled."

"Sir, to your knowledge were the agreements already signed, before the payment was brought hither?" Laurence asked.

Maden offered his upturned hands, without commitment. "What worth is a contract between monarchs? What judge will rule in such a dispute? But Mr. Arbuthnot thought all was settled. Otherwise, would he have taken risks so great, brought such a sum here? All seemed well, all seemed in order."

"Yet if the sum were never handed over—" Laurence said.

Yarmouth had come with written instructions from the ambassador to arrange the delivery, a few days before the latter's death and the former's disappearance. "I did not for a moment doubt the message, and I knew the ambassador's hand most well; his confidence in Mr. Yarmouth was complete," Maden said. "A fine young man, and soon to be married; always steady. I would not believe any underhanded behavior of him, Captain." But he spoke a little doubtfully, and he did not sound so certain as his words.

Laurence was silent. "And you conveyed the money to him as he asked?"

"To the ambassador's residence," Maden confirmed. "As I understood, it was thence to be delivered directly to the treasury; but the ambassador was killed the following day."

He had receipts, signed; in Yarmouth's hand and not the ambassador's, however. He presented these to Laurence with some discomfort, and after leaving him to look at them a while, said abruptly, "Captain, you have been courteous; but let us speak plainly. This is all the proof which I have: the men who carried the gold are mine, of many years' service, and only Yarmouth received it. A smaller sum, lost in these circumstances, I would return to you out of my own funds rather than lose my reputation."

Laurence had been looking at the receipts under the lamp, closely; indeed in some corner of his mind such doubts might have been blooming. He let the papers fall to the table and walked to the window, angry at himself and all the world. "Good God," he said, low, "what a hellish state to be looking in every direction with suspicion. No." He turned around. "Sir, I beg you not repine on it. I dare say you are a man of parts, but that you should have orchestrated the murder of the British ambassador and the embarrassment of your own nation, I do not believe. And for the rest, Mr. Arbuthnot and not you was responsible for safeguarding our interests in the matter; if he trusted too much to Yarmouth, and was mistaken in his man—" He stopped and shook his head. "Sir, if my question is offensive to you, I beg you say so and I will at once withdraw it; but— Hasan Mustafa, if you know him; is it possible he is involved? Either himself the guilty party, or in—in collusion, if I must contemplate it, with Yarmouth? I am certain he has deliberately lied at least so far as claiming the agreements were not concluded."

"Possible? Anything is possible, Captain; one man dead, another gone, thousands upon thousands of pounds of gold vanished? What is *not* possible?" Maden passed a hand over his brow tiredly, calming himself, and answered after a moment, "Forgive me. No. No, Captain, I cannot believe it. He and his family are in passionate support of the Sultan's reforms, and the cleansing of the Janissary Corps—his cousin is married to the Sultan's sister, his brother is head of the Sultan's new army. I cannot say he is a man of stainless honor; can any man be so, who is deep in politics? But that he should betray all his own work, and the work of his house? A man may lie a little to save face, or be pleased to snatch at an excuse for escaping a regretted agreement, without being a traitor."

"Yet why ought they regret it? Napoleon is if anything a greater threat to them now than ever he was, and we all the more necessary allies," Laurence said. "The strengthening of our forces over the Channel must be of native value to them, as drawing more of Napoleon's strength away westward."

Maden looked vaguely discomfited, and at Laurence's urging to speak frankly said, "Captain, there is a popular opinion, since Austerlitz, that Napoleon is not to be defeated, and foolish the nation which chooses to be his enemy. I am sorry," he added, seeing Laurence's grim look, "but so it is said in the streets and the coffeehouses; and by the ulema and the vezirs also, I imagine. The Emperor of Austria now sits his throne by Napoleon's sufferance, and all the world knows it. Better never to have fought him at all."

THARKAY BOWED TO Maden deeply as they were leaving. "Will you be in Istanbul long?" Maden asked him.

"No," Tharkay answered, "I will not come back again."

Maden nodded. "God be with you," he said gently, and stood watching them go.

Laurence was weary, with a more than physical fatigue, and Tharkay utterly withdrawn. They had to wait a while, upon the riverbank, for another ferryman; the wind off the Bosphorus was enough to bring a chill to the air, though the summer weather was yet holding. Laurence roused under the bite of the sea-wind and looked at Tharkay: the man's expression unmoved and unmoving, settled into calm lines and giving no sign of any strong emotion, save perhaps something of a tightness around the mouth, difficult to make out in the lantern-light.

A ferryman at last brought his boat up to the dock; the crossing they accomplished in silence, only the wood-creak and the dipping oars to break it, lopsided and unsteady strokes, the ferryman wheezing, and the water rippling up against the side of the boat; on the far bank the mosques shone from within, candle-light through the stained-glass windows: all the smooth domes together like an archipelago in the dark, and the monumental glory of the Haghia Sophia above them. The ferryman leapt from the boat and held it for them; they climbed up onto the banks into the glimmer of yet another mosque, small only by virtue of comparison; there were gulls flying wildly around the dome, calling in their raucous voices, bellies lit yellow with reflected light.

Too late for merchants, now, even the bazaars and the coffeehouses closed, and too early for the fishermen; the streets were empty as they climbed back towards the palace walls. Perhaps they grew incautious, from the hour or fatigue or distraction; or perhaps it was only ill-fortune; a party of guards had gone by, Tharkay had flung up his grapple; Laurence was at the top of the wall, waiting to offer a hand, with Tharkay halfway up, and abruptly two more guards appeared around the curve of the road, talking quietly together; in a moment they would see him.

Tharkay let go and dropped to the ground, to get his feet under him, as they rushed forward calling; they were already grappling for their swords. One seized his arm; Laurence leapt down upon the other, bore him down in a tumble, and, hooking him by the scruff of the neck, knocked his head against the ground again for good measure, leaving him stunned. Tharkay was sliding a red-washed knife out of the other man's arm, pulling free of his slackened grip; he had Laurence's arm, helping him up, and then they were running down the street together, sprinting, shouts and cries in immediate pursuit.

The noise brought the rest of the guards running back, converging on them out of the rabbit-warren of the streets and alley-ways; the upper floors of the crammed-in houses jutted out inquisitively over the streets, and lights were blooming from the latticed windows in their wake, leaving a trail behind them. The uneven cobbles were treacherous; Laurence flung himself skidding past a corner, just avoiding a swinging sword as two of the guards came out of another side-street, nearly catching them.

The pursuit did not quickly give over; Laurence, following blindly after Tharkay up the hillside, felt his lungs squeezing up against the bands of his ribs; they were dodging with some purpose, he thought, he hoped: no time to stop and ask. Tharkay stopped at last by an old house, fallen into ruin, and turned to beckon him in; only the lowest floor remained, open to the sky, and a moldering trap-door to a cellar. But the guards were too close behind; they would be seen, and Laurence resisted, unwilling to be caught in a mouse-hole with no exit.

"Come!" Tharkay said impatiently, flinging back the trap-door, and led the way down, down; down rotted stairs into a cellar of bare earth, very damp, and far in the back yet another door: or rather a doorway, so low Laurence had nearly to bend double to get through it, and leading further below were steps hewn not of wood but stone, round-edged and slimy with age; up from the deep dark came the soft plucking sound of dripping water.

They went down for a long time. Laurence found one hand on the hilt of his sword; the other he kept on the wall, which as they descended suddenly vanished from under his reaching fingers, and his next step went into water ankle-deep. "Where are we?" he whispered, and his voice went a long hollow way off, swallowed up by dark; the water washed the tops of his boots with every stride along the floor.

The first glow of torchlight dawned behind him as the guards came down after them, and he could see a little: a pale column stood not far away, shining wet on its worn pebbled surface, wider than his arms could span; the ceiling too far above to see, and at his knees a few dull greyish fish bumping in blind hunger, their seeking mouths at the surface of the water making little popping sounds. Laurence caught Tharkay's arm and pointed; they struggled against the weight of the water and the mud thickening the floor, and put themselves behind the pillar as the tentative torch-flickers came further down, widening the circle of dim red light.

A gallery of columns yawned away in every direction around them, strange and malformed; some in separate mismatched blocks, piled atop one another like a child's attempts, held together by nothing it seemed but the weight of the city pressing down upon them: a strain for Atlas to bear, not the crumbling brick and ruin of this hollow place, some cathedral hall long buried and forgotten. For all the cold empty vastness of the space, the air felt queer and very close, as though some share of that weight were bearing down on his own shoulders; Laurence could not help but envision the cataclysm of an eventual collapse: the distant vault of the ceiling disintegrating brick by brick, until one day the arches could no longer hold up their heads and all, houses, streets, palace, mosques, the shining domes, came tumbling down, and drowned ten thousand in this waiting charnel-house.

He clenched his shoulders once against the feeling, and tapping Tharkay silently on the arm pointed at the next pillar: the guards were coming into the water, with enough noise to muffle their own movements. The muck of the bottom stirred up in black swirls as they slogged on, keeping in the shadows of the pillars: thick mud and silt crunching beneath his boots, and gleams of picked-clean bone pale through the water. Not all fish: the jutting curve of a jaw-bone showed above the mud, a few teeth still clinging; a green-stained leg bone leaned against the base of a column, as though washed up by some underground tide.

A sort of horror was gripping him at the notion of meeting his own end here, beyond any simple fear of mortality; something hideous at forming one of the nameless uncounted flung down to rot in the dark. Laurence panted through his open mouth, not only for silence, not only to avoid the stench of mildew and corruption; he was bent over nearly at the waist, oppressed, increasingly conscious of a fierce irrational urge to stop, to turn and fight their way back out into the clean open air. He held a corner of his cloak over his mouth and doggedly went on.

The guards were grown more systematic in their pursuit: they ranged themselves in a line stretched the width of the hall, each one with upraised torch illuminating only a small feeble ring, but the edges of these overlapping to make a barrier which their prey could not cross unseen, as good as a fence of iron. They advanced slow but certain in step, chanted out aloud in unison, voices tolling low, chasing the darkness out of its last clung-to corners with reverberation and light. Laurence thought he glimpsed, ahead, the first reflections off the far wall; they were indeed drawing close to the end of the mouse-hole, where there should be no escape but to try and rush the line, and hope they could outdistance the pursuit again; but now with legs wearied and chilled both by trudging through the deep water.

Tharkay had been touching the pillars as he and Laurence dashed now from one to the other trying to keep ahead; he was running his hand along their sides and squinting at their surfaces; at last he stopped at one, and Laurence touching it also found deep carvings cut into the stone all over it, shapes like drops of rain with soapy-wet muck gathered in the ridges: wholly unlike the other unfinished columns. The line of searchers was growing ever closer, yet Tharkay stopped and began to

prod at the floor with the toe of his boot; Laurence drew his
sword and with mental apology to Temeraire for so insulting the
blade began to run it also over the hard stone underneath the
muck, until he felt the tip slide abruptly into some kind of shallow channel cut in the floor, less than a foot wide and thoroughly clogged.

Tharkay, feeling around, nodded, and Laurence followed
him along the length of the channel, both of them running now
as best they could in the knee-high water: the splashing echoes
were lost in the inexorable chanting behind them, *bir—iki—
üç—dört,* repeated so often Laurence began to recognize the
counting words. The wall was directly before them now, streaked
with shades of green and brown over the thick, flat mortar, and
otherwise unbroken; and the channel had stopped as abruptly as
it had begun.

But Tharkay turned them: a smaller annex stood off to the
side, two pillars holding up its vault, and Laurence nearly jerked
back: a staring monstrous face loomed half out of the water at
the base of the pillar, one blind stone eye fixed upon them, a dim
hellish red. A shout went up: they had been seen.

They fled, and as they ran past the hideous monument, Laurence felt the first thin trickle of moving air upon his face: a
draught somewhere near. Together groping over the wall they
found the black and narrow opening, hidden from the torches
behind a protrusion: stairs half-choked with filth, and the air
fetid and swampy; he took reluctant deep gulps of it as they ran
up the narrow passage and came crawling out at last through an
old rain-gutter, pushing away the crusted iron grate, nearly on
hands and knees.

Tharkay was bent double and gasping; with a tremendous
effort, Laurence put back the grate, and tore a branch from a
low sapling nearby to push through the empty hasp, holding it
in place. He caught Tharkay by the arm and they staggered together drunkenly away through the streets; nothing to cause
much comment, so long as no one looked closely at the state of
their boots and the lower part of their cloaks: the banging upon
the grate was already growing distant behind them, and their

faces had not been seen, surely; not to put a name to, in that mad pursuit.

They found a place at length where the palace walls were a little lower; and taking more care that they were unobserved this time, Laurence boosted Tharkay up, and with his help in turn managed to scramble somehow up and over. They fell into a graceless and grateful heap some little distance into the grounds, beside an old iron water-fountain half buried in greenery, the water trickling but cold, and they cupped up greedy handfuls of it to their mouths and faces, soaking their clothing without regret: it washed away the stench, a little.

The silence was at first complete, but gradually as the roar of his own heart and lungs slackened, Laurence began to be able to hear more clearly the small noises of the night, the rustling of mice and leaves; the faint and far-off sound of the birds singing in the palace aviary beyond the inner walls; the irregular rasp of Tharkay's knife against his whetstone: he was polishing the blade with slow occasional strokes, to draw no attention.

"I would say something to you," Laurence said quietly, "on matters as they stand between us."

Tharkay paused a moment, and the knife-blade trembled in the light. "Very well," he said, resuming his slow, careful work, "say what you will."

"I spoke earlier today in haste," Laurence said, "and in a manner which I would ordinarily disdain to use to any man in my service. And yet even now I hardly know how I should apologize to you."

"I beg you not to trouble yourself further," Tharkay said coolly, never raising his head, "let it all pass; I promise you I will not repine upon it."

"I have considered what to make of your behavior," Laurence said, paying no mind to this attempt at deflection, "and I cannot make you out; tonight you have not only saved my life, but materially contributed to the progress of our mission. And if I consider only the final consequences of your actions, throughout our expedition, there is hardly any room for complaint; indeed you have rather steadfast brought us through one danger and the next, often at your own peril. But twice now you have abandoned your post, in circumstances fraught with innumerable difficulties, with a secrecy both unnecessary and contrived, leaving us as a consequence adrift and prey to grave anxieties."

"Perhaps it did not occur to me my absence would occasion such dismay," Tharkay said, blandly, and Laurence's temper rose at once to meet this fresh challenge.

"Kindly do not represent yourself to me as a fool," he said. "I could more easily believe you the most brazen traitor who has ever walked the earth, and the most inconsistent besides."

"Thank you; that is a handsome compliment." Tharkay sketched an ironic salute with the knife-point in the air. "But there seems to me little point in disputation, when you will not wish my services much longer regardless."

"Whether for a minute or a month," Laurence said, "still I will have done with these games. I am grateful to you, and if you depart, you will go with my thanks. But if you stay, I will have your promise that you will henceforth abide by my command, and cease this haring-off without leave; I will not have a man in my service whom I doubt, and Tharkay," he added, abruptly sure, "I think you like to be doubted."

Tharkay put down the knife and whetstone; his smile had gone, and his air of mockery. "You may say rather, that I like to know if I am doubted; and you will not be far wrong."

"You have certainly done all you could to ensure it."

"That seems to you I suppose perverse," Tharkay said, "but I have long since been taught that my face and my descent bar me from the natural relations of gentlemen, with no action on my part. And if I am not to be trusted, I would rather provoke a little open suspicion, freely expressed, than meekly endure endless slights and whispers not quite hidden behind my back."

"I too have endured society's whispers, and every one of my officers; we are not in service to those small-minded creatures who like to sneer in corners, but to our country; and that service is a better defense of our honor, in the face of petty insult, than the most violent objections we could make," Laurence said.

Tharkay said passionately, "I wonder if you would speak so if you were forced to endure it wholly alone; if not only society but all those on whom you might justly have a claim of brotherhood looked upon you with that same disdain, your superior officers and your comrades-in-arms; if all hope of independence and advancement were denied you and, as a sop, you were offered the place of a superior servant, somewhere between a valet and a trained dog."

He closed his mouth on anything further, though his customary seeming indifference looked now a mask imperfectly put on, and there was some suggestion of color in his face.

"Am I meant to take these charges as laid to my own account?" Laurence demanded, suffering at once indignation and unease; but Tharkay shook his head.

"No, I beg pardon for my vehemence; the injuries of which I speak are no less bitter for their age." With a ghost of his former wryness he added, "What incivilities *you* have offered me, I do not deny I have provoked; I have formed a habit of anticipation: amusing, to me at least, if perhaps unjust to my company."

He had said enough that Laurence might without undue speculation imagine the sort of treatment which had driven Tharkay to abandon country and companionship for his present solitary existence, beholden to none and of none, which to Laurence seemed utterly barren, a waste of a man proven worthy of something better; and stretching out his hand he said earnestly, "If you can believe it so in this case, then give me your word, and take mine—I hope I may in safety promise to give no less than full measure of loyalty to any man who gives me his, and I think I would be sorrier to lose you than I yet know."

Tharkay looked at him, a queer uncertain expression briefly crossing his face, then lightly said, "Well, I am set in my ways; but as you are willing to take my word, Captain, I suppose I would be churlish to refuse to offer it," and reached out his hand with a jaunty air; but there was nothing whatsoever insincere about his grip.

"UGH," TEMERAIRE SAID, having lifted them both over into the garden, examining with distaste the slimy residue on his fore-claws. "But I do not care if you smell bad, so long as you are back; Granby said you were surely only staying late for dinner, and that I must not go look for you; but you were gone so very long," he added more plaintively, before plunging his forehand into a lily-pond to wash it off.

"We were clumsy about it coming back in and were forced to find a bolt-hole for a little, but as you see all ended well; I am very sorry to have given you cause for anxiety," Laurence said, stripping off his own clothes unceremoniously and going directly into the pond himself; Tharkay was already submerging. "Dyer, take those and my boots and see what you and Roland can do with them; and bring me that damned soap."

"I don't see that it would answer if Yarmouth were guilty," Granby said, when Laurence, scrubbed and in shirtsleeves and breeches, had finished making his report of the dinner. "However would he have transported such a mass of gold? He should have needed to take ship, unless he was mad enough to move it away by caravan."

"He would have been noticed," Tharkay agreed quietly. "By Maden's account the gold needed some hundred chests; and there have been no reports from the caravanserai or the dock-yards, of any movement near so large: I spent the morning yes-terday in making inquiries. Indeed he would have been hard-pressed to find any transport; half the drovers have been ferrying in supplies for the harbor fortifications, and the other half have been keeping out of the city because of the dragons."

"Could he perhaps have hired a dragon, then?" Laurence asked. "We saw those dragon-traders in the East; do they ever come so far?"

"I have never seen them this side of the Pamirs," Tharkay said. "In the West men will not have them in the cities, so they could get no profit in any case, and as they are thought nothing other than ferals, they would likely be seized upon and thrust into breeding-grounds, if they came."

"It don't signify; he couldn't move gold by dragon, not if he wanted it back again," Granby said. "I don't believe you could give a dragon great heaps of gold and jewels to carry about for days and then ask him to hand it all back."

They had remained in the garden to hold their low-voiced discussion, and Temeraire now observed, in faintly wistful tones, "It does sound like a very great deal of gold," not disputing Granby's remark in the least. "Perhaps he has put it away somewhere in the city?"

"He would have to be part dragon himself, to be satisfied with hoarding so vast a sum, where he could not show his face again to make use of it," Laurence said. "No; he would not have gone to such lengths, if he had no way of taking away the money."

"But you have all finished saying that the gold cannot have been taken away," Temeraire said reasonably. "So it must still be here."

They were silent, and Laurence finally said, "Then what can be the alternative but at least the connivance of the ministers, if not their active involvement? And such an insult, Britain would have to answer; even if they wish an end to our alliance, would they deliberately provoke a war, which surely would cost them a greater sum than this, and in blood as well as gold?"

"They have been damned busy to see to it we should go away thinking it all Yarmouth's fault," Granby pointed out. "We haven't evidence to go to war over."

Tharkay abruptly stood up from the ground, brushing away dust; they had brought out rugs to recline upon, in the Turkish fashion, there being nothing like chairs in the kiosque. Laurence looked over his shoulder and he and Granby scrambled also to their feet: a woman was standing at the far end of their grove, in the shade of the cypresses. She was perhaps the same they had seen before, on the palace grounds; though in the heavy veil there was scarcely any telling one from another.

"You should not be here," Tharkay said, low, when she had come quickly towards them. "Where is your maid?"

"She is waiting for me at the stairs; she will cough if anyone is coming," the woman answered, cool and steady, her dark eyes never leaving his face.

"Your servant, Miss Maden," Laurence said, awkwardly; he did not know what to do. With all the sympathy in the world he could not in honor endorse a clandestine meeting or worse yet an elopement, and then besides he was in her father's debt; but if they asked him for assistance, he wondered how he could refuse. He fell back on formalities, saying, "May I present Temeraire, and my first lieutenant, John Granby?"

Granby with a start made her a not-very-polished leg. "Honored, Miss Maden," he said, pronouncing her name in a querying tone, and glanced puzzled at Laurence; Temeraire peered down at her with more open inquisitiveness after making his own greeting.

"I will not ask again," Tharkay said to her low.

"Let us not speak of what cannot be," she said, drawing her hand out of the deep pocket of her coat; but not to reach out to him, as Laurence first thought. Instead she held it out flat towards them, saying, "I was able to get inside the treasury, for a moment; though most have been melted down, I am afraid," and upon her palm rested unmistakable a single golden sovereign, stamped with the visage of the King.

"You CANNOT TRUST these Oriental tyrants," Granby said with pessimism, "and after all, we are as good as calling him a thief and a murderer besides. Like as not he will have your head off."

Temeraire was considerably more sanguine, as he had been permitted to go along, and therefore considered all physical dangers rendered negligible by his presence. "I will like to see the Sultan," he said. "Perhaps he may have some interesting jewels, and then we may at last go home again. Although it is a shame that Arkady and the others are not here to see him."

Laurence, not sharing this last sentiment at all, was himself hopeful for a good outcome; Mustafa had regarded the gold coin grimly, and had listened without even an attempt at counterfeiting surprise to Laurence's cold avowal that it had come to his hand from the treasury.

"No, sir; I will not name you my source," Laurence had said, "but if you like, I will go with you to the treasury now, directly; I rather believe we will find more, if you doubt the provenance of this one."

This proposal Mustafa had refused; and though he had made no admission of guilt, no explanations, he had said abruptly, "I must speak with the Grand Vezir," and gone away again; and in the evening a summons had come: at last they were called to an audience with the Sultan.

"I do not mean to put him to the blush," Laurence added now. "Poor Yarmouth deserves better, God knows, and Arbuthnot himself; but when we have got the eggs back to Britain will be soon enough for the Government to decide how they choose to make them answer for it, and I know damned well what they would say to my taking action in *that* matter." Indeed, he suspected dismally there would be a great deal said of his actions even in the matter of the eggs. "In any case, I hope we will learn this is indeed some machination of his ministers, of which the Sultan himself knows nothing."

The two Kazilik dragons Bezaid and Sherazde had returned to escort them once again to the meeting with proper ceremony, even though the three of them were scarcely in the air for a moment, only flying over the palace and landing in the great open lawn of the First Court, outside the front gates of the palace. Absurd though it seemed to Laurence to be ushered with such ceremony into a palace where he had slept three nights already, they were set in a row with the Kaziliks before and after, and marched in stately array through the flung-wide bronze gates and into the courtyard standing just before the gorgeously ornamented portico of the Gate of Felicity: in perfect orderly rows along the pathway stood the ranks of the vezirs, their white turbans brilliant in the sunshine, and farther back along the walls the nervous snorting horses of the cavalry in attendance pranced as they walked by.

The Sultan's throne, wide and gold and blazing all over with polished green gemstones, stood upon a gorgeous rug woven of many-colored wool and elaborately patterned with flowers and ornaments; his dress still more magnificent, a robe of marmalade-orange and yellow satin bordered in black over a tunic of blue and yellow silk, with the diamond-encrusted hilt of his dagger showing above his sash; and an aigrette of diamonds around a great square emerald held a tall spray of stiff feathers affixed to the head of his high white turban. Though the courtyard was large and crowded, there was scarcely any noise; the ranked officials did not speak or whisper amongst themselves, or even fidget.

It was an impressive display, calculated with success to impose a certain natural reluctance to break that silence upon any visitor. But as Laurence stepped forward, Temeraire suddenly hissed behind him, the sound carrying and as purely dangerous as the scrape of a sword-blade leaving its scabbard; Laurence, appalled, turned round to look at him in protest, but Temeraire's gaze was fixed to the left: in the shade cast down by the high tower of the Divan, piled upon herself in glittering white coils, Lien lay watching them with her blood-red eyes.

CHAPTER 9

There was scarcely an opportunity to think, to do anything but stare; the Kazilik dragons had moved to flank Temeraire, and Mustafa was already beckoning them closer to the throne. Laurence numbly stepped forward and made his formal bow with less than his customary grace. The Sultan looked at him without much expression. His face was very broad, his neck disappearing between his clothing and his square brown beard, and rather delicate-featured, with a contemplative look in his handsome dark eyes; he carried within himself an air of repose and of dignity, which seemed rather natural than assumed.

All the prepared speech had gone entirely from Laurence's head, and his rehearsed phrases; he looked up at the Sultan squarely and said in the plainest French, "Your Majesty, you know my errand, and the agreement between our nations. All her obligations under that agreement Britain has fulfilled, and the payment has been delivered. Will you give us the eggs for which we have come?"

The Sultan received this blunt speech calmly and with no sign of anger; he spoke himself in fluent and easy French and said mildly, "Peace be upon your country, and your King; let us pray that friendship will never fail between us." He said a little more in this vein, and spoke of deliberations among his ministers, and promised another audience, and the pursuit of many inquiries. Still laboring under the violent and unhappy shock of finding Lien in the midst of the Sultan's court and his inner councils, Laurence had difficulty in following all he said, but none at all in understanding the meaning underneath: more delay, more refusal, and no intention at all of providing satisfaction. There was indeed little effort made to conceal that meaning: the Sultan made no denials, no explanations, counterfeited no wrath or dismay. Almost he spoke with a touch of pity in his look, though not in the least a softening, and when he had finished, he dismissed them at once, without granting Laurence another opportunity to speak.

Temeraire's attention throughout had never wavered: he had not so much as glanced at the Sultan he had been so eager to see, despite all the glittering display, but rather kept his eyes fixed upon Lien; his shoulders were bunched from moment to moment, and his foreleg crept up by small degrees until it was nearly bumping against Laurence's back, waiting to snatch him away.

The Kaziliks had to nudge him to set him into motion, away along the path, and he went sideways, crab-stepping awkwardly, so as not to face away from her; she for her part never stirred, but as serene as a snake let her eyes follow them back around the curve of the palace and out of the inner courtyard again, until the wall hid her from view.

"Bezaid says she has been here three weeks," Temeraire said; his ruff was spread full and trembling, and had not lowered since the moment they had laid eyes upon Lien. He had made a great protest when Laurence had tried to go into the kiosque, refusing to let him out of his sight; even in the garden he had nudged Laurence insistently to climb upon his foreleg, and his officers had been forced to come out to hear his report.

"Long enough to have knocked us to flinders," Granby said grimly. "If she's of a like mind with Yongxing, *she* wouldn't have scrupled to toss poor Yarmouth into the Med, any more than he would have minded having you knocked on the head; and as for Arbuthnot's accident, it's no great trouble for a dragon to spook a horse."

"She might have done all this and more besides," Laurence said, "and made no headway against us, if the Turks had not been full willing to profit by it."

"They have fallen in with Bonaparte for certain, and make no mistake," Lieutenant Ferris agreed, smoldering, "and I wish they may have joy of it, when they are dancing to his tune; they'll soon enough be sorry for it."

"We will be sorrier, sooner," Laurence said.

The shadow overhead silenced them all, but for Temeraire's savage and rumbling growl; and the two Kaziliks sat up hissing anxiously as Lien circled down and landed gracefully in the clearing. Temeraire bared his teeth at her and snarled.

"You sound like a dog," she said to him, cool and disdainful, in fluent French, "and your manners are not much different. Will you bark at me next?"

"I do not care if you think I am rude," Temeraire said, tail lashing militantly, with much danger to the surrounding trees, walls, statuary. "If you want to fight, I am ready, and I will not let you hurt Laurence or my crew, ever."

"Why should I wish to fight you?" Lien said; she settled herself back upon her haunches, sitting erect like a cat, with her tail coiled neatly around herself, and unblinking stared at them.

Temeraire paused. "Because—because—but do you not hate me? I would hate you, if Laurence had been killed, and it were at all your fault," he said candidly.

"And like a barbarian, you would fling yourself at me and try to claw me to death, I am sure," Lien said.

Temeraire's tail faded slowly to the ground, only the very tip still twitching, and he gazed at her nonplussed; that would certainly have been his very reaction. "Well, *I* am not afraid of *you.*"

"No," she said calmly. "Not yet."

Temeraire stared at her, and she added, "Would your death repay one tenth part of what you have taken from me? Do you think I would count your captain's blood equal to that of my dear companion, a great and honorable prince, as far above yours as pure jade is to the offal that lies in the streets?"

"Oh!" Temeraire said, with indignation, ruffing up even further. "He was not honorable, at *all,* or else he would not have tried to have Laurence killed; Laurence is worth a *hundred* of him or any other prince, and anyway, Laurence is a prince now himself," he added.

"Such a prince you may keep," she said, contemptuous. "For my companion, I will have a truer revenge."

"Well," Temeraire said, snorting, "if you do not want to fight, and you do not mean to hurt Laurence, I do not know why you have come; and you can go away again now, because I do not trust you in the least," he finished defiantly.

"I came," she said, "to be certain that you understood. You are very young and stupid, and you have been badly educated; I would pity you, if I had any pity left.

"You have overthrown the whole of my life, torn me from family and friends and home; you have ruined all my lord's hopes for China, and I must live knowing that all for which he fought and labored was for naught. His spirit will live unquiet, and his grave go untended.

"No, I will not kill you, or your captain, who binds you to his country." She shook out her ruff and leaning forward said softly, "I will see you bereft of all that you have, of home and happiness and beautiful things. I will see your nation cast down and your allies drawn away. I will see you as alone and friendless and wretched as am I; and then you may live as long as you like, in some dark and lonely corner of the earth, and I will call myself content."

Temeraire was wide-eyed and transfixed by the low monotone finality of her words, his own ruff wilting slowly down to lie flat against his neck, and by the time she had finished he was huddled small away from her, clutching Laurence still closer with both his forelegs shielding him like a cage.

She half-unfurled her wings, gathering herself together. "I am leaving now for France, and the service of this barbarian emperor," she said. "It is certain that the miseries of my exile will be many, but I will bear them better now, having spoken to you. We will not meet again perhaps for a long while; I hope you will remember me, and know what joys you have are numbered."

She leapt aloft, and with three quick wing-strokes was away and swiftly diminishing.

"For God's sake," Laurence said strongly, when they had stood all together utterly silent and dismayed awhile, in her wake, "we are not children, to be frightened witless by threats; and that she meant us all the ill in the world we already knew."

"Yes, but I did not know quite so *well*," Temeraire said, in a small voice, and did not seem inclined to let Laurence move away.

"My dear, pray do not let her distress you," Laurence said, laying his hand on Temeraire's soft muzzle. "You would only be giving her what she desires, your unhappiness, and cheap at the cost of a few words. They are hollow: even she, powerful as she is, alone cannot make so great a difference to the war; and Napoleon would exert himself to the fullest towards our destruction regardless of her assistance."

"But she has already done us a great deal of harm, herself," Temeraire said unhappily. "Now they will not let us have the eggs that we need so badly, and have done so much for."

"Laurence," Granby said abruptly, "by God, these villains have bloody well stolen half-a-million pounds, and like as not used the funds to build themselves those fortifications so they could thumb their noses at the Navy. We cannot let it stand; we must do *something*. Temeraire could bring half this palace down on their heads with one proper roar—"

"We will not murder and ruin to revenge ourselves, as she does; such a satisfaction we ought and do disdain," Laurence said. "No," he continued, raising a hand when Granby would have protested. "Do you go and send the men to their supper, and then to take some rest, as much sleep as they can manage, while the light lasts.

"We leave tonight," he continued, very cold and calm, "and we take the eggs with us."

"SHERAZDE SAYS HER egg is being kept inside the harem," Temeraire said, after some inquiry, "near the baths, where it is warm."

"Temeraire, they will not give us away?" Laurence asked with anxiety, looking at the Kaziliks.

"I have not told them why I am asking," Temeraire admitted, with a guilty look. "It does not feel quite proper; but after all," he added, "we will take good care of the eggs, so they will not mind; and the people have no right to object, since they took the gold. But I cannot ask them very much more, or they *will* wonder why I want to know."

"We will have the devil of a time stumbling about looking for them," Granby said. "I suppose the place must be littered with guards, and if the women see us they will surely send up a howl; this mission will be no joke."

"I think we must only a few of us go," Laurence said, low. "I will take a few volunteers—"

"Oh, the devil you will!" Granby exclaimed furiously. "No, this time I damned well put my foot down, Laurence. Send you off to go scrambling about in that warren with no notion where you are going, and nothing more likely than running into a dozen guards round every corner; I should like to see myself do it. I am not going back to England to tell them I sat about twiddling my thumbs whilst you got yourself cut to pieces. Temeraire, you are not to let him go, do you hear me? He is sure to be killed; I give you my word."

"If the party are sure to be killed, I am not going to let anyone go!" Temeraire said, in high alarm, and sat up sharp, quite prepared to physically hold anyone back who made an attempt to leave.

"Temeraire, this is plain exaggeration," Laurence said. "Mr. Granby, you overstate the case, and you overstep your bounds."

"Well, I don't," Granby said defiantly. "I have bit my tongue a dozen times over, because I know it is wretched hard to sit about watching and you haven't been trained up to it, but you are a captain, and you *must* be more careful of your neck. It isn't only your own but the Corps' affair if you snuff it, and mine too."

"If I may," Tharkay said quietly, interrupting when Laurence would have remonstrated further with Granby, "I will go; alone I am reasonably sure I can find a way to the eggs, without rousing any alarm, and then I can return and guide the rest of the party there."

"Tharkay," Laurence said, "this is no service you owe us; I would not order even a man under oath of arms to undertake it, without he were willing."

"But I am willing," Tharkay gave his faint half-smile, "and more likely to come back whole from it than anyone else here."

"At the cost of running thrice the risk, going and coming back and going again," Laurence said, "with a fresh chance of running into the guards every time through."

"So it *is* very dangerous, then," Temeraire said, overhearing to too much purpose, and pricking up his ruff further. "You are *not* to go, at all, Granby is quite right; and neither is anyone else."

"Oh, Hell," Laurence said, under his breath.

"It seems there is very little alternative to my going," Tharkay said.

"Not you either!" Temeraire contradicted, to Tharkay's startlement, and settled down as mulish as a dragon could look; and Granby had folded his arms and wore an expression very similar. Laurence had ordinarily very little inclination to profanity, but he was sorely tempted on this occasion. An appeal to Temeraire's reason might sway him to allow a party to make the attempt, if he could be persuaded to accept the risk as necessary for the gain, like a battle; but he would surely balk at seeing Laurence go, and Laurence had not the least intention of sending men on so deadly an enterprise if he were not going himself, Corps rules be damned.

They were left at a standstill, and then Keynes came out into the gardens. "For the sake of secrecy, it is to be hoped neither of those dragons understands English," he said. "If you have all done shouting like fishwives, Dunne begs the favor of a word, Captain; he and Hackley saw the baths, during their excursion."

"Yes, sir," Dunne said; he was sitting up on his makeshift cot, pale with fever-hot cheeks, in only breeches and a shirt hanging loose over his lacerated skin; Hackley, slighter than he, had taken the flogging worse and was still prostrated. "At least, I am almost sure; they all had the ends of their hair wet, coming out of the place, and the fair ones—the fair ones looked pink with heat." He dropped his eyes ashamedly, not looking Laurence in the face, and finished hurriedly, "And there were a dozen chimneys out of the building, sir, all of them smoking away, though it was midday and hot."

Laurence nodded. "Do you remember the way, and are you strong enough to go?"

"I do well enough, sir," Dunne said.

"He would do well enough to stay lying down," Keynes said caustically.

Laurence hesitated. "Can you draw us a map?" he asked Dunne.

"Sir," Dunne said, swallowing, "sir, please let me come. Truly I don't think I can, without seeing the place around me; we got turned about a great deal."

Despite this new advantage, Temeraire took a great deal more convincing; at last Laurence was forced to yield to Granby's demand, and let him come along, leaving young Lieutenant Ferris in command of the rest of the crew. "There; you may be easy, Temeraire," Granby said with satisfaction, putting the signal-flares in his own belt. "If there's the least danger, I will fire off a flare, and you will come and take Laurence up, eggs or no; I will see to it he is where you can reach him."

Laurence felt a strong sense of indignation; this was all a piece of considerable insubordination, but as it was visibly approved not only by Temeraire but by the entire crew, he had no recourse; and he was privately conscious the Admiralty would be wholly of like mind, except perhaps to censure him even more strongly for going along at all.

Without very good grace he turned to his acting second lieutenant. "Mr. Ferris," he said, "keep all the men aboard and ready. Temeraire, if you have not seen our signal, and a noise begins in the palace, or there is any sign of dragons overhead, go up at once; in the dark you can keep well out of sight for a long time."

"I will; and you needn't think I will go away if I do not see your signal for a long time, so do not try and tell me to do just that," Temeraire said, with a martial light in his eyes.

THANKFULLY, THE KAZILIKS went away before nightfall, to be replaced again by lesser guards, another pair of the middle-weight dragons, who, a little shy of Temeraire, stayed back in the grove and did not trouble him; and the moon was little more than a narrow sliver, enough to give them a little light to place their feet by.

"You will remember I rely upon you to keep all the crew safe," Laurence said to Temeraire softly. "Pray have a care for them, if anything should go awry; do promise me."

"I will," Temeraire answered, "but I will not fly away and leave you behind, so you are to promise me that you will be careful, and send for me if there is any trouble; I do not like to stay here, at all, and be left behind," he finished miserably.

"I do not at all like to leave you, either, my dear," Laurence said, and stroked the soft muzzle, for Temeraire's comfort and his own. "We will try not to be long."

Temeraire made a low unhappy noise, and then he sat up on

his haunches, his wings half-spread to conceal his movements from the guardian dragons, and one after another put the appointed party carefully upon the roof: Laurence and Granby; Tharkay; Dunne; Martin; Fellowes, the harness-master, all his spare leather distributed among them in sacks, to rig out the eggs for carrying; and for their lookout Digby, just made midshipman. With Salyer, Dunne, and Hackley all knocked-down, Laurence had been short of junior officers, and the boy had earned it with his steady work, though young for the promotion; it was pleasanter by far to raise him up than the earlier demotions had been, and they began the desperate adventure with a round of spirits and a quiet toast, to the new midshipman, to the success of their enterprise, and lastly to the King.

The slanting roof was uncertain and difficult footing, but they had to keep low in any case, and steadying themselves with their hands they managed to creep over to where the roof met the harem wall, easily wide enough to stand upon; from the height they could look over the whole ferociously labyrinthine complex: minarets and high towers, galleries and domes, courtyards and cloisters, all standing one atop the other with scarcely any break between them, as though the whole had been almost one single edifice, the work of an architect run mad; the roofs white and grey, plentifully broken up with skylights and attic windows, but all of these which they could make out were barred.

A large marble swimming-pool abutted the wall on the far side, very far down, a narrow walkway of grey slate running all around the border and to a pair of open arches: a way in. They dropped a line and Tharkay slipped down first, all of them tense and watching the lit windows for any passing shadow, the dark for any sudden illumination, any sign they had been seen. No cry was raised; they slung Dunne into a loop and Fellowes and Granby let him down together, the rope braced against their hips and hissing softly through their gloved hands; all the rest of them scrambled down after, one at a time.

They crept single-file along the walkway; the light of many windows shone in the water, rippling yellow, and lanterns were shining on the raised terrace overlooking the pool. They reached the archway; they were inside, and oil lamps flickering from niches upon the floor stretched away along a narrow passage-way, low-ceilinged and ill-lit by guttering candles, broken up with many doors and stairways. There was a whispering draught like a distant conversation coming into their faces.

They went silently and very fast, as fast as they dared; Thar-kay in the lead and Dunne whispering to him about the way, as best he could recall in the darkness. They passed by many small rooms, some still touched with a drifting fragrance, sweet and more fragile than roses, which could only be caught now and again by an accidental breath, and faded into the stronger lin-gering smell of incense and spice if one tried to draw it in. Throughout, flung upon divans and scattered on the floor, lay the beguilements of the harem's idle hours, writing-boxes and books and musical instruments, ornaments for the hair, scarves cast aside, the paints and brushes of beauty. Ducking his head through one doorway, Digby gave a startled gasp, and coming to his side they at first reached for their swords and pistols, see-ing all around them suddenly a crowd of pale distorted faces: they were looking into a graveyard of old mirrors, cracked and gap-toothed and leaning back against the walls, still in their golden frames.

Now and again Tharkay would halt them, and wave them all into one room or another, to crouch in silence, waiting, until in the distance footfalls died away again; once a few women went by laughing in the hallway, clear high voices ringing with hilar-ity. Laurence by degrees grew conscious of a heaviness, a mois-ture in the air, an increase of warmth, and Tharkay looking around caught his eye and nodded, beckoning.

Laurence crept to his side: through a latticework screen they were looking upon a high, well-lit marble hallway. "Yes, that's where we saw them coming out," Dunne whispered, pointing at a tall narrow archway; the floor around it was shining and damp.

Tharkay touched a finger to his lips and motioned them back into the darkness; he crept away, vanishing for minutes that seemed endless, then coming back whispered, "I have found the way down; but there are guards."

Four of the black eunuchs stood in their uniforms at the base of the stairs, idle and drowsy with the late hour, speaking to one another and paying no real attention; but there was no easy way to come towards them without being seen and raising the alarm. Laurence opened his cartridge box and ripped half-a-dozen of the pistol-balls out of their paper twists, scattering the powder upon the ground; they hid to either side of the head of the stairs, and he let the balls go rolling down the stairs, clattering and ringing bright against the smooth marble.

More puzzled than alarmed, the guards came up to investigate and bent low over the black powder; Granby sprang forward, even as Laurence began to give the word, and clubbed one with his pistol-butt; Tharkay another, with a single swift blow to the temple with the pommel of his knife, and lowered him easily to the ground. The third, Laurence caught around the throat with his arm, choking him to silence and then to stillness, but the last, a big man, barrel-chested and thick-necked, managed a strangled shout past Digby's grasp before Martin struck him down.

They stood all panting, listening, but no reply came, no sound of roused vigilance. They bundled the guards into the dark corner where they themselves had been concealed, and tied and gagged them with their neckcloths.

"We must hurry now," Laurence said, and they ran down the stairs and the empty vaulted hallway, their boots loud suddenly on the flagstones. The baths were empty, a great room of marble and stone, vaulted far above with delicate pointed arches of warm yellowed stone, great stone basins and golden spigots set in the wall, with dark wooden screens and little dressing alcoves in the many corners, and platforms of stone in the middle of the room, all of it slick with steam and water-beaded. Archways led out of the room all around, and puffs of steam were issuing into the room from vents set high in the walls; a single narrow stairway built of stone led them a winding way up to an iron door, hot to the touch.

They gathered themselves around and thrust it open, Granby and Tharkay jumping through at once, into a chamber almost scorching-hot and lit with a hellish orange-red glow. A squat many-legged furnace nearly filled the room together with a great boiling-cauldron of shining copper, pipes snaking away and vanishing into the walls, a heap of wood lying beside it to feed the roaring maw, and next to it a brazier of freshly laid coals was just beginning to catch and blaze, little open flames licking up to heat a hanging bowl of stones. Two black slaves naked to the waist stood staring; one held a long-handled ladle full of water, which he had been pouring over the hot stones, and the other an iron poker with which he was stirring the coals.

Granby caught the first and with Martin's help wrestled him to the ground, muffling his sounds; but the second whipped his red-hot poker around and jabbed at Tharkay frantically, opening his mouth to yell; Tharkay gave a queer choked grunt and caught the man's arm, pushing away the poker, and Laurence sprang to clap his hand over the shout; Digby clubbed him.

"Are you all right?" Laurence asked sharply; Tharkay had smothered the little flame which had caught in his trousers with the tails of his coat, but he was putting no weight on his right leg, and leaning with drawn face against the wall; there was a smell of blackened and roasting flesh.

Tharkay said nothing, jaw locked shut, but waved off concern, pointing; a small barred door of ironwork lattice stood behind the furnace, red rust weeping down the bars, and within the slightly cooler chamber behind, in great nests of silken cloth, lay a dozen dragon eggs. The gate was hot to the touch, but Fellowes took out a few wide pieces of leather, and so shielding their hands, Laurence and Granby lifted aside the bar and swung open the door.

Granby ducked inside and went to the eggs, lifting aside the silk and touching the shells with loving care. "Oh, here's our beauty," he said reverently, uncovering one of a dusty reddish hue, speckled lightly with green. "That's our Kazilik all right; and eight weeks at most by the feel of it, we are none too soon." He covered it up again, and with great care he and Laurence lifted it off its perch, silken swaddling and all, and carried it out into the furnace-room where Fellowes and Digby began to lash it into the leather straps.

"Only look at them," Granby said, turning back to survey the rest of the eggs, stroking their shells lightly with the tips of his fingers. "What the Corps would give for the lot. But these are the ones we were promised; an Alaman, that's one of their light-combat fellows, this one," he indicated the smallest of the eggs, a pale lemon-yellow half the size of a man's chest, "and the Akhal-Teke is a middle-weight," a cream-colored egg spotted with red and orange, nearly twice the size.

They all worked now to get the straps on, putting them over the silk coverings, buckling them tight with hands slipping on the leather; they were all of them pouring sweat, great dark stains coming through the backs of their coats. They had closed the door again to work in concealment, and despite the narrow windows, the room was nearly an oven to bake them in alive.

Abruptly voices came in through the vents: they halted with their hands still on the straps, and then a louder voice came through more clearly, a call in a woman's voice. "More steam," Tharkay translated, whispering, and Martin snatched up the ladle and poured some water from the standing basin up and onto the stones; but the clouds of steam did not all go through the vents, and made the room almost impossible to see.

"We must make a dash for it: down the stairs and out the nearest archway, and make for any open air you see," Laurence said quietly, looking to be sure they had all heard.

"I'm no hand in a fight; I'll take the Kazilik," Fellowes said, leaving the rest of his leather in a heap on the floor. "Strap it to my back; and Mr. Dunne can help steady me."

"Very good," Laurence said, and told Martin and Digby off to the Akhal-Teke and the smaller Alaman; he and Granby drew their swords, and Tharkay, who had bound up his leg with some of the leather scraps, took out his knife: there would be no relying on their guns, after they had been soaking a quarter-of-an-hour together in the thick and humid atmosphere.

"Keep all together," he said, and threw all the rest of the

water in one great heave onto the hot stones and the coals themselves, and kicked open the door.

The great white billows of hissing steam carried them down
the stairs and out into the baths; they were halfway to the archway before the air cleared enough to make anything out at all.
Then the trailing steam blew away and Laurence found himself
staring at an exquisitely beautiful woman, perfectly naked and
holding an ewer full of water; her complexion was the exact
color of milky tea, and her hair in long shining-wet ebony ropes
was her only cover; she stared at him with extraordinarily large
sea-green eyes, rimmed in brown, at first in confusion; and then
she gave a piercing shriek, rousing all the other women too:
more than a dozen of them, equally beautiful though of wholly
different style, and all of their voices ringing out in wild and
musical alarm.

"Oh, Christ," Laurence said; deeply ashamed, he caught her
by the shoulders, firmly set her out of the way, and dashed on to
the archway, his men following after him. More of the guards
were running into the room from the far sides, and two came
nearly running directly into Laurence's and Granby's faces.

They were taken aback too much to swing at once, and Laurence was able to knock the sword out of his opposite's hand
and kick it away skittering over the floor. Together Laurence and
Granby shoved them backwards and out into the hall, all of
them half-slipping on the slick floors, and they burst out into the
hallway and ran for the stairs, the two guards, knocked down,
calling to their fellows.

Laurence and Granby ducked under Tharkay's arms and
helped him go limping up the stairs; the others were burdened
with the eggs; yet all of them still went at great speed, the pursuit
boiling up furiously behind them, and the women's screams at-
tracting still more attention. Running footsteps approaching
from ahead warned them their original route had been cut off;
instead Tharkay said sharply, "Go eastward, that way," and
they turned down another hallway to flee.

A draught of cold air, desperately welcome, came into their
faces as they ran; and they emerged from a small marble cloister

into an open-air quadrangle, all the windows blazing around them; Granby at once dropped to one knee and fired up his signal-flares: one and the next refused to go, too wet to fire, and cursing he flung the inert cylinders to the ground, but the third, which had been tucked more deeply into his shirt, at last went off, and the blue glittering trail went smoking up into the black sky.

Then they had to put down the eggs and turn and fight: the first guards were upon them, shouting, more spilling out of the building. One small grace, that for fear of damaging the eggs the Turkish guards had not resorted to their own guns, and were cautious in pressing too closely, trusting to their weight of numbers to overcome the invaders with only a little patience. Laurence struggled to hold off one of the guards, deflecting one blow and then another to either side; he was counting the moments in wingbeats, but he had scarcely reached half his expected total before Temeraire, roaring, swept down over the court, the great wind of his passage nearly flattening them all.

The guards scrambled back, crying out. There was not room for Temeraire to land without crushing the buildings, perhaps bringing them down, but Celestials could hover; his wings beating mightily, Temeraire kept almost directly above them. The thunder of his wings sent loosened bits of brick and stone crumbling down into the courtyard, and the many windows around the court were shattering in sharp explosive bursts, littering the ground with razor shards.

Cables were being flung down to them by the crew already aboard. They frantically tied on the eggs and sent them up, to be stowed away in the belly-rigging; Fellowes did not even take off his precious burden, but let himself be bundled aloft still lashed to the egg and thrust into the belly-netting, many hands reaching to latch his carabiners onto the harness.

"Hurry, hurry," Temeraire called loudly; the alarm was truly given now, horns blowing wildly in the distance, more flares firing up into the sky, and then from the gardens to the north rose a terrible roaring, and a great jet of flame scorched glowing red upon the sky: the Kaziliks were rising into the air, spiraling up through their own smoke and flame. Laurence heaved Dunne up into the reaching hands of the bellmen and jumped for the rigging himself.

"Temeraire, we are aboard, go!" he shouted, dangling by his hands; the bellmen were helping them all get latched on, and Therrows had Laurence's carabiners in hand. Below, the guards were returning with rifles in hand, caution giving way with the eggs so nearly lost to them; they were forming into a company, their rifles aimed together to a single point, the only likely way to injure a dragon with musket-fire.

Temeraire gathered himself, wings sweeping forward, and with a great thrust he was moving straight up and up, heaving himself aloft and higher. Digby cried out, "The egg, 'ware the egg," and lunged for it: the little lemon-yellow Alaman egg, its silk coverings caught on some protrusion on the ground and unfurling in a long glorious red ribbon from underneath the leather straps, leaving the soft, moisture-slick egg too loose in its harness.

Digby's grasping fingers caught on the shell; but still it slid free, easing out between the leather straps and the belly-netting, and he let go the harness and caught it with his other hand. His carabiners dangling loose were not yet latched on. "Digby!" Martin cried, reaching for him; but Temeraire's leap could not be arrested: they were already above the roof and rising still with the force of his great wing-stroke, and Digby fell away startled and open-mouthed, still holding the egg against his breast.

Together the boy and the egg fell tumbling through the air and smashed together upon the courtyard stones, amidst the shouting guards. Digby's arms lay flung wide against the white marble, the curled and half-formed serpentine body of the dragonet in the burst ruins of the shell, and the lantern-light shone grisly upon their small broken bodies lying in a slick of blood and egg-slime, as Temeraire lifted still higher and away.

CHAPTER 10

Along and desperate flight, then, to the Austrian border; all of them sick at heart and only the urgency of the moment keeping them from an indulgence of their grief. Temeraire flung himself onward through the night without speaking, without answering to Laurence's soft calls except to keen back his misery, and behind them a holocaust of fire raged, the wrath of the Kazilik dragons striped across the sky, trying to find them.

The moon had set; they flew on with no light but the clouded stars, and an occasional risked sliver of lantern-light to see the compass by. Temeraire's midnight hide was nearly invisible in the dark, and his ears pricked sharp for the sound of dragon wings. Three times he veered away to one side or another as faster couriers dashed by, carrying the alarm outwards: all the countryside raised against them. But all the while they surged on, Temeraire stretching to the limits of his speed as he had never before done, the cupped wing-strokes like flashing oars dipping into the night, driving them on.

Laurence did not try to hold him back; there was no exhilara-

tion or battle-fever, now, which on other occasions might have
driven Temeraire to exceed the bounds of his own endurance.
Impossible, too, to be sure how quickly they were going; beneath them all was darkness but the occasional faint glow of a
chimney, flashing by. They huddled all silent and close against
Temeraire's body, out of the lashing wind.

The eastern edge of the night, behind them, was beginning to
shine a paler blue; the stars were going out. No use in urging
Temeraire to greater speed; if they could not reach the border
before dawn, they would have to hide, somehow, until the following night; there would be no getting across during the day.

"Sir, I make a light there," Allen said, breaking the silence,
his voice stifled and still thick with tears; he pointed away and
north. One after another the torchlight glimmers came into
view: a thin necklace of lights strung along the border, and the
low wrathful roaring of dragons, calling one to the other in frustration. They were flying along the border in small formations,
back and forth like wheeling birds, all of them roused and peering into the darkness.

"They haven't any night-flyers; they are only venturing a shot
in the dark," Granby said softly into Laurence's ear, cupping his
hand around the noise. Laurence nodded.

The agitation of the Turkish dragons had roused the Austrian
border as well; on the far bank of the Danube, Laurence could
see a fortification not far distant, set on a hill and fully illuminated; he touched Temeraire's side, and when Temeraire looked
around, his great eyes shining and liquid in the dark, Laurence
pointed him at it silently.

Temeraire nodded; he did not go straight at the border, but
flew parallel to the line of fortifications a while, watching the
Turkish dragons in their flights; now and again the crews did
even go so far as to fire off a rifle into the dark, likely more for
the little satisfaction of making a noise than in real hopes of
striking a target. They were sending up flares occasionally, but it
was hopeless, with miles of border, to illuminate it all.

Temeraire gave them only the warning of muscles suddenly
gathered; Laurence pulled down Allen and the other lookout,

Harley, and stayed low to Temeraire's neck himself, and then Temeraire was driving himself forward with short rapid-fire strokes, building up a great deal of speed; ten dragon-lengths from the border he ceased to beat his wings at all, leaving them wide-extended, and drew in a great heaving breath that distended out his sides; gliding he went straight across at one of the dark places between the outposts, and the torches to either side did not so much as gutter.

He did not beat up again for as long as he could; they drifted so low to the ground that Laurence smelled fresh pine-needles before at last Temeraire risked a fresh stroke and then another, to lift himself clear of the tree-tops. He went to north of the Austrian fort, better than a mile, before he came around again; the Turkish border now was more clearly visible against the sky growing paler, and there was no sign they had been noticed in their crossing: the dragons were continuing their search-flights.

Still they had to get under cover before light; Temeraire was too large to easily hide in the countryside. "Run up the colors and hang out a white flag with them, Mr. Allen," Laurence said. "Temeraire, get in and land as quick as you can; better to have them make a noise inside the walls than on our approach."

Temeraire's head was hanging low; he had flown harder than perhaps ever before in his life, and after earlier exertion and grief; his wingbeats were slow now not from caution but from exhaustion. But he drew himself up without complaint for one last sprint: he flung himself up towards the fort and over its walls in a desperate heave, and came down heavily in the court-yard, swaying upon his haunches, scattering in terror a troop of cavalry-horses on one side, and a company of infantrymen on the other, all of them yelling wildly as they fled.

"Hold your fire!" Laurence bellowed out of his speaking-trumpet, then repeated it in French, standing up to wave the British flag. He won some hesitation from the Austrians, and in the pause Temeraire sighed and settled back upon his haunches, head drooping forward over his breast, and said, "Oh, I am so very tired."

COLONEL EIGHER PROVIDED them coffee and beds, and for Temeraire one of the horses which had in its frenzy broken a leg; the rest were hurriedly taken outside the walls of the fort and left in a paddock under guard. Laurence slept through until the afternoon, and rose from his cot still half-submerged in the murk of sleep, while outside Temeraire continued to snore in a manner which would certainly have given him away even to the Turks half-a-mile distant across the border, if he had not been curled up securely behind the thick wooden walls of the fort.

"They mean to dance to Bonaparte's fiddle, do they?" Eigher said, when given a fuller account of their adventure than Laurence had been able to muster up the previous night; his own preoccupation, quite naturally, with the state of relations his nation might expect with her neighbors. "Much joy may they get of him."

He gave Laurence a good dinner, and some sympathy; but he had little to spare. "I would send you on to Vienna," he said, pouring yet another glass of wine, "but God in Heaven, I would be serving you an ill turn. It shames me to say, but there are creatures calling themselves men who would serve you to Bonaparte on a platter; and bend both their knees to him while they were at it."

Laurence said quietly, "I am very grateful for the shelter you have given us, sir, and I would not for all the world embarrass you or your country; I know you are at peace with the French."

"At peace," Eigher said, bitterly. "We are cowering at their feet, you may say; and with more truth."

By the end of the meal he had drunk nearly three bottles; and the slowness with which the wine had any effect upon him betrayed that this was no irregular occurrence. He was a gentleman, but of no high estate, which had limited his advancement and his postings beneath, Laurence suspected, what his competence might have deserved; but it was not resentment drove him to drink but a misery which found voice as the evening drew on, and the combination of brandy and company further unbridled his tongue.

Austerlitz was his demon; he had served under General Langeron in the fatal battle. "The devil gave us the Pratzen Heights," he said, "and the town itself; took his men out of the best ground deliberately and played at a retreat, and why? So that we would fight him. He had then fifty thousand men, and we ninety, with the Russians; and he was luring us to battle." Humorlessly he laughed. "And why not give them to us? He took them back easily enough, a few days later." He waved his hand over the map-table, on which he had laid out a tableau of the battle: a task which had taken him scarcely ten minutes, though he was already thoroughly taken in drink.

Laurence, for his part, had not drunk enough to numb his appalled reaction; he had learned of the great disaster at Austerlitz while already at sea, on his way to China, and only in the vaguest terms; the intervening months had given him no better information, and he had by stages allowed himself to believe the victory exaggerated. Eigher's tin soldiers and wooden dragons in their stately array made a deeply unpleasant impression as the colonel moved them about.

"He let us entertain ourselves by beating upon his right a little while, until we had emptied our center," Eigher said, "and then they appeared: fifteen dragons and twenty thousand men. He had brought them up by forced marches, and not a whisper we had of their coming. We limped on another few hours, the Russian Imperial Guard cost them some blood, but that was the end of it."

Reaching out he tipped over a little mounted figure with a commander's baton, and lay back in his chair, his eyes shut. Laurence picked up one of the little dragon-figures, turning it over in his hands; he did not know what to say.

"Emperor Francis went and begged him for peace the next morning," Eigher said after a little while. "The Holy Roman Emperor, bowing to a Corsican who snatched himself a crown." His voice was thick, and he did not speak again but fell slowly into a stupor.

LAURENCE LEFT EIGHER sleeping and went out to Temeraire, now awake and no less unhappy. "Digby would be bad enough," Temeraire said, "but we have killed that dragonet, too, and it did not have anything to do with all of this; it did not choose to be sold to us, or to be kept back by the Turks, and it could not get away."

He had curled himself brooding around the two remaining eggs, keeping them cuddled against his body, perhaps by instinct, and occasionally putting out his long forked tongue to touch the shells. He only with reluctance admitted even Laurence and Keynes to examine them, and kept hovering so close that the dragon-surgeon impatiently said, "Get your bloody head out of the way, will you; I cannot see anything with you blocking all the light."

Keynes tapped the shells lightly, pressed his ear to the surface and listened, wetted a finger and rubbed them a little and brought it to his mouth. When he was satisfied with his examination, he stepped away again, and Temeraire drew his coils more snugly back around the eggs and looked anxiously to hear his verdict.

"Well, they are in good form, and have taken no harmful chill," Keynes said. "We had better keep them wrapped up in the silk, and," he jerked his thumb at Temeraire, "it will do them no harm to have him playing nursemaid. The middle-weight is in no immediate danger at all; by the sound I should say the dragonet is not yet formed; we might have months to wait there. But for the Kazilik, no more than eight weeks, and no less than six; there is not a moment to lose in getting it home."

"Austria is not safe, nor the German states, with French troops thick on the ground as they are," Laurence said. "I mean to go northward, through Prussia; a week and a half should see us to the coast, and from there a few days' flight to Scotland."

"Whichever way you go, you should go quickly; I will contrive to delay my report to Vienna a little, so you are out of the country before those damned politicians can think of some way they can make use of you to shame Austria a little more," Eigher said, when Laurence spoke to him again, that evening. "I can give you safe-conduct to the border. But should you not go by sea?"

"It would cost us at least another month, going around by Gibraltar, and we would have to find shelter along the Italian coast a good deal of the way," Laurence said. "I know the Prussians have accommodated Bonaparte heretofore, but do you think they will go so far as to surrender us to him?"

"Surrender you? No," Eigher said. "They are going to war."

"Against Napoleon?" Laurence exclaimed; that was a piece of good news he had not expected to hear. The Prussians had long been the finest fighting force in Europe; if only they had joined the earlier coalition in time, surely the outcome would have been very different, and their entry into the struggle now seemed to him a great victory for Napoleon's enemies. But it was plain Eigher saw nothing to be pleased with in this intelligence.

"Yes, and when he has trampled them into the dirt, and the Russians with them, there will be no one left at all in Europe to restrain him," the colonel said.

Laurence kept his opinion of this pessimism to himself. The news made his own heart lift gladly, but an Austrian officer, no matter how passionately he hated Bonaparte, might well not desire to see the Prussian Army succeed where his own had failed. "At least they will have no motive to delay our journey," he said tactfully.

"Go fast and keep ahead of the fighting, or Bonaparte will delay you himself," Eigher said.

THE NEXT EVENING they set out again under cover of dark. Laurence had left several letters with Eigher to be sent on to Vienna and thence to London, though he hoped his own road home would be quicker; but in case of any accident, their progress so far should at least be known, and the situation with the Ottoman Empire.

His report to the Admiralty, laboriously encoded in the year-old ciphers which were all he had to hand, had taken on a more wooden tone than usual. It was not guilt precisely; he was perfectly convinced in his own mind of the justice of his actions, but he was conscious how the whole might appear to a hostile judge: a reckless and imprudent adventure, unsanctioned by any authority higher than himself, entered into on the slightest of evidence. Easy enough to make the change in the sentiments of the Turks the consequence rather than the cause of the theft.

And it could not be defended as a question of duty; no one would ever call it a man's duty to perform so wild and desperate a mission, with profound implications for relations with a foreign power, without orders; it could even be called quite the contrary. Nor was he the sort of sophist who could bald-faced point at Lenton's orders to bring the eggs home and call that justification. There was none, indeed, but urgency; the more sensible reply, in every possible way, would have been an immediate return home, to place the tangled matter into the hands of the Ministry.

He was not sure whether he would have approved his own actions, hearing of them secondhand; just the sort of wild behavior the world expected of aviators, and indeed, perhaps there was something to it; he did not know whether he would have risked so much, knowing himself subject to serve at the pleasure of the Navy. If deliberate, a paltry sort of caution that would be; but no, he had never consciously chosen the politic course; there was only something quite distinct in being captain to a living dragon who entered wholly into his engagements and who was not to be given or taken away by the will of other men. Laurence was uneasily forced to consider whether he might be in danger of beginning to think himself above authority.

"Myself, I do not see what is so wonderful about authority at all," Temeraire said, when Laurence ventured to disclose his anxiety that morning as they settled down for a rest; they had encamped in a clearing high upon the leeward side of a mountain slope, untended but for a handful of former sheep now roasting under Gong Su's careful hand in a fire-pit which did not give off much smoke, the better to avoid notice.

"It seems to me that it is only forcing people to do things

which they do not wish to do, and which they cannot be persuaded to do, with threats," he continued. "I am very glad we are above it. I would not at all be pleased if someone could take you away from me and make me have another captain, like a ship."

Laurence could hardly quarrel with this, and while he might have argued the description of authority, he could not, feeling too false in so doing; he plainly did like being free of restraint at least so far, and if he were ashamed of it he might at least not lie about it. "Well; I suppose it is true any man would be a tyrant an he could," he said ruefully. "All the better reason to deny Bonaparte any more power than he already has."

"Laurence," Temeraire said thoughtfully, "why do people do as he says, when he is so unpleasant a person? And dragons too."

"Oh; well, I do not know he is an unpleasant man in his person," Laurence admitted. "His soldiers love him at least, though that is scarcely to be marveled at, when he keeps winning wars for them; and he must have some charm, to have risen so high."

"Then why is it so terrible that he should have authority, if someone must have it?" Temeraire asked. "I have not heard that the King has ever won any battles, after all."

"The King's authority is nothing like," Laurence answered. "He is the head of the State, but he does not have absolute power; no man in Britain does. Bonaparte has no restraint, no check upon his will; and such gifts as he has he uses only to serve himself. The King and his ministers are all in the end the servants of our nation first, before themselves; at any rate, so the best of them are."

Temeraire sighed, and did not pursue the discussion further, but listlessly curled himself up with the eggs again, leaving Laurence to gaze on him with anxiety. It was not only the unhappy loss; the death of any of his crew always left Temeraire distressed, but rather in frustrated anger than this dragging lethargy; and Laurence feared deeply that the true cause was rather their disagreement over the question of dragon liberties; a more profound disappointment, and one which time would not lay to rest.

He might try and describe for Temeraire a little of the slow political work of emancipation, the long years Wilberforce had already spent nudging one partial act and then another forward through Parliament, and how they were still laboring to ban even the trade; but that seemed to him poor consolation to offer, and not much use as a model: so slow and calculated a progress would never recommend itself to Temeraire's eager soul, and they would have little time to pursue politics while engaged in their duties in any case.

But some hope, he increasingly felt, he must somehow discover; for all that he could not put aside his conviction of their duty to put the war effort first, he could not easily bear to see Temeraire so cast-down.

THE AUSTRIAN COUNTRYSIDE was green and golden with the ripening harvest, and the flocks were fat and contented, at least until Temeraire got his claws upon them; they saw no other dragons and faced no challenge. They crossed into Saxony and moved steadily northward another two days, still with no sign of the mobilizing army; until at last they crossed over one of the last swelling foothills of the final ridges of the Erz Gebirge mountains and came abruptly upon the vast encampment swelling out of the town of Dresden: seventy thousand men or more, and nearly two dozen dragons sprawling in the valley beside.

Laurence belatedly gave the order to have the flag hung out, as below the alarm was raised and men went running to their guns, crews to their dragons; the British flag brought them a very different reception, however, and Temeraire was waved down to a hastily cleared place in the makeshift covert.

"Keep the men aboard," Laurence told Granby. "I hope we need not stop long; we could make another hundred miles today." He swung himself down the harness to the ground, mentally composing his explanations and requests in French, and brushed ineffectually at the worst of his dirt.

"Well, it is about damned time," a voice said, in crisp English. "Now where the devil are the rest of you?"

Laurence turned and stared blankly: a British officer was standing before him, scowling, and snapping his crop against his leg. Laurence would hardly have been more astonished to meet a Piccadilly fish-merchant in the same circumstances. "Good God, are we mobilizing also?" he asked. "I beg your pardon," he added, belatedly recollecting himself. "Captain William Laurence, of Temeraire, at your service, sir."

"Oh; Colonel Richard Thorndyke, liaison officer," the colonel said. "And what do you mean; you know damned well we have been waiting for you lot."

"Sir," Laurence said, ever more bewildered, "I think you have mistaken us for another company; you cannot have been expecting us. We are come from China by way of Istanbul; my latest orders are months old."

"What?" Now it was Thorndyke's turn to stare, and with growing dismay. "Do you mean to tell me you are alone?"

"As you see us," Laurence said. "We have only stopped to ask safe-passage; we are on our way to Scotland, on urgent business for the Corps."

"Well, what more urgent business than the bloody war the Corps has, I should damned well like to know!" Thorndyke said.

"For my part, sir," Laurence said angrily, "I should like to know what occasion justifies such a remark about my service."

"Occasion!" Thorndyke exclaimed. "Bonaparte's armies on the horizon, and you ask me what occasion there is! I have been waiting for twenty dragons who ought have been here two months ago; *that* is the bloody occasion."

PART III

CHAPTER 11

Prince Hohenlohe listened to Laurence's attempted explanations without very much expression: some sixty years of age, with a jovial face rendered dignified rather than unpleasantly formal by his white-powdered wig, he looked nonetheless determined. "Little enough did Britain offer, to the defeat of the tyrant you so profess to hate," he said finally, when Laurence had done. "No army has come across from your shores to join the battle. Others, Captain, might have complained that the British prefer to spend gold than blood; but Prussia is not unwilling to bear the brunt of war. Yet twenty dragons we were assured, and promised, and guaranteed; and now we stand on the eve of war, and none are here. Does Britain mean to dishonor her agreement?"

"Sir, not a thought of it, I swear to you," Thorndyke said, glaring daggers at Laurence.

"There can be no such intention," Laurence said. "What has delayed them, sir, I cannot guess; but that can only increase my anxiety to be home. We are a little more than a week's flying away; if you will give me safe-passage I can be gone and back before the end of the month, and I trust with the full company which you have been promised."

"We may not have so long, and I am not inclined to accept more hollow assurances," Hohenlohe said. "If the promised company appears, you may have your safe-passage. Until then, you will be our guest; or if you like, you may do what you can to fulfill the promises which were made: that I leave to your conscience."

He nodded to his guard, who opened the tent-door, signifying plainly the interview was at an end; and despite the courtliness of his manners, there was iron underlying his words.

"I hope you are not so damned foolish you will sit about watching and give them still more disgust of us," Thorndyke said, when they had left the tent.

Laurence wheeled on him, very angry. "As I might have hoped that you would have taken our part, rather than encourage the Prussians in treating us more as prisoners than allies, and insulting the Corps; a pretty performance from a British officer, when you know damned well our circumstances."

"What a couple of eggs can matter next to this campaign, you have leave to try and convince me," Thorndyke said. "For God's sake, do you not understand what this could mean? If Bonaparte rolls them up, where the devil do you suppose he will look next but across the Channel? If we do not stop him here, we will be stopping him in London this time next year; or trying to, and half the country in flames. You aviators would rather do anything than risk these beasts you are hooked to, I know that well enough, but surely you can see—"

"That is enough; that is damned well enough," Laurence said. "By God, you go too far." He gave the man his back and stalked away in a simmering rage; he was not by nature a quarrelsome man, and he had rarely so wanted satisfaction; to have his courage questioned, and his commitment to duty, and withal an insult to his service, was very hard to bear, and he thought if their circumstances had been anything other than desperate, he could not have restrained himself.

But the prohibition forbidding Corps officers to duel was not an ordinary regulation, to be circumvented; here of all places, in the middle of a war, he could not risk some injury, even short of death, that might not only leave him out of the battle but would cast Temeraire wholly down. But he felt the stain to his honor, deeply, "and I suppose that damned hussar is off thinking to himself I have not the courage of a dog," he said, bitterly.

"You did just as you ought, thank Heaven," Granby said, pale with relief. "There's no denying it's a wrench, but the risk isn't to be borne. You needn't see the fellow again; Ferris and I can go-between with him, if there's anything we must deal with him for."

"I thank you; but I should sooner let him shoot me than let him think I have the least reluctance to face him," Laurence said.

Granby had met him at the entrance to the covert; now together they reached the small, bare clearing which had been assigned them; Temeraire was curled up in what comfort he could find and listening intently to the conversation of the Prussian dragons near him, ears and ruff pricked up with attention, while the men busied themselves at cooking-fires, snatching a hasty meal.

"Are we leaving now?" he asked, when Laurence arrived.

"No, I am afraid not," Laurence said, calling over his other senior officers, Ferris and Riggs, to join them. "Well, gentlemen, we are in the thick of it," he told them grimly. "They have refused us the safe-conduct."

When Laurence had finished giving them the whole of the situation, Ferris burst out, "But sir, we *will* fight, won't—I mean, will we fight with them?" hastily correcting himself.

"We are not children or cowards, to sulk in a corner when there is a battle to hand, and of such vital importance," Laurence said. "Offensive they have been, but I will grant they have been sorely tried, and they might be as outrageous as they liked before I would let pride keep us from doing our duty, and there can scarcely be any question of that; only I wish to God I knew why the Corps has not sent the promised aid."

"There's only one thing it can be; they must be needed more

somewhere else," Granby said, "and likely enough it's the same reason they sent us for the eggs in the first place; only if the Channel is not under bombardment, the trouble must be somewhere overseas—some great upset in India, or trouble in Halifax—"

"Oh! Maybe we are taking back the American colonies?" Ferris offered; Riggs opined that it was more likely the colonials had invaded Nova Scotia, ungrateful rebellious sods; and they wrangled it back and forth a moment before Granby interrupted their fruitless speculation.

"Well, it don't matter where, exactly; the Admiralty will never strip the Channel bare no matter how busy Bonaparte is elsewhere, and if all the spare dragons are coming home by transport, any sort of mess at sea could have held them up. But if they are already two months overdue, surely they must arrive any moment."

"For my part, Captain, I hope you'll forgive my saying, I'd as soon stay and fight if they get here tomorrow," Riggs said, in his bluff forthright way. "We could always pass the eggs to some middle-weight to take home; it would be a damned shame to miss a chance to help give Boney a drubbing."

"Of course we must stay and fight," Temeraire put in, dismissing the entire question with a flick of his tail; and indeed there would have been no restraining him, if the battle were anywhere in his vicinity: young male dragons were not notably reluctant to jump into an affray. "It is a great pity that Maximus and Lily are not here, and the rest of our friends; but I am very glad at last we will get to fight the French again. I am sure we can beat them this time, too, and then maybe," he added suddenly, sitting up; his eyes widened and his ruff mounted up with a visible rush of enthusiasm, "the war will be over, and we can go home and see to the liberty of dragons, after all."

Laurence was startled by the intensity of his own sensation of relief; though uneasy, he had not properly realized how very low Temeraire had sunk, that this burst of excitement should provide so sharply defined a contrast. It wholly overcame any inclination he might have had to voice discouraging cautions; though

a victory here, he was well aware, was necessary but not sufficient to Bonaparte's final defeat. It was entirely possible, he privately argued with his conscience, that Bonaparte might be
forced to make terms, if thoroughly checked in this campaign;
and thus give Britain real peace for at least a little while.

So he merely said, "I am glad that you are all of like mind
with me, gentlemen, so far as engaging to fight; but we must
now consider our other charge: we have bought these eggs too
dear in blood and gold to lose them now. We cannot assume the
Corps will arrive in time to take them safely home, and if this
campaign lasts us more than a month or two, as is entirely likely,
we will have the Kazilik egg hatching in the midst of a battlefield."

They none of them spoke for a moment; Granby with his fair
skin flushed up red to his roots, and then went pale; he dropped
his eyes and said nothing.

"We have them properly bundled up, sir, in a tent with a
good brazier, and a couple of the ensigns watching it every minute," Ferris said, after a moment, glancing at Granby. "Keynes
says they will do nicely, and if it comes to real fighting, we'd best
set the ground crew down somewhere well behind the lines, and
leave Keynes behind to look after the eggs; if we have to fall
back, we can stop and catch them all up quick enough."

"If you are worried," Temeraire put in unexpectedly, "I will
ask it to wait as long as it can, once the shell is a little harder,
and it can understand me."

They all looked blankly at him. "Ask it to wait?" Laurence
said, confused. "Do you mean—the hatchling? Surely it is not a
matter of choice?"

"Well, one does begin to be very hungry, but it does not feel
so pressing until one is out of the shell," Temeraire said, as if this
were a matter of common knowledge, "and everything outside
seems very interesting, once one understands what is being said.
But I am sure the hatchling can wait a little while."

"Lord, the Admiralty will stare," Riggs said, after they had all
chewed over this startling piece of intelligence. "Though perhaps

it is only Celestials who are like that; I am sure I never heard a dragon talk of remembering anything from inside the shell at all."

"Well, there is nothing to talk about," Temeraire said prosaically. "It is quite uninteresting; that is why one comes out."

Laurence dismissed them to go and begin to make some sort of camp, with their limited supplies. Granby hurried away with only a nod; the other lieutenants exchanged a look and followed him. Laurence supposed it was less common with aviators, than with Navy men, that a man got his step only for being in the right place at the right moment, hatchings being under more regular control than captured ships. In the early days of their acquaintance, Granby had himself been one of those officers resentful of Laurence's acquiring Temeraire. Laurence understood his constraint, and his reluctance to speak; Granby could neither speak in favor of a course which would almost certainly result in his being the most senior candidate available when the egg should hatch; nor protest against one which would require him to make the attempt to harness a hatchling under the most dire circumstances, in the midst of a battlefield, the egg barely in their hands for a few weeks, of a rare breed almost unknown to them, and almost certainly no future chance of promotion if he failed.

Laurence spent the evening writing letters in his small tent: all he had in the way of quarters, and that having been put up by his own crew; there had been no offer made to quarter him or his men more formally, though there were barracks for the Prussian aviators erected all around the covert. In the morning he meant to go into Dresden, and see if he could arrange to draw funds on his bank; the last of his money would be gone in a day, provisioning his men and Temeraire at war-time prices, and he had no inclination to go begging to the Prussians under the present circumstances.

A little while after dark, Tharkay tapped one of the tent-poles and came in; the ugly wound at least had not mortified, but he was still limping a little and would bear the deep gouge upon his thigh the rest of his days, a furrow of flesh all seared away. Laurence got up and waved him to the cushion-heaped box which was all he had as a chair. "No, sit; I will do perfectly well here," he said, and himself lay down Turkish-style upon the other cushions on the ground.

"I have only come for a moment," Tharkay said. "Lieutenant Granby tells me we are not to leave; I understand Temeraire has been taken in lieu of twenty dragons."

"Flattering, I suppose, if considered that way," Laurence said wryly. "Yes; we are established here, if against our design, and whether we can fill that tally or no, we mean to do what we can."

Tharkay nodded. "Then I will keep my word to you," he said, "and tell you, this time, that I mean to depart. I doubt an untrained man would be anything other than a dangerous nuisance aboard Temeraire's back in an aerial battle, and you hardly need a guide when you cannot stir out of the camp: I cannot be of any further use to you."

"No," Laurence said slowly, reluctant but unable to argue the point, "and I will not press you to stay, in our present circumstances, though I am sorry to lose you against a future need; and I cannot at the moment reward you as your pains have deserved."

"Let us defer it," Tharkay said. "Who knows? We may meet again; the world is not after all so very large a place."

He spoke with that faint smile, and stood to give Laurence his hand. "I hope we shall," Laurence said, gripping it, "and that I may be of use to you in turn, someday."

Tharkay refused an offer to try and get him a more personal safe-conduct; and indeed Laurence did not have much fear he would need one, despite his game leg. With no further ado, Tharkay put up the hood of his cloak and picking up his small bundle was gone into the bustle and noise of the covert; there were few guards posted around the dragons, and he vanished quickly among the scattered campfires and bivouacs.

LAURENCE HAD SENT Colonel Thorndyke a stiff, short word that they meant to offer their services to the Prussians; in the morning the colonel came again to the covert, bringing with him a Prussian officer: rather younger than other of the senior commanders, with a truly impressive mustache whose tips hung below his chin, and a fierce, hawk-like expression.

"Your Highness, may I present Captain William Laurence, of His Majesty's Aerial Corps," Thorndyke said. "Captain, this is Prince Louis Ferdinand, commander of the advance guard; you have been assigned to his command."

They were forced for direct communication to resort to French. Laurence ruefully thought that at least his mastery of that language was improving, with as much use as he was being forced to make of it; indeed he was for once not the worse speaker, as Prince Louis spoke with a thick and almost impenetrable accent. "Let us see his range, his skill," Prince Louis said, gesturing to Temeraire.

He called over a Prussian officer, Captain Dyhern, from one of the neighboring coverts, and gave him instructions to lead his own heavy-weight, Eroica, and their formation in a drill to give them the example. Laurence stood by Temeraire's head watching, with private dismay. He had wholly neglected formation-drill practice over the long months since their departure from England, and even at the height of their form they could not have matched the skill on display. Eroica was nearly the size of Maximus, Temeraire's year-mate and a Regal Copper, the very largest breed of dragon known; and he was not a fast flier, but when he moved in square his corners nearly had points, and the distance separating him from the other dragons scarcely varied, to the naked eye.

"I do not at all understand, why are they flying that way?" Temeraire said, head cocked to one side. "Those turns look very awkward, and when they reversed there was enough room for anyone to go between them."

"It is only a drill, not a battle-formation," Laurence said. "But you can be sure they will do all the better in combat for the discipline and the precision required to perform such maneuvers."

Temeraire snorted. "It seems to me that they would do better to practice things that would actually be of use. But I see the pattern; I can do it now," he added.

"Are you sure you would not like to observe a little longer?" Laurence asked, anxiously; the Prussian dragons had only gone through one full repetition, and he for his own part would not at all have minded a little time to practice the maneuver in privacy.

"No; it is very silly, but it is not at all difficult," Temeraire said.

This was perhaps not the best spirit in which to enter into the practice, and Temeraire had never much liked formation-flying at all, even the less-rigorous British style. For all Laurence could do to restrain him, he dashed through the maneuver at high speed, a good deal quicker than the Prussian formation had managed it, not to mention than any other dragon over a lightweight in size could have kept up with, spiraling himself about in a flourishy way to boot.

"I put in the turning over, so that I would always be looking out of the formation body," Temeraire added, coiling himself down to the ground rather pleased with himself. "That way I could not be surprised by an attack."

This cleverness plainly did not much impress Prince Louis, nor Eroica, who gave a short coughing snort, as dismissive as a sniff. Temeraire pricked up his ruff at it and sat up on his haunches narrow-eyed. "Sir," Laurence said hurriedly, to forestall any quarreling, "perhaps you are not aware that Temeraire is a Celestial; they have a particular skill—" Here he stopped, abruptly aware that *divine wind* might sound poetical and exaggerated if directly translated.

"Demonstrate, if you please," Prince Louis said, gesturing. There was no appropriate target nearby, however, but a small stand of trees. Temeraire obligingly smashed them down with one deep-chested violent roar, by no means the full range of his strength, in the process rousing the whole covert of dragons into loud calls and inquiries and sparking a terrified distant whinnying from the cavalry on the opposite side of the encampment.

Prince Louis inspected the shattered trunks with some interest. "Well, when we have pushed them back onto their own fortifications, that will be useful," he said. "At what distance is it effective?"

"Against seasoned wood, sir, not very great," Laurence said. "He would have to come too near exposed to their guns; however, against troops or cavalry, the range is greater, and I am sure would have excellent effect—"

"Ah! But too dear a cost," Prince Louis said, waving a hand expressively towards the perfectly audible sound of the shrilling horses. "The army which exchanges its cavalry for dragon-corps will be defeated in the field, if their opponent's infantry hold; this the work of Frederick the Great conclusively has proven. Have you before fought in a ground engagement?"

"No, sir," Laurence was forced to admit; Temeraire had only a few actions at all to his credit, all purely aerial engagements, and despite many years' service Laurence could not claim any experience himself, for while most aviators come up through the ranks would have had some practice at least working in support of infantry, he had spent those years afloat, and by whatever chance had never been at a land battle of any kind.

"Hm." Prince Louis shook his head and straightened up. "We will not try and train you up now," he said. "Better to make of you the best use we can. You will sweep with Eroica's formation, in early battle, then hold the enemy off their flanks; keep with them and you will not spook the cavalry."

HAVING INQUIRED INTO Temeraire's complement, Prince Louis insisted also on providing them with a few Prussian officers and another half-a-dozen ground hands to fill out their numbers; Laurence could not deny the extra hands were of use, after the unhappy losses which he had suffered, without replacement, since their departure from England: Digby and Baylesworth only lately, Macdonaugh killed in the desert, and poor little Morgan slain along with half his harness-men in the French night assault near Madeira so long ago, when they had scarcely weighed anchor. The new men seemed to know their work, but they spoke almost no English and very indifferent French, and he could not like having such perfect strangers aboard; he was anxious a little for the eggs.

The Prussians were plainly not much appeased by his willingness to assist; they had softened a little towards Temeraire and his crew, but the Aerial Corps were still being spoken of as treacherous. Aside from the pain which this could not help but give Laurence, as this justification had been sufficient to make the Prussians comfortable in keeping him against his will, he would not have been wholly astonished if they took the opportunity to commandeer the Kazilik egg, should they become aware of the imminent hatching.

He had made mention of his urgency, without telling them precisely that the egg was so near its time, and he had not said it was a Kazilik, which should certainly provide a great increase of temptation: the Prussians did not have a fire-breather either. But with the Prussian officers about, the secret was in some jeopardy, and they were all unknowing teaching the eggs German by their conversation, which should make a seizure all the easier.

He had not discussed the matter with his own officers, but that had not been necessary to make them share his concerns; Granby was a popular first officer, well-liked, and even if he had been roundly loathed none of the crew could have been happy to see the fruit of all their desperate labors snatched away. Without any instructions, they were standoffish to the Prussian officers and cautious to keep them away from the eggs, which were left in their swaddling-clothes and kept at the heart of their camp under a now-tripled volunteer guard, posted by Ferris, whenever Temeraire was engaged in maneuvers or exercise.

This did not occur very often; the Prussians did not believe in exerting dragons very much, outside of battle. The formations daily drilled and went on reconnaissance missions, probing out a little way into the countryside, but they did not go very far, being constrained by the range of their slowest members. Laurence's suggestion that he should take Temeraire farther afield had been denied, on the grounds that if they were to encounter any French party they should be taken, or lead them back towards the Prussian encampment, providing too much intelligence in exchange for small gain: yet another of Frederick the Great's maxims, which he was growing tired of hearing.

Only Temeraire was perfectly happy: he was rapidly acquiring German from the Prussian crewmen, and he was just as pleased not to have to be constantly performing formation exercises. "I do not need to fly around in squares to do well in a battle," he said. "It is a pity not to see more of the countryside, but it does not matter; once we have beaten Napoleon, we can always come back for a visit."

He regarded the coming battle in the light of an assured victory, as indeed did nearly the whole of the army around them, except for the grumbling Saxons, mostly reluctant conscripts. There was much to give foundation to such hopes: the level of discipline throughout the camp was wonderful to behold, and the infantry drill beyond anything Laurence had ever seen. If Hohenlohe was not a genius of Napoleon's caliber, he certainly seemed a soldierly kind of general, and his swelling army, large as it was, comprised less than half of the Prussian forces; and that not even counting the Russians, who were massing in the Polish territories to the east and would soon march in support.

The French would be badly outnumbered, operating far from their home territory with supply lines stretched thin; they would not be able to bring many dragons with them, and the lingering threat of Austria on their flank and Britain across the Channel would force Napoleon to leave a good portion of his troops behind to guard against a surprise late entry into the war on the part of either power.

"Who has he fought, anyway: the Austrians and the Italians, and some heathens in Egypt?" Captain Dyhern said; Laurence had out of courtesy been admitted to the captains' mess of the Prussian aviators, and they were happy on the occasion of his visits to shift their conversation to French, for the pleasure of describing to him the inevitable defeat of that nation. "The French have no real fighting quality, no morale; a few good beatings and we will see his whole army melt away."

The other officers all nodded and seconded him, and Laurence was as willing as any of them to raise a glass to Bonaparte's defeat, if less inclined to think his victories quite so hollow; Laurence had fought enough Frenchmen at sea to know they were no slouches in battle, if not much in the way of sailors.

Still, he did not think they were soldiers of the Prussian caliber, and it was heartening to be among a company of men so determined on victory; nothing like shyness known among them, or even uncertainty. They were worthy allies; he knew without question he should not hesitate to range himself in line with them, on the day of battle, and trust his own life to their courage; as near the highest encomium he could give, and which made all the more unpleasant his sensations when Dyhern drew him aside, as they left the mess together one evening.

"I hope you will allow me to speak, without offense," Dyhern said. "Never would I instruct a man how his dragon is to be managed, but you have been out in the East so long; now he has some strange ideas in his head, I think?"

Dyhern was a plain-spoken soldier, but he did not speak unkindly, and his words were intended in the nature of a gentle hint; mortifying enough to receive for all that, with his suggestion that "perhaps he has not been exercised enough, or he has been kept from battle too often; it is good not to let them grow preoccupied."

His own dragon, Eroica, was certainly an exemplar of Prussian dragon-discipline: he even looked the role, with the heavy overlapping plates of bone which ringed his neck and traveled up the ridges of his shoulders and wings, giving him an armored appearance. Despite his vast size, he showed no inclination to indolence, instead being rather quick to chide the other dragons if they should flag, and was always ready to answer a call to drill. The other Prussian dragons were much in awe of him, and willingly stood aside to let him take first fruits when they had their meals.

Laurence had been invited to let Temeraire feed from the pen, once they had committed to joining the battle; and Temeraire, inclined to be jealous of his own precedence, would not hang back in Eroica's favor. Nor would Laurence have liked to see him do so, for that matter. If the Prussians did not choose to make more use of Temeraire's gifts, that was their lookout; he could even appreciate the reasoning that kept them from disrupting their beautifully precise formations by introducing at so late a date a new participant. But he would not have stood for a moment any disparagement of Temeraire's qualities, nor tolerated a suggestion Temeraire was in any way not the equal—and to his own mind, the superior—of Eroica.

Eroica did not object to sharing his dinner himself, but the other Prussian dragons looked a little sourly at Temeraire's daring, and they all of them stared when Temeraire did not immediately eat, but took his kill over to Gong Su to be cooked first. "It always tastes just the same, if you only eat it plain," Temeraire said to their very dubious expressions. "It is much nicer to have it cooked; try a little and you will see."

Eroica made no answer to this but a snort, and deliberately tore into his own cows quite raw, devouring them down to the hooves; the other Prussian dragons at once followed his example.

"It is better not to give in to their whims," Dyhern added to Laurence now. "It seems a small thing, I know—why not let them have all the pleasure they can, when they are not fighting? But it is just as with men. There must be discipline, order, and they are the happier for it."

Guessing that Temeraire had once again broached the subject of his reforms with the Prussian dragons, Laurence answered him a little shortly, and went back to Temeraire's clearing, to find him curled up unhappily and silent. What little inclination Laurence had to reproach him vanished in the face of his disappointed droop, and Laurence went to him at once to stroke his soft muzzle.

"They say I am soft, for wishing to eat cooked food, and for reading," Temeraire said, low, "and they think I am silly for saying dragons ought not to have to fight; they none of them wanted to listen."

"Well," Laurence said gently, "my dear, if you wish dragons to be free to choose their own way, you must be prepared that some of them will wish to make no alteration; it is what they are used to, after all."

"Yes, but surely anyone can see that it is nicer to be able to *choose*," Temeraire said. "It is not as though I do not want to fight, whatever that booby Eroica says," he added, with abrupt and mounting indignation, his head coming up off the ground and the ruff spreading, "and what he has to say to anything, when he does not think of anything but counting the number of wingbeats between one turn and the next, I should like to know; at least I am not stupid enough to practice ten times a day just how best to show my belly to anyone who likes to come at me from the flank."

Laurence received this stroke of temper with dismay, and tried to apply himself to soothing Temeraire's jangled nerves, but to little success.

"He said that I ought to practice my formations instead of complaining," Temeraire continued heatedly, "when I could roll them up in two passes, the way they fly; *he* ought to stay at home and eat cows all day long, for the good they will do in a battle."

At last he allowed himself to be calmed, and Laurence thought nothing more of it; but in the morning, sitting and reading with Temeraire—now puzzling laboriously, for his benefit, through a famous novel by the writer Goethe, a piece of somewhat dubious morality called *Die Leiden des jungen Werther*—Laurence saw the formations go up for their battle-drills, and Temeraire, still smarting, took the opportunity to make a great many critical remarks upon their form, which seemed to Laurence accurate so far as he could follow them.

"Do you suppose he is only in a savage mood, or mistaken?" Laurence privately asked Granby, afterwards. "Surely such flaws cannot have escaped them, all this time?"

"Well, I don't say I have a perfectly clear picture of what he is talking about," Granby said, "but he isn't wrong in any of it so far as I can tell, and you recall how handy he was at thinking up those new formations, back during our training. It's a pity we've never yet had a chance of putting them to work."

"I hope I do not seem to be critical," Laurence said to Dyhern that evening. "But though his ideas are at times unusual, Temeraire is remarkably clever at such things, and I would consider myself amiss not to raise the question to you."

Dyhern eyed Laurence's makeshift and hasty diagrams, and then shook his head smiling faintly. "No, no; I take no offense; how could I, when you so politely bore my own interference?" he said. "Your point is well-taken: what's right for one, is not always fair for the other. Strange how very different the tempers of dragons can be. He would be unhappy and resentful, if you were always correcting or denying him, I expect."

"Oh, no," Laurence said, dismayed. "Dyhern, I meant to make no such implication; I beg you believe me quite sincere in wishing to draw to your attention a possible weakness in our defense, and nothing more."

Dyhern did not seem convinced, but he did look over the diagrams a little longer, and then stood up and clapped Laurence on the shoulder. "Come, do not worry," he said. "Of course there are some openings you here have found; there is no maneuver without its points of weakness. But it is not so easy to exploit a little weakness in the air, as it might seem upon paper. Frederick the Great himself approved these drills; with them we beat the French at Rossbach; we will beat them again here."

With this reply Laurence had to be content, but he went away dissatisfied; a dragon properly trained ought be a better judge of aerial maneuvers than any man, it seemed to him, and Dyhern's answer more willful blindness than sound military judgment.

CHAPTER 12

The inner councils of the army were wholly opaque to Laurence; the barrier of language and their establishment in the covert, far from most other divisions of the army, distanced him twice over even from the usual rumors that went floating through the camp. What little he heard was contradictory and vague: they would be concentrating at Erfurt, they would be concentrating at Hof; they would catch the French at the River Saale, or at the Main; and meanwhile the weather was turning to autumnal chill and the leaves to yellow around their edges, without any movement.

Nearly two weeks had crept by in camp, and then at last the word came: Prince Louis summoned the captains to a nearby farmhouse for dinner, fed them handsomely out of his own purse, and to their even greater satisfaction enlightened them a little.

"We mean to make a push south, through the Thuringian forest passes," he said. "General Hohenlohe will advance through Hof towards Bamberg, while General Brunswick and the main army go through Erfurt towards Würzburg," he went on, pointing out the locations on a great map spread out over the dinner table, the destination towns near the known positions where the French Army had been established over the summer. "We have still not heard that Bonaparte has left Paris. If they choose to sit in their cantonments and wait for us, all the better. We will strike them before they know what has happened."

Their own destination, as part of the advance guard, would be the town of Hof, on the borders of the great forest. The march would not be quick; so many men were not easily supplied, and there were some seventy miles to cover. Meanwhile along their route supply-depots had to be established, particularly with herds for the dragons, and the lines of communication secured. But with all these caveats, still Laurence went back to the clearing with much satisfaction: at last, to know something and to be moving was a thousand times better, no matter how slow it would seem to abruptly be bounded by the speed of infantry and cavalry, dragging their guns along in waggons.

"But why do we not go farther out ahead?" Temeraire said, when an easy two hours' flight had brought them, the next morning, to their new covert. "It is not as though we are doing anything of use here but making ourselves some clearings; even those slow dragons can manage flying a little longer, surely."

"They don't want us getting too far off from the infantry," Granby said. "For our sake as much as theirs; if we went off on our own and ran into a troop of French dragons with a regiment of their own infantry and a couple of guns to back them up, we shouldn't enjoy it above half."

In such a case, the enemy dragons would have a clear advantage, the field guns giving them a space of safety in which to regroup and rest, and providing a zone of danger against which the dragons without infantry support could be pinned. But despite this explanation, Temeraire still sighed, and only grumblingly reconciled himself to knocking down some more trees, for firewood and to clear space for himself and the Prussian dragons, while they waited for the marching infantry to catch up.

In this creeping manner they had covered barely twenty-five miles in two days, when abruptly their orders were changed.

"We will be massing first at Jena," Prince Louis said, shrugging ruefully at the vagaries of the senior officers, who continued to meet daily, ferried back and forth by dragon-couriers. "General Brunswick wishes to move all the army together through Erfurt instead."

"First we move not at all, and now we change directions," Laurence said to Granby, with some irritation; they had already gone farther south than Jena and now would have to travel some distance northward as well as west; with the slow pace of the infantry it might mean half-a-day lost. "They would do better to have fewer of these conferences, and to more point."

The army was not assembled around Jena until early October; by then Temeraire was hardly the only one irritated with the pace. Even the most stolid of the Prussian dragons were restless at being held on so short a rein, and strained their necks out westward daily, as if they might win a few more miles by wishing for them. The town was upon the banks of the great Saale River, broad and unfordable, which would serve well as a barrier to defend. Their original destination of Hof lay only twenty miles farther south along its course, and Laurence, studying the maps laid out in the impromptu captains' mess organized in a large pavilion, shook his head; the change of position seemed to him a retreat without cause.

"No, you see, some of the cavalry and infantry have been sent ahead to Hof anyway," Dyhern said. "A little bit of bait, to make them think we are coming that way, and then we pour down on them through Erfurt and Würzburg, and catch them still in parts."

It sounded well enough, but there was a small obstacle to the plan, shortly discovered: the French were already in Würzburg. The news traveled round the camp like wildfire, scarcely moments after the panting courier had ducked into the commander's tent, reaching even the aviators with scarcely any delay.

"They say Napoleon himself is there," one of the other captains said, "the Imperial Guard is at Mainz, and his Marshals are all over Bavaria: the whole Grande Armée is mobilized."

"Well, and so much the better," Dyhern opined. "At least no

more of this damned marching, thank God! Let them come to us
for their thrashing."

Into this sentiment they were all prepared to enter, and a sudden energy gripped the camp; all sensed that battle was close at
hand, as the senior officers again closeted themselves for intense
discussions. There was no shortage of news and rumors now:
every hour, it seemed, some fresh piece of intelligence reached
them, though still the Prussians were sending out scarcely any
reconnaissance missions, for fear of their capture.

"You will enjoy this, gentlemen," Prince Louis said, coming
into their mess. "Napoleon has made a *dragon* an officer: it has
been seen giving orders to the captains of his aerial corps."

"Its captain, surely," one of the Prussian officers protested.

"No, it has none at all, nor any kind of crew," Prince Louis
said, laughing; Laurence, however, found nothing amusing in
the news, particularly when confirmed in his suspicion that the
dragon in question was entirely white.

"We will see to it you have a chance at her on the field, never
fear," Dyhern said only, when Laurence had briefly acquainted
them all with Lien and her history. "Ha ha! Maybe the French
will not have been practicing their formations, if she is in charge?
Making a dragon an officer; next he will promote his horse to
general."

"It does not seem at all silly to *me*," Temeraire said, with a
sniff, when this had been passed along; he was disgruntled at the
news of Lien's preferment among the French, when contrasted
with his own treatment by the Prussians.

"But she can't know a thing about battles, Temeraire, not like
you," Granby said. "Yongxing kicked up such a fuss about Celestials not fighting; she shan't ever have been in one herself."

"My mother said that Lien was a very great scholar," Temeraire said, "and there are many Chinese books about aerial tactics; there is one by the Yellow Emperor himself, though I did
not have a chance to read it," he finished regretfully.

"Oh, things out of books," Granby said, waving a hand.

Laurence said grimly, "Bonaparte is no fool. I am sure he has
their strategy well in his own hands; and if giving Lien rank were

enough excuse to convince her to come into the battle, I am sure he would make her a Marshal of France, and call it cheap at the price; it is the divine wind we must fear now, and what it may do to the Prussian forces, not her generalship."

"If she tries to hurt our friends, I will stop her," Temeraire said, adding, under his breath, "but I am sure *she* is not wasting time on silly formations."

THEY MOVED OUT of Jena early the next morning, with Prince Louis and the rest of the advance guard, for the town of Saal-feld, a cautious ten miles south of the rest of the army, to await the French advance. All was quiet on their arrival; Laurence took a moment to go into the town before the infantry should come in, hoping through the offices of Lieutenant Badenhaur, one of the young Prussian officers added to his crew, to acquire some decent wine and better provender; having replenished his funds in Dresden, he now meant to give his senior officers a din-ner that night, and arrange for some special provision for the rest of his crew. The first battle could come now at any day, and both supplies and the time to prepare them would likely grow short during the ensuing maneuvers.

The Saale River trotted briskly astride their course, energetic though the autumn rains had not yet begun. Laurence paused, halfway across the bridge, and thrust a long branch into the water: down to the limit of his arm, not yet at the bottom, and then as he knelt lower to try and reach a little farther, a surge of the current pulled it roughly from his hand.

"I would not like to try and ford that; and least of all with artillery," Laurence said, wiping his hands as he came off the bridge; though Badenhaur barely knew any English, he nodded in full agreement: translation was scarcely necessary.

The inhabitants were not well-pleased with the coming inva-sion of their sleepy little town, but the shopkeepers were ready enough to be mollified with gold, even if the women closed the shutters on the upper stories of their houses with some vehe-mence as they walked past. They made their arrangements with the keeper of a small inn, who was despondently willing to sell many of his provisions, before the main body of troops should arrive and likely commandeer the rest. He lent them also a couple of his young sons to carry the supplies back. "Pray tell them there is nothing to fear," Laurence told Badenhaur, as they crossed back over the river and drew near the covert, the excited dragons making an unusually loud noise chattering with one another; the boys' eyes had grown saucer-wide in their faces.

They were not much comforted by whatever Badenhaur said, and ran off home almost before Laurence managed to give them each a few pennies in thanks. As they left the food, however, delicious smells rising from the baskets, nobody much minded. Gong Su took charge of the meals; he had by now mostly acquired the role of cook for the men as well as Temeraire, that duty ordinarily rotated about the men of the ground crew, and rarely well-performed. They had all gradually grown used to the creeping inclusion of Oriental spices and preparations in their food, until now they would most likely have noticed their absence more.

The cook was left otherwise unoccupied. Eroica said to Temeraire, as the dragons assembled for their own repast, "Come and eat with us! Fresh meat is what you need, on the eve of a battle; hot blood puts fire into the breast," encouragingly; and Temeraire, who could not conceal he was pleased to be so invited, assented and indeed tore into his cow with great eagerness, if he did lick his chops clean with more fastidiousness than the rest, and wash himself in the river after.

There was nearly a holiday atmosphere by the time the first of the cavalry squadrons began to come across the river, and the sounds and smells of horses reached them through the curtain of trees, the creak and the sharp smell of oil from the gun-carriages: the rest of the men would not arrive until morning. As dusk came on, Laurence took Temeraire for a short solitary flight to let him dissipate some of the nervous energy which had set him to clawing the ground again. They went high up, so as not to alarm the horses, and Temeraire hovered a while squinting through the twilight.

"Laurence, will we not be left very open, on this ground?" Temeraire asked, craning his head around. "We cannot get back across the river very quickly, if there is only that one bridge; and there are all those woods about."

"We do not mean to cross back over; we are holding the bridge for the rest of the army," Laurence explained. "If they came up and the French were in possession of this bank, it would be very difficult to cross over in the face of their resistance, so we must hold it if ever we can."

"But I do not see any more of the army coming," Temeraire said. "What I mean is, I can see Prince Louis and the rest of the advance guard, but no one else behind us; and there are a great many campfires over there, in front."

"That damned infantry is creeping along again, I dare say," Laurence said, squinting northward himself; he could just make out the lights of Prince Louis's carriage, swaying along the road towards the encampment around the town, and beyond that nothing but darkness, far into the distance; while in the south, small smoky campfires were winking in and out of view, like fireflies, brilliant in the thickening dark: the French were less than a mile away.

PRINCE LOUIS WAS not backwards in his response: by dawn his battalions were moving rapidly over the bridge and taking up their positions. Some eight thousand men with more than forty-four guns to support them, though half of them were the conscripted Saxons, whose mutterings were all the louder now that the French were known to be so near. The first musket-shots began to ring out only a little later: not the real beginning of a battle, only the advance outposts trading a little desultory fire with the French scouts.

By nine in the morning, the French were coming out of the hills, keeping well back in the trees where the dragons could not easily get at them. Eroica led his formation in threatening great sweeps over their heads, with Temeraire following after them, but with little effect; Temeraire had been forbidden to use the divine wind, so near to the cavalry. To their general frustration, they were shortly signaled back, so that the cavalry and infantry might make their way forward and engage.

Eroica threw out a signal-flag; "Down, land," Badenhaur, sitting close at Laurence's left, translated, and they all dropped down into the covert again: a panting runner was there with fresh orders for Captain Dyhern.

"Well, my friends, we are in luck," Dyhern called back to all the formation cheerfully, waving the packet overhead. "That is Marshal Lannes over there, and there is a pile of eagles to be won today! The cavalry will have their turn for a while; we are to try and come around behind them, and see if we can scare up a few French dragons to fight with."

They went up again, high over the battlefield: with the pressure of the dragon-formation lifted, the French skirmishers had burst out of the woods to engage the front ranks of Prince Louis's forces, and behind them marched out a single battalion of infantry in line and some squadrons of light cavalry: not yet a great commitment of forces, but the battle was properly joined, and now the guns began to speak in their deep thundering voices. Shadows were moving through the wooded hills; impossible to make out their exact movements, and as Laurence turned his glass upon them, Temeraire let out a ringing roar: a French formation of dragons had lifted into the air, and was coming for them.

The formation was considerably larger than Eroica's, but made almost wholly of smaller dragons, most of them lightweights and even a few courier-types among them. They had none of the crispness that marked the Prussian maneuvers: they had formed into a sort of pyramid, but a shaky one, and were beating up at such different speeds that they were changing places with one another as they came.

Eroica and his formation came about in perfect order to meet the onrushing French, spreading out into a doubled-line, at two heights. Temeraire was nearly turning himself in circles, trying not to overshoot their left flank, where Laurence had set him to take up position; but the Prussians were in formation before the

French reached them, and riflemen aboard each dragon leveled their guns for the devastating volley-fire for which the Prussians were justly feared.

But just as they came into rifle-range, and the guns began to crack, the French formation dissolved into even more complete chaos, dragons darting in every direction; and the Prussian volley made almost no impression. A very neat piece of work, tempting the volley out of them, Laurence was forced to acknowledge; but he did not at once see the point: it would not do them much good, when the little French dragons did not carry the manpower to return fire in kind.

They did not seem to wish to, either; instead, they only circled around in a frantic, buzzing cloud, keeping a safe distance too far for boarding, and their crews firing off shots almost at random, picking off men here and there, dashing in for a moment to claw or snap at the Prussian dragons in any opening they were given. Of those, there were many; Temeraire's peevish criticisms were proving all too accurate, and nearly every dragon of the Prussian force was soon marked and bleeding, here and there, as bewildered they tried to go about in one direction or another, to face their opponents properly.

Temeraire, moving alone, was able best to avoid the skirmishing smaller dragons and pay them back; with no threat of boarding and gunnery only a waste of ammunition against such small quick targets, Laurence only gave him his head, and waved his men to stay low and keep out of the way. Pursuing fiercely, Temeraire caught one after another of the littler French dragons, giving them each a vigorous shake and clawing that had them squalling in pain and retreating hastily from the field.

But he was only one, and there were a great many more of the small dragons than he alone could catch; Laurence would have liked to try and tell Dyhern to break up the formation, and let the single dragons fight as they would: at least they would not have been rendering themselves so predictably vulnerable, over and over, and their heavier weight ought to have told badly against the smaller dragons. He had no opportunity, but after a few more passes Dyhern reached the same conclusion: another signal-flag went up, and the formation broke apart; the blood-ied, pain-maddened dragons threw themselves with renewed energy at the French.

"No, no!" Temeraire cried, startling Laurence; and whipping his head around said, "Laurence, down there, look—"

He leaned over the side of Temeraire's neck, already pulling out his glass: a great body of French infantry were coming out of the woods to the west, enveloping Prince Louis's right flank, and the center was being pressed back by hard, determined fighting: men were falling back over the bridge, and the cavalry had no room to charge. Just now would have been the ideal moment for a dragon-sweep, to drive back the flanking attempt, but with the formation broken up it was almost sure to fail.

"Temeraire, go!" Laurence cried, and already drawing in his breath, Temeraire folded his wings and arrowed downwards, towards the encroaching French troops on the west: his sides swelled out, and Laurence pressed his hands over his ears to muffle a little of that terrible roaring force, as Temeraire unleashed the divine wind. His pass complete, he swept up and away; dozens of men lay crumpled and still upon the ground, blood oozing from their nostrils and their ears and their eyes, and the smaller trees lying cast around them like matchsticks.

The Prussian defenders were a little more dazed themselves than heartened, however, and in their shocked pause a French-man in an officer's uniform leapt from the trees and out amongst his own dead, holding up a standard, and shouted, *"Vive l'Empereur! Vive la France!"* He charged forward, and behind him came all the rest of the French advance guard, nearly two thousand men, and poured down against the Prussians, hacking away with their bayonets and sabers, getting in amongst them so Temeraire could not strike again without killing as many of their own side.

The case was growing desperate: everywhere the infantrymen were being forced into the Saale River and dragged down by the current and the weight of their own boots, the horses' hooves slipping on the banks. With Temeraire hovering, searching for an opening, Laurence saw Prince Louis rally the rest of the cavalry for a charge at the center. The horses massed around him, and with a roar and thunder they threw themselves gallantly forward, to meet the French hussars with an impact like a ringing bell, swords against sabers. The clash stirred up the thick black clouds of gunpowder smoke around them, to cling to the horses' legs and go whirling about them like a storm. Laurence hoped, for a moment; and then he saw Prince Louis fall, the sword spilling from his hand, and a terrible cheer rose from the French as the Prussian colors went down beside him.

NO RESCUE CAME. The Saxon battalions broke first and spilled wildly across the bridge, or flung down their arms in surrender; the Prussians held in small pockets, as Prince Louis's subordinates tried to hold the men together and withdraw in good order. Most of the guns were being abandoned upon the field, and the French were raking the Prussians with a deadly fire, men toppling to the ground or falling into the river in droves as they tried to flee. Others began to retreat northward along the line of the river.

The bridge fell, scarcely after noon; by then, Temeraire and the other dragons were only engaged in defending the retreat, trying to keep the small darting French dragons from turning the withdrawal into a complete rout. They did not meet with much success; the Saxons were in full flight, and the smaller French dragons were snatching up artillery and horses alike away from the Prussian forces, some with screaming men still aboard, and depositing them back into the hands of the French infantry, now establishing themselves upon the far bank of the Saale, amidst the still-shuttered buildings of the town.

The fighting was all but over; the signal-flags *sauve qui peut* fluttered sadly from the ruin of the Prussian position, and the clouds of smoke were drifting away. The French dragons fell back at last, as the retreat drew too far away from their infantry support, and all drooping and weary Temeraire and the Prussian dragons came to earth to catch their breath at Dyhern's signal.

He did not attempt to cheer them; there was no cheer to be

had. The littlest dragon of the formation, a light-weight, was carrying carefully in his talons the broken body of Prince Louis, recovered in a desperate lunge from the battlefield. Dyhern only said briefly, "Collect your ground crews, and fall back on Jena; we will rendezvous there."

CHAPTER 13

Laurence had put down his ground crew deep in the country-side on the far bank of the Saale, tucked into a well-hidden forested defile, not easily seen from above; they were standing all together, the strongest of the hands in front with axes and sabers and pistols held ready, and Keynes and the runners to the back, the eggs tucked safely in their swaddling and harness near a small screened-off fire.

"We heard the guns going near since you left us, sir," Fellowes said, anxiously, even as he and his men began looking over Temeraire's harness for damage.

"Yes," Laurence said, "they overran our position; we are falling back on Jena." He felt as though he were speaking from a great distance; an immense weariness had hold of him, which could not be allowed to show. "A ration of rum for all the flight crew; see to it if you please, Mr. Roland, Mr. Dyer," he said, letting himself down; Emily and Dyer carried the spirit bottles around, with a glass, and the men each drank their tot. Laurence took his own last, with gratitude; the hot liquor was at least an immediate presence.

He went back to speak with Keynes over the eggs. "No harm at all," the surgeon said. "They could keep like this a month without difficulties."

"Have you any better sense of when we may expect the hatching?" Laurence asked.

"Nothing whatsoever has changed," Keynes said, in his peevish way. "We still have anywhere from three weeks to five, or I should have said."

"Very good," Laurence said, and sent him to look over Temeraire, in case there should be any sign of injury to his muscles, a result of overextending himself, which in the heat of battle or the present sorrow he might not have noticed.

"It was mostly that they took us by surprise," Temeraire said miserably, as Keynes clambered over him, "and those wretched formations; oh, Laurence, I ought to have said more, and made them listen."

"There was scarcely any hope of your doing so under the circumstances," Laurence said. "Do not reproach yourself; think rather how the formation movements might most easily be amended, without causing them great confusion. I hope we may persuade them to heed your advice, now, and if so, we will have repaired a grave fault in tactics, at no more cost than the loss of one skirmish; as painful a lesson as it has been, we will then count ourselves fortunate it was no worse."

THEY ARRIVED AT Jena in the small hours of the morning; the army was drawing up close around the town, withdrawing in upon itself. The French had captured a badly needed supply-train at Gera, and the depots in the town were near-empty. There was only a single small sheep for Temeraire to eat; Gong Su stretched it by stewing, with the addition of some aromatics which he had gathered, and Temeraire made a better meal than the men, who had to make do with a sort of hastily cooked porridge, and hard-baked bread.

There was an ugly murmuring all through the camp, as Laurence walked by the fires: Saxon stragglers coming in from the battlefield were murmuring that they had borne the brunt of the attack, sacrificed to try and hold the French; and worse yet, there had been another defeat: General Tauentzein, retreating from Hof in the face of the French advance, had backed out of Marshal Soult's arms and straight into Marshal Bernadotte's, from frying-pan to fire, and had lost four hundred men before at last escaping. Enough to disquiet any man, much less those who had been counting on an easy, assured victory; there was little sign of that early supreme confidence anymore.

He found Dyhern and the other Prussian aviators having claimed a small ramshackle cottage, hastily deserted by its peasant tenants when the dragons descended upon their fields, for their meager comfort. "I am not proposing any wholesale alteration," Laurence said urgently, laying out his diagrams, sketched to Temeraire's orders, "only what changes can easily be accommodated; whatever risks are entailed in so desperate a change in the final hour can scarcely be measured against the certainty of disaster, if nothing be done."

"You are kind enough not to say, *I told you so,*" Dyhern said, "but I hear it nonetheless. Very well; we will let a dragon be our instructor, and see what can be done; at least we will not be sitting in covert licking our wounds, like dogs after a beating."

He and his fellow captains had been sitting gloomily around the mostly bare table, drinking in silence; now he rallied himself and them both with an immense effort, and by sheer force of personality put fresh heart into them, chiding them for getting into the dumps, and very nearly dragged them bodily outside and back to their dragons. The activity perked up their heads and spirits, Temeraire not least of all; he sat up bright-eyed as they all assembled and gladly threw himself into the exercise, showing them the new flying-patterns which he had devised.

To these Laurence and Granby had contributed little but simplified much; elaborate maneuvers which Temeraire could perform without a thought were simply beyond the physical agility of most Western dragon breeds. Even considerably slowed down, the new patterns gave the Prussians, so long inculcated with their formal drills, some difficulty at first, but the precision which informed their regular practice slowly began to tell, and after a dozen passes or so they were tired but triumphant. Some of the other dragons with the army had crept up to observe, and shortly after their officers came too; when Dyhern and his formation dropped down at last for a rest, they were quickly mobbed with questions, and shortly a couple of other formations were in the air trying their own hand.

Their practice was interrupted that afternoon, however, by a fresh change of plans: the army was concentrating anew about Weimar, with intentions of falling back to protect their lines of communications with Berlin, and once again the dragons would lead the way. An angry grumbling met this news; before now all the marching hither and yon, the changing orders, had been taken in good spirits, viewed as the inevitable shifting course of a war. But to fall back again now pell-mell, as if a couple of small French victories were enough to chase them home, was infuriating to all; and the confusion of orders took on the more unsettling cast of a lack of decision among the commanders.

In this hostile mood, the further news reached them that the ill-fated Prince Louis had taken his position across the Saale in answer to unclear orders by Hohenlohe, which had indeed implied an advance in progress, though this same advance had not been properly authorized by Brunswick or the King; the whole army had never stirred southward in the end, Hohenlohe evidently thinking better of his plans.

"He sent fresh orders to fall back," Dyhern said, bitterly, having heard the news from one of Prince Louis's aides-de-camp, who had just struggled back to camp, on foot, his poor horse having foundered crossing the Saale. "But we were already engaged by then, and our prince had not an hour left of life; so has Prussia thrown away one of her finest soldiers."

They could not be said to be mutinous, but they were very angry all, and worse than that discouraged; the sense of achievement built over the afternoon worn away. They went silently to their several clearings to oversee the work of packing.

THE SOUND OF the courier-dragon leaving the covert had begun to be a hateful noise, signifying yet another of the endless futile conferences was under way. Laurence woke to that flurry of wings in the still-black hours of the morning, and rolled out of his tent in bare feet and shirtsleeves to scrub his face at the water-barrel: no frost yet, but more than cold enough to wake a man properly. Temeraire lay sleeping still, breath coming in warm puffs from his nostrils; Salyer looked up alertly when Laurence glanced into the cramped half-sized tent where he and the snoring Allen had kept the night's watch over the eggs: the warmest place in camp, the fabric doubled over and the brazier coals glowing.

They were in covert now a little ways north of Jena, near the eastern edge of the Prussian Army, almost united: the Duke of Brunswick had moved his own forces closer during the night. The whole countryside seemed alive with campfires, whose smoke mingled sadly with the burning town in the distance: something between a panic and a riot had broken out among Hohenlohe's forces the previous night over too little food and too much bad news. The French advance guard had been sighted again just to the south, and several anticipated supply-trains had not arrived; too much, particularly for the Saxons, reluctant allies to begin with and now thoroughly disenchanted.

Separated from the rest of the camp as the covert was, Laurence had not seen much of the unhappy events, but before calm could be restored, fires had caught among the buildings, and now the morning air was acrid and bitter with the floating ash and smoke, damp with dense fog. It was early on the thirteenth of October; almost a month now since their arrival in Prussia, and still he had received no word from England, the post slow and uncertain with the countryside full of armed men. Standing alone with his tea at the edge of the clearing, he looked northwards yearning; he deeply felt the want of connection, so tantalizingly close, and he had rarely known so great a desire to be at home, even when a thousand miles more distant.

The sun was beginning to make some forays towards dawn, but the fog held on grimly, a thick grey mist blanketing all the encampment. Sounds traveled only a short way, deadened queerly, or came seemingly out of nowhere, so one saw ghostly silent figures moving without sound and in another direction heard disembodied voices floating. The men rose sluggishly and went about their work without speaking much one to the other: tired and hungry.

The orders came shortly after ten in the morning: the main body of the army would retreat northwards through Auerstadt, while Hohenlohe's forces kept their position, covering the retreat. Laurence read it silently and handed it back to Dyhern's runner without comment: he would not speak critically of the Prussian command to a Prussian officer. The Prussians were less reticent amongst themselves, loud in their own tongue as the instructions went around.

"They say we ought to give the French a proper battle here, and I think they are quite right," Temeraire said. "Why are we here at all, if not to fight? We might have stayed at Dresden, for all this marching we have been doing; it is as though we are running away."

"It is not our place to say such things," Laurence said. "There may be intelligence which we lack that makes sense of all these maneuvers." This was a small sop to comfort; he did not very much believe it himself.

They were not themselves to move at any time soon, and as the dragons had been fed but poorly three days running now, orders were given not to ask them for any exertions, since at any moment they might be called on for a fresh march or a battle, though that at least seemed now less likely. Temeraire settled to drowse and dream of sheep, and Laurence said to Granby, "John, I am going to go and have a look around from higher ground, outside this blasted fog," leaving him in command.

A FLAT-TOPPED HEIGHT, the Landgrafenberg, commanded the plateau and valley of Jena: Laurence took young Badenhaur as his guide again and together they pushed their way up through a narrow winding ravine that led up its wooded slopes, choked in places by wicked-thorned blackberry bushes. Farther up, the track faded out into the tall grasses: no one had mowed the hay here, the hill too steep to bother, though here and there the taller trees had been cut, and level clearings trampled flat by sheep: a couple of them looked up incuriously and trotted off into the bracken.

Sweating, they gained the summit after almost an hour of toil. "So," Badenhaur said, waving his hand inarticulately at the fine prospect; Laurence nodded. A ring of smoke-blue mountains closed off the view in the far distance, but from their ideal vantage point all the bowl of the valley was spread in a circle around them almost like a living map, its gentler hills furred by yellowing beeches and smaller stands of evergreens, a few white-skinned birches stark among them. The fields were mostly brown-yellow and flat, much of the harvest taken in, muted in the thin autumnal light that made the day seem already far advanced and threw the scattered farmhouses into brilliant relief.

A heavy bank of clouds moving steadily westward presently blocked off the morning sun from their immediate view, the shadow creeping up and over the hills. By contrast a fragment of the Saale River nestled among the hills farther away caught the sunlight full-on and blazed incandescent at them, until Laurence found his eyes almost watering with the brilliance. The wind rose, a low fire-crackling sound of crumpled leaves and dry branches, and under that the deeper hollow roar, rather like a sail first belling out, but going on and on without an end. Otherwise there was an immense silence. The air tasted, smelled, strangely barren: no animal fragrance or rot, the ground already hard with frost.

On the side of the mountain from which they had come, the Prussian Army lay in its serried ranks, mostly obscured under the thick blanket of fog; but here and there the sunlight flickered valiantly on bayonets as Brunswick's legions started to draw away north towards Auerstadt. Laurence cautiously went to peer over the opposite side, where the town lay; there was no definite sign of the French, but the fires in Jena were going out: the orange glowing remnants, like coals from this height, faded one by one amid indistinct voices shouting; Laurence could just dimly make out the forms of horses with carts going to and from the river, carrying water.

He stood a while contemplating the ground, pantomiming to Badenhaur with occasional recourse to the handful of French they both possessed, and then they both went still at once; a breath of wind blew the thick climbing pillar of smoke away from the town, and revealed a dragon coming into view from the east: it was Lien, flying over the river and the town in a quick, hummingbird progress, stopping to hover here and again. There was one startled moment where Laurence had the illusion of her flying directly towards them: a moment only, and then he realized it was no illusion.

Badenhaur pulled on his arm, and together they threw themselves flat to the ground and crawled underneath the blackberry bushes, the long thorns scratching and pulling. Some twenty feet in they found a refuge hollowed out from the ground and the bramble: the work of sheep. The branches kept rustling after they had settled themselves in the low depression, and after a moment a sheep came struggling and kicking to join them in the little hollow, leaving behind great tufts of its wool strung from the thorns, a welcome screen. It flung itself down shivering beside them, perhaps finding some comfort in human company in its turn, as the white dragon folded her great wings and let herself down gracefully onto the summit.

Laurence tensed, waiting; if she had seen them, if she were hunting them, a stand of blackberry would hardly keep her off for long. But she looked away, interested rather in the prospect which they themselves had been examining. There was something different in her appearance: in China he had seen her wear elaborate ensembles of gold and rubies; in Istanbul she had been wholly bare of jewels; but now she wore a very different piece, something like a diadem set around the base of her ruff and hooked cleverly under the edges and the jaw, made of shining steel rather than gold, and secure in the center one enormous diamond nearly the size of a chicken's egg, which blazed insolently even in the thin morning light.

A man in a French officer's uniform let himself down off her back and sprang to the ground. Laurence was deeply surprised to see that she had tolerated a passenger, still less one so undistinguished; the officer was bareheaded, dark hair short and thinning, in only a heavy leather coat flung over a *chasseur*'s uniform, high black boots over breeches, with a serviceable sword slung at his waist.

"Here is a fine thing, all our hosts assembled to greet us," he said, his French oddly accented, opening up a glass to survey over the Prussian Army with particular attention to the ranks flowing away onto the road north. "We've kept them waiting too long; but that will soon be attended to. Davout and Bernadotte will send those fellows back to us presently. I do not see the banner of the King, do you?"

"No, and we should not wait here to find it, with no outposts established. You are too exposed," Lien said, in disapproving tones, looking only indifferently over the field: her blood-red eyes were not very strong.

"Come now, surely I am safe in your company!" the officer chided her, laughing, and his smile, which momentarily he turned flashing up to her, gave light to his whole face.

Badenhaur was gripping Laurence's arm almost with convulsive pressure. "Bonaparte," the Prussian hissed, when Laurence glanced at him. Shocked, Laurence turned back around, leaning closer to the bramble for a better look: the man was not particularly stunted, as he had always imagined the Corsican to be from the depictions in the British newspapers, but rather compact than short. At present, animated with energy, his large grey eyes brilliant and his face a little flushed from the cold wind, he might even have been called handsome.

"There is no hurry," Bonaparte added. "We can give them another three-quarters of an hour, I think, and let them send another division onto the road. A little walking to and fro will put them in just the right frame of mind."

He spent most of this allotted time pacing back and forth along the ridge, gazing thoughtfully out at the plateau below, much of the raptor in his expression, while Laurence and Badenhaur, trapped, were forced to endure an agony of apprehension on the behalf of their fellows. A shudder by his side made Laurence look; Badenhaur's hand had crept towards his pistol, a look of terrible indecision crossing the lieutenant's face.

Laurence put his hand on Badenhaur's arm, restraining, and the young man dropped his eyes at once, pale and ashamed, and let his hand down; Laurence silently gave his shoulder a rough shake for comfort. The temptation he could well understand; impossible not to entertain the wildest thoughts, when scarcely ten yards distant stood the architect of all Europe's woes. If there had been any hope of making him prisoner, it should certainly have been their duty to attempt it, however likely to end in personal disaster; but no attack out of the brush could possibly have succeeded. Their first movement would alert Lien; and Laurence from personal experience knew well how quickly a Celestial could take action. Their only possible chance was indeed the pistol: an assassin's shot, from their concealed position, at his unsuspecting back: no.

Their duty was plain; they would have to wait, concealing themselves, and then bear the intelligence back to camp as quickly as they could muster, that Napoleon was closing upon them the jaws of a trap; the biter might yet be bit, and an honorable victory won. But in this task every minute should count, and it was a thorough-going torture to be forced to lie quiet and still, watching the Emperor at his meditations.

"The fog is blowing off," Lien said, her tail flicking uneasily; she was squinting narrowly down towards the positions of Hohenlohe's artillery, which had the mountain in their view. "You should not be risking yourself like this; let us go at once. Besides, you have had all the reports you need."

"Yes, yes, my nursemaid," Bonaparte said absently, looking again through his glass. "But it is a different thing to see with one's own eyes. There are at least five errors in the elevations on my maps, even without surveying, and those are not three-pounders but six with that horse artillery on their left."

"An Emperor cannot also be a scout," she said severely. "If

you cannot trust your subordinates, you ought to replace them, not do their work."

"Behold me properly lectured!" Bonaparte said, with mock indignation. "Even Berthier does not speak to me like this."

"He ought to, when you are being foolish," she said. "Come; you do not want to provoke them into coming up here and trying to hold the summit," she added, cajolingly.

"Ah, they have missed their chance for that," he said. "But very well, I will indulge you; it is time we got about the business in any case." He put away his glass finally and stepped into her waiting cupped talons as though he had been used to being handled by a dragon all his life.

Badenhaur was scrambling heedlessly through the bramble almost before she was away. Laurence burst out into the clearing behind him and stopped to look over the prospect one last time, searching for the French Army. The fog was turning thin and insubstantial, wisping away, and now he could see clearly around Jena the corps of Marshal Lannes busy heaping up depots of ammunition and food, salvaging for their shelter wood and materials from the burnt-out husks of the buildings, putting up empty pens. But though Laurence pulled out his glass and looked in every direction, he could see no sign of any other mass of French troops immediately visible, certainly not this side of the Saale River; where Bonaparte meant to get his men from, to launch any sort of attack, he could not see.

"We may yet be able to seize these heights, before he can get his men established," Laurence said absently, only half to Badenhaur. A battery of artillery, from this position, would offer a commanding advantage over the plateau; small wonder Bonaparte meant to seize it. But he had been backwards, it seemed, in getting a foothold.

And then the dragons began popping up over the distant woods like jack-in-the-boxes: not the light-weights they had encountered in battle at Saalfeld, but the middle-weights who made up the bulk of any aerial force: Pêcheurs and Papillons, coming at great speed and out of formation. They landed among the French troops securing Jena, something very odd in their appearance. Looking closer through the glass, Laurence realized that they were all of them almost covered over with men: not their own crews only, but whole companies of infantry, clinging on to silk carrying-harnesses, of the same style which he had seen used in China for the ordinary transport of citizens, only far more crowded.

Every man had his own gun and knapsack; the largest of the dragons bore a hundred men or more. And their talons were not empty: they carried, laboring, also whole caissons of ammunition, enormous sacks of food, and, shockingly, nets full of live animals: these, being deposited into the pens and cut free, went wandering about in aimless daze, knocking into the walls and falling over, as visibly drugged as the pigs Temeraire had carried over the mountains, not so very long ago. Laurence sinkingly recognized the damnable cleverness of the scheme: if the French dragons had carried their own rations with them in this manner, there could be any number of them brought along, and not the few dozen which were counted the sum total who could be sustained by an army on the march through hostile territory.

In the course of ten minutes, nearly a thousand men had been assembled on the ground, and the dragons were already turning back for fresh loads; they were coming, Laurence estimated, scarcely a distance of five miles, but five miles with no road, heavily forested and broken by the river. A corps of men would ordinarily have taken a few hours to come across it; instead in minutes they were landing in their new positions.

How Bonaparte had induced his men to consent to attach themselves to dragons and be carried through the air, Laurence could scarcely imagine and had no time to consider; Badenhaur was inarticulately pulling him away. In the distance were rising the heavy-weights of l'Armée de l'Air, the great Chevaliers and Chansons-de-Guerre in all their massive and terrible splendor, on a course for the summit itself, and they were carrying not food nor ammunition but field guns.

Laurence and Badenhaur flung themselves down the hillside and away, both of them skidding and sliding in a cloud of pebbles on the steep trail, clouds of dust and dying leaves stinging their faces as the dragons landed atop the summit. Halfway down the slope, Laurence stopped long enough to risk a final look back: the heavy-weights were discharging battalions by twos and threes, the men running at once to drag the guns into place along the foremost ridge, and the dragons' belly-rigging was being unhooked to deposit great heaps of round-shot and canister-shot beside them.

There would be no challenging them for the summit, and no chance of retreat. The battle would take place as Napoleon had desired, in the shadow of the French guns.

CHAPTER 14

The artillery batteries were trading hot words before Laurence had even left Hohenlohe's tent; already the fastest couriers were flying desperately after Brunswick and the King, and westward to call in the reserves from Weimar. There was no option now but to concentrate as quickly as possible and give battle. For his own part, Laurence could be almost thankful for the French catching them, if not for the suddenness of their assault; it seemed to him as it had to Temeraire, that the commanders had labored desperately the last week to avoid the very war which they had provoked and which all their men were prepared to endure; a stupid cowering sort of delay that could only wear down morale, reduce their supply, and leave detachments exposed and vulnerable to being cut down one by one, as poor Prince Louis had been.

The prospect of action had quite swept away the malaise hanging upon the camp, and the iron discipline and drill was telling in their favor: as he walked swiftly through the ranks he heard laughter and joking tones; the order to stand-to was met everywhere with an instant response, and though the men were themselves in sorry case, wet and pinched with hunger, they had kept their arms in good order, and their colors sprang out gaily overhead, the great banners snapping in the wind like musket-shot.

"Laurence, hurry, hurry, they are fighting already without us!" Temeraire called urgently, sitting up high on his back legs with his head craned out of the covert, spotting Laurence before he had even reached the clearing.

"I promise you we will have enough fighting today, however late we enter the fray," Laurence said, leaping into Temeraire's waiting claw with a speed that belied his counsel of patience, and swinging himself rapidly into place with the aid of Granby's outstretched hand; all the crew were already in their places, the Prussian officers no less than the British, and Badenhaur, who was trained as a signal-officer, sat anxiously beside Laurence's own place.

"Mr. Fellowes, Mr. Keynes, I trust you will make the safety of the eggs your first concern," Laurence called down, locking his carabiners onto the harness just in time: Temeraire was already launching himself aloft, and the only answer Laurence got was their waving hands, any words inaudible in the rush of wing-beats as they drove towards the front lines of the battlefield, to engage the oncoming French advance guard.

SOME HOURS LATER, the morning's first skirmishing done, Eroica led them to ground in a small valley where the dragons might snatch a few swallows of water and catch their breath. Temeraire, Laurence was glad to see, was holding up well and little affected in his spirits, though they might be said to have suffered a repulse. There had been little hope, indeed, of keeping the French from gaining a foothold, not under the guns which had already been established on the heights: at least they had been made to pay for the ground which they had won, and the Prussians had gained enough time to deploy their own regiments.

Far from dismayed, Temeraire and the other dragons were rather more excited at having fought, and full of anticipation of still more battle to come. Too, they had benefited from their work: few were the dragons who had not managed to seize a dead horse or two to eat, so they were better-fed than they had been for many a day, and full of the resultant energy. Waiting their turns to drink, they even engaged in calling across the valley to one another with accounts of their individual bravery, and how they had done for this enemy dragon and that. These Laurence judged to be exaggerated, as the entire plain was not littered with the corpses of their victims, but no scruples on this account arrested their pleasure in boasting. The men stayed aboard, passing around canteens and biscuit, but the captains gathered to consult for a few moments.

"Laurence," Temeraire said to him, as he climbed down to join the others, "this horse I am eating looks very odd to me; it is wearing a hat."

The limp and dangling head was covered with an odd sort of hood, attached to the bridle and made of some thin cotton stuff, very light, but with stiff wooden cuffs almost encircling the eyeholes, and some sort of pouches covering the nostrils. Temeraire held it for him, and Laurence cut away one of the pouches with his knife: a sachet of dried flowers and herbs, and though it was soaked through now with blood and the horse's damp sweating breath, Laurence could still smell the strong perfume beneath.

"Over the nose like that, it must keep them from smelling the dragons and getting spooked," Granby said, having come down to look at it with him. "I dare say that is how they manage cavalry around dragons in China."

"That is bad, very bad," Dyhern said, when Laurence had shared the intelligence with him. "It means they will be able to use their cavalry under dragon-fire, when we cannot use ours. Schleiz, you had better go and tell the generals," he added, to the captain of one of his light-weights, and the man nodded and dashed back to his dragon.

THEY HAD BEEN aground for scarcely fifteen minutes, but they rose up to find the world already changed. The great contest now was unfolding fully beneath them: like nothing Laurence had ever seen. Across full five miles of villages and fields and woods the battalions were forming, ironwork and steel blazing in the sun amid a sea of color, uniforms of green and red and blue in their thousands, in their tens of thousands, all the massed regiments filing into their battle-lines like a monstrous ballet, to the accompaniment of the shrill animal cries of horses, the jar and clatter of the wheels of the supply-carts, the thundercloud-rumble of the field guns.

"Laurence," Temeraire said, "how many of them there are!" The scale might justly make even dragons feel small, a sensation Temeraire could hardly have been less used to; he halted in place and hovered uncertainly, gazing over the battlefield.

Clouds of white-grey gunpowder smoke were blowing across the fields and tangling into the forests of oak and pine. There was some hard fighting continuing on the Prussian left, around a small village; better than ten thousand men engaged, Laurence guessed, and for all that inconsequential. Elsewhere the French had paused to reinforce their lines, in the space which they had already gained: men and horses were pouring over the bridges of the Saale, the eagles of their standards shining gold, and still more coming on dragon-back. Upon the morning's first battle-field the bodies of the dead lay abandoned by both sides; only victory or time would see them buried.

Temeraire said, low, "I did not know battles could be so large; where are we to go? Some of those men are far away; we cannot help all of them."

"We can but play our own part as best we can," Laurence answered him. "It is not for any one man or dragon to win the day; that is the business of the generals. We must look sharp to our orders and our signals, and achieve what they ask of us."

Temeraire made an uneasy rumble. "But what if we should not have very good generals?"

The question was unpleasantly apt; at once the involuntary comparison sprang to mind between that lean and glittering-eyed man on the heights, so full of certainty and command, and the old men in their pavilions with their councils and arguments and endlessly changing orders. Below to the back of the field he could see Hohenlohe on his horse, his white-powdered wig in place, with his knot of aides-de-camp and men running back and forth around him; Tauentzein, Holtzendorf, and Blücher were moving among their separate troops; the Duke of Brunswick was not yet upon the field, his army still hurrying back from their aborted retreat. None of them distant strangers to sixty; and they faced on the French side the Marshals who had fought and clawed their way through the Revolutionary wars and the man who held their reins, any one of whom could have given them twenty years.

"Good or bad, our duty remains the same and that of any man," Laurence said, thrusting aside with an effort such unworthy thoughts. "Discipline on the field may win the day even if the strategy be flawed, and its absence will ensure defeat."

"I do see," Temeraire said, resuming his flight: up ahead, the French light-weight dragons were rising again to harry the unfolding ranks of the Prussian battalions, and Eroica and his formation had turned to meet them. "With so many men, all must obey, or there would be no order at all; they cannot even see themselves as we can, and know how they stand in the whole." He paused and added anxiously and low, "Laurence, if—only if—we were to lose this war, and the French were to try again to come into England, surely we would be able to stop them?"

"Better not to lose," Laurence said grimly, and then they were back into the thick of it, the tableau of the battlefield dissolving into the hundred private struggles of their own corner of the war.

BY THE EARLY afternoon they could feel the tide shifting in their direction for the first time. Brunswick's army was pouring back in double-quick time, long before Bonaparte could have expected them, and Hohenlohe had sent out all his battalions: twenty of them already now deployed in parade-ground form upon the open field and preparing to make an assault against the leading corps of French infantry, who were hunkered down in a small village near the center of the battle.

Still the French heavy-weights had not engaged, and the larger Prussian dragons were growing exasperated. As Temeraire said, "It does not feel right to me, only batting around these little fellows; where are the big dragons from their side? This is not much of a fair fight." By the sound of Eroica's loud and grumbling response, he wholly agreed, and his swipes at the little French dragons were beginning to be desultory.

At last one Prussian courier, a high-flying Mauerfuchs, risked a quick overflight of the French camp while the rest of them engaged the light-weights at close quarters. He winged back almost at once in a flurry to say the larger French dragons were no longer bringing in men, and now were all lying about on the ground, eating and some even napping. "Oh!" Temeraire said, outraged, "they must all be great cowards, sleeping when there is a battle going on; what do they mean by it?"

"We can be grateful for it; they must have worn themselves all out lugging about those guns," Granby said.

"Yet at this rate they will be well-rested enough when they come in," Laurence said; their own side had been flying hours with only the briefest pauses for water. "Perhaps we ought take turns ourselves; Temeraire, will you not land a while?"

"I am not at all tired," Temeraire protested, "and look, those dragons are trying some mischief over there," he added, and dashed away without waiting for an answer, so they all had to cling to his harness to keep from being flung off their feet as he collided mid-air with a startled and squalling pair of French light-weights, who had only been circling around looking over the battlefield, and who promptly fled his attack.

Before Laurence could renew his suggestion, loud cheering rang out below and their attention was distracted: in the teeth of the continuing terrible artillery-fire, Queen Louise herself had come out and was galloping along the Prussian line, escorted only by a handful of dragoons, the Prussian banner streaming out brilliantly behind their little party. She wore a colonel's uniform coat over her clothing and the stiff-sided plumed hat also, with her hair caught up snugly beneath it. The soldiers yelled her name wildly: she was perhaps the heart of the Prussian War Party and had long urged a resistance to Napoleon and his predations of Europe. Her bravery could not fail to put heart into the men; the King also was on the field, his banner showing farther on the Prussian left, and all throughout the ranks the senior officers had exposed themselves with their men to the fire.

She had no sooner cleared the field than the order was given; in another sort of encouragement, bottles were going down across the front ranks, men pouring the liquor straight into their mouths. The drums beat out the signal, and the infantry charged straight out from their lines with bayonets leveled, men screaming with raw voices, and stormed into the narrow lanes of the village.

The death-toll was hideous: from behind every garden wall and window the French sharp-shooters arose and put forth a ceaseless fire, and near enough every bullet found a mark; while down the straight-aways of the main tracks of the village the artillery pounded away, canister-shot breaking apart into deadly shrapnel as it flew from the mouths of the guns. But the Prussians came onward with irresistible force, and one after another the guns were silenced as they poured into the farmhouses, the barns, the gardens, the pigsties, and hacked down the French soldiers at their places.

The village was lost, and the French battalions were pouring out its back, retreating in good order but retreating nonetheless, for nearly the first time that day. The Prussians roared and kept coming onwards: behind the village they drew back together into line again under the shouts of their sergeants and threw the terrible volley-fire upon the retreating French again.

"That is a great success, Laurence, is it not?" Temeraire said jubilantly. "And now surely we will push them back still further?"

"Yes," Laurence said, full of inexpressible relief, leaning over to shake hands with Badenhaur in congratulation, "now we will see some proper work done."

But they had no further opportunity to watch the ground-battle unfold; Badenhaur's hand abruptly tightened on Laurence's with surprise, and the young Prussian officer pointed him around: from the summit of the Landgrafenberg the massed forces of the French aerial corps were rising, the heavy-weights coming to the battle at last.

The Prussian dragons gave almost as one a loud roar of delight, and full of renewed energy began to shout out taunting remarks on the subject of the French dragons' late entry to the field as they waited for the others to move into formation and close. The French light-weights, who had so valiantly held the field all day, made now one heroic final effort and kept up a sort of screen before the oncoming dragons, darting back and forth around the Prussians' heads to obscure their view, wings flapping distractingly in their faces. The bigger dragons impatiently snorted and lashed out here and there, but without much attention, rather craning their heads to see. Only at the last moments did the light-weights pull away, and Laurence saw the French were not coming in formation at all.

Or almost—there was one formation, the plainest imaginable, only a wedge, but made entirely of heavy-weights: in the lead one Grand Chevalier, leaner but with broader shoulders than Eroica, and behind him three Petit Chevaliers, each one bigger than Temeraire, and behind them a row of six Chansons-de-Guerre only a little smaller, incongruously cheerful in appearance with their orange and yellow markings. They might all have been formation-leaders in their own right; instead they made one enormous if lumbering group, surrounded by a vast unformed crowd of middle-weights.

"Well, that's never a Chinese strategy?" Granby said, staring. "—what the devil are they trying now?" Laurence shook his head perplexed; they had seen a few military reviews amongst the Chinese dragons, who operated aloft more nearly as men did upon the ground, drilling in lines and columns, and never in so confused a manner.

Eroica and his formation anchored the center of the Prussian line, and now with bared teeth he threw himself forward to meet the Grand Chevalier, crying out in a ringing challenge. The Prussian colors were streaming out from his shoulders like another pair of wings. The two formations increased their speed as they drew nearer one another; the miles turned into yards and then feet and then vanished all together. The collision was at hand—and then the moment was past, and Eroica turned round bewildered and indignant in mid-air: the big French dragons had one and all swerved to go past him and gone straight for the wings of his formation, the ranks of smaller middle-weights.

"*Feiglinge!*" Eroica bellowed after them at the top of his lungs as they clawed and scattered his wing dragons. He had been left flying almost alone, and even as he came around to the attack again, three of the French middle-weights seized the opening and drew up alongside him. They were too small to do him any direct harm, and did not even try, but their backs were crammed full of men. No less than three boarding parties leapt over, almost twenty men, swords and pistols in their hands, grabbing at his harness.

Eroica's crew burst into activity to hold off the new threat, all the riflemen bringing up their guns, and a sudden spatter of musket-shot rang out, making the raised sword-blades sing in high, clear notes as the bullets struck them. Thick streams of gunpowder smoke boiled away as Eroica thrashed in the air frantically, head going this way and that as he tried to see what was going toward and protect his captain.

His efforts threw off many of the hapless boarders, who went flailing through the air, but others had already latched themselves on securely; and Eroica was throwing his own crew off their feet as well as the boarders. The confusion served the French with a lucky stroke: two lieutenants clinging to one another for support kept their feet after one of these mid-air convulsions, when all the crew had been flung down, and in the momentary gap they sprang forward and hacked off the carabiner straps of some eight men, sending them tumbling free to their deaths.

The rest of the struggle was sharp but brief, as the boarding parties advanced in force upon the dragon's neck. Dyhern shot two men and killed another with a saber-thrust, but then his blade lodged in the man's chest and would not come out again; and the falling body ripped it from his hands. The French seized his arms and put a blade to his throat, calling to Eroica, *"Gib auf,"* while they pulled down the Prussian flags and put the tricolor in its place.

It was a terrible loss, and one which they could not avert: Temeraire himself was being hotly pursued by five middleweights, similarly overburdened with men, and all his speed and ingenuity were required to avoid them. Now and again a few men would take the desperate risk and leap across onto his back even though they were not very close; but few enough that Temeraire flung them off at once, with a quick writhing turn, or the topmen cut them down with sword or pistol.

But an Honneur-d'Or, greatly daring, flung herself directly at Temeraire's head; he ducked instinctively, and as she whisked by overhead a couple of her bellmen let go and dropped aboard directly onto Temeraire's shoulders, flattening young Allen and knocking Laurence and Badenhaur into a tangled sprawl of straps and limbs. Laurence grabbed blindly for some purchase; Badenhaur was with an excess of courage trying to throw himself atop Laurence protectively, and getting in the way of his putting himself back on his feet.

But the act was justified: he sank back gasping into Laurence's arms, blood spreading dark from a stab-wound through his shoulder; the Frenchman who had dealt the blow was drawing back the sword for another attempt. Granby with a shout threw himself against the handful of attackers and heaved them back three paces. Laurence at last righted himself and cried out— Granby had thrown off his straps to make the attack, and the pair of French officers seizing him by the arms flung him over the side.

"Temeraire!" Laurence shouted. *"Temeraire!"*

The earth dropped out from beneath his feet: Temeraire doubled on himself and plunged after Granby's falling body, wings driving. Laurence could not breathe for the sickening, dizzying speed of it, the blurred ground hurtling towards them and a

humming like the sound of bees all around them from the flight
of bullets through the air as they came low over the battlefield.
And then Temeraire corkscrewed up and away, his tail smashing
to flinders a slim young oak-tree. Laurence clawed himself hand-
over-hand up the straps and looked over Temeraire's shoulder:
Granby lay in Temeraire's talons gasping, trying to staunch the
blood streaming from his nostrils.

Laurence rolled to his feet and went for his sword. The
Frenchmen were leaping to the attack again; he smashed the
pommel into the first one's face, savagely, and felt the bone crush
beneath his gloved fist; then he ripped the blade free from the
sheath and swung at the second. It was the first time he had
struck a flesh-blow with the Chinese sword: it bowled the man's
head off with scarcely any resistance.

From startlement and reaction, Laurence stood gawking at
the headless body, its hand still clinging to its sword. Then belatedly Allen jumped to his duty and cut the Frenchmen's straps, so
their bodies fell away, and Laurence was recalled to himself. He
wiped his sword hurriedly and put it back away; hauling himself
gratefully back into his place on Temeraire's neck.

The French had turned their successful maneuver against the
other formations one at a time: the heavy-weights throwing
themselves en masse against the wings, isolating the leaders so
the middle-weights could pounce. Eroica was flying away
wretchedly with hang-dog head, and not alone; three more Prussian heavy-weight dragons followed him in short order, all of
them beating so slowly they were descending towards the ground
between each wing-stroke and the next. The other members of
their formations were milling uncertainly without them, slow to
comprehend the abrupt losses: ordinarily the members of a formation so stripped of its leader would have at once gone to support a different formation, but having been all stricken at once,
they were now mostly flying into each other's way, at the mercy
of their enemies. The French heavy-weights massed again and
brutally scattered them over and over, riflemen firing terrible
barrages into their crews. Men were falling like hailstones, and
the loss was so dreadful that many of the dragons cried out and

yielded themselves in desperation, unboarded, to save their captains and the remnants of their crews.

The last three Prussian formations, forewarned by their comrades' fate, had drawn up in tight close ranks, protecting their leaders; but though they were successfully fending off the attempts at breaking in, they were paying with distance and position, drifting farther and farther afield under the steady pressure. Temeraire's own situation was growing increasingly desperate; he twisted and turned this way and that, constantly under fire with his own riflemen returning their own shot in bursts: Lieutenant Riggs bawling out the firing drill to keep them steady, though they were all of them reloading as fast as they could go.

Temeraire's scales and the chainmail with which he was girt turned aside most of those balls which came towards him by accident, though here and again one tore through the more delicate membrane of his wings, or lodged shallowly in his flesh. He did not flinch, too full of battle-fever to even feel the small wounds, but concentrated all his powers on the evasion. Even so Laurence thought in anguish that they too would soon be forced to flee the field or be taken; the long day's labors were telling on Temeraire, and his turns were slowing.

To quit the field, to desert under fire without an order to retreat, he could hardly imagine; yet the Prussians themselves were giving way, and if he did not withdraw, aside from the very great evil of their own capture, the eggs were almost sure to fall into enemy hands as well. Laurence had no desire to so recompense the French for having taken Temeraire's egg from them; he was on the point of calling Temeraire away, at least for a breath, when his conscience was spared: a clarion roar sounded, musical and terrible at once, and with breathtaking suddenness their enemies vanished away. Temeraire whirled around three times before he was satisfied he had indeed been left in peace, and only then risked hovering long enough for Laurence to see what was going forward.

The ringing call was Lien's voice: she had not herself taken part in the battle, but she was hovering now in mid-air, behind the lines of the French dragons. She had no harness nor crew, but the great diamond upon her forehead was glowing fiery orange with the reflected sunset, almost to match the virulence of her red eyes. She cried out again, and Laurence heard another drumming below: signals flying from the French ranks, and at the crest of the hill on a grey charger Bonaparte himself watching over the field, the breastplates of the feared Imperial Guard behind him molten gold in the light.

The Prussian formations dispersed or driven off, the French dragons had acquired a clear dominance over the aerial arena. Now in answer to Lien's call, they all moved together into a straight-line formation. Below, the French cavalry all as one wheeled and broke away to either side of the battlefield, all the horses spurred as quick as they could go, and the infantry fell back from the front lines, though keeping up a steady musket- and artillery-fire as they went.

Lien rose higher into the air and drew a great breath, her ruff under its steel diadem spreading wide around her head, her sides belling out like sails overpressed with wind, and then from her jaws burst the terrible fury of the divine wind. She directed it against no target; she struck down no enemy and dealt not a single blow; but the hideous force of it left the ears ringing as though all the cannon in the world had gone off at once. Lien was some thirty years of age to Temeraire's two, a little larger and more experienced by far, and there was not only the power of her greater size behind it but a sort of resonance, a rise and fall in her voice, which carried on the roaring a seemingly endless time. Men reeled back from it, all along the battlefield; the Prussian dragons huddled themselves away; even Laurence and his crew, familiar with the divine wind, jerked instinctively away so that their carabiner straps drew taut.

A complete silence followed, broken only by small shocked cries, the moans of the wounded on the field below; but before the echoes had stopped ringing away, all the line of French dragons lifted up their own heads and, roaring in full voice, plunged earthwards. They pulled up their dive just short of collision with the ground; some few, indeed, were unable to do so, and tumbled out of the sky to crush great swaths of the Prussian ranks beneath their bodies, though crying out in agony as they rolled over their own wings. But the rest did not even pause: dragging their claws and tails as they skimmed just above the ground, they went tearing through the stunned and unprepared ranks of the Prussian infantry, and they left great bloody ranks of the dead behind them as they lifted away again into the air.

The men broke. Before even the dragons struck the front ranks, the lines to the rear were dissolving into utter confusion, a wild panicked attempt at flight, men struggling with one another and trying to flee in different directions. King Frederick was standing in his stirrups, three men holding his frantic and heaving charger to keep it from throwing him off; he was shouting through a speaking-trumpet while signal-flags waved. "Retreat," Badenhaur said, gripping Laurence's arm: his voice sounded utterly matter-of-fact, but his face was streaked and dirty with tears, which he did not seem even to notice he was shedding; down on the field below, the Duke of Brunswick's limp and blood-spattered body was being carried back towards the tents.

But the men were in no frame to listen or to obey; some few battalions managed indeed to form into square for defense, the men standing shoulder to shoulder with their bayonets bristling outwards, but others went running half-mad back through the village, through the woods, which they had only just won with so much labor; and as the French dragons dropped to the earth to rest, their blood-spattered sides heaving, the French cavalry and infantry poured all down off the hill and streamed past them, roaring in human voices, to complete the ruin and defeat.

CHAPTER 15

"No, I am all right," Granby said, hoarsely, when they laid him out in the covert. "For God's sake don't hold up on my account; I am only damned tired of always getting knocked about the head." He was shaken and ill, for all he said, and when he tried to drink a little portable soup he vomited it up again at once; so his crewmates contented themselves with giving him enough liquor to knock him over yet again, of which he drank only a swallow or two before falling asleep.

Laurence meant to take aboard as many of the ground crews as he could, of the dragons taken prisoner. Many of the men almost refused to come, in disbelief; the covert was well to the south of the battlefield, and they had not seen the day's events. Badenhaur argued with them a long time, all of them growing increasingly loud and tense. "Keep your damned voices down," Keynes snapped, while the crew carefully bundled the eggs back aboard into the belly-rigging. "That Kazilik is mature enough by now to understand," he said to Laurence in an undertone. "The last thing we need is for the blessed creature to be frightened in the shell; it often makes a timid beast."

Laurence nodded grimly, and then Temeraire lifted his weary head up from the ground and looked into the darkening sky above. "There is a Fleur-de-Nuit up there, I hear its wings."

"Tell those men they may stay and be damned, or get aboard now," Laurence said to Badenhaur, waving his own crew aboard, and they landed outside Apolda cold and tired and cramped.

The town was nearly a ruin: windows smashed, wine and beer running in the gutters, stables and barns and pens all emptied; no one in the streets but drunken soldiers, bloody and ragged and belligerent. On the stoop of the largest inn Laurence had to step past one man weeping like a child into the palm of his right hand; his left was missing, the stump tied up in a rag.

Inside there were only a handful of lower officers, all of them wounded or half-dead of exhaustion; one had enough French to tell him, "You must go; the French will be here by morning if not sooner. The King has gone to Sömmerda."

In the back cellars Laurence found a rack of wine bottles unbroken, and a cask of beer; Pratt heaved the last onto his shoulder and carried it, while Porter and Winston took armfuls of bottles, and they went back to the clearing. Temeraire had smashed up an old dead oak, lightning-blasted, and the men had managed to kindle a fire; he lay curved round it while the men huddled against his sides.

They shared the bottles and breached the cask for Temeraire to drink; little enough comfort, when they had at once to get aloft again. Laurence hesitated; Temeraire was so exhausted he was swallowing with his eyes almost shut. But that fatigue was itself a danger; if a French dragon-patrol came on them now, he doubted Temeraire could rouse quickly enough to escape. "We must be away, my dear," he said gently. "Can you manage?"

"Yes, Laurence; I am perfectly well," Temeraire said, struggling up onto his feet again, though he added, low, "Must we go *very* far?"

The fifteen-mile flight seemed longer. The town bloomed out of the dark suddenly, with a bonfire on the outskirts; a handful of Prussian dragons looked up anxiously as Temeraire landed heavily beside it, in the trampled field which was their bivouac:

light-weights and a few couriers, a couple of middle-weights; not a single formation entire, and not another heavy-weight among them. They crowded gladly around him for reassurance, and nudged towards him a share of the horse-carcasses that were their dinner, but he tore off only a little of the flesh before he sank down quite asleep, and Laurence left him dead to the world, many of the smaller dragons tucking themselves against his sides.

He sent the men to find what cheer they could to make their camp more comfortable and walked across the fields to the town alone. The night was quiet and beautiful: an early frost made all the stars shine bright, and his breath only briefly hung white in the air. He had not done very much fighting, but he was aching in all his parts, a clenching hot pain around his neck and shoulders, legs stiff and cramped; he stretched them gratefully. Tired cavalry-horses crowded into a paddock raised their heads and whickered anxiously as he went past the fence: they smelled Temeraire upon him, he supposed.

Little enough of the army had yet reached Sömmerda: most fugitives had escaped on foot, and would be walking through the night, if they even knew to come. The town had not been looted, and some measure of order was kept; the groans of the wounded marked the field-hospital in a small church, and the King's hussar guards were drawn up still in ranks outside the largest building: not quite a fortress, only a solid and respectable manor.

He could find no other aviators at all, nor any senior officer to make his report to, with poor Dyhern captured; he had spent some of the day in support of General Tauentzein's command, and another part under Marshal Blücher; but so far as anyone could tell him, neither was in the town. At last he went to Hohenlohe directly, but the prince was engaged in conference, and a young aide, with an officious brusqueness hardly excusable even by the weight under which they all were laboring, took him to the room and told him to wait in the hallway outside. After half-an-hour cooling his heels outside the door without so much as a chair, hearing only the occasional muffled sound of voices, Laurence sat down on the floor and put out his legs, and fell asleep leaning against the wall.

Someone was speaking to him in German. "No, thank you," he said, still asleep, and then opened his eyes. A woman was looking down at him, with a kind expression but half-amused; abruptly he recognized the Queen, and a couple of guards were standing with her. "Oh, good Lord," Laurence said, and sprang to his feet with much embarrassment, begging her pardon in French.

"Oh, what a nothing," she said, and looked at him curiously, "but what are you doing here?" She opened the door, when he had explained, and put her head in, to Laurence's discomfort: he had much rather have waited a longer time than seem a complainer.

Hohenlohe's voice answered her in German, and she beckoned Laurence in with her. A good fire was laid on in the room, and heavy tapestries on the walls kept the cold stone from leaching away all the heat. The heat was very welcome; Laurence had stiffened up even further from sitting in the hall. King Frederick stood leaning against the wall near the fireplace: a tired man, not as handsome or vital as his wife, with a long pale face and hair set high up on his broad white forehead; his mouth was thin, and he wore a narrow mustache.

Hohenlohe stood at a large table covered over with maps; Generals Rüchel and Kalkreuth were with him; also several other staff-officers. Hohenlohe stared at Laurence unblinkingly a long moment, then with an effort said, "Good God, are you still here?"

Laurence did not immediately understand how to take this, as Hohenlohe had not even known he was in the town; then he was abruptly wide-awake and furiously angry. "I am sorry that I should have troubled you," he bit out. "As you have been expecting my desertion, I am perfectly happy to be gone."

"No, nothing of the kind," Hohenlohe said, somewhat incoherently adding, "and God in Heaven, who could blame you."

He ran his hand over his face; his wig was disordered and dingy grey, and Laurence was sorry; plainly Hohenlohe did not have full command of himself.

"I have only come to make my report, sir," Laurence said, with more moderation. "Temeraire has taken no serious injury; my losses are three wounded, none dead, and I have brought in some three dozen ground crewmen from Jena, and their equipment."

"Harness and forges?" Kalkreuth asked quickly, looking up.

"Yes, sir, though only two of the latter, besides our own," Laurence said. "They were too heavy to bring more."

"That is something, thank God," Kalkreuth said. "Half our harnesses are coming apart at the seams."

After this no one else spoke for a long time. Hohenlohe was gazing fixedly at the maps, but with an expression which suggested he was not properly seeing them; General Rüchel had slipped into a chair, his face grey and tired, and the Queen was at her husband's side, murmuring to him in a low private voice in German. Laurence wondered if he ought to ask to be excused, though he did not think they were keeping silent from any scruple at his presence: there was a very miasma of fatigue thickening the atmosphere of the room. Abruptly the King shook his head and turned back to face the room. "Do we know where he is?"

There was no need to ask who *he* was. "Anywhere south of the Elbe," one young staff-officer muttered, and flushed as it came out over-loud in the dull room, earning him glares.

"Jena tonight, Sire, surely," Rüchel said, still scowling at the young man.

The King was perhaps the only one who took no notice of the slip of the tongue. "Will he give us an armistice?"

"That man? Not a moment to breathe," Queen Louise said, with scorn, "nor any kind of honorable terms. I would rather throw myself completely into the arms of the Russians than grovel for the pleasure of that *parvenu*." She turned to Hohenlohe. "What can be done? Surely something can be done?"

He roused himself a little and went through his maps, pointing at different garrisons and detachments, speaking half in French and half in German of rallying the troops, falling back on the reserves. "Bonaparte's men have been marching for weeks and fighting all day," he said. "We will have a few days, I hope, before they can organize a pursuit. Perhaps a large share of the army has escaped; they will come this way and towards Erfurt: we must gather them and fall back—"

Heavy boots rang on the stones in the hallway, and a heavy hand on the door. The newcomer, Marshal Blücher, did not wait to be asked in, but came in with no more warning. "The French are in Erfurt," he said, without ceremony, in plain blunt German even Laurence could understand. "Murat landed with five dragons and five hundred men and they surrendered, the fuckers—" He cut off in great confusion, blushing fiery red under his mustaches: he had just seen the Queen.

The others were more preoccupied with his intelligence than his language; a confused babble of voices arose, and a scramble among the staff-officers through the disordered papers and maps. Laurence could not follow the conversation, mostly in German, but that they were brangling was noisily clear. "Enough," said the King, suddenly and loud, and the quarreling faltered and stilled. "How many men do we have?" he asked Hohenlohe.

The papers were shuffled through again, more quietly; at last the descriptions of the various detachments were all collected. "Ten thousand under Saxe-Weimar, somewhere on the roads south of Erfurt," Hohenlohe said, reading the papers. "Another seventeen in Halle, under Württemburg's command, our reserves; and so far we have another eight thousand here from the battle: more will surely come in."

"If the French do not overtake them," another man said quietly; Scharnhorst, the late Duke of Brunswick's chief of staff. "They are moving too quickly. We cannot wait. Sire, we must get every man we have left across the Elbe and burn the bridges at once, or we will lose Berlin. We should send couriers to begin even now."

This provoked another furious explosion, nearly every man

in the room shouting him down and in their disagreement finding a vent for all the raw violence of their feelings, which were all that one might expect from proud men, seeing their honor and that of their country rolled in the dust, and forced to learn humility and fear at the hand of a deadly and implacable enemy, whom even now they all could feel drawing close upon their heels.

Laurence too felt an instinctive revulsion for so ignominious a withdrawal, and the sacrifice of so much territory; madness, it seemed to him, to give so much ground without forcing the French to do battle for any of it. Bonaparte was not the sort of man who would be satisfied even with a large bite when he could devour the whole, and with as many dragons as he had in his train, the destruction of the bridges seemed at once an insufficient obstacle, and an admission of weakness.

In the tumult, the King beckoned to Hohenlohe and drew him aside before the windows to speak with him; when the rest had spent themselves in shouting, they came back to the tables. "Prince Hohenlohe will take command of the army," the King said, quietly but with finality. "We will fall back on Magdeburg to gather our forces together, and there consider how best to organize the defense of the line of the Elbe."

A low murmuring of obedience and agreement answered him, and with the Queen he quitted the room. Hohenlohe began to issue orders, sending men out with dispatches, the senior officers one by one slipping away to organize their commands. Laurence was by now almost desperate for sleep, and tired of being left waiting; when all but a handful of staff-officers remained and he still had been given no orders nor dismissed, and Hohenlohe showed every sign of once again burying himself in the maps, Laurence finally lost patience and put himself forward.

"Sir," he said, interrupting Hohenlohe's study, "may I ask to whom I am to report; or failing that, your orders for me?"

Hohenlohe looked up and stared at him again with that hollow expression. "Dyhern and Schliemann are made prisoner," he said after a moment. "Abend also; who is left?" he asked, looking around. His aides seemed uncertain how to answer him; then finally one ventured, "Do we know what has become of George?"

Some more discussion, and several men sent to make inquiries, all returned answers in the negative; Hohenlohe said finally, "Do you mean to say there is not a single damned heavy-weight left, out of fourteen?"

Lacking either acid-spitters or fire-breathers, the Prussians organized their formations to maximize strength rather than, like the British, to protect a dragon with such critical offensive capabilities; the heavy-weights were nearly all formation-leaders, and as such had come in for particular attention in the French attack. Too, they had been peculiarly vulnerable to the French tactics, being slower and more ponderous than the middle-weights who had spearheaded the boarding attempts, and much of their strength and limited agility already worn down from a day of hard flying. Laurence had seen five taken on the battle-field; he did not find it wonderful that the rest should have been snapped up afterwards, or at best driven far away, in the chaotic aftermath.

"Pray God some will come in overnight," Hohenlohe said. "We will have to reorganize the entire command."

He paused heavily and looked at Laurence, both of them silenced by the awareness that Temeraire was the only heavy-weight left at hand; at one stroke thus become critical to their defenses, and impossible to restrain: Hohenlohe could not force them to stay. Laurence could not help being torn; in some wise his first duty was to protect the eggs, and given the disaster, that surely meant to see them straightaway to England; yet to desert the Prussians now would be as good as giving the war up for lost, and pretending they could do no more to help.

"Your instructions, then, sir?" he said abruptly; he could not bring himself to do it.

Hohenlohe did not make any expressions of gratitude, but his face relaxed a little, a few of the lines easing out. "Tomorrow morning I will ask you to go to Halle. All our reserves are there: tell them to fall back, and if you can carry some guns for them, so much the better. We will find some work for you then; God knows there will be no shortage."

"Ow!" TEMERAIRE SAID, loudly. Laurence opened his eyes already sitting up, his back- and leg-muscles protesting loudly, and his head thick and clouded besides from so little sleep: there was only a little dim light filtering in. He crawled out of his tent and discovered that this was rather the fault of the fog than the hour: the covert was already alive, and even as he stood up he saw Roland coming to wake him as she had been told to do.

Keynes was scrambling over Temeraire, digging out the bullets; their precipitous departure from the battlefield after the fighting had kept him from attending to the wounds then. Though Temeraire had borne them up to now without even noticing, and far worse wounds without complaint, he flinched from their extraction, stifling small cries as Keynes drew each one out; though not very thoroughly.

"It is always the same," Keynes said sourly; "you will get yourselves hacked to pieces and call it entertainment, but only try and stitch you back together and you will moan without end."

"Well, it hurts a great deal more," Temeraire said. "I do not see why you must take them out; they do not bother me as they are."

"They would damned well bother you when you got blood-poisoning from them. Hold still, and stop whimpering."

"I am not whimpering, at all," Temeraire muttered, and added, "ow!"

There was a rich, pleasant smell in the air. Three meager horse-carcasses were all that had been delivered to the covert that morning to feed more than ten hungry dragons; before the inevitable jostling could begin, Gong Su had appropriated the lot. The bones he roasted in a fire-pit and then stewed with the flesh in some makeshift cauldrons, the dragons' breastplates temporarily put to this new use and all the youngest crewmen set to stirring. The ground crews he peremptorily sent out to scavenge by means best not closely examined whatever else they could find, which varied ingredients he picked over for inclusion.

The Prussian officers looked on anxiously as their dragons' provisions all went into the vats, but the dragons caught a sort of excitement at the process of choosing which items would go in, and offered their own opinions by here nudging forward a heap of knotted yellow onions, there surreptitiously pushing away some undesirable sacks of rice. These last, Gong Su did not let go to waste; he reserved some quantity of the liquid when the dragons had been served their portions, and cooked the rice separately in the rich broth swimming with scraps, so the aviators breakfasted rather better than much of the camp; a circumstance which went far to reconciling them to the strange practice.

The harnesses of the dragons were all in sorry shape, clawed and frayed, some down to the wires threaded through the leather for strength, some straps entirely severed; and Temeraire's was in particularly wretched case. They had neither the time nor the supplies to make proper repairs, but some patchwork at least had to be done before their departure for Halle.

"I'm sorry sir, with all we can do it'll be rising noon before we can get him under leather again," Fellowes came to say apologetically, having made a first survey of the damage and set the harness-men to work. "It's the way he twists about, I expect: widens the tears."

"Do what you can," Laurence said briefly; no need to press them: every man was working to his limits, and there were as many as could be asked for, volunteers from the ground crews they had rescued. In the meantime, he coaxed Temeraire to sleep and conserve his energy.

Temeraire was not unwilling, and laid himself out around the still-warm ashes of the cooking fires. "Laurence," he said after a moment, softly, "Laurence, have we lost?"

"Only a battle, my dear; not the war," Laurence said, though honesty compelled him to add, "but a damnably important battle, yes; I suppose he has taken half the army prisoner, and scattered the rest." He leaned against Temeraire's foreleg, feeling very low; he had so far staved off with activity any serious contemplation of their circumstances.

"We must not yield to despair," he said, as much for himself as for Temeraire. "There is yet hope, and if there were none at all, still sitting on our hands bewailing our fate would do no good."

Temeraire sighed deeply. "What will happen to Eroica? They will not hurt him?"

"No, never," Laurence answered. "He will be sent along to some breeding-grounds, I am sure; he may even be released, if they settle upon terms. Until then they will only keep Dyhern under lock and key; what the poor devil must feel." He could well imagine all the horrors of the Prussian captain's situation; to be not only himself prevented from doing any good for his country, but the instrument of his inexpressibly valuable dragon's imprisonment. Temeraire evidently shared some very similar train of thought, with respect to Eroica; he curled his foreleg in to draw Laurence nearer, and nudged him a little anxiously for petting; this reassurance only let him drop off at last.

The harness-men managed the repairs quicker than promised, and before eleven o'clock were beginning the laborious process of getting aboard all the enormous weight of straps and buckles and rings, with much assistance from Temeraire himself: he was the only one who could possibly have raised up the massive shoulder-strap, some three feet wide and full of chain-mesh within, which anchored the whole.

They were in the midst of their labors when several of the dragons looked up together, at some sound which only they could hear; in another minute they could all see a little courier coming in towards them, his flight oddly unsteady. He dropped into the center of the field and sank down off his legs at once, deep bloody gashes along his sides, crying urgently and twisting his head around to see his captain: a boy some fifteen years of age if so many, drooping in his straps, whose legs had been slashed badly by the same strokes which marked his dragon.

They cut off the bloody harness and got the boy down; Keynes had put an iron bar in the hot ashes the moment both came down, and now clapped the searing surface to the open and oozing wounds, producing a terrible roasting smell. "No arteries or veins cut; he'll do," was his brusque remark after he had inspected his handiwork, and he set to giving the same treatment to the dragon.

The boy revived with a little brandy splashed into his mouth and smelling-salts under his nose; and he got out his message in German, gasping long stuttering breaths between the words to keep from breaking into sobs.

"Laurence, we were to go to Halle, were we not?" Temeraire said, listening. "He says the French have taken the town; they attacked this morning."

"WE CANNOT HOLD Berlin," Hohenlohe said.

The King did not protest; he only nodded. "How long until the French reach the city?" the Queen asked; she was very pale, but composed, with her hands lying in her lap folded over lightly. "The children are there."

"There is no time to waste," Hohenlohe said; enough of an answer. He paused and said, his voice almost breaking, "Majesty— I beg you will forgive—"

The Queen sprang up and took his shoulders in her hands, kissing him on the cheek. "We will prevail against him," she said fiercely. "Have courage; we will see you in the east."

Regaining some measure of self-control, Hohenlohe rambled on a little longer, plans, intentions: he would rally more of the stragglers, send the artillery trains west, organize the middleweights into formations; they would fall back to the fortress of Stettin, they would defend the line of the Oder. He did not sound as though he believed any of it.

Laurence stood uncomfortably in the corner of the room, as far away as he could manage. "Will you take their Majesties?" Hohenlohe had asked, heavily, when Laurence had first told him the news.

"Surely you will need us here, sir," Laurence had said. "A fast courier—" but Hohenlohe had shaken his head.

"After what happened to this one, bringing the news? No; we cannot take such a risk. Their patrols will be out in force all around us."

The King now raised the same objection and was answered the same way. "You cannot be taken," Hohenlohe said. "It would be the end, Sire, he could dictate whatever terms he desired; or God forbid, if you should be killed, and the crown prince still in Berlin when they come there—"

"O God! My children in that monster's power," the Queen said. "We cannot stand here talking; let us go at once." She went to the door and called her maid, waiting outside, to go and fetch a coat.

"Will you be all right?" the King asked her quietly.

"What, am I a child, to be afraid?" she said scornfully. "I have been flying on couriers; it cannot be very different," but a courier twice the size of a horse was not to be compared with a heavy-weight bigger than the whole barn. "Is that your dragon, on the hill over there?" she asked Laurence, as they came into view of the covert; Laurence saw no hill, and then realized she was pointing at the middling-sized Berghexe sleeping on Temeraire's back.

Before Laurence could correct her, Temeraire himself lifted up his head and looked in their direction. "Oh," she said, a little faintly.

Laurence, who remembered when Temeraire had been small enough to fit into a hammock aboard the *Reliant,* still in some part did not think of him being quite so large as he really was. "He is perfectly gentle," he said, in an awkward attempt at reassurance; also a brazen lie, since Temeraire had just enthusiastically spent the previous day in the most violent pursuits imaginable; but it seemed the thing to say.

All the dragon-crews sprang up startled to their feet as the royal couple entered the makeshift covert, and remained at stiff and awkward attention; aviators were not used to being so graced, as the little couriers who ordinarily bore important passengers went to their lodgings to carry them to and fro. Neither monarch looked very easy, particularly when all the dragons, catching their crews' excitement, began craning their heads to peer at them; but with true grace the King took the Queen's arm in his and went around to speak to the captains and give each a few words of approval.

Laurence seized the moment and beckoned hurriedly to Granby and Fellowes. "Can we get a tent put up for them aboard?" he asked urgently.

"I don't know we can, sir; we left all behind what we could spare, running from the battlefield, and that lummox Bell had out the tents to make room for his kit, as though we couldn't work him up a tanning-barrel anywhere we went," Fellowes said, rubbing at the back of his neck nervously. "But we'll manage something, if you can give me a turn of the glass; maybe some of these other fellows can lend us a bit of scrap."

The tent was indeed managed out of two pieces of spare leather sewn together; personal harnesses were cobbled together; a half-respectable cold supper was hastily assembled and packed into a basket with even a bottle of wine, though how this should be opened mid-flight without disaster, Laurence had not the least idea. "If you are ready, Your Majesty," he said tentatively, and offered the Queen his arm when she nodded. "Temeraire, will you put us up? Very carefully, if you please."

Temeraire obligingly put down his claw for them to step into. She looked at it a little palely; the nails of his talons were roughly the length of her forearm and of polished black horn, sharp along the edges and coming to a wicked point. "Shall I go first?" the King said to her quietly; she threw her head back and said, "No, of course not," and stepped in, though she could not help but throw an anxious look at the talons curving above her head.

Temeraire was regarding her with great interest, and having let her step off again onto his shoulder, he whispered, "Laurence, I always thought queens would have a great many jewels, but she has none at all; have they been stolen?"

Fortunately he spoke in English, as otherwise this remark would not have been much of a secret, issuing as it did from jaws large enough to swallow a horse. Laurence hurried the Queen into the tent before Temeraire could shift to German or

French and take to questioning her on the state of her array; she very sensibly wore a plain heavy overcoat of wool over her gown, adorned with nothing more elaborate than silver buttons, and a fur pelisse and hat, practical enough on a flight.

The King had the benefit at least of a military officer's experience of dragons, and showed no hesitation, if he felt any; but the retinue of guards and servants looked more deeply anxious even at coming near. Looking at their pale faces, the King said something briefly in German; Laurence guessed from the looks of shamefacedness and relief that he was giving them permission to stay behind.

Temeraire took this opportunity to put in his own remarks in that language, provoking startled looks all around; and he then stretched out his foreleg towards the group. This did not quite have the effect that Laurence imagined Temeraire had intended, and a few moments later there were left only four of the royal guard, and one old woman servant, who snorted profoundly and climbed without ceremony into Temeraire's hand to be put aboard.

"What did you say to them?" Laurence asked, half-amused and half-despairing.

"I only told them they were being very silly," Temeraire said in injured tones, "and that if I meant to do them any harm, it would be much easier for me to reach them where they were standing, anyway, than if they were on my back."

BERLIN WAS IN a ferment; the townspeople looked without love on soldiers in uniform, and Laurence, going through the town in haste, trying to get what supplies he could, heard muttering about the "damned War Party" in every shop and corner. News of the terrible loss had already reached them, along with news of the French drive on the city, but there was no spirit of resistance or revolt, or even any great unhappiness; indeed the general impression was a kind of sullen satisfaction at being proven right.

"They drove the poor King to it, you know, the Queen and all those other young hotheads," the banker told Laurence. "They would prove that they could beat Bonaparte, and they could not, and who is it that pays for their pride but us, I ask you! So many poor young men killed, and what our taxes will be after this I do not want to think."

Having delivered himself of these criticisms, however, he was quite willing to advance Laurence a good sum in gold. "I had rather have my money in an account at Drummonds' than here in Berlin with a hungry army marching in," he said candidly, while his two sons lugged up a small but substantial chest.

The British embassy was in turmoil; the ambassador already gone, by courier, and scarcely anyone left could give him good information, or would; his green coat commanded not the least attention, beyond queries if he were a courier, bringing dispatches.

"There has been no trouble in India these three years, whyever should you ask such a thing?" a harried secretary said, impatiently, when Laurence at last resorted to halting him in the corridor by main force. "I have not the least understanding why the Corps should have failed in our obligations, but it is just as well we had not more committed to this rout."

This political view Laurence could not easily subscribe to, still more angry and ashamed to hear the Corps described in such a way. He closed his mouth on the reply which first sprang to mind and said only, very cold, "Have you all safe route of escape?"

"Yes, of course," the secretary said. "We will embark at Stralsund. You had best get back to England straightaway yourself. The Navy is in the Baltic and in the North Sea, to assist with operations in support of Danzig and Königsberg, for whatever good that will do; but at least you will have a clear route home once you are over the sea."

If a craven piece of advice, this at least was reassuring news. But there were no letters of his own waiting, which might have given him an explanation less painful to consider, and of course none would find them now. "I cannot even send a new direction home with them," Laurence said to Granby as they walked back towards the palace. "God only knows where we shall be in two days, much less a week. Anyone would have to address it to William Laurence, East Prussia; and throw it into the ocean in a bottle, too, for all the likelihood it should find me."

"Laurence," Granby said abruptly, "I hope to God you will not think me chickenhearted; but oughtn't we be getting home, as he said?" He gazed straight ahead down the street and avoided Laurence's eyes as he spoke; there was alternating color and pallid white in his cheeks.

It abruptly occurred to Laurence, to be compounded with his other cares, that his decision to stay might look to the Admiralty as though he were keeping the egg out in the field intentionally, delaying until Granby might have his chance. "The Prussians are too badly short of heavy-weights now to let us go," he said finally, not really an answer.

Granby did not answer again, until later, when they had come to Laurence's quarters and might shut the door behind them; in that privacy he bluntly said, "Then they can't stop us going, either."

Laurence was silent over the brandy-glasses; he could not deny it, nor even criticize, having entertained much the same thought himself.

Granby added, "They've lost, Laurence: half their army, and half the country too; surely there's no sense in staying now."

"I will not allow their final loss to be certain," Laurence said strongly at this discouraged remark, turning around at once. "The most terrible sequence of defeats may yet be reversed, so long as men are to be had and they do not despair, and it is the duty of an officer to keep them from doing so; I trust I need not insist upon your confining such sentiments to your breast."

Granby flushed up crimson and answered with some heat, "I am not proposing to go running around crying that the sky is falling. But they'll need us at home more than ever; Bonaparte is sure to already be looking across the Channel with one eye."

"We did not stay only to avoid pursuit or challenge," Laurence said, "but because it is better to fight Bonaparte farther from home; that reason yet remains. If there were no real hope, or if our efforts could make no material difference, then I would say yes; but to desert in this situation, when our assistance may be of the most vital importance, I cannot countenance."

"Do you honestly think they will manage any better than they have so far? He's overmatched them, start to finish, and they are in worse case now than they were to start."

This there was no denying, but Laurence said, "Painful as the lesson has been, we have surely learnt much of his mind, of his strategy, from this meeting; the Prussian commanders cannot fail to now revise their strategy, which I fear before this first contest of arms had too much to do with overconfidence."

"As far as that goes, too much is better than too little," Granby said, "and I see precious little reason for any confidence at all."

"I hope I will never be so rash as to say I am *confident* of dealing Bonaparte a reversal," Laurence said, "but there remains good and practical reason to hope. Recall that even now the Prussian reserves in the east, together with the Russian Army, will outmatch Bonaparte's numbers by half again. And the French cannot venture forward until they have secured their lines of communication: there are a dozen fortresses of vital strategic importance, fended by strong garrisons, which they will first have to besiege and then leave troops to secure."

But this was only parroting; he knew perfectly well numbers alone did not tell the course of battle. Bonaparte had been outnumbered at Jena.

He paced the room for another hour when Granby had at last gone. It was his duty to show himself more certain than he was, and besides that to not permit himself to be downhearted, sentiments which should surely convey themselves to the men. But he was not wholly sure of the course he was following, and he knew that his decision was in some part formed by his disgust for the notion; desertion, even from a situation into which he had effectively been pressed, had too much an ugly and dishonorable ring to it, and he had not the happy turn of character which might have allowed him to call it by another name, and lose the odium thereby.

"I DO NOT want to give up, either, though I would like to be at home," Temeraire said, with a sigh. "It is not so nice, losing battles, and seeing our friends taken prisoner. I hope it is not upsetting the eggs," he added, anxious despite all of Keynes's reassurances, and bent over to nudge them gently and carefully with his nose where they lay in their nests, presently tucked between two warming braziers under a ledge in the main courtyard of the palace, waiting to be loaded aboard.

The King and Queen were saying their farewells: they were sending the royal children away by courier to the well-protected fortress of Königsberg, deep in East Prussia. "You ought to go with them," the King said softly, but the Queen shook her head and kissed her children good-bye swiftly. "I do not want to go away, either, Mother; let me come, too," said the second prince, a sturdy boy of nine, and he was only packed off with difficulty and in the face of loud protests.

They stood together watching until the little courier-dragons dwindled to bird-specks and vanished, before at last they climbed back aboard Temeraire for the journey eastward with the handful of their retinue brave enough to venture it: a small and sad party.

Overnight a steady stream of bad news had flowed into the city, though at least these pieces of intelligence had been largely expected, if not so soon: Saxe-Weimar's detachment caught by Marshal Davout, every last man of ten thousand killed or taken prisoner; Bernadotte already at Magdeburg, cutting Hohenlohe off; the Elbe crossings falling into French hands, not a single bridge destroyed; Bonaparte himself already on the road to Berlin, and when Temeraire rose up into the air, they could see, not very distant, the smoke and dust of the oncoming army: marching, marching, with a cloud of dragons overhead.

They spent the night at a fortress on the Oder River; the commander and his men had not even heard rumors, and were bitterly shocked by news of the defeat. Laurence suffered through the dinner which the commander felt it necessary to give, a black and silent meal, quenched by the officers' depression and the natural embarrassment attendant on dining in the presence of royalty. The small walled covert attached to the fortress was barren and dusty and uncomfortable; and Laurence escaped to it and his meager bivouac of straw with great relief.

He woke to a soft rolling patter like fingertips on a drum: a steady grey rain falling against Temeraire's wings, which he had spread over them protectively; there would be no fire that morning. Laurence had a cup of coffee inside, looking over the maps and working out the compass-directions for the day's flight; they were trying to find the eastern reserves of the army, under command of General Lestocq, somewhere in the Polish territories which Prussia had lately acquired.

"We will make for Posen," the King said tiredly; he did not look as though he had slept very well. "There will be at least a detachment in the city, if Lestocq is not there yet himself."

The rain did not slacken all the day, and sluggish bands of fog drifted through the valleys below them; they flew through a grey formlessness, following the compass and the turns of the hourglass, counting Temeraire's wingbeats and marking his speed. Darkness was almost welcome; the cross-wind that blew the rain in their faces slackened, and they could huddle a little warmer in their leather coats. Villagers in the fields disappeared as they flew overhead; they saw no other signs of life until, crossing a deep river valley, they flew over five dragons, ferals, sleeping upon a sheltered ledge, who lifted up their heads at Temeraire's passage.

They leapt off the ledge and came flying towards Temeraire; Laurence grew anxious, lest they either provoke a quarrel or try and follow them, like Arkady and the mountain ferals; but they were small gregarious creatures and only flew alongside Temeraire a while, jeering wordlessly and making demonstrations of their flying abilities, backwing swoops and steep dives. Half-an-hour's flight brought them to the edge of the valley, and there the ferals with piercing cries broke off and circled back away into their territory. "I could not understand them," Temeraire said, looking over his shoulder after them. "I wonder what that language is, that they are speaking; it sounds a little bit like Durzagh in places, but it was too different to make out, at least when they spoke so quickly."

They did not reach the city that night after all: some twenty miles short they came upon the small and sodden campfires of the army, settling into miserable wet bivouacs for the night. General Lestocq came to the covert himself to greet the King and Queen, with sedan-chairs drawn up as close as he could persuade the bearers to come; he had evidently been warned to expect them, likely by a courier.

Laurence was naturally not invited to accompany them, but neither was he offered the simple courtesy of a billet, and the staff-officer who stayed to see to their supply was offensively short in his hurry to be gone. "No," Laurence said with mounting impatience, "no, half a sheep will *not* do; he has had a ninety-miles' flight today in bad weather, and he damned well will be fed accordingly. You do not look to me as though this army were on short commons." The officer was at length compelled to provide a cow, but the rest of them had a wet and hungry night, receiving only some thin oat porridge and biscuit, and no meat ration at all; perhaps a spiteful revenge.

Lestocq had with him only a small corps: two formations of smallish heavy-weights, nowhere near Temeraire's size, with four middle-weight wing dragons apiece, and a few courier-dragons for leaven. Their comfort had been equally neglected: the men were sleeping mostly distributed upon the backs of their dragons, only a few smallish tents posted for officers.

After they had unloaded him, Temeraire nosed around here and there, trying to find some drier place to rest, without success: the bare ground of the covert was nothing but mud two full inches down.

"You had better just lie down," Keynes said. "The mud will keep you warm enough, once you are in it properly."

"Surely it cannot be healthy," Laurence said dubiously.

"Nonsense," Keynes said. "What do you think a mustard-plaster is but mud? So long as he does not lie in it for a week, he will do perfectly well."

"Wait, wait," Gong Su said, unexpectedly; he had been gradually acquiring English, being isolated otherwise, but he was still shy of speaking out, save where his business of cookery was concerned. He went through his jars and spice-bags hurriedly and brought out a jar of ground red pepper, a few pinches of which Laurence had seen him use to flavor an entire cow. He put on a glove and ran beneath Temeraire's belly, scattering a double handful of it upon the ground, while Temeraire peered at him curiously from between his legs.

"There, now will be warm," Gong Su said, stepping out and sealing tight the jar again.

Temeraire gingerly let himself down into the muck, which made rude noises as it squelched up around his sides. "Ugh," he said. "How I miss the pavilions in China! This is not at all pleasant." He squirmed a little. "It *is* warm, but it feels quite odd."

Laurence could not like having Temeraire thus marinated, but there was little hope of doing better by him tonight at least. Indeed, he recalled that even while with the larger corps, under Hohenlohe's command, they had received little better accommodations; only the milder weather had rendered their circumstances more comfortable.

Granby and his men did not seem to take it as he did, shrugging. "I suppose it's what we're used to," Granby said. "When I was with Laetificat in India, once they put us on the day's battlefield, with the wounded moaning away all night and bits of swords and bayonets everywhere, because they didn't want to be put to the trouble of clearing some brush away for us to sleep elsewhere; Captain Portland had to threaten to desert to get them to move it the next morning."

Laurence had spent his career as an aviator so far entirely in the highly comfortable training-covert at Loch Laggan and in the long-established one at Dover, which—if nothing like what the Chinese considered adequate—at least offered well-drained clearings, shaded by trees, with barracks for the men and junior officers, and rooms at the headquarters for the captains and senior lieutenants. He supposed perhaps he was unrealistic, to expect good conditions in the field, with an army on the march, but surely something better might have been arranged: there were hills visible not very distant, certainly within an easy quarter-of-an-hour's flight, where the ground would not have been so thoroughly soaked.

"What can we do for the eggs?" he asked Keynes; at present the two large bundles were standing upon a handful of chests, draped over with an oilskin. "Will they take any harm from the cold?"

"I am trying to think," Keynes said irritably; he was pacing around Temeraire. "Will you be sure not to roll onto them in the night?" he demanded of the dragon.

"Of course I am not going to roll onto the eggs!" Temeraire said, outraged.

"Then we had better wrap them in oilskins and bury them up against his side in the mud," Keynes said to Laurence, ignoring Temeraire's muttered indignations. "There's no hope of starting a fire that will keep in this rain."

The men were already all as wet as they could be; by the time they had finished digging a hole they were also all over mud, but at least they had warmed up by the exercise; Laurence himself had stood out the whole while being drenched, feeling it his place to share the discomfort. "Share out the rest of the oilskins, and let everyone sleep aboard," he said, once the eggs were safely tucked into their nest, and gratefully climbed up to his own shelter for the night: the tent, now vacant, had been left up on Temeraire's back for him.

HAVING COVERED NEARLY two hundred miles in two days of flying, it was an unwelcome reversion to find themselves once again leashed by the infantry and, worse, by the endless trail of supply-waggons, which it seemed were stuck as often they were moving. The roads were terrible, unpaved sand and dirt that churned and squelched under every step, and littered with fallen leaves, wet and slippery. The army was moving eastward in hopes of a rendezvous with the Russians; even in the wretched conditions, laboring under the news of defeat, the discipline did not fail, and the column marched along in steady order.

Laurence found he had been unjust to the supply-officer: they were indeed on short rations. Though the harvest had just been brought in, there seemed to be nothing available anywhere in the countryside; at least not to them. The Poles showed empty hands when asked to sell, no matter what money they were offered. The crops had been bad, the herds had been sick, they said if pressed, and showed empty granaries and pens; though the black shiny eyes of pigs and cattle might occasionally be glimpsed peeking out from the dark woods behind their fields, and occasionally some enterprising officer unearthed a cache of grain or potatoes hidden in a cellar or beneath a trap-door. There were no exceptions, not even for Laurence's offers of gold, not even in houses where the children were too thin and scantily dressed against the coming winter; and once, in a small cottage little better than a hovel, when in exasperation he doubled the gold in his palm and held it out again with a pointed look at the baby lying scarcely covered in its cradle, the young matron of the house looked at him with mute reproach, and pushed his fingers closed over it before she pointed at the door.

Laurence went out again rather ashamed of himself; he was anxious for Temeraire, who was not getting enough to eat, but he could hardly blame the Poles for resenting the partition and occupation of their country; it had been a shameful business, much deplored in his father's political circles, and Laurence thought perhaps the Government had made some sort of formal protest, though he did not properly remember. It would hardly have made a difference; hungry for land, Russia and Austria and Prussia would not have listened. They had all pushed their borders out piece by piece, ignoring the cries for justice from their weaker neighbor, until at last they had met in the middle and there was no more country left in between; small wonder that the soldiers of one of those nations should meet a cool reception now.

They took two days to cross the twenty miles to Posen and

found an even colder welcome there; and a more dangerous one. Rumors had already reached the town: with the arrival of the army, the disaster at Jena could hardly be a secret, and more news came pouring in. Hohenlohe had finally surrendered with the tattered remnants of his infantry; and with that all of Prussia west of the Oder was falling like a house of cards.

The French Marshal Murat was repeating all over the country the same trick that had worked so nicely for him at Erfurt, seizing fortresses one after another with no weapon but brass cheek. His simple method was to present himself at their stoop, announce that he had come to receive their surrender, and wait until the doors were opened and the governor let him in. But when the governor at Stettin, several hundred miles from the battlefield and as yet wholly ignorant of what had occurred, indignantly refused this charming request, the iron beneath the brass plating was revealed: two days later there were thirty dragons and thirty guns and five thousand men outside the walls, busily digging trenches and piling up bombs in very noticeable heaps for a full assault, and the governor meekly handed over the keys and his garrison.

Laurence overheard this story told some five times in one walk around the town's marketplace square; he did not understand the language, but the same names would keep ringing out together, in tones not merely amused but exultant. Men sitting together murmuring in alehouses were raising their vodka-glasses to *Vive l'Empereur* when there was no Prussian in hearing distance, and sometimes even when there was, depending on how low the level in the bottle had gone; there was an atmosphere of belligerence and hope mingled.

He put his head in at every market-stall he could find; here at least the merchants could not refuse to sell what was plainly in sight, but supplies in the town were not much more plentiful and had for the most part already been appropriated. After much searching, Laurence was able only to find one poor small pig; he paid some five times its value and at once had it knocked smartly over the head with a cudgel to stun it and trundled to its doom in a wheelbarrow by one of his harness-men. Temeraire took it and ate it raw, too hungry to wait for cooking, and painstakingly licked clean his talons afterwards.

"SIR," LAURENCE SAID, restraining his temper, "you have not the proper supply for a heavy-weight, and the daily distance you cross is a tenth of what he can do."

"What difference does that make?" General Lestocq said, bristling. "I do not know what kind of discipline you run in England, but if you are with this army, you march with it! Good God, your dragon is hungry; so are all my men hungry. A fine form we should be in, if I began letting them run fifty miles afield to feed themselves."

"We would be at every evening's camp—" Laurence said.

"Yes, you will be," Lestocq said, "and you will be at the morning camp, and at the noon camp, and with the rest of the dragon-corps at every moment, or I will have you down as a deserter; now get out of my tent."

"I take it things went well," Granby said, looking at his face when Laurence came back into the small abandoned shepherd's hut which was their day's shelter, the first time they had slept dry in the week of slow and miserable marching since Posen; Laurence threw his gloves down on the cot with violence, and sat down to pull off his boots, ankle-deep in mud.

"I have half a mind to take Temeraire and be gone after all," Laurence said furiously. "Let that old fool put us down as deserters if he likes, and be damned to him."

"Here," Granby said, and picked up some of the straw from the floor to take hold of the boot-heel, so Laurence could get his foot out. "We could always go hunting, and join up again if we see a fight coming," he said, wiping off his hands and sitting back down on his own cot. "They'll hardly turn us away."

Laurence almost gave it consideration, but he shook his head. "No; but if this continues as it is—"

It did not; instead their pace slowed even further, and the only thing in shorter supply than food was good news. Rumors had gone around the camp for several days that a peace settlement had been offered by the French; an almost general sigh of relief had issued from the weary troops, but as the days passed and no announcement came, hope failed. Then fresh rumors followed about the shocking terms: the whole vast swath of Prussian territory east of the Elbe to be surrendered, and Hanover, too; huge indemnities to be paid; and, outrageously, the crown prince to be sent to Paris, "under the care of the Emperor, to the improvement of understanding and friendship between our nations, desirable to all," as the sinister phrasing had it.

"Good Lord, he does begin to think himself a proper Oriental despot, doesn't he," Granby said, hearing this news. "What would he do if they broke the treaty, send the boy to the guillotine?"

"He had D'Enghien murdered for less cause," Laurence said, thinking with sorrow of the Queen, so charming and courageous, and how this fresh and personal threat should act upon her spirits. She and the King had gone on ahead to meet with the Tsar; that, at least, was a piece of encouragement: Alexander had pledged himself wholly to continue the war, and the Russian Army was already on its way to rendezvous with them in Warsaw.

"LAURENCE," TEMERAIRE SAID, and Laurence shuddered up out of an old familiar night-terror: finding himself utterly alone on the deck of the *Belize,* his first command, in a gale; all the ocean lit up by lightning-flashes and not a human face anywhere in sight; with the unpleasant new addition of a dragon egg rolling ponderously towards the open forward hatch, too far for him to reach in time: not the green-speckled red of the Kazilik egg, but the pale porcelain of Temeraire's.

He wiped the dream from his face and listened to the distant sounds: too regular for thunder. "When did it begin?" he asked, reaching for his boots; the sky was only just growing lighter.

"A few minutes ago," Temeraire said.

They were three days from Warsaw, on the fourth of November. All through that day's march they heard the guns to the east, and during the night a red glow of fire shone in the distance. The guns were fainter the next day and silent by the afternoon. The wind had not changed. The army did not break from its mid-day camp; the men scarcely stirred, as if they all collectively held their breath, waiting.

The couriers, sent off that morning, came back hurrying a few hours later, but though the captains went directly to the general's quarters, before they even came out again the news was somehow already spreading: the French had beaten them to Warsaw. The Russians had been defeated.

CHAPTER 16

The small castle had been built of red brick, a long time ago: wars had battered it; peasants looking for building materials had dismantled it; rain and snow had melted down its edges. It was little more than a gutted shell now, one wall held up between half-crumbled towers, windows that faced onto open fields on both sides. They were grateful for the shelter nonetheless, Temeraire huddling for concealment into the square made by the ruined walls, the rest of them sheltering in the single narrow gallery, full of red brick dust and crumbled white mortar.

"We will stay another day," Laurence said in the morning; more an observation than a decision: Temeraire was grey and limp with exhaustion, and the rest of them hardly in better state. He asked for volunteers to go hunting and sent Martin and Dunne.

The countryside was alive with French patrols, and Polish also, formed of dragons released from the Prussian breeding-grounds where they had been pent up since the final partition ten years before. During the intervening years, many of their captains had died in Prussian captivity or from age or sickness; the bereft dragons were full of bitterness, which had easily enough been turned to Napoleon's use. They might not answer to discipline well enough to serve in battle, without captain or crew, but they could profitably be set to scouting; and no harm done if they should take it on themselves to attack some hapless group of Prussian stragglers.

And the army was nothing but stragglers now, all of them making only loosely for the last Prussian strongholds in the north. There was no more hope of victory; the generals had spoken only of securing some position that might strengthen their hands at the bargaining table a little. It seemed to Laurence folly; he doubted himself whether there would be any table at all.

Napoleon had sent his armies speeding across the sodden roads of Poland with not a single waggon to hold them back, dragons carrying all the supply: gambling that he could catch and beat the Russians before his food ran out and his men and beasts began to starve. He had risked all on one throw of the dice, and won; the Tsar's armies had been strung out along the road to Warsaw, wholly unsuspecting, and in three days and three battles he had smashed them in their separate parts. The Prussian army he had carefully skirted on the road; they had served him, they understood only too late, as bait to draw the Russians more quickly from their borders.

Now the jaws of the Grande Armée were closing in on them for the final bite. The army had spilled northward in desperation, whole battalions deserting at a time; Laurence had seen artillery and ammunition abandoned on the road, supply-waggons surrounded by clouds of birds feasting on grain spilled in struggles among the starving men. Lestocq had sent orders to the covert to send the dragon-corps to their next post, a small village ten miles away; Laurence had crumpled the dispatch in his hand and let it fall to the ground to be trampled into the mud, and then he had put his men aboard, with all the supplies they could find, and flown north as long as Temeraire's strength would allow.

What so complete a defeat should mean for Britain, he would

not now consider. He had one goal only: to get Temeraire and his men home, and the two dragon eggs. They seemed now piti- fully inadequate, when they should have to help be a wall around Britain, to defend her against an Emperor of Europe in search of more worlds to conquer. If he had been once again on that hill, in the brush, with Napoleon standing so close to hand, Laurence did not know what he would do; he wondered occasionally, in the sleepless hours of the night, if Badenhaur blamed him for staying his hand.

He did not feel any kind of black mood or anger, such as had occasionally fallen upon him after a defeat; only a great dis- tance. He spoke calmly to his men, and to Temeraire; he had managed to get his hands on a map, at least, of their route to the Baltic Sea, and spent most of his hours studying how to skirt the towns, or how to get back on course after a patrol had forced them to flee out of their way, to a temporary safety. Though Temeraire could cover ground by far more quickly than infan- try, he was by far more visible as well, and their progress north- ward did not much outstrip the rest of the army after all their dodging and evasions. There was little left in the countryside to forage, and they were all going hungry, giving whatever could be spared to Temeraire.

Now, in the ruins of the castle, the men slept, or lay listless and open-eyed against the walls, not moving. Martin and Dunne came back after nearly an hour with one small sheep, shot neatly through the head. "I'm sorry for having to use the rifle, sir, but I was afraid it would get away," Dunne said.

"We didn't catch sight of anyone," Martin added anxiously. "It was off alone; I expect it had wandered away from its herd."

"You did as you ought, gentlemen," Laurence said, without attending very much; if they had done anything badly, it would still hardly have been worth reproaching them.

"I take it first," Gong Su said urgently, catching his arm, when Laurence would have given it straight to Temeraire. "Let me, it will go further. I make soup for everyone; there is water."

"We haven't much biscuit left," Granby ventured to him very

quiet and tentatively, at this suggestion. "It would put heart into the fellows, to have a taste of some meat."

"We cannot risk an open flame," Laurence said with finality.

"No, not open fire." Gong Su pointed to the tower. "I build inside, smoke comes out slow, from this," and he tapped the crevices between the bricks in the wall beside them. "Like smokehouse."

The men had to come out of the closed gallery, and Gong Su could only go in to stir for a few minutes at a time, coming out coughing and with his face covered with black, but the smoke seeped out only in thin, flat bands which clung to the brick and did not send up any great column.

Laurence turned back to his maps, laid out on top of a broken table-sized block of wall; he thought a few more days would see them to the coastline, and then he would have to decide: west for Danzig, where the French might be, or east to Königsberg, almost surely still in Prussian hands, but farther from home. He was all the more grateful, now, to his meeting with the embassy secretary in Berlin who had given him the now-priceless information that the Navy was out in the Baltic in force— Temeraire had only to reach the ships, and they would be safe; pursuit could not follow them into the teeth of the ships' guns.

He was working out the distances for the third time when he lifted his head, frowning; men were stirring a little across the camp. The wind was shifting into their faces and carrying a snatch of song, not very tuneful but sung with great enthusiasm in a girl's clear voice, and in a moment she came into view around the wall. She was just a peasant girl, bright-cheeked with exercise, with her hair neatly braided back beneath a kerchief and carrying a basket full of walnuts and red berries and branches laden with yellow and amber leaves. She turned the corner and saw them: the song stopped mid-phrase, and she stared at them with wide startled eyes, still open-mouthed.

Laurence straightened up; his pistols were lying in front of him, weighting down the corners of his maps; Dunne and Hackley and Riggs all had their rifles right in their hands, being that moment engaged in reloading; Pratt, the big armorer, was leaning against the wall in arm's reach of the girl; a word and she would be caught, silenced. He put his hand out and touched the pistol; the cold metal was like a shock to his skin, and abruptly he wondered what the devil he was doing.

A shudder seized him, shoulders to waist and back; and suddenly he was himself again, fully present in his own skin and astonished by the change of sensation: he was at once painfully, desperately hungry, and the girl was running away wildly down the hill, her basket flung away in a hail of golden leaves.

He continued the movement and put the pistols back into his belt, letting the maps roll up. "Well, she will have everyone in ten miles roused in a moment," he said briskly. "Gong Su, bring the stew out; we can have a swallow at least before we must get about it, and Temeraire can eat while we pack. And Roland, Dyer, do you two go and collect those walnuts and crack the shells."

The two runners hopped over the wall and began to gather up the spilled contents of the peasant girl's basket, while Pratt and his mate Blythe went in to help carry out the big soup-pot. Laurence said, "Mr. Granby, let us see a little activity here, if you please; I want a lookout up on that tower."

"Yes, sir," Granby said, jumping at once to his feet, and with Ferris began rousing the men from their own separate lethargies to begin pushing the broken stone and brick into something like steps up the side of the tower. The work did not go quickly, with the men all tired and shaky, but it gave them more life, and the tower was not so very high; soon enough they had a rope thrown over one of the crenellations of the parapet, and Martin was scrambling up to keep watch, calling, "And don't you fellows eat my share, either!" to more laughter than this feeble sally deserved. The men turned eagerly to get out their tin cups and bowls as the cauldron came very carefully out, not a drop spilling.

"I am sorry we must go so quickly," Laurence said to Temeraire, stroking his nose.

"I do not mind," Temeraire said, nuzzling him with particular energy. "Laurence, you are well?"

Laurence was ashamed that his queer mood should have been so noticeable. "I am; forgive me for having been so out of sorts," he answered. "You have had the worst of it all along; I ought never have committed us to this enterprise."

"But we did not know that we were going to lose," Temeraire said. "I am not sorry to have tried to help; I would have felt a great coward running away."

Gong Su ladled out the still-thin soup in small sparing portions, half-a-cupful to each man, and Ferris doled out the biscuit; at least there was as much tea as anyone could want to drink, situated as the castle was between two lakes. They all ate involuntarily slowly, trying to make each bite count for two, and then Roland and Dyer went around with the odd unexpected treat of fresh walnuts, a little young and bitter, but delicious; the purplish sloes, too tart for their palates, Temeraire licked up out of the basket as a single swallow. When all had eaten their share, Laurence sent Salyer up in Martin's place, and had the midshipman down for his own meal; and then Gong Su began heaving the dismembered joints of the sheep's carcass out of the cauldron one at a time directly into Temeraire's waiting jaws, so the hot juice would not run out of them and go to waste.

Temeraire too lingered over each swallow, and he had scarcely consumed the head and one leg before Salyer was leaning over and shouting, and scrambling down the rope. "Air patrol, sir, five middle-weights coming," he panted; a worse threat than Laurence had feared: the patrol must have been sheltering just at the nearby village, and the girl must have run straight to them. "Five miles distant, I should think—"

The meal behind them and the immediate danger before gave them all a burst of fresh energy; in moments the equipment was back aboard, the light mesh armor laid out: they had left behind the armor plates, several escapes ago. Then Keynes said, "For the love of Heaven, don't eat the rest of the meat," sharply to Temeraire, who was just opening his mouth for Gong Su to tip in the last mouthfuls.

"Why not?" Temeraire demanded. "I am still hungry."

"The blasted egg is hatching," Keynes said. He was already tearing and heaving at the silken swaddling, throwing off great shining panels of green and red and amber. "Don't stand there gawking, come and help me!" he snapped.

Granby and the other lieutenants sprang to his assistance at once while Laurence hurriedly organized the men to get the second egg, still wrapped up, back into Temeraire's belly-rigging; it was the last of the baggage.

"Not now!" Temeraire said to the egg, which was now rocking back and forth so energetically that they were having to hold it in place with their hands; it would otherwise have gone rolling end-over-end across the ground.

"Go and get the harness arranged," Laurence told Granby, and took his place bracing the egg; the shell was hard and glossy and queerly hot to the touch under his hands, so he even took a moment to pull on his gloves; Ferris and Riggs, on the other side, were wincing their hands away alternately.

"We must leave at this moment, you cannot hatch now; and anyway there is almost no food," Temeraire added, to no apparent effect but a furious rapping noise from inside against the shell. "It is not paying me any mind," he said, aggrieved, sitting back on his haunches, and looked rather unhappily at the remnants in the cauldron.

Fellowes had long since put together a dragonet's rig out of the softest scraps of harness, just in case, but it had been rolled up snugly with the rest of the leather deep in their baggage. They finally got it out, and Granby turned it over with almost shaking hands, opening some buckles and adjusting others. "Nothing to it, sir," Fellowes said softly; the other officers clapped him on the back with encouraging murmurs.

"Laurence," Keynes said in an undertone, "I ought to have thought of this before; but you had better draw Temeraire away at once, as far as you can; he won't like it."

"What?" Laurence said, just as Temeraire said, with a flare of belligerence, "What are you doing? Why is Granby holding that harness?"

Laurence thought at first, in deep alarm, that Temeraire was speaking out against the harnessing of the dragon in principle. "No, but Granby is in *my* crew," Temeraire said, obstinately, an objection which disqualified every man in sight, unless perhaps he had not yet formed an attachment to Badenhaur or the handful of other Prussian officers. "I do not see why I must give it my food, *and* Granby."

The shell was beginning to crack, now; none too soon. The patrol had slowed their approach out of caution, perhaps imagining that the British meant to make a stand from behind the shelter of the walls, since evidently they were not fleeing. But caution would only keep them off so long; soon one of them would make a quick dart overhead, see what was going on, and then they would instantly attack in force.

"Temeraire," Laurence said, backing away a distance and trying to distract Temeraire's attention from the hatching egg, "only consider, the little dragon will be quite alone, and you have a large crew all for yourself. You must see it is not fair; there is no one else for the dragonet, and," he added with sudden inspiration, "it will have no jewels at all, such as you have; it must surely feel very unhappy."

"Oh," Temeraire said. He put his head down very close to Laurence. "Perhaps it could have Allen?" he suggested quietly, with a darting look over his shoulder to make sure he was not overheard by that awkward young ensign, who was presently engaged in surreptitiously running his finger around the rim of the pot, and licking it clean of a few more drops of soup.

"Come, that is unworthy of you," Laurence said reprovingly. "Besides, this is Granby's chance of promotion; surely you would not deny him the right to advance himself."

Temeraire made a low grumbling noise. "Well, if he *must*," he said, ungraciously, and curled up to sulk, taking up his sapphire breastplate in his foreclaws to nose over and rub to a higher shine with the side of his cheek.

His agreement was only just in time; the shell did not so much break open as burst with a cloud of steam, speckling them all with tiny fragments of shell and egg-slime. "*I* did not make such a mess," Temeraire said, disapprovingly, brushing at the bits stuck to his hide.

The dragonet itself spat bits of shell in every direction; it was hissing below its breath in a strangled sort of way. It was almost a miniature in form of the adult Kaziliks, with the same bristling thorny spines all over, scarlet with shining purplish armor plates over its belly; even the impressive horns were there, smaller in scale; only the green leopard-spots were missing. The baby dragon looked up at them with glaring yellow eyes, hot and indignant, coughed once, twice, and then drew in and held a deep breath that made its sides puff out like a balloon. Abruptly thin jets of steam issued out of its spines, hissing, and it opened its mouth and jetted out a little stream of flame some five feet long, sending the nearest men jumping back in surprise.

"Oh, *there*," she said, pleased, sitting up on her haunches. "That is much better; now let me have the meat."

Granby had been looking perfectly white beneath his sunburn, but he managed a steady voice as he stepped nearer her. He was holding the harness draped across his right arm, where she could see it plainly, without thrusting it at her. "My name is John Granby," he said. "We will be happy to—"

"Yes, yes, the harnessing," she interrupted, "Temeraire has told me about that."

Laurence turned and eyed Temeraire, who looked vaguely guilty and pretended to be very occupied polishing away a scratch on his breastplate; Laurence began to wonder what else he might have instructed the eggs in, as he had been nursemaiding them now nearly two months.

Meanwhile the dragonet put her head out to sniff at Granby; she tilted her head first to one side and then the other, looking him up and down. "And you have been Temeraire's first officer?" she said interrogatively, with the air of one asking for references.

"I have," Granby said, rather flustered, "and should you like a name of your own? It is a very nice thing to have; I would be happy to give you one."

"Oh, I have already decided that," she said, much to Granby's further consternation and that of the other aviators. "I want to be Iskierka, like that girl was singing about."

Laurence had harnessed Temeraire more by accident than design, and since then had never seen another hatching; he did not have any very clear idea of how it was supposed to go, but judging by the expressions of his men this was not characteristic. However, the baby Kazilik added, "But I should like to have you as my captain anyway, and I do not mind being harnessed and fighting to help protect England; but hurry, because I am *very* hungry."

Poor Granby, who had likely been dreaming of this day since he had been a seven-year-old cadet, every moment planned out with full ceremony and the name long-since chosen, looked tolerably blank for a moment; then abruptly he laughed out loud. "All right, Iskierka it is," he said, recovering handsomely, and held up the neck-loop of the harness. "Will you put your head in here?"

She cooperated quite willingly, except for stretching her head impatiently out towards the pot while he hurried to fasten the last few buckles, and when finally loosed, she thrust her entire head and forelegs into the still-hot cauldron to devour the remains of Temeraire's dinner. She did not need any encouragement to eat quickly; the contents vanished with blazing speed, the pot rocking back and forth as she finished licking it clean. "That was very good," she said, lifting her head out again, her little horns dripping with soup, "but I would like some more; let us go hunting." She experimentally fluttered out her wings, still soft and crumpled against her back.

"Well, we can't now, we must get out of here," Granby said, keeping a prudent hold of her harness; and a sudden storm of wings came above, as one of the patrol-dragons finally came and put its head over the wall to see what they were doing. Temeraire sat up and roared, and it backwinged hastily away, but the damage was done; it was already calling to its fellows.

"All aboard, no ceremony!" Laurence shouted, and the crew hastily flung themselves onto the harness. "Temeraire, you must carry Iskierka, will you put her aboard?"

"I can fly myself," she said. "Is there going to be a battle? Now? Where is it!" She did indeed lift off into the air a little ways, but Granby managed to keep his grip on her harness, and she ended by bouncing back and forth.

"No, we are not going to have a battle," Temeraire said, "and anyway you are too little to fight just yet." He bent down his head and closed his jaws around her body: the gap between his sharp front teeth and those to the rear held her neatly, and though she squalled in angry protest, he picked her up and laid her down across his shoulders. Laurence gave Granby a leg up to the harness, so he could scramble to her straightaway, and followed himself. All the crew were aboard, and Temeraire launched himself with a leap even as the patrol came charging over the wall: roaring, he threw himself straight up into their midst, and knocked them all away like ninepins.

"Oh! Oh! They are attacking us! Quick, let us kill them!" Iskierka said with appalling bloodthirstiness, trying to leap off into the air.

"No; for Heaven's sake, stop that!" Granby said, clinging to her desperately while with his other hand he struggled to get carabiner straps on her, to latch her harness securely to Temeraire's. "We're going a dashed sight faster right now than you could manage; be patient! We'll go flying as much as you like, only give it a little while."

"But there is a battle now!" she said, squirming around to try and see the enemy dragons; she was hard to get a proper hold of, with all her spiky thorn-like protrusions, and she was scrabbling at Temeraire's neck and harness with her claws; still soft, but evidently ticklish from the way Temeraire snorted and tossed his head.

"Hold still!" Temeraire said, looking around; he had taken advantage of the temporary disarray of the enemy dragons to put on a burst of speed, and was flying fast for a thick cloud-bank to the north, which might conceal them. "You are making it very difficult for me to fly."

"I don't want to be still!" she said shrilly. "Go back, go back! The fighting is that way!" For emphasis she fired off another jet of flame, which only narrowly escaped singeing off Laurence's hair, and danced with impatience from one foot to the other, with all Granby could do to hold her.

The patrol came on rapidly after them, and they did not give up after the cloud cover hid Temeraire from their sight, but kept on, calling out to one another in the mist to make sure of their positions, and advancing more slowly. The cold damp was unpleasant to the little Kazilik, who coiled herself around Granby's chest and shoulders in loops for warmth, narrowly avoiding strangling him or jabbing him with spikes, and kept up a muttering complaint about their running away.

"Do hush, there's a dear creature," Granby said, stroking her. "You'll give away our place; it is like hide-and-seek, we must be quiet."

"We would not need to be quiet or stay in this nasty cold cloud if only we went and thrashed them," she said, but finally subsided.

At length the sound of the searchers died away, and they dared to slip out again; but now a fresh difficulty presented itself: Iskierka had to be fed. "We will have to risk it," Laurence said, and they flew cautiously away from the thick woods and lakes, and closer to farmland territory, while they searched the ground with spyglasses.

"How nice those cows would be," Temeraire said wistfully after a little while; Laurence hurriedly turned his glass to the far distance and saw them, a herd of fine cattle grazing placidly upon a slope.

"Thank Heaven," Laurence said. "Temeraire, go to ground if you please; that hollow there will do, I think," he added, pointing. "We will wait until after dark and take them then."

"What, the cows?" Temeraire said, looking around with some confusion as he descended. "But Laurence, are those not property?"

"Well, yes, I suppose they are," Laurence said, in embarrassment, "but under the circumstances, we must make an exception."

"But how are the circumstances any different than when Arkady and the others took the cows in Istanbul?" Temeraire demanded. "They were hungry then, and we are hungry now; it is just the same."

"There we were arriving as guests," Laurence said, "and we thought the Turks our allies."

"So it is not theft if you do not like the person who owns the property?" Temeraire said. "But then—"

"No, no," Laurence said hastily, foreseeing many future difficulties. "But at present—the exigencies of war—" He fumbled through some explanation, trailing off lamely. Of course it would seem rather like theft; although this was, at least on the maps, Prussian territory, so it might reasonably be called requisition. But the distinction between requisition and theft seemed difficult to explain, and Laurence did not at all mean to tell Temeraire that so had all their food the past week been stolen, and likely near enough all the supply from the army, too.

In any case, call it bald-faced theft or some more pleasant word, it was still necessary; the little dragon was too young to understand having to go hungry, and was in more desperate need: Laurence well remembered the way Temeraire had gone through food in his early weeks of rapid growth. And they were in great need too, of her silence: if thoroughly fed she would probably sleep away all the time between meals for her first week of life.

"Lord, she's a proper terror, isn't she," Granby said, lovingly, stroking her glossy hide; despite her impatient hunger, she had fallen into a nap while they waited for the night to come. "Breathing fire straight from the shell; it will be a fright to manage her." He did not sound as though he objected.

"Well, I hope she will soon become more sensible," Temeraire said. He had not quite recovered from his earlier disgruntlement, and his temper had not been improved by her accusations of cowardice and demands to go back and fight: certainly his own instinctive inclination, if an impractical one. More generally it seemed his devotion to the eggs had curiously not translated to immediate affection for the dragonet; though perhaps he was merely still annoyed at being robbed to feed her.

"She is precious young," Laurence said, stroking Temeraire's nose.

"I am sure *I* was never so silly, even when I was first hatched," Temeraire said, to which remark Laurence prudently made no answer.

An hour after sunset they crept up the slope from downwind and made their stealthy attack; or so it might have been, save in a frenzy of excitement Iskierka clawed through the carabiner straps holding her on, and flung herself over the fence and onto the back of one of the sleeping, unsuspecting cows. It bellowed in terror and bolted away with all the rest of the herd, with the dragonet clinging aboard and shooting off flames in every direction but the right one, so the affair took on the character more of a circus than a robbery. The house lit up, and the farmhands dashed out with torches and old muskets, expecting perhaps foxes or wolves; they halted at the fence staring, as well they might; the cow had taken to frantic bucking, but Iskierka had her claws deeply embedded in the roll of fat around its neck, and was squealing half in excitement, half in frustration, ineffectually biting at it with her still-small jaws.

"Only *now* look what she has done," Temeraire said self-righteously, and jumped aloft to snatch the dragonet and her cow in one claw, a second cow in the other. "I am sorry we have woken you up, we are taking your cows, but it is not stealing, because we are at war," he said, hovering, to the white and frozen little group of men now staring up at his vast and terrible form, whose incomprehension came even more from terror than from language.

Feeling pangs of guilt, Laurence hastily fumbled at his purse and threw some gold coins down. "Temeraire, do you have her? For Heaven's sake let us be gone at once; they will have the whole country after us."

Temeraire did have her, as was proven once in the air by her muffled but audible yelling from below, "It is my cow! It is mine! I had it first!" which did not greatly improve their chances of hiding. Laurence looked back and saw the whole village shining like a great beacon out of the dark, one house after another illuminating; it would certainly be seen for miles.

"We had better have taken them in broad daylight, blowing a fanfare on trumpets," Laurence said with a groan, feeling that it was a judgment on him for stealing.

They put down only a little way off out of desperation, hoping to feed Iskierka and make her quiet. At first she refused to let go of her cow, now quite dead, having been pierced through by Temeraire's claws, though she could not quite get through its hide and begin eating. "It is *mine*," she kept muttering, until at last Temeraire said, "Be quiet! They only want to cut it open for you, now let go. Anyway, if I wanted your cow I would take it away."

"I should like to see you try!" she said, and he whipped his head down and growled at her, which made her squeak and jump straight for Granby, who was knocked sprawling by her landing unexpectedly in his arms. "Oh, that was not nice!" she said indignantly, coiling around Granby's shoulders. "Only because I am still small!"

Temeraire had the grace to look a little ashamed of himself, and he said a little more placatingly, "Well, I am not going to take your cow anyway, I have one of my own, but you should be polite while you are still so little."

"I want to be big now," she said sulkily.

"You shan't get bigger unless you let us feed you properly," Granby said, which drew her quick attention. "Come and you shall watch us make it ready for you; how will that do?"

"I suppose," she said, reluctantly, and he carried her back over to the carcass. Gong Su slit open the belly and cut out first the heart and the liver, which he held out to her with a ceremonial air, saying, "Best first meal, for little dragons to get big," and she said, "Oh, is it?" and snatched them in both claws to eat with great gusto, blood pouring out the sides of her jaws as she tore and swallowed one bite and another from each one in turn.

One of the leg joints was all the rest which she could manage, despite her best efforts, and then she collapsed into a stupor to their general and profound gratitude; Temeraire devoured the rest of his own cow while Gong Su crudely and quickly butchered the remnants of the second and packed it away in his pots; and they were back aloft in some twenty minutes, with the dragonet now lying heavy and asleep in Granby's arms, quite dead to all the world.

But there were dragons circling over the illuminated village in the distance now, and as they rose up one of them turned to look at them, its luminous white eyes shining: a Fleur-de-Nuit, one of the few nocturnal breeds. "North," Laurence said, grimly, "straight north as quick as you can, Temeraire; to the sea."

They fled all the rest of the night, the queer low voice of the Fleur-de-Nuit sounding always behind them, like a deep brass note, and the answering higher voices of the middle-weights following its lead. Temeraire was burdened more heavily than their pursuers, carrying all his ground crew and supplies and Iskierka to boot; it seemed to Laurence she had already visibly grown. Still Temeraire managed to keep ahead, but only just, and there was no hope of losing them; the night was cold and clear, the moon barely short of full.

The miles spilled away, the Vistula River beneath them unwinding towards the sea, black and glistening occasionally with ripples; they loaded all their guns fresh, readied the flash-powder charge, and Fellowes and his harness-men struggled all the way up Temeraire's side notch by notch with a square of spare chainmesh to lay over Iskierka for protection. She murmured without waking and snuggled closer to Granby as they draped it over her body, hooking it to the rings of her little harness.

Laurence thought at first that the enemy had started shooting at them from too far away; then the guns sounded again and he recognized the sound: not rifles but artillery, in the distance. Temeraire turned towards it at once, to the west; out before them was opening the vast unbroken blackness of the Baltic, and the guns were Prussian guns, defending the walls of Danzig.

CHAPTER 17

"I am sorry you should have shut yourself into this box with us," General Kalkreuth said, passing to him the bottle of truly excellent port, which Laurence could appreciate sufficiently to tell it was being wasted on his palate after the past month of drinking weak tea and watered rum.

It followed on several hours full of sleep and dinner, and the still-better comfort of seeing Temeraire eat as much as he wished. There was no rationing, at least not yet: the city's warehouses were full, the walls fortified, and the garrison strong and well-trained; they would not easily be starved out or demoralized into surrender. The siege might last a long time; indeed the French seemed in no hurry to begin it properly.

"You see we are a convenient mousetrap," Kalkreuth said, and took Laurence to the southern-facing windows. In the waning daylight, Laurence could see the French encampments arranged in a loose circle around the city, out of artillery-fire range, astride the river and the roads. "Daily I see our men coming in from the south, the remnants of Lestocq's division, and falling into their hands as neatly as you please. They must have taken five thousand prisoners already at least. From the men, they only take their muskets and their parole and send them home, so as not to have the feeding of them; the officers they keep."

"How many men do they have?" Laurence asked, trying to count tents.

"You are thinking of a sortie, and so have I been," Kalkreuth said. "But they are too far away; they would be able to cut the force off from the city. When they decide to start besieging us in earnest and come a little closer, we may have some action; for what good it will do us, now that the Russians have made peace.

"Oh yes," he added, seeing Laurence's surprise, "the Tsar decided he would not throw a good army after bad, in the end, and perhaps that he did not want to spend the rest of his life as a French prisoner; there is an armistice, and they are negotiating a treaty in Warsaw, the two Emperors, as the best of friends." He gave a bark of laughter. "So you see, they may not bother getting us out; by the end of this month I may be a *citoyen* myself."

He had only just escaped the final destruction of Prince Hohenlohe's corps, having been ordered to Danzig by courier to secure the fortress against just such a siege. "They first appeared on my doorstep less than a week later, without warning," he said, "but since then I have had all the news I could want: that damned Marshal keeps sending me copies of his own dispatches, of all the impudence, and I cannot even throw them in his face because my own couriers cannot get through."

Temeraire himself had barely made it over the walls; most of the French dragons enforcing the blockade were presently on the opposite side of the city, barring it from the sea, and surprise had saved them from the artillery below. However, they were now properly in the soup: several more pepper-guns had made their appearance amid the French guns since that morning, and long-range mortars were being dug into place all around.

The walled citadel itself was some five miles distant from the ocean harbor. From Kalkreuth's windows Laurence could see the last shining curve of the Vistula River, its mouth broadening as it spilled into the sea, and the cold dark blue of the Baltic was dotted over with the white sails of the British Navy. Laurence could even count them through the glass: two sixty-fours, a seventy-four with a broad pennant, a couple of smaller frigates as escort, all of them standing only a little way off the shore; in the harbor itself, protected by the guns of the warships, lay the big lumbering transport hulks which had been waiting to go and fetch Russian reinforcements to the city: reinforcements that now would never come. Five miles distant and as good as a thousand, with the French artillery and aerial corps standing in between.

"And now they must know that we are here and cannot reach them," Laurence said, lowering the glass. "They could hardly have avoided seeing us come in, yesterday, with the fuss the French made."

"It's that Fleur-de-Nuit who chased us here that is the worst trouble," Granby said. "Otherwise I should say let us just wait until the dark of the moon and make a dash for it; but you may be sure that fellow will be waiting for us to try just such a thing; he'd have all the rest of them on us before we clear the walls." Indeed that night they could see the big dark blue dragon as a shadow against the moonlit ocean, sitting up alertly on his haunches in the French covert, his enormous pallid eyes almost unblinking and fixed on the city walls.

"YOU ARE A good host," Marshal Lefèbvre said cheerfully, accepting without demur another tender pigeon upon his plate, and attacking it and the heap of boiled potatoes with gusto and manners perhaps more suited to a guard-sergeant than a Marshal of France: not surprising, as he had begun his military career as such, and life as the son of a miller. "We've been eating boiled grass and crows with our biscuit these two weeks."

He wore his curly hair grey and unpowdered over a round peasant's face. He had sent emissaries to try and open negotiations, and had accepted sincerely and without hesitation Kalkreuth's caustic reply: an invitation to dine in the city itself to discuss the matter of surrender. He had ridden up to the gates with no more escort than a handful of cavalrymen. "I'd take more risk for a dinner like this," he said with a rolling laugh, when one of the Prussian officers commented ungraciously on his courage. "It's not as though you'd get anything for long by putting me in a dungeon, after all, except to make my poor wife cry; the Emperor has a lot of swords in his basket."

After he had demolished every dish and mopped up the last of the juices from his plate with bread, he promptly let himself doze off in his chair while the port went around, and woke up only as the coffee was set before them. "Ah, that gives life to a man," he said, drinking three cups in quick succession. "Now then," he went on briskly without a pause, "you seem like a sensible fellow and a good soldier; are you going to insist on dragging this all out?"

The mortified Kalkreuth, who had not meant in the least to suggest he would truly entertain a suggestion of surrender, said coolly, "I hope I will maintain my post with honor until I receive orders to the contrary from His Majesty."

"Well, you won't," Lefèbvre said prosaically, "because he's shut up in Königsberg just like you are here. I'm sure it's no shame to you. I won't pretend I'm a Napoleon, but I hope I can take a city with two-to-one odds and all the siege guns I need. I'd just as soon save the men, yours and mine both."

"I am not Colonel Ingersleben," Kalkreuth said, referring to the gentleman who had so quickly handed over the fortress of Stettin, "to surrender my garrison without a shot fired; you may find us a tougher nut to digest than you imagine."

"We'll let you out with full honors," Lefèbvre said, refusing to rise to the bait, "and you and your officers can go free, so long as you give parole not to fight against France for twelve months. Your men too, of course, though we'll take their muskets. That's the best I can do, but still it'll be a damned sight nicer than getting shot or taken prisoner."

"I thank you for your kind offer," Kalkreuth said, getting up. "My answer is no."

"Too bad," Lefèbvre said without dismay, and got up also, putting on the sword he had casually slung over the back of his chair. "I don't say it'll stay open forever, but I hope you'll keep it in mind as we go on." He paused on turning, seeing Laurence, who had been seated some distance down the table, and added, "Though I'd better say now it doesn't apply to any British soldiers you have here. Sorry," he said to Laurence apologetically, "the Emperor has a fixed notion over you English, and anyway we've orders about you in particular, if you're the one with that big China dragon who came sailing over our heads the other day. Ha! You caught us sitting on the pot and no mistake."

With this final laugh at his own expense, he tramped out whistling to collect his escort and ride back out of the walls, leaving all of them thoroughly depressed by his good cheer; and Laurence to spend the night imagining all the most lurid sorts of orders which Lien might have persuaded Bonaparte to make concerning Temeraire's fate.

"I hope I need not tell you, Captain, that I have no thoughts of accepting this offer," Kalkreuth said to him the next morning, having summoned him to breakfast to receive this reassurance.

"Sir," Laurence said quietly, "I think I have good reason to fear being made a French prisoner, but I hope I would not ask to have the lives of fifteen thousand men spent to save me from such a fate, with God only knows how many ordinary citizens killed also. If they establish their batteries of siege guns, and I do not see how you can prevent it forever, the city must be surrendered or reduced to rubble; then we would be killed or taken in any case."

"We have a long road to travel before then," Kalkreuth said. "They will have slow going on their siege works, with the ground frozen, and a cold unhealthy winter sitting outside our gates; you heard what he said about their supplies. They will not make any headway before March, I promise you, and a great deal can happen in so long a time."

His estimate seemed good at first: seen through Laurence's glass, the French soldiers picked and spaded the ground in an unenthusiastic manner, making little headway with their old and rust-bitten tools against the hard-packed earth: saturated through, so near to the river, and frozen hard already in the early winter. The wind brought drifts and flurries of snow off the sea, and frost climbed the window-panes and the sides of his morning washbasin each day before dawn. Lefèbvre himself looked to be in no rush: they could see him, on occasion, wandering up and down the shallow beginnings of the trench, trailed by a handful of aides and his lips puckered in a whistle, not dissatisfied.

Others, however, were not so content with the slow progress: Laurence and Temeraire had been in the city scarcely a fortnight before Lien arrived.

She came in the late afternoon, out of the south: riderless, trailed only by a small escort of two middle-weights and a courier, beating hard away from the leading edge of a winter gale that struck the city and the encampment scarcely half-an-hour after she had landed. She had been sighted by the city lookouts only, and for all the two long days of the storm, with snow obscuring all their sight of the French camp, Laurence entertained some faint hope that a mistake had been made; then he woke heart thundering the next day to a clear sky and the dying echoes of her terrible roar.

He ran outside in nightshirt and dressing gown, despite the cold and the ankle-deep snow not yet swept from the parapet; the sun was pale yellow, and dazzling on the whitened fields and on Lien's marble-pale hide. She was standing at the edge of the French lines, inspecting the ground closely: as he and the appalled guards watched, she once again drew her breath deep, launched aloft, and directed her roar against the frozen earth.

The snow erupted in blizzard-clouds, dark clods of dirt flying, but the real damage was not to be recognized until later, when the French soldiers came warily back to work with their pickaxes and shovels. Her efforts had loosened the earth many feet down, to below the frost-line, so that their work now moved at a far more rapid pace. In a week the French works outstripped all their prior progress, the labor greatly encouraged by the presence of the white dragon, who often came and paced back and forth along the lines, watchful for any sign of slackening, while the men dug frantically.

Almost daily the French dragons now tried some sortie against the city's defenses, mostly to keep the Prussians and their guns occupied while the infantry dug their trenches and set up their batteries. The artillery along the city walls kept the French dragons off, for the most part, but occasionally one of them would try and make a high aerial pass, out of range, to drop a load of bombs upon the city fortifications. Dropped from so great a height, these rarely hit their mark, but more often fell into the streets and houses with much resulting misery; already the townspeople, more Slavic than German and feeling no particular enthusiasm for the war, began to wish them all at Jericho.

Kalkreuth daily served his men a ration of gunnery to return upon the French, though more for their morale than for what effect it would have upon the works, still too far away to reach. Once in a while a lucky shot would hit a gun, or carry away a few of the soldiers digging, and once to their delight struck a posted standard and sent it with its crowning eagle toppling over: that night Kalkreuth ordered an extra ration of spirits sent round to all, and gave the officers dinner.

And when tide and wind permitted, the Navy would creep in closer from their side and try a fusillade against the back of the French encampment; but Lefèbvre was no fool, and none of his pickets were in range. Occasionally Laurence and Temeraire could see a small skirmish go forward over the harbor, a company of French dragons running a bombardment against the transports; but the quick barrage of canister- and pepper-shot from the warships as quickly drove them back in turn: neither side able to win a clear advantage against the other. The French might, with time enough, have built artillery emplacements enough to drive off the British ships, but they were not to be so distracted from their real goal: the capture of the city.

Temeraire did his best to fend off the aerial attacks, but he was the only dragon in the city barring a couple of tiny couriers and the hatchling, and his strength and speed had their limits. The French dragons spent their days flying idly around the city, over and over, taking it in shifts; any flagging of Temeraire's attention, any slackening of the guard at the artillery, was an opportunity to pounce and do a little damage before dashing away again, and all the while the trenches slowly widened and grew, the soldiers as busy as an army of moles.

Lien took no part in these skirmishes, save to pause and sit watching them, coiled and unblinking of eye; her own labors were all for the siege works going steadily forward. With the divine wind, she could certainly have perpetrated a great slaughter among the men on the ramparts, but she disdained to venture herself directly on the field.

"She is a great coward, if you ask me," Temeraire said, glad of an excuse to snort in her direction. "I would not let anyone make *me* hide away like that, when my friends were fighting."

"*I* am not a coward!" Iskierka threw in, briefly awake enough to notice what was going on around her. No one could have doubted her claim: increasingly massive chains were required to restrain her from leaping into battle against full-grown dragons as yet twenty times her size, though daily that proportion was decreasing. Her growth was a fresh source of anxiety: though prodigious, it was not yet sufficient to enable her either to fight or to fly effectively, but would soon make her a serious burden upon Temeraire should they attempt to make their escape.

Now she rattled her latest chain furiously. "I want to fight too! Let me loose!"

"You can only fight once you are bigger, like she is," Temeraire said hurriedly. "Eat your sheep."

"I *am* bigger, much," she said resentfully, but having dismantled the sheep, she fell shortly fast asleep again, and was at least temporarily silenced.

Laurence drew no such sanguine conclusions; he knew Lien was lacking neither in physical courage nor in skill, from the example of her duel with Temeraire in the Forbidden City. Perhaps she might yet be governed, to some extent, by the Chinese proscription against Celestials engaging in combat. But Laurence suspected that in her refusal to engage directly they rather saw the cunning restraint appropriate to a commander: the position of the French troops was thoroughly secure, and she was too valuable to risk for only insignificant gain.

The daily exhibition of her natural authority over the other dragons, and her intuitive understanding of how best they could be put to use, soon confirmed Laurence in his sense of the very material advantage to the French of her taking on what seemed so curious a role. Under her direction, the dragons forwent formation drill in favor of light skirmishing maneuvers; when not so engaged, they lent themselves to the digging, further speeding the progress of the trenches. Certainly the soldiers were uneasy at sharing such close quarters with dragons, but Lefèbvre managed them with displays of his own unconcern, walking among the laboring dragons and slapping them on their flanks, joking loudly with their crews; though Lien gave him a very astonished look on the one occasion when he used her so, as a stately duchess might to a farmer pinching her on the cheek.

The French had the advantage of superior morale, after all their lightning victories, and the excellent motive of getting inside the city walls before the worst of the winter struck. "But the essential point is, it is not only the Chinese, who grow up among them, who can grow accustomed: the French *have* gotten used to it," Laurence said to Granby amid hasty bites of his bread-and-butter; Temeraire had come down to the courtyard for a brief rest after another early-morning skirmish.

"Yes, and these good Prussian fellows also, who have Temeraire and Iskierka crammed in amongst them," Granby said, patting her side, which rose and fell like a bellows beside him; she opened an eye without waking and made a pleased drowsy murmur at him, accompanied with a few jets of steam from her spines, before closing it again.

"Why shouldn't they?" Temeraire said, crunching several leg bones in his teeth like walnut shells. "They must recognize us by now unless they are very stupid, and know that we are not going to hurt them; except Iskierka might, by mistake," he added, a little doubtfully; she had developed the inconvenient habit of occasionally scorching her meat before she ate it, without much attention to who if anyone might be in her general vicinity at the time.

KALKREUTH NO LONGER spoke of what might happen, or of long waits; his men were drilling daily to make ready for an attack on the advancing French. "Once they are in range of our guns, we will sortie against them at night," he said grimly. "Then, if we accomplish nothing more, we can at least make some distraction that may give you a chance at escaping."

"Thank you, sir; I am deeply obliged to you," Laurence said; such a desperate attempt, with all the attendant risk of injury or death, nevertheless recommended itself greatly when laid against the choice to quietly hand himself and Temeraire over. Laurence did not doubt for an instant that Lien's arrival was owed to their presence: the French might be willing to take their time, more concerned with the capture of the citadel; she had other motives. Whatever Napoleon's plans and hers for the discomfiture of Britain, to witness them as helpless prisoners, under a sure sentence of death for Temeraire, was as terrible a fate as Laurence could conceive, and any end preferable to falling into her power.

But he added, "I hope, sir, that you do not risk more than you ought, helping us so: they may resent it sufficiently to withdraw the offer of honorable surrender, should their victory seem, as I fear it now must, a question merely of time."

Kalkreuth shook his head, not in denial: a refusal. "And so? If we took Lefèbvre's offer; even if he let us go, what then?—all the men disarmed and dismissed, my officers bound by parole not to lift a hand for a year. What good will it do us to be released honorably, rather than to make unconditional surrender; either way the corps will be utterly broken up, just like all the rest. They have undone all the Prussian Army. Every battalion dissolved, all the officers swept into the bag—there will be nothing even left to rebuild around."

He looked up from his maps and despondency and gave Laurence a twisted smile. "So, you see, it is not so great a thing that I should offer to hold fast for your sake; we are already looking total destruction in the face."

They began their preparations; none of them spoke of the batteries of artillery which would be directed upon them, or the thirty dragons and more who would try and bar their way: there was after all nothing to be done about them. The date of the sortie was fixed for two days hence on the first night of the new moon, when the gloom should hide them from all but the Fleur-de-Nuit; Pratt was hammering silver platters into armor plates; Calloway was packing flash-powder into bombs. Temeraire, to avoid giving any hint of their intentions, was hovering over the city as was his usual wont; and in one stroke all their planning and work was overthrown: he said abruptly, "Laurence, there are some more dragons coming," and pointed out over the ocean.

Laurence opened up his glass and squinting against the glare of the sun could just make out the approaching forces: a shifting group of perhaps as many as twenty dragons, coming in fast and low over the water. There was nothing more to be said; he took Temeraire down to the courtyard, to alert the garrison to the oncoming attack and to take shelter behind the fortress guns.

Granby was standing anxiously by the sleeping Iskierka in the courtyard, having overheard Laurence's shout. "Well, that has torn it," he said, climbing up to the city walls with Laurence and borrowing his glass for a look. "Not a prayer of getting past two dozen more of—"

He stopped. The handful of French dragons in the air were hurriedly taking up defensive positions against the newcomers. Temeraire rose up on his hind legs and propped himself against the city wall for a better view, much to the dismay of the soldiers stationed on the ramparts, who dived out of the way of his great talons. "Laurence, they are fighting!" he said, in great excitement. "Is it our friends? Is it Maximus and Lily?"

"Lord, what timing!" Granby said, joyfully.

"Surely it cannot be," Laurence said, but he felt a sudden wild hope blazing in his chest, remembering the twenty promised British dragons; though how they should have come now, and here to Danzig of all places—but they had come in from the sea, and they *were* fighting the French dragons: no formations at all, only a kind of general skirmishing, but they had certainly engaged—

Taken off their guard and surprised, the small guard of French dragons fell back in disarray little by little towards the walls; and before the rest of their force could come to their aid, the newcomers had broken through their line. Hurtling forward, they set up a loud and gleeful yowling as they came tumbling pell-mell into the great courtyard of the fortress, a riot of wings and bright colors, and a preening, smug Arkady landed just before Temeraire and threw his head back full of swagger.

Temeraire exclaimed, "But whatever are you doing here?" before repeating the question to him in the Durzagh tongue. Arkady immediately burst into a long and rambling explanation, interrupted at frequent junctures by the other ferals, all of whom clearly wished to add their own mite to the account. The cacophony was incredible, and the dragons added to it by getting into little squabbles amongst themselves, roaring and hissing and trading knocks, so that even the aviators were quite bewildered with the noise, and the poor Prussian soldiers, who had only just begun to be used to have the well-behaved Temeraire and the sleeping Iskierka in their midst, began to look positively wild around the eyes.

"I hope we are not unwelcome." The quieter voice drew Laurence around, away from the confusion, and he found Tharkay standing before him: thoroughly windblown and disarrayed but with his mild sardonic look unchanged, as though he regularly made such an entrance.

"Tharkay? Most certainly you are welcome; are you responsible for this?" Laurence demanded.

"I am, but I assure you, I have been thoroughly punished for my sins," Tharkay said dryly, shaking Laurence's hand and Granby's. "I thought myself remarkably clever for the notion until I found myself crossing two continents with them; after the journey we have had, I am inclined to think it an act of grace that we have arrived."

"I can well imagine," Laurence said. "Is this why you left? You said nothing of it."

"Nothing is what I thought most likely would come of it," Tharkay said with a shrug. "But as the Prussians were demanding twenty British dragons, I thought I might as well try and fetch these to suit them."

"And they came?" Granby said, staring at the ferals. "I never heard of such a thing, grown ferals agreeing to go into harness; how did you persuade them?"

"Vanity and greed," Tharkay said. "Arkady, I fancy, was not unhappy to engage himself to *rescue* Temeraire, when I had put it to him in those terms; as for the rest—they found the Sultan's fat kine much more to their liking than the lean goats and pigs which are all the fare they can get in the mountains; I promised that in your service they should receive one cow a day apiece. I hope I have not committed you too far."

"For twenty dragons? You might have promised each and every one of them a herd of cows," Laurence said. "But how have you come to find us here? It seems to me we have been wandering halfway across Creation."

"It seemed so to me, also," Tharkay said, "and if I have not lost my sense of hearing in the process it is no fault of my company. We lost your trail around Jena; after a couple of weeks terrorizing the countryside, I found a banker in Berlin who had seen you; he said if you had not been captured yet, you would likely be here or at Königsberg with the remains of the army, and here you behold us."

He waved a hand over the assembled motley of dragonkind, now jostling one another for the best positions in the courtyard. Iskierka, who had so far miraculously slept through all the bustle, had the comfortable warm place up against the wall of the barracks' kitchens; one of Arkady's lieutenants was bending down to nudge her away. "Oh, no," Granby said in alarm, and dashed for the stairs down to the courtyard: quite unnecessarily, for Iskierka woke just long enough to hiss out a warning lick of flame across the big grey dragon's nose, which sent him hopping back with a bellow of surprise. The rest promptly gave her a wide respectful berth, little as she was, and gradually arranged themselves in other more convenient places, such as upon the roofs, the courtyards, and the open terraces of the city, much to the loud shrieking dismay of the inhabitants.

"TWENTY OF THEM?" Kalkreuth said, staring at little Gherni, who was sleeping peacefully on his balcony; her long, narrow tail was poking in through the doors and lying across the floor of the room, occasionally twitching and thumping against the floor. "And they will obey?"

"Well; they will mind Temeraire, more or less, and their own leader," Laurence said doubtfully. "More than that I will not venture to guarantee; in any case they can only understand their own tongue, or a smattering of some Turkish dialect."

Kalkreuth was silent, toying with a letter opener upon his desk, twisting the point into the polished surface of the wood, heedless of damage. "No," he said finally, mostly to himself, "it would only stave off the inevitable."

Laurence nodded quietly; he himself had spent the last few hours contemplating ways and means of assault with their new aerial strength, some kind of attack which might drive the French away from the city. But they were still outnumbered in the air three dragons to two, and the ferals could not be counted on to carry out any sort of strategic maneuver. As individual skirmishers they would do; as disciplined soldiers they were a disaster ready to occur.

Kalkreuth added, "But I hope they will be enough, Captain, to see you and your men safely away: for that alone I am grateful to them. You have done all you could for us; go, and God-speed."

"Sir, I only regret we cannot do more, and I thank you," Laurence said.

He left Kalkreuth still standing beside his desk, head bowed, and went back down to the courtyard. "Let us get the armor on him, Mr. Fellowes," Laurence said quietly to the ground-crew master, and nodded to Lieutenant Ferris. "We will leave as soon as it is dark."

The crew set about their work silently; they were none of

them pleased to be leaving under such circumstances. It was impossible not to look at the twenty dragons disposed about the fortress as a force worth putting to real use in its defense; and the desperate escape they had planned to risk alone felt now selfish, when they meant to take all those dragons with them.

"Laurence," Temeraire said abruptly, "wait; why must we leave them like this?"

"I am sorry to do it also, my dear," Laurence said heavily, "but the position is untenable: the fortress must fall eventually, no matter what we do. It will do them no good in the end for us to stay and be captured with them."

"That is not what I mean," Temeraire said. "There are a great many of us, now; why do we not take the soldiers away with us?"

"CAN IT BE done?" Kalkreuth asked; and they worked out the figures of the desperate scheme with feverish speed. There were just enough transports in the harbor to squeeze the men aboard, Laurence judged, though they should have to be crammed into every nook from the hold to the manger.

"We will give those jack tars a proper start, dropping onto them out of nowhere," Granby said dubiously. "I hope they may not shoot us out of the air."

"So long as they do not lose their heads, they must realize that an attack would never come so low," Laurence said, "and I will take Temeraire to the ships first and give them a little warning. He at least can hover overhead, and let the passengers down by ropes; the others will have to land on deck. Thankfully they are none of them so very large."

Every silk curtain and linen sheet in the elegant patrician homes was being sacrificed to the cause, much against their owners' wishes, and every seamstress of the city had been pressed into service, thrust into the vast ballroom of the general's residence to sew the carrying-harnesses under the improvisational direction of Fellowes. "Sirs, begging your pardon, I won't stand on oath they'll any of them hold," he said. "How these things are rigged in China, ordinary, I'm sure I don't know; and as for what we are doing, it'll be the queerest stuff dragon ever wore or man ever rode on, I can't say plainer than that."

"Do what you can," General Kalkreuth said crisply, "and any man who prefers may stay and be made prisoner."

"We cannot take the horses or the guns, of course," Laurence said.

"Save the men; horses and guns can be replaced," Kalkreuth said. "How many trips will we need?"

"I am sure I could take at least three hundred men, if I were not wearing armor," Temeraire said; they were carrying on their discussion in the courtyard, where he could offer his opinions. "The little ones cannot take so many, though."

The first carrying-harness was brought down to try; Arkady edged back from it a little uneasily until Temeraire made some pointed remarks and turned to adjust a strap of his own harness; at which the feral leader immediately presented himself, chest outthrust, and made no further difficulties: aside from turning himself round several times in an effort to see what was being done, and thus causing a few of the harness-men to fall off. Once rigged out, Arkady promptly began prancing before his comrades; he looked uncommonly silly, as the harness was partly fashioned out of patterned silks that had likely come from a lady's boudoir, but he plainly found himself splendid, and the rest of the ferals murmured enviously.

There was rather more difficulty getting men to volunteer to board him, until Kalkreuth roundly cursed them all for cowards and climbed on himself; his aides promptly followed him up in a rush, even arguing a little over who should go up first, and with this example before them the reluctant men were so shamed they too began clamoring to board; to which Tharkay, observing the whole, remarked a little dryly that men and dragons were not so very different in some respects.

Arkady, not the largest of the ferals, being leader more from force of personality than size, was able to lift off the ground easily with a hundred men dangling, perhaps a few more. "We can fit nearly two thousand, across all of them," Laurence said, the trial complete, and handed the slate to Roland and Dyer to make them do the sums over, to be sure he had the numbers correct: much to their disgruntlement; they felt it unfair to be set back to schoolwork in so remarkable a situation. "We cannot risk over-loading them," Laurence added. "They must be able to make their escape if we are caught at it in the middle."

"If we don't take care of that Fleur-de-Nuit, we will be," Granby said. "If we engaged him tonight—?"

Laurence shook his head, not in disagreement but in doubt. "They are taking precious good care he is not exposed. To get anywhere near we would have to come in range of their artillery, and get directly into their midst; I have not seen him stir out of the covert since we arrived. He only watches us from that ridge, and keeps well back."

"They would hardly need the Fleur-de-Nuit to tell them we were doing something tomorrow, if we made a great point of singling him out tonight," Tharkay pointed out. "He had much better be dealt with just before we begin."

No one disagreed, but puzzling out the means left them at sixes-and-sevens a while. They could settle on nothing better than staging a diversion, using the littler dragons to bombard the French front ranks: the glare would interfere with the Fleur-de-Nuit's vision, and in the meantime the other dragons would slip out to the south, and make a wider circle out to sea.

"Though it won't do for long," Granby said, "and then we will have all of them to deal with, and Lien, too: Temeraire can't fight her with three hundred men hanging off his sides."

"An attack such as this will rouse up all the camp, and some-one will see us going by sooner or late," Kalkreuth agreed. "Still it will gain us more time than if the alarm were raised at once; I would rather save half the corps than none."

"But if we must circle about so far out of the way, it will take a good deal more time, and we will never get so many away," Temeraire objected. "Perhaps if we only went and killed him very quickly and quietly, we might then get away before they know what we are about; or at least thumped him hard enough he could not pay any more attention—"

"What we truly need," Laurence said abruptly, "is only to put him quietly out of the way; what about drugging him?" In the thoughtful pause, he added, "They have been feeding the dragons livestock dosed with opium all through the campaign; if we slip him one more thoroughly saturated, likely he will not notice any queer taste, at least not until it is too late."

"His captain will hardly let him eat a cow if it's still wandering in circles," Granby said.

"If the soldiers are eating boiled grass, the dragons cannot be eating as much as they like, either," Laurence said. "I suspect he will prefer to ask forgiveness than permission, if a cow goes by him in the night."

Tharkay undertook to manage it. "Find me some nankeen trousers and a loose shirt, and give me a dinner-basket to carry," he said. "I assure you I will be able to walk through the camp quite openly; if anyone stops me I will speak pidgin to them and repeat the name of some senior officer. And if you give me a few bottles of drugged brandy for them to take from me, so much the better; no reason we cannot let the watch dose themselves with laudanum, too."

"But will you be able to get back?" Granby asked.

"I do not mean to try," Tharkay said. "After all, our purpose is to get out; I can certainly walk to the harbor long before you will have finished loading, and find a fisherman to bring me out; they are surely doing a brisk business with those ships."

KALKREUTH'S AIDES WERE crawling around the courtyard on hands and knees, drawing out a map in chalks, large enough for the feral dragons to make out and, by serendipity, colorful and interesting enough to command their attention. The bright blue stripe of the river would be their guide: it passed through the city walls and then curved down to the harbor, passing through the French camp as it went.

"We will go single-file, keeping over the water," Laurence

said, "and pray be sure the other dragons understand," he added anxiously to Temeraire, "they must go very quietly, as if they were trying to creep up on some wary herd of animals."

"I will tell them again," Temeraire promised, and sighed a very little. "It is not that I am not happy to have them here," he confided quietly, "and really they have been minding me quite well, when one considers that they have never been taught, but it would have been so very nice to have Maximus and Lily here, and perhaps Excidium; he would know just what to do, I am sure."

"I cannot quarrel with you," Laurence said; apart from all considerations of management, Maximus alone could likely have taken six hundred men or more, being a particularly large Regal Copper. He paused and asked, tentatively, "Will you tell me now what else has been worrying you? Are you afraid they will lose their heads, in the moment?"

"Oh; no, it is not that," Temeraire said, and looked down, prodding a little at the remains of his dinner. "We are running away, are we not?" he said abruptly.

"I would be sorry to call it so," Laurence said, surprised; he had thought Temeraire wholly satisfied with their plan, now that they meant to carry out the Prussian garrison with them, and for his own part thought it a maneuver to applaud: if they could manage it. "There is no shame in retreating to preserve one's strength for a future battle, with better hope of victory."

"What I mean is, if we are going away, then Napoleon really has won," Temeraire said, "and England will be at war for a long time still; because he means to conquer us. So we cannot ask the Government to change anything, for dragons; we must only do as we are told, until he is beaten." He hunched his shoulders a little and added, "I do understand it, Laurence, and I promise I will do my duty and not always be complaining; I am only sorry."

It was with some awkwardness in the face of this handsome speech that Laurence recognized, and had then to convey to Temeraire, the change in his own sentiments, an awkwardness increased by the bewildered Temeraire's dragging out, one after another, all of Laurence's own earlier protests on the subject.

"I have not, I hope, changed in essentials," Laurence said, struggling for justification in his own eyes as well as his dragon's, "but only in my understanding. Napoleon has made manifest for all the world to see the marked advantages to a modern army of closer cooperation between men and dragons; we return to England not only to take up our post again, but bearing this vital intelligence, which makes it not merely our desire but our duty to promote such change in England."

Temeraire required very little additional persuasion, and all Laurence's embarrassment, at seeming to be fickle, was mitigated by his dragon's jubilant reaction, and the immediate necessity of presenting him with many cautions: every earlier objection remained, of course, and Laurence knew very well they would face the most violent opposition.

"I do not care if anyone else minds," Temeraire said, "or if it takes a long time; Laurence, I am so very happy, I only wish we were at home already."

ALL THAT NIGHT and the next day they continued to labor over the harnesses; the cavalry-horses' tack was soon seized upon and cannibalized, and the tanners' shops raided. Dusk was falling and Fellowes was still frantically climbing with his men all over the dragons, sewing on more carrying-loops, of anything which was left—leather, rope, braided silk—until they seemed to be festooned with ribbons and bows and flounces. "It is as good as Court dress," Ferris said, to much muffled hilarity, as a ration of spirits was passed around, "we ought to fly straight to London and present them to the Queen."

The Fleur-de-Nuit took up his appointed position at the usual hour, settling back on his haunches for the night's duty; as the night deepened, the edges of his midnight blue hide slowly faded into the general darkness, until all that could be seen of him were his enormous dinner-plate eyes, milky white and illuminated by the reflections of the campfires. Occasionally he stirred, or turned round to have a look towards the ocean, and the eyes would vanish for a moment; but they always came back again.

Tharkay had slipped out a few hours before. They watched, anxiously; for an eternity counting by the heartbeat, for two turns counting by the glass. The dragons were all ranged in lines, the first men aboard and ready to go at once. "If nothing comes of it," Laurence said softly, but then the palely gleaming eyes blinked once, twice; then for a little longer; then again; and then with the lids drooping gradually to cover them, they drifted slowly and languorously to the ground, and the last narrow slits winked out of sight.

"Mark time," Laurence called down to the aides-de-camp standing anxiously below, holding their hourglasses ready; then Temeraire leapt away, straining a little under the weight. Laurence found it queer to be conscious of so many men aboard, so many strangers crowding near him: the communal nervous quickening of their breath like a rasp, the muffled curses and low cries silenced at once by their neighbors, their bodies and their warmth muting the biting force of the wind.

Temeraire followed the river out through the city walls: staying over the water so that the living sound of the current running down to the sea should mask the sound of his wings. Boats drawn up along the sides of the river creaked their ropes, murmuring, and the great brooding bulk of the harbor crane protruded vulture-like over the water. The river was smooth and black beneath them, spangled a little with reflections, the fires of the French camp throwing small yellow flickers onto the low swells.

To their either side, the French encampment lay sprawling over the banks of the river, lantern glims showing here and there the slope of a dragon's body, the fold of a wing, the pitted blue iron of a cannon-barrel. Lumps that were soldiers lay sleeping in their rough bivouacs, huddled near one another under blankets of coarse wool, overcoats, or only mats of straw, with their feet poking out towards the fires. If there were any sounds to be heard from the camp, however, Laurence did not know it; his heart was beating too loudly in his ears as they went gliding by, Temeraire's wingbeats almost languidly slow.

And then they were breathing again as the fires and lights fell behind them; they had come safely past the edges of the encampment with one mile of soft marshy ground to the sea, the sound of the surf rising ahead: Temeraire put on eager speed, and the wind began to whistle past the edges of his wings; somewhere hanging off the rigging below, Laurence heard a man vomiting. They were already over the ocean; the ship-lanterns beckoned them on, almost glaring bright with no moon for competition. As they drew near Laurence could see a candelabrum standing in the stern-windows of one of the ships, a seventy-four, illuminating the golden letters upon her stern: she was the *Vanguard*, and Laurence leaned forward and pointed Temeraire towards her.

Young Turner crept out onto Temeraire's shoulder and held up the night-signal lantern where it could be seen, showing the friendly signal out its front, one long blue light, two short red, with thin squares of cloth laid over the lantern-hole to make the colors, and then the three short white lights to request a silent response; and again, as they drew nearer and nearer. There was a delay; had the lookout not seen? was the signal too old? Laurence had not seen a new signal-book in almost a year.

But then the quick blue–red–blue–red of the answer shone back at them, and there were more lights coming out on deck as they descended. "Ahoy the ship," Laurence called, cupping his hands around his mouth.

"Ahoy the wing," came the baffled reply, from the officer of the watch, faint and hard to hear, "and who the devil are you?"

Temeraire hovered carefully overhead; they flung down long knotted ropes, the ends thumping hollowly upon the deck of the ship, and the men began to struggle loose from the harness with excessive haste to be off. "Temeraire, tell them to go carefully, there," Laurence said sharply. "The harness won't stand hard use, and their fellows will be next aboard."

Temeraire rumbled at them low, in German, and the descent calmed a little; still further when one man, missing his grasp, slipped and went tumbling down with a too-loud cry that broke only with the wet melon-thump sound of his head striking against the deck. Afterwards the others went more warily, and below, their officers began to force them back against the ship's rails and out of the way, using hands and sticks to push them into place instead of shouted orders.

"Is everyone down?" Temeraire asked Laurence; only a handful of the crew were left, up on his back, and at Laurence's nod, Temeraire carefully let himself down and slipped into the water beside the ship, scarcely throwing up a splash. There was a great deal of noise beginning to rise from the deck, the sailors and soldiers talking at one another urgently and uselessly in their different tongues, and the officers having difficulty reaching one another through the crowd of men; the crew were showing lanterns wildly in every direction.

"Hush!" Temeraire said to them all sharply, putting his head over the side, "and put away those lights; can you not see we are trying to keep quiet? And if any of you do not listen to me or begin to scream, like great children, just because I am a dragon, I will pick you up and throw you overboard, see if I do not," he added.

"Where is the captain?" Laurence called up, into a perfect silence, Temeraire's threat having been taken most seriously.

"Will? Is that Will Laurence?" A man in a nightshirt and cap leaned over the side, staring. "The devil, man, did you miss the sea so much you had to turn your dragon into a ship? What is his rating?"

"Gerry," Laurence said, grinning, "you will do me the kindness to send out every last boat you have to carry the message to the other ships; we are bringing out the garrison, and we must get them embarked by morning, or the French will make the country too hot to hold us."

"What, the whole garrison?" Captain Stuart said. "How many of them are there?"

"Fifteen thousand, more or less," Laurence said. "Never mind," he added, as Stuart began to splutter, "you must pack them in somehow, and at least get them over to Sweden; they are damned brave fellows, and we aren't leaving them behind. I must get back to ferrying; God only knows how long we have until they notice us."

Going back to the city they passed over Arkady coming with his own load; the feral leader was nipping at the tails of a couple of the younger members of his flock, keeping them from meandering off the course; he waved his tail-tip at Temeraire as they shot by, Temeraire stretched out full-length and going as fast as he might, as quiet as he might. The courtyard was in controlled havoc, the battalions marching out one after another in parade-ground order to their assigned dragons, boarding them with as little noise as could be managed.

They had marked each dragon's place with paint on the flag-stones, already scratched and trampled by claws and boots. Temeraire dropped into his large corner, and the sergeants and officers began herding the men quickly along: each climbed up the side and thrust his head and shoulders through the highest open loop, getting a grip on the harness with his hands or clinging to the man above, trying for footholds on the harness.

Winston, one of the harness-men, flew over gasping, "Anything that needs fixing, sir?" and ran off instantly on hearing a negative, to the next dragon; Fellowes and his handful of other men were dashing about with similar urgency, repairing loose or broken bits of harness.

Temeraire was ready again; "Mark time," Laurence called.

"An hour and a quarter, sir," came back Dyer's treble; worse than Laurence had hoped, and many of the other dragons were only getting away with their second loads alongside them.

"We will get faster as we go along," Temeraire said stoutly, and Laurence answered, "Yes; quickly as we can, now—" and they were airborne again.

Tharkay found them again as they dropped their second load of men down to one of the transports in the harbor; he had somehow gotten on deck, and now he came swarming hand-over-hand up the knotted ropes, in the opposite direction from the descending soldiers. "The Fleur-de-Nuit took the sheep, but he did not eat the whole thing," he said quietly, when he had gotten up to Laurence's side. "He ate only half, and hid the rest; I do not know it will keep him asleep all night."

Laurence nodded; there was nothing to be done for it; they had only to keep going, as long as they could.

A suggestion of color was showing in the east, now, and too many men still crowded the lanes of the city, waiting to get aboard. Arkady was showing himself not useless in a time of crisis; he chivvied along his ferals to go quicker, and himself had already managed eight circuits. He came sailing in for his next load even as Temeraire finally lifted away with his seventh: his larger loads took more time to get aboard and disembark. The other ferals too were holding up bravely: the little motley-colored one whom Keynes had patched up, after the avalanche, was showing himself particularly devoted, and ferrying his tiny loads of twenty men with great determination and speed.

There were ten dragons on the decks of the ships, unloading, as Temeraire landed, mostly the larger of the ferals; the next pass would see the city close to empty, Laurence thought, and looked at the sun: it would be a close-run race.

And then abruptly from the French covert rose a small, smoking blue light; Laurence looked in horror as the flare burst over the river: the three dragons who were in transit at the moment squawked in alarm, jerking from the sudden flash of light, and a couple of men fell from their carrying-harnesses screaming to plunge into the river.

"Jump off! Jump, damn you," Laurence bellowed at the men still climbing down from Temeraire's harness. "Temeraire!"

Temeraire called it out in German, almost unnecessarily; the men were leaping free from all the dragons, many falling into the water where the ships' crews began frantically to fish them out. A handful were stuck still on the carrying-harnesses, or clinging to the ropes, but Temeraire waited no longer; the other dragons came leaping into the air behind him, and as a pack they stormed back to the city, past the shouts and now-blazing lanterns of the French encampment.

"Ground crew aboard," Laurence shouted through his speaking-trumpet as Temeraire came down into the courtyard for the last time, and outside the French guns sounded their first tentative coughing roars. Pratt came running with the last dragon egg in his arms, wrapped and bundled around with padding and oilskin, to be thrust into Temeraire's belly-rigging; and Fellowes and his men abandoned their makeshift harness-repairs. All the ground crew came swarming aboard with the ease of long practice on the ropes, getting quickly latched to the harness proper.

"All accounted for, sir," Ferris yelled from farther along Temeraire's back; he had to use his speaking-trumpet to be audible. Above their heads, the artillery was sounding from the walls, the shorter hollow coughs of howitzers, the whistling whine and fall of mortar shells; in the courtyard, shouting now, Kalkreuth and his aides were directing the last battalions aboard.

Temeraire picked Iskierka up in his mouth and slung her around onto his shoulders. She yawned and picked up her head drowsily. "Where is my captain? Oh! Are we fighting now?" Her eyes opened all the way at the rolling thunder of the guns going off one after another over their heads.

"Here I am, don't fret," Granby called, clambering up the rest of the way to catch her by the harness, just in time to keep her from leaping off again.

"General!" Laurence shouted; Kalkreuth waved them on, refusing, but his aides snatched him bodily and heaved him up: the men let go their own grips on the harness to take hold of him and hand him up along, until he was deposited next to Laurence, breathing hard and with his thin hair disarrayed: his wig had vanished in the ascent. The drummer was beating the final retreat; men were running down from the walls, abandoning the guns, some even leaping from the turrets and ledges straight onto the dragons' backs, grabbing blindly for some purchase.

The sun was coming up over the eastern ramparts, the night breaking up into long, narrow ranked clouds like rolled cigars, blue and touched all along their sides with orange fire; there was no more time. "Go aloft," Laurence shouted, and Temeraire gave a shattering roar and leapt away with a great thrust of his hindquarters, men dangling from his harness; some slipped away grasping vainly at the air, and fell down to the stones of the courtyard below, crying out. All the dragons came rising into the air behind him, roaring with many voices, with many wings.

The French dragons were coming out of their covert and going to the pursuit, their crews still scrambling to get into battle-order; abruptly Temeraire slowed, to let the ferals pass him, and then he put his head around and said, "There, *now* you may breathe fire at them!" and with a squeak of delight, Iskierka whipped her head around and let loose a great torrent of flame over Temeraire's back and into their pursuers' faces, sending them recoiling back.

"Go, now, quickly!" Laurence was shouting; they had won a little space, but Lien was coming: rising from the French camp bellowing orders; the French dragons, milling about in their riders' confusion, fell instantly in line with her. There was no sign of her earlier self-restraint: seeing them now on the verge of escape, she was beating after them with furious speed, outdistancing all the French dragons but the littlest couriers, who desperately fought to keep pace with her.

Temeraire stretched long and went flat-out, legs gathered close, ruff plastered against his neck, wings scooping the air like oars; they devoured the miles of ground as Lien did the distance between them, the thunder-coughing of the long guns of the warships beckoning them to the safety of their sheltering broadside. The first acrid wisps were in their faces; Lien was stretching out her talons, not yet in reach, and the little couriers were making wild attempts on their sides, snatching away a few men in their talons; Iskierka was gleefully firing off at them in answer.

Abruptly they were blind, plunging into a thick black-powder cloud; Laurence's eyes were streaming as they came out again, clear and away past the encampment and still going fast. The city and its fading lights was dwindling behind them with every wing-stroke; they shot out low over the harbor, the last of the men being hauled up out of the water and into the transports, and here came the great rolling drum-beat of the cannon: canister-shot whistling by thick as hailstones behind them, to halt the French dragons.

Lien burst through the cloud and tried to come after them, even through the rain of hot iron, but the little French couriers shrilled, protesting; some threw themselves on her back, clinging, to try and drag her out of range. She shook them all off with a great heave, and would have pressed on, but one more, crying out, flung himself before her with desperate courage: his hot black blood was flung spattering upon her breast as the shot which would have struck her tore instead through his shoulder, and she halted at last, her battle-fury broken, to catch him up when he would have fallen from the sky.

She withdrew then with the rest of her anxious escort of couriers; but hovering out of range over the snow-driven shore, she voiced one final longing and savage cry of disappointment, as loud as if she might crack the sky. It chased Temeraire out of the harbor and beyond, leaving a ghost of itself still ringing in their ears, but the sky ahead was opening up to a fierce deep cloudless blue, an endless road of wind and water before them.

A signal was flying from the mast of the *Vanguard*. "Fair wind, sir," Turner said, as they passed the ships by. Laurence leaned into the cold sea-wind, bright and biting; it scrubbed into the hollows of Temeraire's sides to clean away the last of the pooled eddies of smoke, spilling away in grey trailers behind them. Riggs had given the riflemen the order to hold their fire, and Dunne and Hackley were already calling habitual insults to each other as they sponged out their barrels and put their powder-horns away.

It would be a long road still; as much as a week's flying, with this contrary wind in their faces and so many smaller dragons to keep in company; but to Laurence it seemed he already beheld the rough stone coast of Scotland, heather gone brown and purplish-sere and the mountains mottled with white, past the green hills. A great hunger filled him for those hills, those mountains, thrusting up sharp and imperious, the broad yellowing squares of harvested farmland and the sheep grown fat and woolly for winter; the thickets of pine and ash in the coverts, standing close around Temeraire's clearing.

Out ahead of them, Arkady began something very like a marching-song, chanting lines answered by the other ferals, their voices ringing out across the sky each to each; Temeraire added his own to the chorus, and little Iskierka began to scrabble at his neck, demanding, "What are they saying? What does it mean?"

"We are flying home," Temeraire said, translating. "We are all flying home."

EXTRACTS FROM A LETTER PUBLISHED IN THE
PHILOSOPHICAL TRANSACTIONS OF THE ROYAL SOCIETY, APRIL 1806

March 3, 1806

Gentlemen of the Royal Society:

It is with trepidation that I take up my pen to address this august body regarding Sir Edward Howe's recent discourse upon the subject of draconic aptitude for mathematics. For an amateur of so little distinction as myself to make reply to so illustrious an authority must smack of vainglory, and I tremble at the notion of offering offense to that gentleman or his many and justly deserved supporters. Only the sincerest belief in the merits of my case, and, beyond this, a grave concern for the deeply flawed course upon which the study of dragons seems bent, would suffice to overcome the natural scruple I must feel at setting myself in opposition to the judgment of one whose experience so greatly outstrips my own, and to whom I would show unhesitating deference, if not for evi-

dence I must consider irrefutable; which, after much
anxiety, I herein submit to the consideration of this
body. My qualifications for this work are by no
means substantial, my time for the pursuit of natural
history being sadly curtailed by the demands of my
parish, so if I am to persuade it must be with the
force of my argument alone, and not through influence or impressive references. . . .

By no means do I intend any disparagement of
those noble creatures under discussion, nor to
quarrel with any man who would call them admira-
ble; their virtues are manifest, and among the highest
of these the essential good-humour of their nature,
evident in their submitting to the guidance of man-
kind for the sake of affection, rather than through a
compulsion it were quite impossible for any man to
bring to bear upon them. In this they have shown
themselves very like that more familiar and most
amiable creature the dog, who will shun the company
of his own kind and cleave in preference unto his
master, thus displaying almost alone among the
beasts a discrimination for the society of his betters.
This same discrimination dragons show, greatly to
their credit, and certainly no one can deny that with
it is matched an understanding superior to virtually
all of the animal world that renders them arguably
the most valuable and useful of all our domestic
beasts. . . .

And yet it has been some years now since many
eminent gentlemen, unsatisfied with these considerable encomiums, have begun to put before the world,
cautiously and in measured stages, a body of work
which in its sum total, almost as if by joint intention,
leads the thinking man to the inevitable and seduc-
tive conclusion that dragons rise beyond the animal
sphere entirely: that they possess, in full measure
equal to man, the faculty of reason and intellect.

The implications of such an idea I scarcely need enumerate. . . .

The foremost argument of these scholars to date has been that dragons alone among the beasts possess language, and show in their speech to the observer all the attributes of feeling and free will. Yet this argument I cannot allow even to be persuasive, much the less conclusive. The parrot, too, has mastered all the tongues of men; dogs and horses may be trained to comprehend some scattered words: if the latter possessed the facile throats of the former, would they not speak to us also, and solicit of us greater attentions? And as for these other arguments, who that has heard a dog whine, left behind by his master, would deny that animals know affection, and who that has set a horse at a fence and had it refused would deny that beasts possess their own—and often lamentably contrary!—will. Apart from these examples drawn from the animal kingdom, we have further seen in the famous work of Baron von Kempelen and M. de Vaucanson that the most astonishing automata may be produced, from a little tin and copper, which may produce speech through the operation of a few levers, or even mimic intelligent motion and persuade the uninformed observer of a lifelike animation, though they are nothing but clockwork and gears. Let us not mistake these simulacra of intelligence in brutish or mechanical behavior for true reason, the province only of man. . . .

Once we have set these aside as insufficient proofs of draconic intelligence, we come to Sir Edward Howe's most recent essay, which puts forth an argument not so easily dismissed: the ability of dragons to perform advanced mathematical calculations, an achievement which eludes many an otherwise educated man and is not to be found anywhere in the animal world, nor imitated by machinery. However, upon closer examination, we discover that . . . these feats we are to accept, upon the scantiest of evidence—the testimony of the dragon's captain and his officers, his fond and affectionate companions, affirmed by Sir Edward Howe only through one examination made personally, over the course of a few hours. This may seem sufficient to some number of my readers, the essay made more plausible by its less-ambitious forerunners in the field. However, permit me to point out that a similarly fragile body of evidence serves as the foundation of many of these earlier works as well. . . .

My audience may justly demand to know why such a claim might be pressed, intentionally or no; without making any accusation, I will for the satisfaction of this demand speculate not upon the *actual*, but upon *plausible* motives, though only considering those which may be called disinterested. I trust that these are sufficient to allay any suspicion that I mean to suggest any sordid conspiracy, for nothing could be further from my mind. It is natural that the huntsman should love his hounds and see in their brute devotions a human affection, that he should read into the tenor of their barks and the gleam of their eyes a deeper communication; it is the huntsman's own sensitivity which makes truth of this illusion, and makes him all the better a custodian of his flock. That the officers of the Aerial Corps have a communication of this sort with their dragons I do not doubt; but this must be laid to the credit of the men and not the beasts, even if the men deny the credit of it in all sincerity. . . . Furthermore, all those who have affection for these noble creatures must desire the improvement of their condition, and an acknowledgment of, as it were, the humanity of these beasts, must surely oblige us to deal with them more kindly than heretofore, which cannot be called anything but a generous motive. . . .

So far I have only endeavored to cast doubt upon the work of others. If positive evidence to the contrary be desired, however, we need only to contemplate the condition of feral dragons to have this truth at once illustrated before us. I have spoken at length with those good herdsmen who tend the breeding-grounds at Pen Y Fan, whose work daily brings them into the circles of the wild dragons, and who, rough as they themselves are, view these beasts with an unromantic disposition. Left to their own devices, unharnessed and free, these feral dragons display native cunning and an animal intelligence, but no more. They make no use of language, save the grunting and hissing common among animals; they form no society nor civilized relations; they have no art and no industry; they manufacture nothing, neither shelter nor tools. The same cannot be said of the meanest savage in the most barren part of the earth; what dragons know of higher things, they have learned only from men, and the impulse is not native to the species. Surely this is sufficient evidence of distinction between man and dragon, if such evidence be necessary. . . .

If with these arguments I have failed to convince, I will close with the final assertion that a conclusion so extravagant, flying in the face of all recorded and Scriptural authority and much observation to the contrary, must rather be proven *true* than *false,* and if even eligible for consideration ought to endure challenge greater than what my own small powers have enabled me to offer herein, with however good a will upon my part, and requires a far more substantial body of evidence, obtained and affirmed by impartial observers. It is in hopes of provoking wiser men than myself to doubt and to fresh investigations that I have ventured to make this attempt at refutation, and I most sincerely beg pardon of any man whom I may have herein offended, whether through my opinions or my lack of skill in expounding upon them.

Pray permit me to style myself, with the highest respect, your most humble obedient servant,

D. Salcombe
Brecon, Wales

ACKNOWLEDGMENTS

In working out the revised history of the campaign of 1806, I have relied especially on *The Campaigns of Napoleon*, by David G. Chandler, and *A Military History and Atlas of the Napoleonic Wars*, by Brigadier General Vincent J. Esposito and Colonel John R. Elting, both of which share the virtue of enabling even an amateur to grasp at understanding. Mistakes and implausibilities are my own; any accuracy may be laid at their door.

Many thanks to my beta readers on this one for all their help: Holly Benton, Francesca Coppa, Dana Dupont, Doris Egan, Diana Fox, Vanessa Len, Shelley Mitchell, Georgina Paterson, Sara Rosenbaum, L. Salom, Rebecca Tushnet, and Cho We Zen. I am as ever indebted to Betsy Mitchell, Emma Coode, and Jane Johnson, my splendid editors, and to my agent, Cynthia Manson.

And most of all, to Charles.

READ ON FOR AN EXCERPT OF

EMPIRE OF IVORY

THE FOURTH BOOK
IN THE TEMERAIRE SERIES BY

NAOMI NOVIK

"Send up another, damn you, send them all up, at once if you have to," Laurence said savagely to poor Calloway, who did not deserve to be sworn at: the gunner was firing off the flares so quickly his hands were scorched black, skin cracking and peeling to bright red where some powder had spilled onto his fingers; he was not stopping to wipe them clean before setting each flare to the match.

One of the little French dragons darted in again, slashing at Temeraire's side, and five men fell screaming as a piece of the makeshift carrying-harness unraveled. They vanished at once beyond the lantern-light and were swallowed up in the dark; the long twisted rope of striped silk, a pillaged curtain, unfurled gently in the wind and went billowing down after them, threads trailing from the torn edges. A moan went through the other Prussian soldiers still clinging desperately to the harness, and after it followed a low angry muttering in German.

Any gratitude the soldiers might have felt for their rescue from the siege of Danzig had since been exhausted: three days flying through icy rain, no food but what they had crammed into their pockets in those final desperate moments, no rest but a few hours snatched along a cold and marshy stretch of the Dutch coast, and now this French patrol harrying them all this last endless night. Men so terrified might do anything in a panic; many of them had still their small-arms and swords, and there were more than a hundred of them crammed aboard, to the less than thirty of Temeraire's own crew.

Laurence swept the sky again with his glass, straining for a glimpse of wings, an answering signal. They were in sight of shore, the night was clear: through his glass he saw the gleam of lights dotting the small harbors all along the Scottish coast, and below heard the steadily increasing roar of the surf. Their flares ought to have been plain to see all the way to Edinburgh; yet no reinforcements had come, not a single courier-beast even to investigate.

"Sir, that's the last of them," Calloway said, coughing through the grey smoke that wreathed his head, the flare whistling high and away. The powder-flash went off silently above their heads, casting the white scudding clouds into brilliant relief, reflecting from dragon scales in every direction: Temeraire all in black, the rest in gaudy colors muddied to shades of grey by the lurid blue light. The night was full of their wings: a dozen dragons turning their heads around to look back, their gleaming pupils narrowing; more coming on, all of them laden down with men, and the handful of small French patrol-dragons darting among them.

All seen in the flash of a moment, then the thunderclap crack and rumble sounded, only a little delayed, and the flare dying away drifted into blackness again. Laurence counted ten, and ten again; still there was no answer from the shore.

Emboldened, the French dragon came in once more. Temeraire aimed a swipe which would have knocked the little Pou-de-Ciel flat, but his attempt was very slow, for fear of dislodging any more of his passengers; their small enemy evaded with contemptuous ease and circled away to wait for his next chance.

"Laurence," Temeraire said, looking round, "where are they all? Victoriatus is in Edinburgh; he at least ought to have come. After all, we helped him, when he was hurt; not that I *need* help, precisely, against these little dragons," he added, straightening his neck with a crackle of popping joints, "but it is not very convenient to try and fight while we are carrying so many people."

This was putting a braver face on the situation than it deserved: they could not very well defend themselves at all, and Temeraire was taking the worst of it, bleeding already from many small gashes along his side and flanks, which the crew could not bandage up, so cramped were they aboard.

"Only keep everyone moving towards the shore," Laurence said; he had no better answer to give. "I cannot imagine the patrol will pursue us over land," he added, but doubtfully; he would never have imagined a French patrol could come so near to shore as this, either, without challenge; and how he should manage to disembark a thousand frightened and exhausted men under bombardment he did not like to contemplate.

"I am trying; only they *will* keep stopping to fight," Temeraire said wearily, and turned back to his work. Arkady and his rough band of mountain ferals found the small stinging attacks maddening, and they kept trying to turn around mid-air and go after the French patrol-dragons; in their contortions they were flinging off more of the hapless Prussian soldiers than the enemy could ever have accounted for. There was no malice in their carelessness: the wild dragons were unused to men except as the jealous guardians of flocks and herds, and they did not think of their passengers as anything more than an unusual burden; but with malice or none, the men were dying all the same. Temeraire could only prevent them by constant vigilance, and now he was hovering in place over the line of flight, cajoling and hissing by turns, encouraging the others to hurry onwards.

"No, no, Gherni," Temeraire called out, and dashed forward to swat at the little blue-and-white feral: she had dropped onto the very back of a startled French Chasseur-Vocifère: a courier-beast of scarcely four tons, who could not bear up under even her slight weight and was sinking in the air despite the frantic beating of its wings. Gherni had already fixed her teeth in the French dragon's neck and was now worrying it back and forth with savage vigor; meanwhile the Prussians clinging to her harness were all but drumming their heels on the heads of the French crew, crammed so tightly not a shot from the French side could fail of killing one of them.

In his efforts to dislodge her, Temeraire was left open, and the Pou-de-Ciel seized the fresh opportunity; this time daring enough to make an attempt at Temeraire's back. His claws struck so near that Laurence saw the traces of Temeraire's blood shining black on the curved edges as the French dragon lifted away again; his hand tightened on his pistol, uselessly.

"Oh, let me, let me!" Iskierka was straining furiously against the restraints which kept her lashed down to Temeraire's back. The infant Kazilik would soon enough be a force to reckon with; as yet, however, scarcely a month out of the shell, she was too young and unpracticed to be a serious danger to anyone besides herself. They had tried as best they could to secure her, with straps and chains and lecturing, but the last she roundly ignored, and though she had been but irregularly fed these last few days, she had added another five feet of length overnight: neither straps nor chains were proving of much use in restraining her.

"Will you hold still, for all love?" Granby said despairingly; he was throwing his own weight against the straps to try and pull her head down. Allen and Harley, the young lookouts stationed on Temeraire's shoulders, had to go scrambling out of the way to avoid being kicked as Granby was dragged stumbling from side to side by her efforts. Laurence loosened his buckles and climbed to his feet, bracing his heels against the strong ridge of muscle at the base of Temeraire's neck. He caught Granby by the harness-belt when Iskierka's thrashing swung him by again, and managed to hold him steady, but all the leather was strung tight as violin strings, trembling with the strain.

"But I can stop him!" she insisted, twisting her head sidelong as she tried to work free. Eager jets of flame were licking out of the sides of her jaws as she tried once again to lunge at the enemy dragon, but their Pou-de-Ciel attacker, small as he was, was still many times her size and too experienced to be frightened off by a little show of fire; he only jeered, backwinging to expose all of his speckled brown belly to her as a target in a gesture of insulting unconcern.

"Oh!" Iskierka coiled herself tightly with rage, the thin spiky protrusions all over her sinuous body jetting steam, and then with a mighty heave she reared herself up on her hindquarters. The straps jerked painfully out of Laurence's grasp, and involuntarily he caught his hand back to his chest, the numb fingers curling over in reaction. Granby had been dragged into mid-air and was dangling from her thick neck-band, vainly, while she let loose a torrent of flame: thin and yellow-white, so hot the air about it seemed to twist and shrivel away, it made a fierce banner against the night sky.

But the French dragon had cleverly put himself before the wind, coming strong and from the east; now he folded his wings and dropped away, and the blistering flames were blown back against Temeraire's flank. Temeraire, still scolding Gherni back into the line of flight, uttered a startled cry and jerked away while sparks scattered over the glossy blackness of his hide, perilously close to the carrying-harness of silk and linen and rope.

"*Verfluchtes Untier! Wir werden noch alle verbrennen,*" one of the Prussian officers yelled hoarsely, pointing at Iskierka, and fumbled with shaking hand in his bandolier for a cartridge.

"Enough there; put up that pistol," Laurence roared at him through the speaking-trumpet; Lieutenant Ferris and a couple of the topmen hurriedly unlatched their harness-straps and let themselves down to wrestle it out of the officer's hands. They could only reach the fellow by clambering over the other Prussian soldiers, however, and while too afraid to let go of the harness, the men were obstructing their passage in every other way, thrusting out elbows and hips with abrupt jerks, full of resentment and hostility.

Lieutenant Riggs was giving orders, distantly, towards the rear; "Fire!" he shouted, clear over the increasing rumble among the Prussians; the handful of rifles spoke with bright powder-bursts, sulfurous and bitter. The French dragon made a little shriek and wheeled away, flying a little awkward: blood streaked in rivulets from a rent in his wing, where a bullet had by lucky chance struck one of the thinner patches around the joint and penetrated the tough, resilient hide.

The respite came late; some of the men were already clawing their way up towards Temeraire's back, snatching at the greater security of the leather harness to which the aviators were hooked by their carabiner straps. But the harness could not take all their weight, not so many of them: if the buckles stretched open, or some straps gave way, and the whole began to slide, it would entangle Temeraire's wings and send them all plummeting into the ocean together.

Laurence loaded his pistols fresh and thrust them into his waistband, loosened his sword, and stood up again. He had willingly risked all their lives to bring these men out of a trap, and he meant to see them safely ashore if he could; but he would not see Temeraire endangered by their hysteric fear.

"Allen, Harley," he said to the boys, "do you run across to the riflemen and tell Mr. Riggs: if we cannot stop them, they are to cut the carrying-harness loose, all of it; and be sure you keep latched on as you go. Perhaps you had better stay here with her, John," he added, when Granby made to come away with him: Iskierka had quieted for the moment, her enemy having quitted the field, but she still coiled and re-coiled herself in sulky restlessness, muttering in disappointment.

"Oh, certainly! I should like to see myself do any such thing," Granby said, taking out his sword; he had for-gone pistols since becoming Iskierka's captain, to avoid the risk of handling open powder around her.

Laurence was too unsure of his ground to pursue an argument; Granby was not properly his subordinate any longer, and the more experienced aviator of the two of them, counting years aloft. Granby took the lead as they crossed Temeraire's back, moving with the sureness of a boy trained up from the age of seven; at each step Laurence handed forward his own lead-strap and let Granby lock it on to the harness for him, which he could do one-handed, that they might go more quickly.

Ferris and the topmen were still struggling with the Prussian officer in the midst of a thickening clot of men; they were disappearing from view under the violent press of bodies, only Martin's yellow hair visible. The soldiers were near full riot, men beating and kicking at one another, thinking of nothing but an impossible escape. The knots of the carrying-harness were tightening, giving up more slack, so all the loops and bands of it hung loose and swinging with the thrashing, struggling men.

Laurence came on one of the soldiers, a young man, eyes wide and staring in his wind-reddened face and his thick mustache wet-tipped with sweat, trying to work his arm beneath the main harness, blindly, though the buckle was already straining open, and he would in a moment have slid wholly free.

"Get back to your place!" Laurence shouted, pointing to the nearest open loop of the carrying-harness, and thrust the man's hand away from the harness. Then his ears were ringing, a thick ripe smell of sour cherries in his nostrils as his knees folded beneath him. He put a hand to his forehead slowly, stupidly; it was wet. His own harness-straps were holding him, painfully tight against his ribs with all his weight pulling against them. The Prussian had struck him with a bottle; it had shattered, and the liquor was dripping down the side of his face.

Instinct rescued him; he put up his arm to take the next blow and pushed the broken glass back at the man's face; the soldier said something in German and let go the bottle. They wrestled together a few moments more; then Laurence caught the man's belt and heaved him up and away from Temeraire's side. The soldier's arms were spread wide, grasping at nothing; Laurence, watching, abruptly recalled himself, and at once he lunged out, reaching to his full length; but too late, and he came thumping heavily back against Temeraire's side with empty hands; the soldier was already gone from sight.

His head did not hurt over-much, but Laurence felt queerly sick and weak. Temeraire had resumed flying towards the coast, having rounded up the rest of the ferals at last, and the force of the wind was increasing. Laurence clung to the harness a moment, until the fit passed and he was able to make his hands work properly again. There were already more men clawing up: Granby was trying to hold them back, but they were overbearing him by sheer weight of numbers, even though struggling as much against one another as him. One of the soldiers grappling for a hold on the harness climbed too far out of the press; he slipped, landed heavily on the men below him, and carried them all away; as a tangled, many-limbed mass they fell into the slack loops of the carrying-harness, and the muffled wet noises of their bones cracking together sounded like a roast chicken being wrenched hungrily apart.

Granby was hanging from his harness-straps, trying to get his feet planted again; Laurence crab-walked over to him and gave him a steadying arm. Below he could just make out the washy seafoam, pale against the black water; Temeraire was flying lower and lower as they neared the coast.

"That damned Pou-de-Ciel is coming round again," Granby panted as he got back his footing; the French had somehow got a dressing over the gash in the dragon's wing, even if the great white patch of it was awkwardly placed and far larger than the injury made necessary. The dragon looked a little uncomfortable in the air, but he was coming on gamely nonetheless; they had surely seen that Temeraire was vulnerable. If the Pou-de-Ciel and his crew were able to catch the harness and drag it loose, they might finish deliberately what the soldiers had begun in panic, and the chance of bringing down a heavy-weight, much less one as valuable as Temeraire, would surely tempt them to great risk.

"We will have to cut the soldiers loose," Laurence said, low and wretched, and looked upwards, where the carrying-loops attached to the leather; but to send a hundred men and more to their deaths, scarce minutes from safety, he was not sure he could bear; or ever to meet General Kalkreuth again, having done it; some of the general's own young aides were aboard, and doing their best to keep the other men quiet.

Riggs and his riflemen were firing short, hurried volleys; the Pou-de-Ciel was keeping just out of range, waiting for the best moment to chance his attack. Then Iskierka sat up and blew out another stream of fire: Temeraire was flying ahead of the wind, so the flames were not turned against him, this time; but every man on his back had at once to throw himself flat to avoid the torrent, which burnt out too quickly before it could reach the French dragon.

The Pou-de-Ciel at once darted in while the crew were so distracted; Iskierka was gathering herself for another blow, and the riflemen could not get up again. "Christ," Granby said; but before he could reach her, a low rumble like fresh thunder sounded, and below them small round red mouths bloomed with smoke and powder-flashes: shore batteries, firing from the coast below. Illuminated in the yellow blaze of Iskierka's fire, a twenty-four-pound ball of round-shot flew past them and took the Pou-de-Ciel full in the chest; he folded around it like paper as it drove through his ribs, and crumpled out of the air, falling to the rocks below: they were over the shore, they were over the land, and thick-fleeced sheep were fleeing before them across the snow-matted grass.

The townspeople of the little harbor of Dunbar were alternately terrified at the descent of a whole company of dragons onto their quiet hamlet, and elated by the success of their new shore battery, put into place scarcely two months ago and never before tried. Half-a-dozen courier-beasts driven off and one Pou-de-Ciel slain, overnight became a Grand Chevalier and several Flammes-de-Gloire, all hideously killed; the town could talk of nothing else, and the local militia strutted through the streets to general satisfaction.

The townspeople grew less enthusiastic, however, after Arkady had eaten four of their sheep; the other ferals had made only slightly less extravagant depredations, and Temeraire himself had seized upon a couple of cows, shaggy yellow-haired Highland cattle, sadly reported afterwards to be prize-winning, and devoured them to the hooves and horns.

"They were very tasty," Temeraire said apologetically; and turned his head aside to spit out some of the hair.

Laurence was not inclined to stint the dragons in the least, after their long and arduous flight, and on this occasion was perfectly willing to sacrifice his ordinary respect for property to their comfort. Some of the farmers made noises about payment, but Laurence did not mean to try and feed the bottomless appetites of the ferals out of his own pocket. The Admiralty might

reach into theirs, if they had nothing better to do than sit before
the fire and whistle while a battle was carrying on outside their
windows, and men dying for lack of a little assistance. "We will
not be a charge upon you for long. As soon as we hear from
Edinburgh, I expect we will be called to the covert there," he
said flatly, in reply to the protests. The horse-courier left at once.

The townspeople were more welcoming to the Prussians,
most of them young soldiers pale and wretched after the flight.
General Kalkreuth himself had been among these final refugees;
he had to be let down from Arkady's back in a sling, his face
white and sickly under his beard. The local medical man looked
doubtful, but cupped a basin full of blood, and had him carried
away to the nearest farmhouse to be kept warm and dosed with
brandy and hot water.

Other men were less fortunate. The harnesses, cut away,
came down in filthy and tangled heaps weighted by corpses already turning greenish: some killed by the French attacks, others
smothered by their own fellows in the panic, or dead of thirst or
plain terror. They buried sixty-three men out of a thousand that
afternoon, some of them nameless, in a long and shallow grave
laboriously pickaxed out of the frozen ground. The survivors
were a ragged crew, clothes and uniforms inadequately brushed,
faces still dirty, attending silently. Even the ferals, though they
did not understand the language, perceived the ceremony, and
sat on their haunches respectfully to watch from a distance.

Word came back from Edinburgh only a few hours later, but
with orders so queer as to be incomprehensible. They began reasonably enough: the Prussians to be left behind in Dunbar and
quartered in the town; and the dragons, as expected, summoned
to the city. But there was no invitation to General Kalkreuth or
his officers to come along; to the contrary, Laurence was strictly
adjured to bring no Prussian officers with him. As for the dragons, they were not permitted to come into the large and comfortable covert itself at all, not even Temeraire: instead Laurence
was ordered to leave them sleeping in the streets about the castle, and to report to the admiral in command in the morning.

He stifled his first reaction, and spoke mildly of the arrangements to Major Seiberling, now the senior Prussian; implying as best he could without any outright falsehood that the Admiralty meant to wait until General Kalkreuth was recovered for an official welcome.

"Oh; must we fly again?" Temeraire said; he heaved himself wearily back onto his feet, and went around the drowsing ferals to nudge them awake: they had all crumpled into somnolence after their dinners.

Their flight was slow and the days were grown short; it lacked only a week to Christmas, Laurence realized abruptly. The sky was fully dark by the time they reached Edinburgh; but the castle shone out for them like a beacon with its windows and walls bright with torches, on its high rocky hill above the shadowed expanse of the covert, with the narrow buildings of the old medieval part of the city crammed together close around it.

Temeraire hovered doubtfully above the cramped and winding streets; there were many spires and pointed roofs to contend with, and not very much room between them, giving the city the appearance of a spear-pit. "I do not see how I am to land," he said uncertainly. "I am sure to break one of those buildings; why have they built these streets so small? It was much more convenient in Peking."

"If you cannot do it without hurting yourself, we will go away again, and orders be damned," Laurence said; his patience was grown very thin.

But in the end Temeraire managed to let himself down into the old cathedral square without bringing down more than a few lumps of ornamental masonry; the ferals, being all of them considerably smaller, had less difficulty. They were anxious at being removed from the fields full of sheep and cattle, however, and suspicious of their new surroundings; Arkady bent low and put his eye to an open window to peer inside at the empty rooms, making skeptical inquires of Temeraire as he did so.

"That is where people sleep, is it not, Laurence? Like a pavilion," Temeraire said, trying cautiously to rearrange his tail into a more comfortable position. "And sometimes where they sell jewels and other pleasant things. But where are all the people?"

Laurence was quite sure all the people had fled; the wealthiest tradesman in the city would be sleeping in a gutter tonight, if it were the only bed he could find in the new part of town, safely far away from the pack of dragons who had invaded his streets.

The dragons eventually disposed of themselves in some reasonable comfort; the ferals, used to sleeping in rough-hewn caves, were even pleased with the soft and rounded cobblestones. "I do not mind sleeping in the street, Laurence, truly; it is quite dry, and I am sure it will be very interesting to look at, in the morning," Temeraire said consolingly, even with his head lodged in one alley-way and his tail in another.

But Laurence minded for him; it was not the sort of welcome which he felt they might justly have looked for, a long year away from home, having been sent halfway round the world and back. It was one thing to find themselves in rough quarters while on campaign, where no man could expect better, and might be glad for a cow-byre to lay his head in. To be deposited like baggage on the cold unhealthy stones, stained years-dark with street refuse, was something other; the dragons might at least have been granted use of the open farmland outside the city.

And it was no conscious malice: only the common unthinking assumption by which men treated dragons as inconvenient if elevated livestock, to be managed and herded without consideration for their own sentiments; an assumption so ingrained that Laurence had recognized it as outrageous only when forced to do so by the marked contrast with the conditions he had observed in China, where dragons were received as full members of society.

"Well," Temeraire said reasonably, while Laurence laid out his own bedroll inside the house beside his head, with the windows open so they might continue to speak, "we knew how matters were here, Laurence, so we cannot be very surprised. Besides, I did not come to make myself more comfortable, or I might have stayed in China; we must improve the circumstances of all our friends. Not," he added, "that I would not like my own pavilion; but I would rather have liberty. Dyer, will you pray get that bit of gristle out from between my teeth? I cannot reach forward to put my claw upon it."

Dyer startled up from his half-doze upon Temeraire's back and, fetching a small pick from their baggage, scrambled obediently into Temeraire's opened jaws to scrape away.

"You would have more luck in achieving the latter, if there were more men ready to grant you the former," Laurence said. "I do not mean to counsel you to despair; we must not, indeed. But I had hoped to find on our arrival more respect than when we left, not less; which must have been a material advantage to our cause."

Temeraire waited until Dyer had climbed out again to answer. "I am sure we must be listened to on the merits," he said, a large assumption, which Laurence was not at all sanguine enough to share, "and all the more, when I have seen Maximus and Lily, and they are ranged with me. And perhaps also Excidium, for he has been in so many battles: no one could help but be impressed with him. I am sure *they* will see all the wisdom of my arguments; *they* will not be so stupid as Eroica and the others were," Temeraire added, with shades of resentment. The Prussian dragons had at first rather disdained his attempts at convincing them of the merits of greater liberty and education, being as fond of their tradition of rigorous military order as ever were their handlers, and preferring instead to ridicule as effete the habits of thought which Temeraire had acquired in China.

"I hope you will forgive me for bluntness; but I am afraid even if you had the hearts and minds of every dragon in Britain aligned with your own, it would make very little difference: as a party you have not very much influence in Parliament," Laurence said.

"Perhaps we do not, but I imagine if we were to *go* to Parliament, we would be attended to," Temeraire said, an image most convincing, if not likely to produce the sort of attention which Temeraire desired.

Laurence said as much, and added, "We must find some better means of drawing sympathy to your cause, from those who have the influence to foster political change. I am only sorry I cannot apply to my father for advice, as relations stand between us."

"Well, I am *not* sorry, at all," Temeraire said, putting back his ruff. "I am sure he would not have helped us; and we can do perfectly well without him." Aside from his loyalty, which would have resented coldness to Laurence on any grounds, he not unnaturally viewed Lord Allendale's objections to the Aerial Corps as objections to his own person; and despite their never having met, he felt violently as a matter of course towards any-one whose sentiments would have seen Laurence separated from him.

"My father has been engaged with politics half his life," Laurence said: with the effort towards abolition in particular, a movement met with as much scorn, at its inception, as Laurence anticipated for Temeraire's own. "I assure you his advice would be of the greatest value; and I do mean to effect a repair, if I can, which would allow our consulting him."

"I would as soon have kept it, myself," Temeraire muttered, meaning the elegant red vase which Laurence had purchased in China as a conciliatory gift. It had since traveled with them five thousand miles and more, and Temeraire had grown inclined to be as possessive of it as any of his own treasures; he now sighed to see it finally sent away, with Laurence's brief and apologetic note.

But Laurence was all too conscious of the difficulties which faced them; and of his own inadequacy to forward so vast and complicated a cause. He had been still a boy when Wilberforce had come to their house, the guest of one of his father's political friends, newly inspired with fervor against the slave trade and beginning the parliamentary campaign to abolish it. Twenty years ago now; and despite the most heroic efforts by men of ability and wealth and power greater than his own, in those twenty years surely a million souls or more had yet been carried away from their native shores into bondage.

Temeraire had been hatched in the year five; for all his intel-ligence, he could not yet truly grasp the weary slow struggle which should be required to bring men to a political position, however moral and just, however necessary, in any way con-trary to their immediate self-interest. Laurence bade him good-night without further disheartening advice; but as he closed the windows, which began to rattle gently from the sleeping dragon's breath, the distance to the covert beyond the castle walls seemed to him less easily bridged than all the long miles which had brought them home from China.

The Edinburgh streets were quiet in the morning, unnaturally so, and deserted but for the dragons sleeping in stretched ranks over the old grey cobbles. Temeraire's great bulk was heaped awkwardly before the smoke-stained cathedral, and his tail running down into an alley-way scarcely wide enough to hold it. The sky was clear and cold and very blue, only a handful of terraced clouds running out to sea, a faint suggestion of pink and orange early light on the stones.

Tharkay was awake, the only soul stirring when Laurence came out; he was sitting, crouched against the cold, in one of the other narrow doorways to an elegant home, the heavy door standing open behind him, looking into the entry hall, tapestried and deserted. He had a cup of tea, steaming in the air. "May I offer you one?" he inquired. "I am sure the owners would not begrudge it."

"No, I must go up," Laurence said; he had been woken by a runner from the castle, summoning him to a meeting at once. Another piece of discourtesy, when they had only arrived so late; and to make matters worse, the boy had been unable to tell him of any provisions made for the feeding of the hungry dragons. What the ferals should say when they awoke, Laurence did not like to think.

"You need not worry; I am sure they will fend for themselves," Tharkay said, not a cheering prospect, and offered Laurence his own cup for consolation; Laurence sighed and drained it, grateful for the strong, hot brew. He gave Tharkay back the cup, and hesitated; the other man was looking across the cathedral square with a peculiar expression—his mouth twisted at one corner.

"Are you well?" Laurence asked; conscious he had thought not enough about his men, in his anxiety over Temeraire; and Tharkay he had less right to take for granted.

"Oh, very; I am quite at home," Tharkay said. "It is some time since I was last in Britain, but I was tolerably familiar with the Court of Session, then," nodding across the square at Parliament House, where the court met: Scotland's highest civil court, and a notorious pit of broken hopes, endless dragging suits, and wrangling over technicalities and estates; presently deserted by all its solicitors, judges, and suitors alike, and only a scattering of harried papers blown up against Temeraire's side like white patches, relics of old settlements. Tharkay's father had been a man of property, Laurence knew; Tharkay had none; the son of a Nepalese woman perhaps would have been at some disadvantage in the British courts, Laurence supposed, and any irregularity in his claims easily exploited.

At least he did not look at all enthusiastic to be home; if home he considered it, and Laurence said, "I hope," tentatively, and tried awkwardly to suggest that Tharkay might consider extending his contract, when they had settled such delicate matters as payment for those services already rendered: Tharkay had been paid for guiding them along the old silk trading routes from China, but since then he had recruited the ferals to their cause, which demanded a bounty beyond Laurence's private means. And his services could by no means be easily dispensed with now, not until the ferals were settled somehow into the Corps, Tharkay being, apart from Temeraire, almost the only one who could manage more than a few words of their odd, inflected language. "I would gladly speak to Admiral Lenton at Dover, if you would not object," Laurence added; he did not at all mean to discuss any such irregular question with whichever notable was commanding here, after the treatment which they had so far received.

Tharkay only shrugged, noncommittal, and said, "Your messenger grows anxious," nodding to where the young runner was fidgeting unhappily at the corner of the square, waiting for Laurence to come along.

The boy took him the short distance up the hill to the castle gates; from there Laurence was escorted to the admiral's office by an officious red-coated Marine, their path winding around to the headquarters building through the medieval stone court-yards, empty and free from hurry in the early-morning dimness. The doors were opened, and he went in stiffly, straight-shouldered; his face had set into disapproving lines, cold and rigid. "Sir," he said, eyes fixed at a point upon the wall; and only then glanced down, and said, surprised, "Admiral Lenton?"

"Laurence; yes. Sit, sit down." Lenton dismissed the guard, and the door closed upon them and the musty, book-lined room; the Admiral's desk was nearly clear, but for a single small map, a handful of papers. Lenton sat for a moment silently. "It is damned good to see you," he said at last. "Very good to see you indeed. Very good."

Laurence was very much shocked at his appearance. In the year since their last meeting, Lenton seemed to have aged ten: hair gone entirely white, and a vague, rheumy look in his eyes; his jowls hung slack. "I hope I find you well, sir," Laurence said, deeply sorry, no longer wondering why Lenton had been trans-ferred north to Edinburgh, the quieter post; he wondered only what illness might have so ravaged him, and who had been made commander at Dover in his place.

"Oh . . ." Lenton waved his hand, fell silent. "I suppose you have not been told anything," he said, after a moment. "No, that is right; we agreed we could not risk word getting out."

"No, sir," Laurence said, anger kindling afresh. "I have heard nothing, and been told nothing; with our allies asking me daily for word of the Corps, until there was no more use in asking."

He had given his own personal assurances to the Prussian commanders; he had sworn that the Aerial Corps would not fail them, that the promised company of dragons, which might have turned the tide against Napoleon, in this last disastrous cam-paign, would arrive at any moment. He and Temeraire had stayed and fought in their place when the dragons did not arrive, risking their own lives and those of his crew in an increasingly hopeless cause; but the dragons had never come.

Lenton did not immediately answer, but sat nodding to himself, murmuring. "Yes, that is right, of course." He tapped a hand on the desk, looked at some papers without reading them, a portrait of distraction.

Laurence added more sharply, "Sir, I can hardly believe you would have lent yourself to so treacherous a course, and one so terribly shortsighted; Napoleon's victory was by no means assured, if the twenty promised dragons had been sent."

"What?" Lenton looked up. "Oh, Laurence, there was no question of that. No, none at all. I am sorry for the secrecy, but as for not sending the dragons, that called for no decision. There were no dragons to send."

Victoriatus heaved his sides out and in, a gentle, measured pace. His nostrils were wide and red, a thick flaking crust around the rims, and a dried pink foam lingered about the corners of his mouth. His eyes were closed, but after every few breaths they would open a little, dull and unseeing with exhaustion; he gave a rasping, hollow cough that flecked the ground before him with blood; and subsided once again into the half-slumber that was all he could manage. His captain, Richard Clark, was lying on a cot beside him: unshaven, in filthy linen, an arm flung up to cover his eyes and the other hand resting on the dragon's foreleg; he did not move, even when they approached.

After a few moments, Lenton touched Laurence on the arm. "Come, enough; let's away." He turned slowly aside, leaning heavily upon a cane, and took Laurence back up the green hill to the castle. The corridors, as they returned to his offices, seemed no longer peaceful but hushed, sunk in irreparable gloom.

Laurence refused a glass of wine, too numb to think of refreshment. "It is a sort of consumption," Lenton said, looking out the windows that faced onto the covert yard; Victoriatus and twelve other great beasts lay screened from one another by the ancient windbreaks, piled branches and stones grown over with ivy.

"How widespread—?" Laurence asked.

"Everywhere," Lenton said. "Dover, Portsmouth, Middlesbrough. The breeding grounds in Wales and Halifax; Gibraltar; everywhere the couriers went on their rounds; everywhere." He turned away from the windows and took his chair again. "We were inexpressibly stupid; we thought it was only a cold, you see."

"But we had word of that before we had even rounded the Cape of Good Hope, on our journey east," Laurence said, appalled. "Has it lasted so long?"

"In Halifax it started in September of the year five," Lenton said. "The surgeons think now it was the American dragon, that big Indian fellow: he was kept there, and then the first dragons to fall sick here were those who had shared the transport with him to Dover; then it began in Wales when he was sent to the breeding grounds there. *He* is perfectly hearty, not a cough or a sneeze; very nearly the only dragon left in England who is, except for a handful of hatchlings we have tucked away in Ireland."

"You know we have brought you another twenty," Laurence said, taking a brief refuge in making his report.

"Yes, these fellows from where, Turkestan?" Lenton said, willing to follow. "Did I understand your letter correctly; they were brigands?"

"I would rather say jealous of their territory," Laurence said. "They are not very pretty, but there is no malice in them; though what use twenty dragons can be, to cover all England—" He stopped. "Lenton, surely something can be done—must be done," he said.

Lenton only shook his head briefly. "The usual remedies did some good, at the beginning," he said. "Quieted the coughing, and so forth. They could still fly, if they did not have much appetite; and colds are usually such trifling things with them. But it lingered on so long, and after a while the possets seemed to lose their effect—some began to grow worse—"

He stopped, and after a long moment added, with an effort, "Obversaria is dead."

"Good God!" Laurence cried. "Sir, I am shocked to hear it—so deeply grieved." It was a dreadful loss: she had been flying with Lenton some forty years, the flag-dragon at Dover for the last ten, and though relatively young had produced four eggs already; perhaps the finest flyer in all England, with few to even compete with her for the title.

"That was in, let me see; August," Lenton said, as if he had not heard. "After Inlacrimas, but before Minacitus. It takes some of them worse than others. The very young hold up best, and the old ones linger; it is the ones between who have been dying. Dying first, anyway; I suppose they will all go in the end."

NAOMI NOVIK is the *New York Times* bestselling author of *A Deadly Education* and *The Last Graduate*, the award-winning novels *Uprooted* and *Spinning Silver*, and the Temeraire series. She is a founder of the Organization for Transformative Works and the Archive of Our Own. She lives in New York City with her family and six computers.

naominovik.com
Facebook.com/naominovik
Twitter: @naominovik
Instagram: @naominovik

About the Type

This book was set in Sabon, a typeface designed by the well-known German typographer Jan Tschichold (1902–74). Sabon's design is based upon the original letter forms of sixteenth-century French type designer Claude Garamond and was created specifically to be used for three sources: foundry type for hand composition, Linotype, and Monotype. Tschichold named his typeface for the famous Frankfurt typefounder Jacques Sabon (c. 1520–80).

Explore more wondrous worlds with
NAOMI NOVIK!

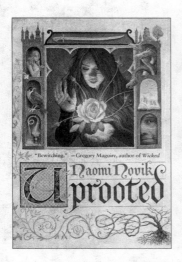

EXPLORE THE WORLDS OF DEL REY BOOKS

READ EXCERPTS
from hot new titles.

STAY UP-TO-DATE
on your favorite authors.

FIND OUT about exclusive
giveaways and sweepstakes.

CONNECT WITH US ONLINE!
⊙ f 🐦 @DelReyBooks

DelReyBooks.com

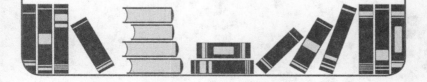